Charlotte Grimshaw is the author of three critically acclaimed novels, *Provocation* and *Guilt*, published in Britain and New Zealand, and *Foreign City*, published in New Zealand in 2005. She has been named by the *New Zealand Listener* as one of the ten best New Zealand writers under forty. In 2000 she was awarded the Buddle Findlay Sargeson Fellowship for literature. She has been a double finalist and prizewinner in the *Sunday Star-Times* short story competition, and in 2006 she won the Bank of New Zealand Katherine Mansfield award for short fiction. She lives in Auckland.

For Conrad, Madeleine and Leo

Opportunity

Charlotte Grimshaw

VINTAGE

This collection was written with the assistance of a grant from
Creative New Zealand.

A catalogue record for this book is available from the National Library of New Zealand.

A VINTAGE BOOK
published by
Random House New Zealand
18 Poland Road, Glenfield, Auckland, New Zealand
www.randomhouse.co.nz

Random House International
Random House
20 Vauxhall Bridge Road
London, SW1V 2SA
United Kingdom

Random House Australia (Pty) Ltd
20 Alfred Street, Milsons Point, Sydney,
New South Wales 2061, Australia

Random House South Africa Pty Ltd
Isle of Houghton
Corner Boundary Road and Carse O'Gowrie
Houghton 2198, South Africa

Random House Publishers India Private Ltd
301 World Trade Tower, Hotel Intercontinental Grand Complex,
Barakhamba Lane, New Delhi 110 001, India

First published 2007

Design: Katy Yiakmis
Cover images: Katy Yiakmis, Matthew Trbuhovic, gettyimages (truck)
Cover design: Matthew Trbuhovic
Printed in Australia by Griffin Press

contents

And as one of the old playwrights said, what was virtue
compared to an opportunity?
Frank Sargeson, *En Route*

animals

There were red swirls. I fought my way out of them. A metal object was eased out of my throat. They were asking a question.

'Nine,' I said, after a long time.

They conferred. They tried again. 'Mr James? Jack? What is your level of pain on a scale of one to ten?'

'Fifteen,' I groaned. Above me shapes loomed and split off from one another. I heard mumbled words. The pain came at me again. I twisted and sighed. Then the red swirls again. I dreamed I was walking towards my wife. I was following her down a long corridor, through red light. Out the window was a red plain. She laughed and asked, 'How much did you love me, on a scale of one to ten?'

'Zero!' I shouted. 'Zero, you cow!'

I woke in a room in which everything looked liquid. A plastic bag above me reflected sunlight. There was a window, a square of blue sky, sparkling dust in the air. There were shining chrome bars. When I turned my head I felt a tug — a tube had been inserted in my nose. Other tubes emerged from the bedclothes and ran down to the floor. I peered over. Two bottles — one red, one clear — stood upright on the floor. They were connected to me. How disgusting, I thought, in a light, tired, teary way. The red swirls had gone. Everything was too bright.

I lay thinking. Sometimes I moved parts of my body, in a cautious, experimental fashion. I remembered my wife, the way she'd skipped and danced through the loops of my pain. She hadn't really been there, of course. My sister Karen had volunteered to help me, now I was separated from my wife and, as Karen put it, 'all alone'.

Karen sat by my bed. She filled my water jug and punched her fist into my pillows. She chattered about her family. Then her voice deepened slightly and she said, 'It'll take you a long time to get over this.'

'How long?' I asked.

'You'll be exhausted for *months*.'

'I've got to go back to work.'

Karen looked secretive, as if that might never be possible. She said, 'Did they tell you? The operation destroys the stomach muscles. You'll have a pot belly for the rest of your life.'

'I'll have to wear a corset,' I said, wearily.

There was a short silence.

'Of course in Auckland it's too hot for a corset.'

I looked at her. 'Oh yes,' I said.

'I'll be back soon,' she promised.

Don't hurry, I thought. I said goodbye without smiling. She would tell you I've always been like that. Rude. Male. Ungrateful. She stood above me, in the liquidy light. She's still one of the most beautiful women I've ever seen. Big blue eyes, blonde hair. She has the face of an angel, people used to say. And she's so good. She goes to church every Sunday, works behind the stall at the church fair, runs tirelessly after her kids. And still finds time to stand at the bedside of her elder brother . . .

The surgeon came. He complained about the petrol tax. I waited, not wanting to ask. Finally he remembered to say,

'Everything went very well. You'll be a new man. You'll just need time to recuperate. And some check-ups after that.'

I stopped listening. Something in me subsided. I realised I'd been afraid.

I slept for a day and a night. The next night I began to look about my room. There was a small TV on a metal bracket that I drew up close to my face. I watched reruns of old shows far into the night. Out my window I could see the city lights.

In the morning two nurses took me, tubes and all, into a bathroom and washed me with a shower nozzle. I slept after this ordeal and woke to a terrible wall of sound. Panicked, I struggled up, looked out, and saw twenty people grouped in the dayroom, singing hymns. When the song ended I shouted, 'Shut up!' There was a shocked silence. Then someone quietly closed my door. I laughed. I almost felt myself again. I arranged the bedclothes and straightened my fresh pyjamas. A nurse took out some of my tubes and I feasted on half a cup of soup. I threw it all up again, but pressed on later, with half a cup of tea. It was Sunday. Soon Karen would come, fresh from church, with her blue eyes, her beautiful smile. I want to get out of here, I thought.

Our mother, Karen's and mine, was a big, powerful woman with a soft voice. She made us go to church on Sundays and Wednesdays. She taught Sunday School. She was stern and took no nonsense, but wasn't punitive or hard. I was a thin, sickly child. I must have taken up a lot of her time. Was Karen parked in front of the TV while everyone fussed around me? Did something wither in her, grow disappointed and hard? I see a little blonde girl, picking the scabs on her knees, her blue eyes glazed with *Good Times*, with *Happy Days*. I think my mother was a powermonger, who made us yearn to please her. And my sister could please her with goodness but not with her talk, because, unlike me, Karen didn't have our mother's brains. So my little sister grew gooder and gooder, and badder and badder, until she was the beautiful Christian fiend appearing at the door, with flowers and cards, with messages of sibling love.

'People get secondaries,' she said. 'It starts with one thing and then . . .'

'It just gets worse,' I chimed in softly. I smiled at her. She didn't understand that I'd always loved her. I patronised her when we were young, but I was proud of her. Or maybe she did understand, and that made her hate me more. There was a lot of the powermonger in her too. She used to dislike my wife Gina because she thought she fancied herself. Gina said Karen was *sinister*.

I worked on eating. I did well with some rice pudding, but threw up an omelette. I watched TV. I tried to read but the pages blurred. I went for a walk along the corridor, dragging my tubes and bottles, like a ghost — robed, wavering, clanking. Visitors averted their eyes. I limped past photos of nuns, and one of the Pope wearing a Maori cloak. My insides groaned, something laboriously rearranging itself, then there was a loud report that made my ears burn. Laughter came to me, a wave of weakness. I had to be helped back into bed.

Karen said, 'I hear you've been shouting at people.'

'Only at the Christians.'

I thought about writing. Would I ever have the strength again? I couldn't think straight. But I was getting stronger. In the middle of the night a nurse inserted a painkiller up my arse. 'You're in the paper,' she said.

'Do you read my column?' It was a strange moment to have to be polite.

'Your interviews are funny. That one on . . . the TV guy.'

'Thank you,' I said. Then my body made a terrible sound. I wondered whether I'd blown the pain pill out again.

She bent down. 'Not to worry,' she said.

Mornings, a Samoan woman cleaned the ensuite bathroom. Usually she sang. One day she was angry. She rushed into the bathroom and closed the door. Then there were crashes and bangs, metallic pings. She threw the door open, snatched my tray and banged it onto her trolley.

'You. In the paper,' she said.

'Yes.'

She stood, hands on hips. 'I say to my children, "Only *nosy people* read the paper".'

I nodded. She smiled vindictively and pushed the trolley out the door. I watched her go. What were her children *allowed* to think about? What extraordinarily limited lives some people led. I decided I would write a novel. But what about? This had me absorbed for a long time, until a German nurse, my bête noire, entered with her equipment, her instruments of torture. 'The thing about cancer is,' she began, and told me terrible things while she yanked and pummelled and pushed needles into my arms.

On a sunny morning the surgeon told me I was fit to go. We discussed my case. Karen came, and joined in. Struck by her radiance, the surgeon lingered, drawing her a diagram of my insides, pressing pamphlets into her hands. He outlined my diet. 'Mostly puréed, please.'

Karen joked and beamed. Then she said to him, 'Could I just have a word with you outside?'

'Tell her nothing,' I said. They laughed.

'She's not my wife,' I whispered, but they'd gone. I sank into a chair. I had to wait while she walked him up the corridor. I couldn't even carry my bag.

Karen helped me into her Landcruiser. I was high up, behind tinted glass. The enormous truck, the juggernaut, started with a roar. I felt fragile, wincing as we throbbed around corners, swayed onto the motorway.

We pulled up outside my first-floor flat. Gina had kept our villa in Grey Lynn and I rented a place in Parnell. The sitting room looked over a sunny yard in which, on alternate mornings, a playgroup was held for local toddlers.

Karen helped me onto the couch. I sat in the sunlight. She brought me a cup of soup.

'Jack, the surgeon says . . .'

I held up my hand. I gave her a very hard look. I'm used to warfare, but this was a difficult moment. For one thing, after the hospital, the flat looked messy, unsanitary, threatening. I sensed dust and germs.

'You'll be getting some home visits. I've arranged . . . since you're all alone . . .'

'Tell me later.'

I played the answerphone messages. Four were from a novelist I'd interviewed just before going into hospital. He said, 'It's Tony Irons. I've had a couple of extra thoughts!' He left a number.

Karen left. I made a complicated trip to the lavatory. On the way back to the couch I picked up a magazine. The sun shone hot through the window. I reached up to open it. My innards groaned.

In the yard outside, two women were setting up toys for the playgroup. Small children staggered about. More women came, more children. I dropped the magazine and watched. Time passed. I was absorbed.

Later Karen came with a puréed meal. A nurse paid a visit. I spent the night watching shadows of car headlights moving on the wall. I thought about Gina. I imagined she was lying on my arm, and we talked.

Some days went by. The playgroup came regularly and I set myself up on the couch to watch. The leader was a tall redhead. Other women conferred with her, deferred to her. There were cliques, a couple of loners. There were grandmothers, and some very young women, probably nannies. One woman was the life and soul; others gathered about her laughing. One, a large woman with a sharp face, watched the clownish woman constantly, a disdainful look on her face.

I watched and made notes on a jotter pad. I began to look forward to playgroup days. I didn't like it when Karen interrupted me. I said little, willing her to go. One day she left me a pile of videotapes, another some magazines. She brought casseroles full of frozen puréed food. The nurse came and made me do exercises.

'What are you staring at down there?' she said. She leaned over. 'Oh. Kiddies.' She looked at me. 'Do you have children of your own?'

'I have twin daughters. My wife and I are separated,' I

added, with dignity. I saw her lift up one of my magazines with the tip of her pen, sneaking a look at the cover.

One morning, while deep in thought, I picked up my keys and went out. I opened the door and stood watching the street. It was a still, sunny morning. People were going to work. The playgroup leader began unloading children from a car. Mothers were arriving with pushchairs. They glanced at me and at one another. I had the impression they were saying something about me.

A young, slim woman came along the street. I shaded my eyes against the sun. There was something familiar.

'Dee,' I called. She began crossing the road away from me. The mothers watched. 'Dee!'

She hesitated, came back.

'Oh, hi,' she said.

I was terribly excited. 'Will you come in? How about a coffee?'

She looked unwilling.

'Please, Dee,' I said. 'I'm dying to talk to you.' I took her arm and started dragging her towards the door. The playgroup leader watched, a wriggling child in her arms.

'Come on.' I pulled Dee inside.

She started laughing. 'Hey, you'll blow a valve.'

'Humour me,' I said.

We got upstairs and I made her a cup of coffee. 'Okay. Tell me what's been going on.'

Dee shrugged. 'The usual. She goes for long walks. She makes eccentric meals.'

'Does she go out much?'

'Yes, quite often.'

'And what's the deal with you?'

'I clean. I babysit if she wants me at night and when the girls get home from school.'

'Has she got a boyfriend?'

'Not sure.'

I said, 'I want you to work for me.'

She argued a bit, but in the end we hammered out a deal.

She would clean my apartment and I would pay her a lot, but only if she gave me information about Gina.

'Don't tell her about this,' I said.

'Why not?'

'Because she'll fire you,' I said. I felt weak. 'Come and sit here.' I patted the couch. 'Look down there.' I pointed at the playgroup.

She looked at me. 'Are you all right?'

'I had bowel cancer. I had this operation.'

'I heard about that.'

'Did she tell you about it?'

'She said your sister is evil.'

I thought about this. 'Did the girls want to come and see me?'

'I don't know.'

'Gina said things about ... "floozies". But I was trying to find someone like her. And none of them were any good. I just want her back.'

'Yeah,' Dee said.

'Look down there. See the playgroup? I've been watching them. I've been taking notes.' I flipped the pages at her.

'Whoa,' Dee said. She raised one eyebrow. I leaned close to her face. It was narrow, with hollow cheeks, fine freckles on the nose. Her eyes were watchful, intelligent.

'The granny there. She brings that kid.' I pointed. 'And see that young woman — she's bored. When the granny's kid gets stuck, is about to fall over, that young woman just stares. She's willing it to fall. Once I saw it fall and there was something in her face. Satisfaction. Like she was thinking *Yes. Smash.* But if her own kid looks like falling, she's there in a flash, saving him. The granny's started to notice that the young woman stares at her kid. And if her kid goes near the young woman the granny watches like a hawk.'

Dee didn't say anything.

'That kid goes around attacking the others. The mothers stop him, but that same young woman only rears up if he heads for *her* kid.'

Dee traced her name on the window.

'The mothers have a radar — when something's going wrong they turn. The nannies don't have it. They don't favour the kid they're looking after.'

'You need to get out more,' Dee said.

'Young women might be the worst people to be nannies. What if they're programmed to dislike other people's kids, because they're gearing up to have their own?'

'O-kay,' she said.

'The thing is, Dee, we're all animals. Creatures.'

She turned.

'We're all animals,' I said again. I looked into her eyes and saw a kind of darkness there.

'I look after your kids,' she said.

'Well, you're all right.' I sighed.

She got up. 'I'm going to see a lawyer. My ex-boyfriend was arrested. They took us to the police station.'

'Were you charged?'

'No. And I've split up with him now.'

'Did they put you in a cell? What was it like?'

She stared down at the yard. 'There's something about being put in a cell. It's bad out of all proportion. Don't tell Gina,' she added.

She left. Karen came. 'Who's been here?'

'No one.'

'I know about all your "friends",' she said impressively. She removed Dee's lipstick-smeared cup from the coffee table. 'I'm glad you're feeling better.' She sniffed.

Outside, the yard was empty. Rain drummed on the blue sandpit cover. Karen sat down. 'I talked to Gina.' She smoothed the arm of the couch with her fingers. 'She wanted to know how you were.'

'Really? What did she say? Exactly?'

She smiled. 'She's so over the top. What are you writing?'

'A piece about the playgroup mothers. About how they're animals.'

'Animals?'

I went quiet. I was angry with her for not telling me about Gina. I hated the way she said 'over the top'. She was repressive, bigoted, right-wing. She worshipped money. She was aggressive, two-dimensional. But I knew why I loved her. Because she was always little sister, putting on a front. Dressed up in her outfits, acting important. She was good at organising, she was 'steady' and 'sensible'; she was never over the top. But it was all armour, and just the foot-stamping dumb little girl underneath. Only a big brother would see her so clearly.

I felt tired. I stood up and put my hand on her shoulder as I passed on my way to the bathroom, where I hunched over the bowl, waiting to be sick. Oh, nausea, with its browns and greens. A terrible sense of complexity came over me. I was known for being funny in my weekly column. I'd written something about the playgroup, but it was too dark. That we're all animals — it isn't very *funny*. I would have to concentrate on my novel. But how was I going to write it when I couldn't leave the house?

Karen said, 'I got you this.'

It was a tiny, rectangular, satin pillow, embroidered in beautiful colours. She made me lie down and put it over my eyes. It was unexpectedly heavy, pressing down, cool and soothing on the contours of my face.

'It's fantastic,' I said.

She read from a pamphlet. 'Slows rapid eye movement. Good for headache, hangover, insomnia.'

'Thanks.' I grabbed her wrist.

'S'all right,' she said.

I began to invent a character. He would be very sick, very old. He would have lost most of his connection to the world. Confronting death, he would see life for what it was — a struggle for survival, among animals. His view would be detached and clear. He would see himself, having come from the earth, soon to return to the earth.

I made pages of notes. I exhausted myself. I woke in the night, switched on the lamp and wrote down thoughts I was afraid I would have lost by morning. I started transferring my ideas onto my laptop. The only thing that stopped me was visitors. Dying Larry, wheeled out onto the sunporch, would be contemplating an object — a telephone, say — in his simple, pared-down way, when Karen would arrive with another casserole of horrible puréed food. I got quite irritable with her. I had Larry crutching along a sun-striped hall, looking at pictures of nuns and the Pope in a Maori cloak, Larry menaced by a Samoan cleaner, Larry shouting at a choir. He knew he would never leave the Institution. He lived minute by minute. His life was intense, full of dazed revelation . . .

The phone rang. 'It's Tony Irons,' said the voice. It was the writer I'd interviewed before hospital. 'I've got a couple of points,' he told me. I made him hang on. I got the piece I'd written about him up on my screen. It was good. I wasn't changing it. His hands, I remembered, had shaken throughout the interview.

'You asked me about sources for my fiction.' His voice was nervous. I heard him drag on a cigarette and blow out.

'Did I?'

He rustled some papers. 'Do I base my characters on real people or do I make them up?' He drew a big breath. 'Jack, the answer is both. Things have to be psychologically accurate. When I create a character, even if it's based on a real person, it takes on its own identity. The fictional filter changes it. Changes it utterly!'

I twiddled the keys on the laptop. 'Mmm, good,' I said.

'And there was a point you raised about my childhood. If I could just take you back . . .'

He went on. He had a list of twenty-five points. I thought he would never go away.

Tuesday morning. I was in the bathroom. The doorbell rang three times before I got to it. I saw Dee at the bottom of the stairs, walking away. The door slammed.

'Stop! I'm here!' I called. I hobbled downstairs as fast as I could and shouted after her, 'Dee!'

The mothers were arriving. 'Dee!' I had a pain. I hunched over and a loud noise ripped through the air. (Did the

playgroup mothers stiffen? Did they exchange stony, significant looks?)

She was coming back. I hung on to the door handle.

'You all right?'

'I'm much better.' I crept up the stairs after her, praying that
my insides would behave.

'Sit down,' I said. I cleared papers and books off the couch.

She gave me a characteristic look: tolerant, incredulous.
'I thought I was supposed to clean?'

'Oh yes. Clean.'

'Or did you just want me to sit and talk?'

'That too. No, really, cleaning first.'

'You *are* going to pay me?'

I settled down to watch the playgroup. One of the women
gestured towards my window. I nodded gravely. I imagined
going down there, the women gathering around as I unfurled
my notes. They would be flattered by my interest, struck by
the accuracy of my observations. They would laugh, covering
their faces shyly.

The vacuum cleaner started up. The phone rang.

'You asked about plot structure,' Irons said. 'I meant to say
there's something that Chekhov (I think) said about fiction.
That a, um, work of art, a work of fiction, must have good
architecture. By which he meant it has to have a pleasing, a
beautiful *structure.*'

'Actually, Tony, I'm writing a novel of my own.'

'Oh. Great!'

I clapped down the phone. I worked. Larry had escaped
from his carers. A cliff above a beach, the sun spilling into the
horizon. He looked at the sky and thought he could feel the
earth rolling away beneath him. A wave boomed like a
slamming door, the islands were turning to black silhouettes.
There was a ship strung with lights out at sea.

The vacuum cleaner popped and died. Dee thumped it.
The mothers glanced up at me. There was laughter, grimaces.
I went back to my work. I had the pleasing feeling I'd become
a fixture for them — a benign presence, almost part of the group.

I interrogated Dee. Gina had talked of 'going on a trip with a friend'. She had bought a daringly short skirt. She'd scraped the side of the car again. She'd had a fight on the phone, after which she'd stood on the lawn swearing. Someone had rung back and she'd cried and smiled. She'd been out one night until 3 a.m.

Dee left. I felt cold. So Gina was being unfaithful. She would have some ridiculous rationale to do with our separation, some nonsense about needing to move on.

Oh, you vicious tramp! I wanted to tell her: I miss you. I see you everywhere. Nobody matters but you.

There was a knock on the door. I opened it, my eyes full of tears, expecting to be throwing myself on Dee. (Deadpan Dee, how many of our quarrels had she witnessed over the years?)

It was a policeman.

He got straight to the point. There had been a complaint. I had been watching the children in the yard. Had caused discomfort. There was talk of 'intense peering'. Strange behaviour. Shouting in the street. Note-taking, or sketching. Someone had mentioned a camera.

'What camera?' Outrage was added to hurt. My playgroup friends had *complained*.

I snatched up my notebook. 'I don't look at the children. It's the women I'm interested in. I've had thoughts about animals. That they are animals.'

'*Animals?*'

'We're all animals,' I said.

He didn't want to hear it. He took a heavy tone. I wasn't to upset anyone else. He didn't want to have to come back again. I told him I'd been sick. He said I ought to see someone about it. 'We know where you are,' was his parting shot.

Wounded, I took refuge in the mind of Larry. Karen came, the nurse came. I ignored them and worked on. Larry was captured by his carers and brought back to the Institution. He was taken on an outing in a minibus and some amusing incidents took place . . .

The next day there was an easterly storm, driving rain,

purple sheet lightning, rain drumming on the sandpit cover, water pooling on the concrete. Larry, labelled as a rebel, was locked in a battle of wills with a sinister nurse, and mused late at night about death. I watched the rain falling over the city, falling through city lights. The nurse tried to inject Larry with a painkiller; he refused, fearing her motives. The struggle exhausted him. In a black moment he had a sense of the void.

When Dee came the following day I gave her a package and some money. 'Post this to Gina,' I said. 'It's the start of my novel.'

Her report: a man had come to collect Gina in a big car. He was introduced as Nigel. Gina had giggled a lot. She was elaborately, yet minimally, dressed.

Listening, I bared my teeth, mangled this 'Nigel' between my fingers. 'No!' I shouted. I pressed my forehead against the window. Below, women hurried children inside, arms around little shoulders.

Dee hitched the parcel under her arm. I lay down after she'd gone, too exhausted to move.

The phone rang. I let it switch to the answerphone. Tony Irons said, 'Jack? If you feel like a drink sometime? I'm interested in the idea of a journalist who wants to write a novel. You, in other words!'

I couldn't get up. I didn't eat anything. I lay with my face to the wall. Karen came, rang the nurse, and they both tried to bully me into moving. I ignored them. Karen got upset, called me childish. She offered me soup and tea. I shook my head until the nurse put her foot down and said I'd have to be seen by a doctor.

I told Karen I was dying. 'It's what you want,' I said.

She shouted at me. 'How can you *say* that? I've looked after you. I've been here day after day!'

'I'm still dying,' I said. I heard her crying. I kept my face to the wall. She said my name. She sounded despairing. By the time I'd made up my mind to turn over, she'd gone.

When I woke there was a woman by my bed.

'Gina!' I sat up, full of joy. I put my arms around her. I told her I was dying. I told her I missed her. I begged her to come back. I said: 'I see you everywhere; in passing cars, in dreams. No one matters except you.'

She said, 'I read the stuff you sent. It's funny. It's bleak, though. Just lonely old Larry. Can't you pad it out a bit? Make a plot, add other characters?'

'What other characters? I've been ill, and nothing's happened. I've been completely alone.'

'There must be real people you can write about.'

'What people? There's only Karen and the nurse.' (I didn't mention Dee.)

'You could put me in it.'

'But I haven't got you!'

'I'm here, aren't I?'

I woke again. The sky out the window was pink. I was alone. I lay looking at the pearly sky. After a while I went to my computer, sat down and began to write: *There were red swirls. I fought my way out of them.* I wrote my way to this point, here. Because Gina always puts me straight, you see. She tells me what's important and what to throw away, and that is why I love her.

stories

I was sitting at my desk. It was a cold morning in June. The wind was rattling the windows and the rain had bits of hail in it. I was watching my neighbour, Ron Cassidy. He was up on his roof trying to fix a loose bit of iron. The wind was blowing his sweatshirt up over his broad, pale, freckled back. He was wearing shorts, calf-length socks and carpet slippers. His feet were slipping about on the wet iron.

I've lived here for five years. I live by myself, with two cats. There are the Cassidys on one side, and on the other a friendly old couple I don't talk to much. We say hello on the driveway. I'm on good terms with the man down the back. We sometimes have a chat. But it's the Cassidys I talk to most. As soon as I moved in here we started having words.

Ron Cassidy used to be an athlete a long time ago. He never managed to find anything to do after his sporting career was finished. These days he presents himself as a sort of builder or odd-job man. He has a battered truck filled with paints and hardware and tools, a trailer attached to it, piled high with more odds and ends. Often he sets off in this vehicle looking purposeful, only to return a short time later, perhaps with more junk piled on his trailer, or less junk, or the junk rearranged. Some afternoons he ties junk to his trailer and moves it from one end of the driveway to the other. He is always trotting around his property with some kind of appliance, repeating, mechanically, to anyone who comes near, 'It's got to be done. It's got to be done.' And everything he does makes his house older, messier, sadder, closer to being ruined.

One day he unloaded an ancient portable generator from his trailer. He set it up under my bedroom window and attached it to a high-pressure hose. Then he ran the generator continuously for two days, while he water-blasted his roof. It was so loud I couldn't shut it out of any part of my house. I couldn't work. I couldn't read. At the end of the second day he'd scoured the paint off half his roof. He stopped work and took the generator away. Months later, the roof is still half scoured and half covered in old paint. The walls of the house are also half painted. At the front a set of windows is covered in black polythene, half fixed. He has a homemade security gate, half of which is broken.

Under the house is Ron's workshop. This neon-lit, cobwebby basement, full of dead machinery, is where he and his son Blake apply themselves to their most serious passion: tinkering with cars. I have sometimes sat here working while Blake and his dad have sawed a car in half. When they stop work I can hear the murmur of their earnest talk. Something like: 'Yeah, the fuggin. Yeah. The wrench. The fuggin wrench. Yeah. The fuggin.'

They have the usual trouble with their tools. Whole days are devoted to fixing the dodgy saw they've borrowed to cut the car in half. In the evenings young Blake, an apprentice mechanic, likes to invite his friends over. After the traffic has died down in the street, after the long and stressful day, I relax to the sound of Blake's engine, with its souped-up oversized exhaust being revved into a scream, until it sounds as if it's begging for mercy. The youths cluster around the open bonnet, humourlessly smoking. In the lull after the screaming the car steams, its guts splayed — the tortured corpse. Blake's face is intent, white, tiny-eyed. Sometimes he breaks into a sharp-toothed grin: 'Eh! Look a' that!' As he might have done when the kitten exploded that time, when the puppy sighed and died, when the helpless thing he was fucking with finally gave up the ghost, and whimpered no more, and hung limp from the clothesline . . .

Oddly, I don't hate Blake. (I do hate his parents. I do.) Once, when I'd been in the paper and on TV, Blake went through a phase of greeting me in the street. He did a sort of wave — ceremonious. It was my being on TV that did it. I'm sure TV is the ultimate reality for Blake. Reading and writing are not his thing. Once he put a sign on an old car he'd dumped outside my house: 'Some FCKWIT stole my plates. Please RETURE.' He has a large tattoo on one arm and clumsy, boyish hands. It's hard to hate a boy. It's hard to hate a boy who can't spell 'return'.

Anyway, you'd think from all this that I live somewhere a bit scruffy, wouldn't you? Somewhere out west, or quite far south? Henderson, Mangere. But no. The Cassidys live in Remuera. We live in Remuera. It's not supposed to be like this.

So we have words. I'm no shrinking violet. I'm a writer, and I need quiet. (I've had a reasonably successful career. I'm old now, and a few people know my name.) Like Ron Cassidy, I need to be home all day. Unlike him, I like getting a bit of work done. And I've done a fair bit of raging out into the drive and telling them to turn down or off whatever machine they're operating.

But the thing about the Cassidys, apart from their living in Remuera and being so disreputable, is that they're fantastically paranoid and aggressive. If you complain, they do not apologise. They rear up and fight back. And if I've ever taken any direct action (sometimes I write angry letters; once, despairing, I threw two large tomatoes at the revving youths) they're not slow to take revenge. My car has been attacked with a brick, my windscreen wipers stolen. My tomatoes arrived back on my doorstep soon after, accompanied by a mountain of rubbish.

Mrs Cassidy — Glenda — who works in a bank, is as sharp and stringy as her husband is flabby and dull. She's not above leaning over the fence and giving me what for, when I've been cramping Ron and Blake's style with some mean-minded complaint. She stands by her men. She has a great sense of drama, and is always scurrying out to see what I've done to Ron and Blake this time. Sometimes I get a cold feeling when I'm out, and turn, and there is terrible Glenda, stooped, pitched sideways with the strain of the blackest scowl she can sustain without turning her face inside out.

The tumbledown house, moody Blake, glowering Glenda, moronic Ron, the piles of junk on Ron's trailer going back and forth all day — all of this has unsettled me so much that I've often thought of moving. I haven't managed to yet, even though I've been so sorely tried.

The Cassidys' latest trick (revenge for one of my complaints) is to park a couple of derelict cars outside my house so I have nowhere to park my own. They're always 'trailing their coat', as the Irish saying goes. They're always itching for a fight . . .

It was a cold June morning. I was sitting at my desk watching Ron Cassidy fixing a loose bit of iron on his roof. The wind rattled the windows and the rain had bits of hail in it. Ron was wearing carpet slippers. His feet slipped about on the iron. I started writing: an elderly woman was sitting in her house. She was watching her neighbour, an aggressive, unpleasant man who, for years, had made her life difficult. She was thinking about hate. She was thinking: there are very few people I hate, but that man is one of them. He has made me unhappy in my own house. And he hates me. She thought: if this were the Balkans or Rwanda, if society broke down and that man suddenly had the opportunity, he would kill me. Given the chance, I wouldn't kill him, even though I hate him, because I am a better class of person. But he would kill me.

She watched him sliding about on the roof. He had a hammer and a mouthful of nails and he was trying to hold down a section of iron. The wind tore at his clothes and hair. He slipped, threw up his arms and dropped the hammer. She saw him catch hold of a rusty overflow pipe to steady himself. It broke and came away. He teetered for a second, his body twisting, his hands clutching the air. The pipe tilted with him. There was a scattering of pieces of iron, nails, broken pipe. The wind got under the iron and made it shriek. He fell into the yard below. She heard his heavy body hit the concrete.

She sat still. Some minutes went by. No one came out to help him. No one was home over there. She could see his legs. She waited, looking at his legs. They didn't move. It started raining hard. He lay in the rain. She felt very strange sitting there, looking at her neighbour's legs. She picked up her coat and umbrella and went slowly out into the street. She stood outside her gate, the rain drumming on her umbrella. She got in her car and drove away.

The Writers' Festival was on. There had already been two days of appearances by local and overseas writers. At three that afternoon I was to appear in An Hour With Celia Myers, in which I would talk about my career and read from my work. I'd already chaired a session with three young women novelists, and taken part in panel discussions with some overseas writers. It had all gone well. The sessions were lively, and I'd managed to avoid any disasters or embarrassments. I'd been told that my Hour With session had sold reasonably well. I enjoyed festivals. My books were especially popular with women. After the session with the young novelists the crowd had been enthusiastic, and I'd realised how much I enjoyed the crush, the warmth of all those bodies pressing towards us. I live alone. My husband died years ago, and my daughters, Dee and Viola, have long since grown up. Mostly it suits me, being alone. But I crave the human touch.

I left my car in the parking building and walked down to the Hilton. The cold rain was sheeting down, but the Hilton was the perfect place to be on such a melancholy afternoon. The building was at the end of the wharf and the windows looked out onto the harbour all tossed with foam and white-caps, and the container ships in the rain, and the ferries crossing the water. In the late afternoon the water took on a silvery sheen and the air just above it was a haggard yellow. The cold light on the water only made it seem cosier inside. People rushed in, folding their umbrellas and shaking off the water. Inside, in the crush and heat and chatter, there were tables loaded with books for sale, long queues for tickets and coffee, people filing into sessions or gathering for signings. I walked in and stood for a moment, feeling myself gently bumped and buffeted by the crowd. There was a smell of wet wool. I was nervous about my forthcoming session; this gave me a feeling of inertia, of uneasy, drowsy luxury. I could have sneaked off to one of the rooms upstairs and lain across the bed drinking, sprawled and stalled, while time went on somewhere else without me . . .

I stood still, calming myself. I looked across the crowd. I saw a man standing against the high windows, the grey sea behind him. I wasn't sure until he moved and looked towards me. He was older and heavier, slightly stooped, but it was him. After all these years. The memory came rushing back. I remembered a scene long ago: a hotel room, the opened mini-bar, myself much younger — a beautiful, blonde younger self. The yellow light on the walls. The expensive linen. The rain drifting past the windows and outside the canyon made of city walls, the browns, the tans, the desolate spaces. Shirred water on a roof far below. No sound, the concrete silence. The bed where he lay, where he lounged and smiled. I saw him. And I saw him. Long ago, in the room of my nerves. And here, between the hotel pillars! And there, appearing again, and walking up the stairs now, a programme in his hand. Walking up the stairs to where a crowd was gathering: for An Hour With Celia Myers. The woman he . . . The woman whose marriage . . . Long ago, in the room where he lay, where he grinned and smoked and made a joke, I'd looked out at the darkening city and thought of my husband Joe, at home, not knowing. At home with our daughters.

I followed him up the stairs. I looked at his back, his shoulders. Let's call him Martin. Long ago I fell in love with him, and went to bed with him, and Joe found out and left me. And then Martin told me: 'I don't love you. I love someone else. I love another woman.'

Joe and I got back together after a while, but things were never the same. And now he's dead I look back and think about what our life would have been like. I know it would have been better if I'd never met Martin.

He had joined the queue. He was going to my Hour With. It was impossible. I couldn't allow it. I would yank him out of the line. 'I'm not having you sitting there ruining my hour. Smirking. Making your smartarse jokes.' I moved towards him. I used to yearn to hurt him. I had such violent dreams. But I only did it on paper in the end. On paper, and in my head.

'Celia! Celia!' Now here came Sarah, weaving though the crowd. 'Celia, I've been looking all over for you. Come this way. What can I get you? Water? Coffee?'

She hustled me to the Green Room. I let her push me gently into a chair. I stared at the coffee she put in front of me. I thought about the affair, how it had felt back then. I had been happily married with two children. I met Martin at a party. He made me laugh. He sent me witty notes. Some of the things he wrote were quite beautiful. We started meeting secretly. I remembered the hotel room. My nerves. The rain drifting past the window, the yellow light inside. The joy and the fear. I was right up at the sharpest, sweetest peak of feeling. I'd been married for so long, a hard-working mother for so long, and then, suddenly, I was back in the time when feelings overwhelmed me, when everything was vivid.

He felt none of those things — I know that now. He'd never been married. He didn't have the sense of 'coming alive again'. He was just doing the same jaded thing he'd always done: having a fling. After a while he told me he loved someone else.

Just like that. He didn't mince words. I fled back to Joe. But Joe found out and he left me. I was distraught. I got Joe back, but the hurt didn't go away. There was a new distance between us.

I researched Martin afterwards. He went for women who weren't available. A classic type. I raged at him. I had dreams in which I punched him until I was exhausted. In my dreams I scorned and sneered and jeered. I tied him up and tortured him. He hadn't loved me. He had hurt me and my family. He needed punishing for that.

I wrote a story about him. I invited him to a café and made him read it. A contemptible tear slid down his cheek. 'Look at you, playing at feeling,' I said. 'You crocodile. Go away and learn to be a human being.'

The story was about a loveless playboy, a dishonourable man, good for nothing except suicide. I described his faithless ways, his self-pity. At the end I had him lying on a couch dying of booze, of lousiness . . .

'Celia?' Sarah was leaning over me. 'Are you ready?'

I never asked Joe what he thought of the story. If Martin had asked me to, would I have left Joe? If Joe had been a writer, what sort of story would he have written about me?

Sarah was hovering. 'Celia. Can I get you . . . ?'

'I'm just a bit faint.' I wiped my face. I was crying.

'There's a *huge* crowd out there. They're even standing at the back.'

I got up and gathered my notes. The chairperson was waiting at the door. She was flushed and nervous. She whispered a lot of instructions about the microphone. I nodded and smoothed my shirt. We went out onto the stage.

Beyond the bright lights there was a collective rustle and sigh. I smiled into the hot dazzle. I could see rows and rows of heads. Impossible to see who any of them were. The chair was already up at the podium, introducing me. I sat down and set my expression: modest, polite.

I couldn't keep my mind on the notes I'd prepared. Why had he come? Did he have some kind of feeling for me back then? Was he sorry?

The introduction was winding down. I wanted to be in a room upstairs, lying across the bed, the mini-bar open, looking out at the drifting rain, crying for myself, for my poor lost Joe. One thing about Martin, standing in the queue: he was alone. Always alone.

'Introducing Celia Myers!' Polite applause. And then the questions. Do you see yourself as. Are your stories a form of. Women see you as a.

Some guardian angel took over. I felt as though I were listening to someone else. I answered all the questions. In front of me were hundreds of nodding heads.

The chair announced that I would read. I rose and opened a book of short stories. I read a short funny one, then a more serious one. (More scattered clapping.) Then, my hands trembling, I opened an old collection. I read the story I'd written about Martin long ago. He was out there somewhere in the black spaces beyond the lights. Did he know I'd seen him outside? He would know now. He would guess. I was reading the story to him, no one else. It was a hate letter, a message of hate, directed only at him. I read in a clear, strong voice. I finished. I listened to the clapping. I thought, there is a circle, and love and hate are on it. At some point they are very close. And neither will change the immutable, the thing you send them towards.

I felt rather light and dizzy. I didn't know whether I had been a disaster or a success. But afterwards they told me that, of all the events, my session had been the 'most consistent'. Whatever that means.

I signed books in the foyer. There was a long line. (There were other authors there too.) I kept looking along it, but there was no Martin. It took more than an hour to get through the queue, and then Sarah and others took me for a drink at the bar. I looked around at the crowd. I signed some more books. I talked to a radio journalist who poked a big microphone at me. He asked me about new work. 'I'm writing a collection of stories,' I told him. 'One that contains all of my crimes.'

I felt bad suddenly. I made an excuse and went outside. The rain was still pouring down. The sea was churned up, full of choppy waves. I looked along the wharf. And then I saw him, walking away. He was carrying an umbrella. There was a woman beside him, keeping step. He was holding the umbrella over her. I stood watching them until they went around the corner. I looked up into the white sky and let the rain fall on my face. I went back inside. In the toilets I faced the mirror. I pulled out some paper towels and wiped my eyes.

I drove home. Ron Cassidy was under his veranda, taking a piece of engine apart. Blake squatted nearby, smoking and watching. A broken pipe spouted water into the grass behind them. They looked like creatures in a lush green habitat at the zoo. I thought of my idea: Ron teetering, falling, the spray of iron and pipe and nails. The thud as he hit the concrete. His body lying inert in the yard. The woman standing at the gate, then driving slowly away.

I didn't finish the story about Ron falling off the roof. I might go back to the idea one day. I might use it. I did write the story about Martin, though, and I did read it to him, only him, at the festival, while hundreds of people looked on. But I wrote it a long time ago, when I was young and raw. I wrote it before I lost my sense of who was good and who was bad, before I started feeling sorry for everyone, and living my life and recording it — and everyone else's — as truly as I can.

pity

I saw my client to the door. 'You'll be fine, Dee,' I said. 'Just tell them exactly what I told you to say.'

I watered the plants and fed the birds. The hot sun shone through the windows and the room was full of yellow light. The birds cheeped and fluttered. In the street below, a woman was pushing a child in a pushchair. She wore a mini-skirt and her back was tattooed under her sleeveless shirt. I watched her. The canary made his cage swing. I whistled to him. He looked at me with one round, shiny, empty eye.

I checked my diary. I had some time. No more clients, nothing until an appearance in the afternoon. I spent a lot of time in the local district court, dealing with remands and bail applications and defended hearings. Most of my clients were criminal, although I made money with a bit of conveyancing. I was ambitious. I'd done a rape trial and I'd acted in a major aggravated robbery case, with multiple defendants. What I wanted was a murder trial, or a serious drugs charge. Those were the big cases, the ones that got you noticed.

My secretary, Sharon, had given me the canary for my

birthday, and then a client had given me a couple of budgies. I had a parakeet for a while. It shat everywhere and climbed claw-over-beak up the curtain. Sharon thought it was hilarious but I soon put my foot down. It was too much of a distraction, not to mention the muck it left everywhere. Without my having much to do with it, the birds had become a trademark. I knew they made me seem friendly, quirky, eccentric. They suited my sunny office above the shopping centre, where people trudged in and out clutching summonses for shop-lifting, assault, burglary, car conversion, disorderly behaviour.

My client, Dee Myers, was good-looking, and I'd wanted her to like me. I'd gone into a spiel about the birds — a bit of patter I usually gave to put people at ease. When I'd finished she didn't coo or smile or get up and pretend to look into the cages. She just stared at me. There was an expression on her face. Boredom? Impatience? She was all angles — thin shoulders, a long straight nose, intense, direct eyes. I was disconcerted. I picked up the file and got down to business.

Thinking about it now, I swung the canary cage. The bird clung to its perch, fluttering. Tiny shreds of birdseed hung from its rashy beak. I looked at it with dislike.

I went down to the café, ordered a takeaway coffee and a muffin and leaned against the counter reading the newspaper. I walked slowly back, sipping my coffee, thinking out a letter I needed to write.

Sharon was at the top of the stairs. With small shakes of her head she poked an afro comb into her frizzy hair. 'There's someone waiting for you. A Duane Mitchell?' We looked at each other and shrugged.

He stood up when I came in. He was short — no more than five foot six. He was about thirty, with dark hair, pale grey eyes and a handsome, angular face. His hair was fashionably cut. His teeth were crooked. You could see a bit of gold when he talked.

'Duane Mitchell,' he said in a deep, harsh voice. 'I haven't got an appointment.' He gave off a strong male smell of sweat and cigarettes. His shoulders were broad and his chest was strong, but the big torso was mounted on short legs.

He made a chirping noise at the canary. 'I know a guy who can get you this stuff wholesale. Birdcages and that? This guy I know, imports exotic pets. If you want tropical fish. Axolotls.'

'I've got too many pets already.'

'Pets are good for you. I read that. They're good for your health.'

'What can I do for you?' From his manner I was guessing some kind of fraud charge. Using a document for pecuniary advantage. Or a pyramid scam.

He lowered his eyes, pompous. 'I've got some information that concerns you. It's about your wife.'

'My wife and I are separated,' I said quickly. I picked a file up off the desk and opened it.

'Yeah. She told me.'

He looked at me with his pale eyes. He thought he had some kind of power over me, and he was enjoying it. He brushed a streak of ash off his black jacket. A thread hung from a frayed sleeve.

'Are you a friend of my wife?'

'I met her in a bar.' His smile was insinuating. He seemed to probe me with it, to dig for signs of weakness.

I was about ready to throw him out. He realised I was getting angry, stopped smiling. 'I'm a personal trainer. But I have a bit to do with the fashion industry. We'd done a show.' He named some fashion designer. 'I went to a bar afterwards with a couple of the models.' He paused, winked. I looked away. 'I saw this beautiful lady at the bar, all by herself, and I offered to buy her a drink. She accepted. Then she buys me one. She tells me she doesn't go out much but she'd went out with her "book group", right,' — he put two fingers up, scratching quotation marks in the air — 'and the last ones had just gone home and she was waiting for a taxi.

'Anyway she was a cheap drunk. One drink and she was away. It turned into a bit of a party. We got on well, chatting about this and that. By the end we were both a bit smashed and she starts telling me about her life. As you do. She told me a whole lot about her ex. Which was you.'

'Really.' I looked at my watch. I felt cornered and he knew it.

His voice altered. 'She told me about your divorce.' His tone went higher — there was something challenging, goading. I saw how aggressive, how ready he was.

'What do you want?' I said.

'The reason I've come to see you is that your wife said something. She said it more than once. Come to think of it, after we'd had a few, it was the only thing she wanted to talk about.'

I thought about telling him to leave. What would that involve? A scuffle? Punches thrown? I looked at him with disgust. 'So what was it?'

He looked down, fiddled with his hands, pursed his lips. He sighed and said in a voice that was light, scandalised, 'She said she wanted to have you killed.'

I laughed. I threw down my pen. 'Right.'

He screwed himself around in his chair, rolling his shoulders, gearing himself up. He put his hands out, steadying something — himself — a small gesture, melodramatic, but it worked. I felt the adrenalin surge. I swallowed.

'Now. She wasn't just going off. I thought she was at first, but she was serious. She talked about things you'd done to her. She said you'd hurt her. She said you'd mess up your kid, too — that you'd turn the kid into someone like you. You'd corrupt him, she said. She wanted to find someone who would get rid of you for money. She'd read an article in a magazine, about how you could hire people, through the gangs.'

We stared at each other. There was something very bad in his face. He was hard, coiled, malevolent. He was angry that I'd laughed.

'You think she was serious?'

'Oh, I know she was,' he said in a lilting voice.

There was a silence.

'Because she asked *me* to do it.'

He made a quick movement. My throat closed. A second of fear: I thought we were going to fight and I pushed my chair back. But he was a salesman. He wanted to create an effect. He was selling me the idea, drawing me in. Now there was a little smile on his face.

I was furious, but I stayed sitting. 'I don't believe you,' I said.

He eyed me. He could see how rattled I was. He waited. I tried to gather my thoughts. Was it possible? It was true that relations between Carita and me were very bad.

'Let's think about this,' I said. I raised my eyes. Duane Mitchell was watching. 'What do you want?'

He knew he'd scored. He couldn't have imagined it would be so easy. I saw in his eyes some predatory calculation going on. He also looked disconcerted and conscientious, as though the situation were almost too rich, too testing for him to handle.

'I want you to know I turned her down.' He coughed. 'But that's not to say she hasn't gone somewhere else. She was pretty set on it.'

I pressed my fingers against my temples. 'I hope you tried to talk her out of it?'

'Mate, she wasn't going to listen. There was something in her eyes. Crazy. Freaked me out, you know?'

'How did you know where to find me?'

'She told me your name. I know your reputation. I've seen you at the court.'

'Really.'

'I've had a few run-ins. Traffic and that. Couple of minor things.'

'You'd better leave,' I said. I couldn't think with him sitting there.

He didn't move.

'I'm expecting someone,' I said loudly. He stood up. He was trying to decide what to say. He didn't want to disconnect so soon. Having unloaded his information he wanted to make sure he profited from it.

'Thought you'd be grateful for the warning,' he said.

'Thank you.'

I felt his aggression again. He struck a pose: wounded, incredulous, like someone who'd been ripped off.

'Do you want money?' I wondered what it would be like to hit him. Satisfying — for the split-second before he smashed your head in. His forearms bulged with muscle.

He hesitated. He looked cunning, then high-minded. 'She ought to be stopped,' he said.

I rubbed my eyes. It hit me again, what we were discussing. How surreal it was. Should I be afraid? I almost laughed. Something made me say, 'Have you got a card?'

He produced a rectangle of cheap white paper.

'She ought to be stopped,' I repeated. I took the card. We stood up. Weirdly, we shook hands.

'Mind how you go,' he said.

'Goodbye.'

I sat down. Then I jumped up and went after him.

'Duane? Would you know how to find her again?'

He turned, nodded. 'She give me her phone number.'

He went out. I heard him talking to Sharon, and Sharon's high laugh. I threw myself down in my chair.

We'd been fighting — for how long? — over custody of our son. I'd endured countless sessions in the Family Court, a gruelling year of her accusations. She claimed I was unfit to look after Lars even part time, that I shouldn't have any access at all. She cited my recent car accident, a fight I'd had with my neighbour. These things were trivial, but she'd tried to paint a picture of permanent chaos. She told the court I was a binge drinker. She said I had an unhealthy lifestyle (but to her, eating a burger was 'suicide'). She got people to spy on me, my neighbour for instance, which is why I'd had an argument with him — he knew Carita from the tennis club, and told her once when I'd had a woman to stay the night.

I'd been baffled by her vitriol at first. I'd responded calmly to each new salvo, and so far I'd managed to convince the court I should go on seeing Lars. But she was persuasive, tireless, inventive. It hung over me that she might succeed in taking my boy away from me. She had engaged Andrea Sykes as her lawyer — and Andrea was effective. Bland, humourless and relentless, she was a bureaucratic automaton. I had to keep myself very calm around her. It was my money paying for this steel-spectacled robot, my money that funded Carita's spectacularly defamatory affidavits. After court sessions I sometimes hid stinging tears — how had we got to this? We used to love each other. It was only after the latest session (when there'd been something so heightened and hysterical in Carita's performance that even Andrea had looked slightly perturbed) that it had dawned on me: my ex-wife had changed, changed utterly. My terrible little Finnish beauty: she had gone completely mad.

If Duane Mitchell wasn't lying, then she was very mad indeed. She'd realised she couldn't malign me or trick me or defame me in court. And she'd flipped her lid. Suddenly I believed it. A weird, stunned laugh rose in me, as if I'd seen something marvellous and freakish, too crazy to be real. Then I thought of Lars. He was little and trusting and round-eyed. He was only five. I loved him more than anything in the world. He was living with a lunatic.

She ought to be stopped. Little Carita. She was pretty and blonde. She was *tiny*. When I first met her she was wearing a furry pink jumper and tight white jeans. We were in a student café. She turned to me in the queue, with her kohl-rimmed eyes and her Finnish accent and her giggling; she was holding something up for me to see — a sandwich in a plastic packet. She just *couldn't*. Would I? Manful, grinning like an idiot, I wrenched the staples apart. How she applauded and fell about, how charmingly she mocked her own ineptitude. Later I performed other feats. I opened jam jars, pickle jars, doors, stuck windows. I reached up to high shelves. I jump-started her car, and taught her how to do the self-serve at petrol stations. She had round eyes, long hair, slightly buck teeth. Her figure was perfect. When I walked with her in the street, men followed her with their eyes. She'd been in the country for a year. She was studying to be a dietician. She was sexy, comical. Once when she was angry she followed me down the hall in her see-through nightie, beating me with her toothbrush. We used to sleep with our arms around each other. How had we come to this?

She beat me with a toothbrush, and one night she threw three carrot sticks at me. She had been offering them to Lars. Before she left I grabbed her wrist in anger, and left red finger-marks on her tender skin. That was the extent of the violence between us.

It was after Lars's birth that things went wrong. She was obsessive about his schedules, about the whole domestic scene. She decided I was a slob. I thought I was about averagely messy, but she said I was an unsanitary pig. Worse, I wasn't interested in healthy eating. This started to bother her out of all proportion — the fact that after one of her salads or nut cutlets I'd be likely to sneak off for a burger and fries.

There was another kind of progression: as her English improved, I began to understand what she was really like, and she got a better idea of me, too. The language barrier had shielded us from certain subtleties, problematic nuances. Meanwhile she'd started to scream at me every time I left a curtain crooked or a ballpoint pen on the floor. I used to think it was atavistic, the sudden post-natal fixation with scouring and sterilising and vitamins. Some Scandinavian spirit had risen in her; she was panicking, in a strange land, half frantic with disgust.

When she left for good, taking Lars with her, I'd expected to 'let myself go'. I thought it would be burgers in front of the TV, old pizza boxes strewn over the bed. Instead I found myself in a constant state of vigilance. Coming home, I cleaned and tidied and sat by the window eating some rudimentary scrap. I was waiting — not for her, but for Lars. It took me some time, numb and dazed as I was, to understand that I needed my boy to come home. When I realised, I succumbed to the kind of hysterical tears I hadn't shed since I was a child. I cried all night; the next day I set about making sure I would be raising Lars too. From then on I asserted my rights. Carita put up only minimal resistance at first, but there began to be incidents. She said I fed him the wrong food, showed him the wrong films, read the wrong books. She started throwing tantrums every time she had to drop him at my house. Then she hired Andrea Sykes.

I turned Duane Mitchell's card over in my hand. Carita could well succeed in limiting my access to Lars. Andrea Sykes was very good at her job. Another possibility lay at the back of my mind: what if Carita decided to take him back to Finland? I didn't think she'd be able to, but what if my case were weakened by some new lie, some fresh calumny? What if she took him for a visit and never came back? Such things happened all the time.

This was what she was threatening. When Lars was a baby I loved him so much my eyes sometimes ached and prickled when I held him. Now, when I took him for a walk, the grave five-year-old with his too-short flared trousers, his frown, his big sandals, I would turn and wait and watch with such tender pride. He was thoughtful, charming, comical, terrified of blood, confident in shops and cafés, fierce, interested in all kinds of insects, given to collecting, so that when we arrived home from a walk around the block I (the faithful Sherpa) would be carrying (say) a coil of wire, some interesting leaves and a paint tin, while he would be toting some stick or nail-studded plank, which he would then 'work on' in the garden all afternoon.

Then he would bring a book and I would read to him for an hour while we lay on my bed, Lars curled against my side and fiddling dreamily with my hair. He loved stories. He was clever at school. Sometimes he woke in the night and was afraid of the dark. He and I played verbal games, where I was Spiderman and he was Batman. These games could go on, exhaustingly, for hours. 'Make Spiderman talk,' he'd say. 'Now make the baddie talk.' Each time Carita came to fetch him I wanted to kill *her*. I could see how she'd got the idea. But to act upon it? Even if it was just drunken ranting in a bar, she'd definitely crossed a line. And where was Lars while she was cavorting with Duane Mitchell? Not alone, I assumed. Surely not alone.

But was it just drunken ranting? I sat up straight. This needed to be ascertained. I was justified, obviously, in wanting to know exactly what Carita was planning. (What she was *planning* — my mouth twisted into another incredulous smirk.) One thing I was sure of: if I told anyone about this, she would deny it. No one would believe Carita capable of even thinking about violence. If I accused her now, Andrea Sykes would convince the court I was mad.

The card said, tersely: *Duane Mitchell — Personal Trainer*. There was a mobile number. I started to ring it, then hung up. I got up, maddened by the cheeping of the birds.

I couldn't do nothing. I couldn't wait for her to hire some thug. But I couldn't make any kind of accusation while I only had Duane Mitchell to back me up. (Accused, Carita would bat her eyelashes, she would look 'stunned' and 'bewildered'. She would ring Andrea 'in tears'.)

I picked up the phone. I told Duane I wanted him to meet me at the café on the corner in half an hour. I told Sharon I was going to see a client. Then I went downstairs, crossed the little square and sat in the window drinking a double-shot coffee.

Duane arrived twenty minutes late, looking uneasy. He fidgeted and scratched. He refused my offer of a coffee. He burped and there was a bad smell. He barged up out of his seat and said he'd get himself a muffin. I waited.

He said in my ear, 'Mate, you'll probably find she's forgotten all about it. Just the piss talking.' He sat heavily down.

I stared at the square outside. 'She has to be stopped.'

'Yeah, but like I said, she's probably woken up with a hangover and thought what the hell was I on about last night, and forgotten.'

'We need to know how far she'll go.'

'How far?'

'I want you to tell her you're on for it.'

He spread out his hands, laughed. 'Me? No way. I'm not killing anyone.'

'No,' I said patiently. 'I want you to tell her you know someone who will.'

He stared. 'Pardon?'

'It's a test,' I explained. 'If she wants to go ahead, then we'll know she's for real. If she backs off and says, "Ooh no, I wasn't serious", then we'll know where we stand.'

'Why should I do this?' He picked fussily at his muffin.

'You came to me.'

'That was a public service,' he said promptly. 'Done you a favour. Thought you might help me with some problems I've got and that, maybe. In court.'

'I can help you. I can make it worthwhile for you.'

'But she's probably forgotten all about . . .'

'We need to know how far she'll go,' I repeated. 'This is a way of containing her. If she thinks she's got you she won't go to anyone else.'

'And will you help me?'

'I will.'

'But who do I say I've got? Some killer? How do I know any killer?'

'You tell her you've thought about what she's said. You've asked around. You've been recommended a guy. Through the gangs. Make up some Hell's Angels connection. I'll worry about the rest. You've just got to let her think it's possible. Then we'll know what we're dealing with.'

'But what if she says she wasn't serious?'

'You told me she was serious, Duane.' My face was hot. I felt like grabbing him by the neck.

'Yeah.' He hesitated. 'She seemed to be. But she mightn't . . .' He put his head on one side. His expression was sly, cunning, filthy — and baffled. He couldn't quite see where we were going. He grinned and tapped his temple. 'You want her to kill you?'

'No, Duane. I want you to remind her of your previous conversation, and then tell her you've got the man for her.'

I gave him my phone numbers. I left him sitting there. I walked over to the courthouse in a state of frigid calm, made a success of a highly unlikely bail application, exchanged banter afterwards with some colleagues, and then, since I didn't have Lars the next day, accepted an invitation to go out for a Friday night drink. Much later I staggered home, slept, and woke with a hangover. I hadn't eaten anything the night before and I'd drunk myself stupid. My stomach was in ruins. I went to the bathroom and threw up. Then I lay in bed thinking about Carita and Duane Mitchell. I spent a fevered morning going over it in my mind.

Later, gingerly, I went to the shops for supplies: fizzy water, icecream, painkillers, antacids. The walk took a long time — I was as hunched as an old man. I watched a video, then read a book while the rain streamed down the windows. I ate a sandwich in bed, listening to the downpour drumming on the iron roof. I watched the TV news. I was lonely. I longed for Lars. I wished I had a woman in bed with me. I went to sleep, a tub of icecream melting on the bedside table.

The next morning, Sunday, I went out for a walk. When I came home the phone was ringing. It was Duane. 'She's not into it,' he said.

'What?'

'I rung her. She got all shitty and that. Said it was a bad time. She didn't know what I was on about. Looks like you're okay, mate. She's not going to top ya.'

I sat down. I looked straight ahead. I said quietly, 'I don't know why you think that means I'm okay.'

'She's not on for it.'

'I can't rely on that. She said it was a bad time. She's telling you to call later. She probably had someone there. We don't know what she's up to.'

I could hear him scratching his chin. 'Nothing. Far as I know.'

'Perhaps you'll have to remind her what a good idea it was.'

'What?'

I said, 'You're a salesman, Duane. Make her remember how much she wanted it.'

Then I told him all the things I could do for him if he helped me.

I spent the afternoon painting Lars's bedroom. He kept a lot of his toys here, but the room still didn't seem properly his. He was always a little visitor, with his overnight bag. I ached and burned for him. A red point of rage glowed inside me. That she could threaten to take him away, that she had threatened us for months. And now she'd gone really crazy, and still I couldn't fight her, because no one would believe me if I told.

I tossed and turned all night and went to work white-faced. I dealt with my clients efficiently, but I was in a bad state of nerves. Duane Mitchell didn't call.

The next day I had a defended hearing set down for the whole day. When the court closed at five I went back to the office. Sharon said, 'That Mitchell person's here again.'

I hurried in. We shook hands. He said, 'I don't know what I'm getting into here.'

I waited. He seemed jovial, over-excited. He smelled of alcohol. 'I've only spun her the biggest line of shit. You should of heard it. About the Highway 61s and the Hell's Angels and how I'd met a guy who met a guy in jail. Anyway, you were right: she is on for it. I didn't even have to get her drunk. She just accepted it all. We were in the car down on the waterfront. I told her I could introduce her to a "friend" — my supposed killer mate. She didn't argue. I said he'd charge about five grand. She said, "Oh yes." I go, "You got five grand, darling?" and she goes, "Yes." Just like that. "Yes." I told her the guy'll break in and kill you, probably strangle you or smack you one over the head, right, and then fuck off to Australia. People think it's just a burglary turned nasty. No problem. I told her it happens all the time. She was quite interested in that. She said, "Oh does it really?" She's all pretty and polite and that, but it's creepy when you think about it. It's like she's not all there.'

'You seem to have found it all quite invigorating,' I said. I was pacing and rubbing my hands together. I felt — odd. Sick, odd and triumphant. There was going to be a contract out on me. Now we were getting somewhere.

'I think she's a pill-popper, mate,' Duane said. 'When I've been with her she takes these pills. She reckons they're herbal but they look like painkillers. That might be why she's gone a bit drifty.'

'You think she's a drug user,' I said, pacing.

'Well, yeah. Could be.'

'Duane, you've saved my life.'

'Yeah. Done meself out of five grand.' He did a big laugh. There was a short silence. We looked at each other.

'It'll be worth your while,' I said.

He coughed. 'Yeah, good,' he muttered.

'All you have to do now is ring her and arrange for her to meet the "killer".'

'Your guy . . . And who's he going to be?'

'Don't you worry. I'll tell you the time and place and you get her there, okay? Then it's done. Thank you, Duane.'

'No worries,' he said.

After he'd gone I closed my office door and rang the Central Police Station. I spoke to a policeman I knew, Detective Sergeant Damon Lee. I arranged to meet him the next day. I said I'd received some disturbing information. I'd been threatened. A certain criminal transaction was going to take place. The situation would call for the use of an undercover detective.

I went home. I sat out on my deck drinking beer. I thought about ringing Carita. I decided it would be too hard to act natural. I wanted to talk to Lars. But it was dark now; it was late. He would be tucked in with his teddies, his Tintin comics. I would confuse him.

She would have read to him. He would be wearing his blue pyjama suit. Beside his bed the drink and sandwich. The dim light on his small, dreamy face. Carita was a good mother. She loved him. She never shouted at him, never hit him. When he had nightmares she let him crawl into the big bed. She played games with him. She was never late to pick him up from school. The only thing she did wrong was to try to take him away from me. What had she told Duane Mitchell — that I would ruin Lars, corrupt him? What did she mean?

When we first went out together she overlooked certain things. I told crass jokes at the dinner table. When drunk in restaurants, my fellow lawyers and I sometimes burst into song, and quaffed and guffawed, and clashed our tankards, while she sat to one side, her face creased with dismay. Some of the things she said to me: 'Do you never talk about anything serious? What about politics? Don't your friends have any ideas, any views?' No, we were a joke a minute, a barrel of laughs, we had nothing to say about anything unless it was sport, and she put up with it because she loved me. But when she was pregnant she started to panic — she couldn't tolerate it any more. She was in a serious state — of culture shock, of recoil. She was even repelled by what I ate.

I made sausage sandwiches and washed them down with beer. I went to bed drunk, and fell asleep straight away. I started having a dream. I was at the mouth of a railway tunnel. There was snow outside and it was freezing cold. There was a small boy pulling himself through the snow. He was dirty and neglected. He came into the tunnel. He said, 'I'm cold.' I picked him up and held him, and I was filled with terrible grief. Great, deep, rhythmic sobs came out of me. The boy wasn't Lars, then he was. I wept in regular gasps, woke dry-eyed, then started crying properly. I was struck by the sensation, the lingering power of the dream-sobs. The emotion was deeper than any I'd felt while awake.

I lay and dozed. The boy wasn't Lars, then he was. It made me think the dream wasn't just about Lars. It was about pity. Was it about pity for all people? For Carita?

daughters

I grew up in a big house in Remuera with my father, who was a wealthy businessman, and my stepmother, Rania. Rania was beautiful and elegant. She was obsessed with my father. He was unfaithful to her and it made her insecure. She was clinging and neurotic and terrified of getting old. She spent a lot of time in spas, having beauty treatments. When she was fifty-five, she looked thirty-five. She went to a plastic surgeon and had her eyes done and her breasts and neck lifted. She was nearly six feet tall, with a perfect figure, a smooth oval face and green eyes. When she was in a bad frame of mind she looked at the world with hatred, as if it were something that was polluting, that would destroy her.

I was an only child. My mother died when I was four. My father married Rania, one of his girlfriends, soon after. He and I always got on well but Rania tried to keep him away from me. They wanted to have children but she wasn't able to conceive. Rania stayed childless, and pencil slim, and girlish. She didn't understand that her husband was my father. She behaved as though I were a female rival who had to be kept at bay. She winced when my father and I came near each other. She threw tantrums, sulked and raged. When I hit puberty she could hardly stand it. She looked at me with a kind of horrified prudishness. I would walk in on her telling her friends how impossible I was. If she and my father met me in the street, he would say, 'Come with us, Claudine, we're going to such-and-such a place', and Rania would nudge me with her sharp elbow and say, 'No, let her go; she won't want to come with us.' It used to amaze me, the amount of energy my stepmother spent fending me off. She liked to tell a story about how, when I was a young child, she'd suffered a bout of depression (she was 'highly strung') and had had to fight the urge to smother me. She told this story at dinner parties — while I was there. Her eyes went moist when she told it. Her nostrils flared and she smoothed her hair away from her bony face. The story moved her: how she had suffered. She said I had been an extremely difficult child.

My father worked long hours. He had an importing business. When Rania and I argued he rolled his eyes and sloped off to his study. Then, later, through the study door, I would hear his low voice on the telephone. He was a compulsive seducer, an adept womaniser. He was handsome, suave, evasive. I can picture him now, slipping out the back door, ducking neatly into his car as his name was shrieked, with incredible force, from an upstairs room.

Rania's family had escaped from some Egyptian slum and come to New Zealand with nothing. She had certain feelings about money. If I brought friends home she wanted to know what cars their parents drove, what school they went to, and how big their houses were. You could see her sneaking looks under the table, checking their shoes. She wanted to wrench them to her chest and turn over the labels on their clothes. If they had slightly less money than us she was pleased. If they had more she was narrow-eyed but polite. If they were poor, she was cold. For Rania, to be poor, or just ordinarily struggling, was distasteful. She shuddered away from cheap things. She dressed in matching outfits, in designer suits and shoes and sunglasses. She drove a white Mercedes convertible. She looked like a vamp in an airport thriller. Her fingernails were blood red, and an inch long.

I went to an expensive private girls' school: St Cuthbert's. I got into plenty of trouble there. Rania gave me spending money, and my friends and I spent days in town, hanging about in music stores, sneaking into pubs, buying cosmetics. In the weekends we went to nightclubs. On the way home we set fire to cars. I knew a boy called Blake who lived in our street. He was expert at it: you got some rubbish, wedged it under the chassis and lit it. The car would burn, and eventually there was a muffled pop and it exploded. You could blow up two or three cars at once and get away before the police and firemen turned up. Or you could just hang around and watch the show, as if you'd just come around the corner and it was nothing to do with you.

During the day we burgled houses. We stole clothes, TVs, stereos, gadgets. I liked looking around other people's houses. While Rania was leafing through *House & Garden* under the sunray lamp at Spa Sierra, Blake and I were out in the field inspecting the real thing: some conservatory or water feature, or laboratory-sized kitchen. We dawdled around the suburbs in the daytime, and if there was an open window you could just reach in and take something — a radio or a clock, say — while people were in the house. Or swim in the pool of an empty house, or stroll through gardens, picking fruit. Long afternoons in the sunlit grids of the suburb, other people's property: the real, the personal — I wonder what I thought I was doing with it. I was just as likely to throw away the things I stole. I didn't want any of it. Not really.

I kept one thing: a clock, it belonged to the old lady who lived next door to Blake. He said she was a writer. While we were burgling her house Blake kept threatening to burn it down. One thing I remember, we were still in the house when she came home. We hid in one of the bedrooms. She heard us and went quiet, then shouted something and rushed to the front door. She was frightened. We ran out the back door and climbed over the fence.

We disliked school for the usual reasons. The teachers were humourless and mealy-mouthed; they rewarded dullness and crushed originality; they valued only the nice and the drab. You know how it was: the pallid girl with the hairy legs and the big mane of dead hair, the girl who was *no trouble at all*, was cooed over and admired and cherished. Girls with talent, on the other hand, had to have it squashed out of them, had to be punished and ostracised and belittled.

'The teachers are cunts,' I said to Rania.

She looked at me, with her Arabian eyes. She was drinking iced tea and smoking a gold-tipped cigarette. 'Is good school,' she said. 'Cunts or not.'

'I'm checking out,' I told her. It was a Sunday morning in winter. I was seventeen. My father eyed me over the top of the fridge. He was wearing a white robe and holding a phone to his ear. Now he clamped the phone to his chest. 'Checking out? Of where?'

'Of school. And out of here.'

Rania looked down. She coughed harshly: she liked to go down to the summerhouse at the bottom of the garden and smoke hash. Only once a week. She was moderate in her habits.

'You can't do that,' my father said.

'When did you leave school? Sixteen? And look at you. Rolling in money.'

'You have to get a . . . a . . . degree!' He twitched the phone irritably back up to his ear. Rania made a tsking sound and shook her head. I levelled my gaze at her.

'What've you got a degree in, Rania? Nail polish? Fucking?'

'Hey!' they both said.

I went on, tonelessly. 'In handbags? Facelifts?'

Rania picked up the folded newspaper and threw it at me. My father ducked. 'Say that again?' he said intently into the phone.

'Frocks? Hair dye?'

Rania reached across the table to slap me but she was too slow. She made an animal noise through her teeth and held her red nails against her face. 'Gnaaaa,' she said. Her fingers quivered.

'Go on, rip your face off. You can always get a new one. Yeah, get them to rig you up a new one!'

Unable to talk over the screaming match that now gained pace and volume, my father put his phone away and leaned on the top of the fridge, his chin on his hand. There was a moment when Rania and I couldn't hear each other, or ourselves. Her face was contorted. I could see her back teeth. Then there was a lull.

'What are you going to do, then?' he asked. 'In life,' he added, delicately. He pinched his fingers over his brow.

'Can't you give me a job?'

The phone on the kitchen bench rang. Rania snatched at it, but my father was too quick. 'Call you back,' he muttered into it, and ducked his head. 'I'll think about a job,' he said to me, and slipped out of the room. We listened to him thud up the stairs. Rania made another sound: weary, cynical: 'Eeeeyah.'

That afternoon my father and I conferred in the summer-house. He offered me a job in the waterfront office from which his associate, Mr Ling, conducted some of his deals. The winter sun was setting over the big house. Somewhere within, in a trance of Egyptian cunning, Rania plotted and lurked. The camellia bushes were flowering, and covered in the dead brown blobs of flowers already gone bad. My father smoked a brown cheroot, smoothed his bottle-brown hair and told me, eyes glazed, fist cupped protectively around his pungent smoke, 'If you ever need money, you come to me. You come to me.'

'You sound like a gangster, Dad,' I said.

He took my arm. 'Let me tell you a few things about Mr Ling,' he said.

Later I was in my bedroom, among the magazines and cuddly toys. While packing a single reproachful sports bag — six impractically flimsy outfits, four cartons of Rania's cigarettes and a ton of makeup — I was busy regretting Rania's shoe size. It was only the canoeish length of her feet that stopped me stealing a swag bag of gold stilettos, of jewelled mules. Below, a fresh fight was breaking out. My father's new girlfriend kept ringing the house and it was getting on Rania's nerves.

Their voices rose. He threw her cigarettes into the pool. She told him to get a hairpiece. 'You are very nearly bald!' She told him she'd suffered enough. 'My bags are packed! The lawyers are poised!'

He went down on one knee and begged her not to go. Her gaze travelled ironically upwards, her eye caught mine as I leaned from the upstairs window. I saw his hunched shoulders, his head bowed at the level of her crotch. There was a thin moon above the plum tree, and tinselly Venus beside it, shining down. Rania was brown and slant-eyed, like a witch. My father had his fingers crossed behind his back. She let him win her over — her long fingers suffered themselves to unclench, to run over his hair; he rose and clasped her hands in his — but it was beginning to be over. I could see it all. It wouldn't be Rania who packed her bags and called the lawyers. My father would never let that happen. No, unquestionably, he would be the one to go first. And only once he'd worked out what to do with his money.

There were reversals and re-workings. After all, they'd been together a long time. I'd left the big house by then, and wasn't witness to their final parting. I heard about it later from Rania. He moved into a penthouse with his new girlfriend, but kept sneaking back home (to be mauled and punished and slashed with Rania's six-inch heels). After a couple of nights he would flee, scratched and bloodied, back to the penthouse. He was working out his old addiction. Eventually his girlfriend put her foot down. She told him he needed a change. He came to me at the offices of Mr Ling, and told me he was heading overseas. 'To Thailand first. Business interests. Then we'll take it from there.'

He left me a lot of money. And the job, which gave me a lot

more money than it should have, being a job that was all about doing very little. He left the big Remuera house to Rania, for me to inherit when she died. I haven't seen him or heard from him since. I know he's moved about all over the place. Vietnam. Brazil. Georgia. The Ukraine. I've wondered, sometimes, whether I have any half-siblings out there. I mean, he's always put it about to such an extent, you'd think there'd be someone (some Thai or Australian or Arab or American) who looks uncannily like me.

But I have no word of anyone so far.

Mr Ling and I hit it off when I went to work for him, down there at John John G. Shipping. He taught me to play mahjong. He made deals and I managed the office. There were shady things going on with the business, but I only did light office work and arranged the files. If I'd dug a bit deeper I would have found that John John G. Shipping was a front. But I didn't care about that.

I lived in an apartment on the waterfront with two St Cuthbert's old girls, Mackenzie and Nadine. They were in their early twenties. Both knew my father. Mackenzie was a PR agent who liked to snort coke and go out with awful, crass, rich property dealers, and Nadine was a presenter on a children's TV show. We went out every night, drinking and clubbing. I spent all the money I earned. Nadine had a permanently stuffed-up nose and a squeaky Mickey Mouse voice because of all the drink and drugs and blowjobs she got through. Her cartoon voice made her popular with children, and whenever we went near kids we were mobbed by her teeny fans. Like most of us private-school girls Mackenzie and Nadine talked about money all the time, wouldn't be seen dead in a cheap car, and had nasty faux St Cuthbert's accents. (That accent of ours: what's it supposed to sound *like*? And where does it think it comes *from*?) We were always bawling for whaite waine and calling it naice and, like true private-school girls, we were good at shouting and drinking and being unbelievably aggressive in the traffic. Nights we spent in the waterfront bars, days I sat in the office, making phonecalls for

Mr Ling. During lunchtimes I played mahjong. And then, one day, it all came crashing down.

I went to work and found the glass doors locked. There were men in suits inside, carrying boxes of files. They had Mr Ling on a plastic chair and someone was sticking a bit of paper under his nose. I walked away. I went and stood at the edge of the wharf looking down at the water. I couldn't think what to do. For a while I had the irrational idea that if I kept very still no one would see me. I had the office keys in my hand; I let them fall into the water. I saw them sink under the green swell. The sun was shining on the water; the light was very bright. There was a man in a suit walking towards me. 'Good morning,' he said. 'Claudine Zambucka? Would you please come with me?'

They sat me on a plastic chair next to Mr Ling. They held bills of lading in front of me and asked me what they were for. I told them I didn't know. A bit later they took me and Mr Ling to the police station, in separate cars. I went on saying I'd been hired to carry out light office duties. I tried to impress on them how stupid I was. I acted hurt and pompous, as though I thought the menial tasks I performed were vitally important to the running of John John G. Shipping. None of them mentioned my father — I suppose he'd disguised his connection to the place. And I hoped nice Mr Ling wouldn't divulge the staggering sum I was being paid for doing practically nothing. 'What's this all about?' I kept asking. They let me out eventually, with threats, and warnings of a bruising rerun. 'We'll be in touch,' they said.

By the time I got out the day had gone. The day had disappeared while I was sweating it out at Central Police. The town hall clock told me it was 4 a.m. I had no money and no coat. It was freezing, and, unusually, there was thick mist hanging in the streets. It took me a long time to walk home, and then I remembered I'd thrown away my keys. *That* was a stupid thing to have done. I couldn't get into the building.

Workmen had been reshaping the path, and there was a patch of broken stones and concrete. I was looking around in it for something to throw up onto the balcony, when a man walked out of the fog. I straightened up, a bit of concrete in my hand. I remember thinking how extremely pale he was. I waited for him to pass but he stopped. He was about thirty, with a round face and curly hair. He was wearing a suit. He said something about himself. He clutched his arms to his stomach. I told him to go away. And he attacked me. Just like that. Or was something else said? Perhaps I swore at him and he . . . Anyway he attacked me. He stumbled forward and took hold of my shoulders. I hit him with the stone I had in my hand. It wasn't very heavy — maybe as big as half a brick. He clawed my face. I hit him in the head. He bent over, staggering. And then I ran away.

When the sun came up I was walking along Tamaki Drive. I had a scratched eye, laddered stockings, and half the buttons wrenched from my shirt. One of my shoes flip-flopped against my foot, the heel left somewhere on Quay Street.

It was high tide. On the harbour side the water glimmered all silvery and cold, the sky was high and pale and tinged with rose. Over in Judges Bay the water was deep green and still under the pohutukawas. I looked at the water and thought how beautiful it was — the rippled silver, the slow green. When the dawn came an idea had got into my head. There was something missing. The man at the waterfront — I couldn't remember what he'd said. Something about himself. Or about his body. Had he told me he was hurt? Out in the harbour a current — smooth water crossing ripples — formed a snaky question mark. Was it possible he had asked for my help? I laughed. You came to the wrong place, mister. Sorry about that. I turned into Ngapipi Road. Still about a mile to go. Where was I heading? Back to the big house I'd left a year before. I couldn't think of anywhere else to go.

I knocked on the door. Piles of leaves lay along the path. The lawn had been mown, the hedges trimmed, the summer-house freshly painted. Looking around, I was having to re-work the picture I'd built up in my mind over the year, a scenario I'd relished during my quiet hours at John John G. Shipping:

that of Rania, now abandoned, gone speechlessly to rack and ruin. Instead, when she wrenched open the door and stood staring down her nose with the highest, snootiest Arabian disgust, she looked more burnished and coppery than ever. She looked like an ad.

'Pooh,' she kept saying after I'd persuaded her to let me in. 'What please is that horrible smell?'

'Police stations.'

'Pooh!'

I waited, patiently. 'Can I have a shower?'

'Pooh!'

Eventually I was sitting at the kitchen table, wrapped in one of her old robes, while she pretended to look through the fridge. 'Nothing much here,' she said with sprightly malice. 'But you're not exactly fading away!'

I settled for one of her powerful coffees, and an International Gold. 'How are things with you, Rania?' I asked.

Her expression went dark. 'Your father left me with nothing. No money. How could I pay the bills?'

'So what did you do?' I could tell she hadn't had to scrimp or save. Her face, her hair, her clothes, all bore evidence of the costliest attention.

She smiled coldly. 'I have a business.'

'What sort of business?'

'Gentlemen's club.'

'A brothel?'

'Sauna, massage, brothel. Sure. Very good business. Ling and I . . .'

'Mr Ling!'

'Ling is silent partner.' She hummed and looked out the window.

'Oh really.' I told her why I'd been at the police station. Then I regretted having told her, because I had to spend a long time getting her to not throw me out.

'This is *my* house,' I protested, after a while.

'Not yet it isn't! Only when I die! I don't want trouble here! Go away!'

'Don't be ridiculous.' I was weary. 'I want to go to bed.'

'No! Get out!'

'Oh, shut up, Rania,' I said. I went to my old room. I dragged a chest of drawers in front of the door. I took out an empty drawer and put it next to the bed, as a weapon. I crawled into the cold sheets.

I dreamed Rania was coming at me, a satin cushion in her hands. She said, intently, 'He's gone now. He's gone. There's only *you and me . . .*'

For two days I hid in the upstairs room. In the mornings she rattled the doorknob and threatened to call the police, and told me to be out by the time she came back. When I heard her convertible on the drive I went down to the kitchen. In the evening we watched television together in the sitting room. Rania lived on cigarettes and diet pills and sparkling wine. On the third day I went out to the shops, and withdrew some money from my bank account, slumping with relief when they let me do it. I'd feared there might be some sort of freeze on my funds. That night I cooked her a meal. She watched me prepare it and waited for me to start eating, as though suspecting I'd slipped in some poison. She had a few mouthfuls and then lit a moody cigarette. I ate all mine and then finished hers.

She stared at me. Then she drummed her fingers on the table and said, 'So. Fatty boomsticks. You want a job?'

'In a brothel? No thanks.'

'Administration,' she said smoothly. 'Strictly no contact work. Managing the girls.'

I thought about it. I was curious. 'Yeah, go on then. When and where?'

'You come with me. Tomorrow.' She pulled her long black hair away from her face. There were rich, raisiny shadows under her eyes. Her eyes were black-lined and almond-shaped, in the painted face. I looked at her: my Egyptian stepmummy, with her hating eyes.

'And now I must go and watch *Antiques Weekly*,' she announced, and swept from the room. I heard the fizz and crackle of the TV. Her mad scent hung in the air.

The next morning we stood outside her brothel. It was called The Land of Opportunity. It was a grand old stone house with stained-glass windows, at the end of a row of shops.

'We are strictly upmarket,' Rania said. 'Lot of doctors, lawyers. Judges. Pillars of community. Top civil servants, policemen . . .'

She ran on. Like most people in this game, she liked to make it sound as if everyone did it, they just didn't admit it. Especially people of great talent and distinction. 'Politicians, captains of the industry, artists, television executives . . .'

I followed her up the stairs.

'Actors, diplomats, visiting dignitaries . . .'

We entered a velvety bar, with couches and heaped cushions.

'And no Maoris,' Rania finished.

'No *Maoris*?'

'Customers maybe. If tidy. Girls, no.' Her eyes were slits.

'You can't do that. It's not . . . It's against the . . . Human Rights Convention.'

'Is my place.'

'God. You're supposed to have left all that behind when you came here. You can't go on like that.'

'Is classy place.'

'God, Rania!'

She told me what I had to do. I sat in a kind of nook up the front and matched the girls with all the captains of industry and diplomats and judges. Except of course there weren't any of those. If you checked out the conversation in the lounge, pre-date, you'd find it wasn't very intellectual. Or very classy. Mostly the men were drunk, or needing to get drunk very quickly; most were sweating yobs whose eyes bulged with all the things they were planning to do, once they'd loosened up enough there in the lounge. And none of them looked like they had any money.

After a month I knew my way around. I was well established

in The Land of Opportunity. Rania seemed resigned to having me back in the house, too. She and I went on arguing about the race issue. I was pretty shocked by her attitude. I tried to put it in her terms: 'Okay. Forget the civil rights question. You're turning away good merchandise. I mean, they tend to be better-looking, for a start.'

'Not than the Asians.'

'Okay, not better than the Asians. But better than the whites. Better than all that pastiness and freckles and flab you've got going out there.'

In the end she said she would have a few Maoris if they pretended to be Arab. That was a good laugh, but Rania seemed to believe it was possible. Or she pretended to. She hired a Maori woman called Diana, who was very good-looking and who, pretending with satirical insouciance to be an Arab, got on well with Rania. When Diana was taking a break they sat in the office together, smoking and watching the lounge through the one-way glass. They were both brown and narrow-eyed and mad and hard. Sometimes they were joined by Mr Ling, for a session of mahjong. Mr Ling had done some work on his identity: he now sported a perm, and everyone called him Mr Long. In the evenings the place stank of coffee and cigarettes and booze. And sex and crime. And money.

A few months after Diana arrived, she brought her little cousin Darlene in to work at The Land. Darlene was an awkward girl with a witless, compulsive laugh. It was a chuckle, characteristically Maori, but with the charm hammered out of it — a dull, reflexive plea for peace-not-violence. I sat in my nook listening to her. The laugh was unbelievable. What terrible forces, what deprivation, had produced that abject sound?

'I told the fulla eh, ih ih ih ih, stick it up yor arse, eh, ih ih ih ih. Got a smoke? Ih ih ih. And he goes, nah, cuz, gunna stick it up *yor* arse, ih ih ih.'

That was Darlene off duty. When she was entertaining clients she was nice and polite and put on a few airs: 'And where do youse fullas stay? Eh? *True?* Long way to come, eh? My cousin's from there, eh. He's a mean bugger, eh. Ih ih ih ih.'

She was a useful girl, just turned seventeen. She didn't usually baulk at anything. But one night, when a stag party had taken over the lounge and the men looked, to me in my corner, like predatory animals, with their watchful, calculating eyes, Darlene had some sort of meltdown or failure of courage. Her laugh got higher and stranger, and more repetitive, until it was like panting, like a full-blown panic attack. Diana got up from her place on the couch. She drew Darlene to her bosom and took her into my corner, whispering in her ear, stroking her hands.

'Baby,' she said. 'Baby.' Darlene looked blankly at me, over Diana's shoulder. Her breathing slowed. Her eyes closed.

Diana gave her a little shake. 'There now. Hush now. Okay, kid? Okay?'

They hugged. Diana wiped Darlene's tears.

Then she forced a couple of pills down the girl, mopped her makeup and booted her back to work. It was a bumper evening. Rania and Mr Long were up all night afterwards, talking tax evasion.

I had an idea after that, thinking about their faces — Diana's and Darlene's. The eyes, the cheekbones, the beautifully curved lips. I decided Diana was Darlene's mum. I put it to Rania but she just looked at me over her champagne flute and made a hissing sound between her teeth, '*Sssssss.*' Mr Long appeared at the door behind her, his face folded into a smile. When he smiled his eyes disappeared. He lounged there in his black suit, with his no-eyes smile.

At home one afternoon, I sat smoking in the summerhouse. The days were lengthening, the light was bright, the winter chill had gone. The garden was full of flowers. Above the house the sky was delicately striped with cloud. I remembered my father standing by the dropping buds of the camellia bush, cupping his hand around his brown cigarette. I remembered my dead mother. One memory: she was sitting on the couch, it was raining, a man had just come to the door and gone, and she was crying. I looked out at the liquid world and listened to a story record while I waited for her to stop crying, and when I moved my head the ripples in the windowpane made trenches in the lawn. I remembered the man who came at me out of the fog that time, down on the wharf. He said to me . . . what did he say? *They took my. Please. I need your. I need your . . .*

A car was nosing down the drive. It was Mr Long, in his black Mercedes. Rania came out of the house. She walked with him, talking. He nodded. Soon we would head across town, to The Land. The girls would be waiting — the battered merchandise, their use-by dates near expired. And the men, the clients — they reminded me of something. They reminded me of myself. Long ago, in all those back yards, the empty houses in the drifting afternoons. The breaking and entering. The searching, the rummaging. And then the emptiness of a white courtyard, ribbons of light glancing off a pool, the strewn pile of knick-knacks and trinkets. A kind of daze afterwards, a confusion in the lull. What did the men want? What did I want? What I stole I threw away. I didn't want it. Not really. What was the thing we looked for, and couldn't find?

I crossed the lawn. We were wearing black that day, Rania and I. A sentimental acknowledgement (to placate the girls) of Darlene's death the day before. Her substance issues (her smorgasbord drug habit) had finally finished her off. All evening I would be boredly soothing deluded clients: 'She understood me,' they would say. 'She listened.' 'She was the only one who cared.' I wouldn't set them straight. I wouldn't tell them: she barely noticed you. She was out of her mind. And if you did swim into focus, she was out of her mind with fear.

Now I stepped up to the black car. Mr Long opened the door. I sank into the plush seat. In the front Rania lit a gold-tipped cigarette. She angled the mirror at me and raised her eyebrows. I smiled. Mr Long drove up the drive. The iron gates closed with a heavy clunk on the high walls. Soft music played. We cruised across town. At The Land of Opportunity we got out. The three of us, Rania, Mr Long and I. In our black sunglasses. In our mourning weeds.

him

There are some unsolved murders in this city, and I think three of them are connected.

I think they were done by the same man. The first was a woman found murdered in a city office block. In the second, a woman walking downtown went missing and turned up dead behind a suburban building. The third was a man found dead at the bottom of another office block. The killer is operating in a small area. He lives somewhere central. How do I know this? It's instinct. I just know I'm on the right track.

I used to have lunch with my husband, Max, in the city. We'd go to a café in the mall and there was a security guard stationed at the entrance. He had cold blue eyes and an intent expression. When I passed him I always had the strange fancy that he was making a noise, a sort of low, avid exhalation, like a beast. I thought of the noise as *ravening*. My husband didn't have any fancies about noises, and when I described this impression he smiled tolerantly and glazed over as usual. But I thought, that man is a killer.

When the woman was found dead in the very same building the man worked in as a guard, I didn't have any trouble figuring out who was responsible. The next time we went to the mall for lunch the place was full of cops. I don't remember seeing the guard there again. But I did see him soon after, in Remuera, when I was buying a cake for a big lunch party I was having. I stared and stared. He looked up and I saw that he'd noticed me. I was worried then, in case he realised I suspected him. Imagine if he turned up outside my house!

A week or so later, when I was with the boys in Foodtown, I turned around and the same man was standing right behind me. This is the sort of thing that happens to me: I go looking for trouble and then find I've bitten off more than I can chew. I got a fright, but I knew what I had to do. I glanced at him in a completely neutral way. I went on talking to the boys and dawdling through the aisles. I thought, if I show anything, it'll confirm that I know, and he *will* follow me to the house. The boys had no idea what was going on, and he stopped following after a while, and went away. It was a test of my nerve. I realised how careful you have to be, especially when you're the mother of young children.

I didn't see the man again, but I didn't stop thinking about him. When I heard about the woman who'd gone missing and turned up dead I thought *him* again. And now he's thrown someone off a building in the city. The police haven't made any progress, although they don't tell the public everything. But I'm sure I'm the only one who's worked it out. It all comes from being observant, and noticing what people are really like.

Max only ever paid attention to things that affected him. We had a relative who started growing a tumour behind his eye. Each time we saw him his eye had got more prominent, until he looked like a monster. After one lunch I said to Max, 'I'm glad John's getting his eye seen to at last.' Max looked completely blank. He said what was I talking about. If you don't notice a huge eyeball you're not going to pick up the subtleties.

Max and I didn't talk much about anything, to tell the truth.

He was always too busy. I told my friends Karen and Trish about my theories, but they laughed a lot and strayed off the point. We ended up talking about the kids and complaining about our schedules. Karen and Trish each had two children. My two, Charles and Max junior, were nine and four. We'd taken Charles out of his state primary school and sent him to King's School. Max went to a private kindergarten.

I had to do a lot of driving, what with all the children's activities. There was golf, cricket, swimming, piano, extra maths, violin, gymnastics. There seemed to be a competition at King's about who was paying the biggest fortune to turn out the most talented kid. It struck me as a bit rude the way the mothers went on about money. They brought it into the conversation all the time, either explicitly or by hints. They complained about how much they'd spent, just so you'd know how much. That's what the school was like.

'Nothing but the best for my boy,' Max said. 'You get what you pay for,' he said.

I shared the driving with Karen and Trish, and I supposed it was good the boys had so many activities. My childhood was different. I remember my mother coming home from work and asking, 'What've you been doing?' and we always said, 'Playing under the house.' We spent hours down there in the dirt and cobwebs. There were no adults around. We made huts. We pretended. We ran wild.

Sometimes, when we were driving to golf, I looked back at the boys. They had their faces pressed against the window. I wondered what they were thinking. I tried to talk to them but they just grunted and glowered. I tried to keep to the speed limit. In the back the trolleys and golf bags rattled with a cold, clinking sound.

Charles was playing soccer and I was standing on the sideline, warming my hands with a takeaway coffee.

Karen said, 'And I picked up some cute ski suits from Baby Gap?'

There was a man coming across the field. He was in jeans

and a T-shirt, although it was cold and showery. He had strong shoulders and a nice lean body. I'd seen him somewhere before.

'It had to be the five series. Then the Porsche Cayenne. There's no pleasing . . .' Karen stopped. She nudged me.

The man was smiling at us. His glasses were smeared with rain.

'Hi, Kim,' he said.

I remembered: he was Dan Weston, the father of one of Charles's school friends.

'I had a word with the coach. Tom's changed to Charles's team.'

'Oh *good.*'

Dan was young and good-looking. We started talking. Karen made it obvious she thought he was pretty nice. He said he worked in TV, some technical role. Tom was his only child. He lived near the soccer ground, and he said why didn't we get together after the game so Charles and Tom could play. Karen dropped hints that she'd like to come too, but he didn't pick up on them. She turned huffy after that. Dan smiled at me and I thought he knew she was annoyed, and that he was sharing a little joke with me about it. His eyes were sharp and alert. He looked as if he noticed things about people.

I walked along with Dan after the game. Charles looked surprised when I said we were going to Tom's, but soon the boys were racing ahead, shouting and kicking the ball to each other. Karen stood by her car, watching.

Dan and Tom lived in a stucco building a few streets back from the beach. They had a small flat on the ground floor. The sitting room was full of pot plants and the winter sun shone directly in. There were shelves full of books. They had a yard out the front, and a picnic table. There were some big tubs with palms, the dirt filled with cigarette butts. The kitchen was tiny but clean.

Dan said, 'I've only got instant coffee. Is that okay?'

It all seemed so sunny and simple; it made me feel light and happy. I thought: why do we need all the stuff we have? There was a ramshackle garage in the front of the yard, with a battered car that Max wouldn't have been seen dead in. It made me feel embarrassed, but in a rich, pleasurable way, as if Dan had told me a family secret.

We sat at the picnic table. He had an opinion about everything: books, politics, TV, the arts. The time went by fast. It seemed all right to ask, 'What does Tom's mother do?' He said they'd split up and that she'd gone home to the Wairarapa, leaving him to bring up Tom as best he could.

He seemed so hard up I wondered how he could afford to send Tom to King's. Straight away, as if he could read my mind, he told me that his ex-wife's parents paid. They were wealthy farming people. He got very serious and said he wanted only the best for Tom, even if it meant he had to go without things himself. He said he believed fiercely in education, and that he wanted to make sure Tom worked hard. He said he thought Charles would be a good influence on Tom, because Tom was lazy, whereas Charles was a studious, bright boy.

'Charles is tall for his age isn't he?' he said. 'Well co-ordinated, too. He looks great on the soccer field.'

He got up suddenly and called out, 'Tom! Keep the noise down!'

He explained that the other tenants were old and complained.

When we were leaving, the boys kept kicking the ball. Dan grabbed Tom's arm and said, 'Tom. Manners.'

'Thank you for coming,' Tom said.

On school days Dan parked his old Holden among the expensive cars and SUVs. There was a kind of dignity about it. He never looked embarrassed, even though some of the other parents made jokes about his car. On sports day he stayed the whole afternoon and sat with us on the grass. He said he worked flexible hours so he could be around for Tom. He stayed to watch Charles high-jumping. When Charles came first I hugged him, and Dan did too. He'd told me he'd had a word with the headmaster and that Tom was to move into

Charles's class. He was pleased, because he thought their friendship was so good for Tom. There was something about the way he said it that made me think he was pleased for his own sake too. I blushed. Then he said, boyishly, 'So we can spend a lot of time together.' And I blushed even more.

'You fancy him,' Karen said.

'No,' I said. But I thought about him, in his jeans and T-shirt, waiting for Tom in the carpark while the big cars purred and throbbed by. Once I saw him and Tom having a sword fight with long grass stalks, laughing, falling down.

'I don't like him,' Karen said. She made a spiteful face.

Tom started coming to our house after school. Afterwards Dan picked him up and he always stopped to talk. He repeated that he wanted Charles and Tom to be best friends; it was a kind of refrain with him, but he made it clear he was glad for his own reasons. He said how lucky it was that we'd got together, two people who were interested in the same things. He said we had the same ideas about bringing up children. Too many people didn't really think about it, he said, and that amounted to negligence. They spoiled their kids and let them behave like slobs. He and I were going to have a really terrific pair of boys, because we thought about things and knew what mattered. He talked as if he and I had a secret pact, and the rest of the world could do what it liked.

He was observant. He imitated the teachers: their walks, the way they talked. He made me laugh. He said things that I'd thought myself, privately, but hadn't had anyone to tell. I began inviting Tom over myself, without asking Charles whether he wanted me to.

Dan didn't approve of the boys watching TV. He liked them to have healthy outdoor activity. He was very serious about that. He said that Charles had such a good physique, it would be criminal to let him sit around. We had a rope swing that went right over the bank at the back of our garden and Dan went down with me and the boys to have a look at it. We were talking, and the next moment he leapt onto the swing. I watched him flying through the air, his shirt riding up, his legs kicking. He was a big, strong man, but sometimes he used his body as if he was still a boy.

Dan invited Charles to their place, but Charles told me he wouldn't go.

'Why?' I demanded.

Charles scowled and wouldn't say. I went on at him.

He said, 'It's too small and you have to be quiet because of the tenants and he hasn't got anything to play with.'

'You're a spoiled middle-class brat,' I told him. I kept inviting Tom to our place instead. I liked to think he enjoyed our big house and the pool. And I looked forward to talking to Dan.

Every week at soccer Dan watched Charles and praised his skill. He paid more attention to him than to Tom, who wasn't so sporty. 'Charles is a real athlete,' he said, following him with his eyes. Each time he said nice things about Charles I had the impression that he was really saying something about me. But there was a shy side to him, and so he communicated in this sideways way, through Charles. Once, after he'd watched Charles for a long time, he said to me, 'I think Charles takes after you, not Max.' I smiled and looked at the ground.

One day Dan told me he'd had to move house. He said the flat wasn't a suitable environment for a child. He'd rented a villa with a garden. I felt sorry for him. He was so keen to do the right thing for Tom, and it couldn't be easy when he was short of money. A few weeks later he told me they'd moved again. The house hadn't worked out. This time he was going to try a flat in the inner city. I didn't think that sounded very nice for Tom, but I didn't say anything. I was a bit surprised when I discovered they'd moved yet again. It became quite a pattern. I can't remember how many times Dan came up with a new address, a new phone number. Tom seemed resigned to packing up and moving on, and I thought Dan must be one of those restless people who's always thinking somewhere else will be better, more interesting.

Dan wanted to have a sleepover at his place for the boys.

He said he would pitch a tent in the garden. The boys would love it. I was a bit embarrassed, because every time I put this to Charles he refused, and I had to keep making excuses. Dan wasn't put off. He kept raising the subject. I didn't like to think Charles was too soft and spoiled to sleep in a tent.

I bought a computer, and when I told Dan this he said he would help me set it up. He was an expert on the internet. He knew everything about computers, and I asked his advice because I didn't know much. He said, 'I'll be your computer fixer. You'll never need anyone else. Call me for advice any time.' He said he wanted to create a website for Tom. 'It's a fun thing. I'll get Charles's photo and we can post it on the web. Then they can communicate with kids all over the world. It'll be educational.'

Another thing Dan knew about was cameras. He videoed sports days, school outings. Karen got him to video the school play.

In March I invited Tom to Charles's birthday party. It was already a riot by the time Dan and Tom arrived. The boys were throwing themselves into the pool and shooting one another with water guns. Max was already talking about needing a gin and tonic. Dan pushed Tom ahead of him and said, 'Make sure you behave yourself.' Tom walked away, towards the pool.

'About four o'clock, then,' I said, putting on a wry, brave face, because of the bedlam.

'Actually, I thought I'd stay, if that's all right,' Dan said. 'It's a long drive home and my car's making a funny noise.'

'Oh. Okay, fine.' I was flustered. I went to my room and looked in the mirror. I put on some makeup, to cover my blushing. I thought about offering him some wine.

When I looked out, Dan was running across the lawn with a water gun, shooting the boys. I watched him wrestle a boy to the ground. It was strange to see a man throwing himself about in that way. His shirt came up and I saw his chest. I felt hot watching him. He put his foot on the boy and did a Tarzan pose, showing his arm muscles. The boys stopped running and watched uncertainly, trailing their guns. The boy under Dan suddenly twisted away, and Dan fell. He got up, marched over, took hold of the boy's collar and put his face up close, talking. The boy bowed his head, hunching his small shoulders. Dan said something and flipped the boy away. Then they were all running again, hooting and shrieking.

I went out on the deck and offered him a glass of wine. He came over, sweating. He refused the wine. He said, 'Honestly. Kids.'

'What happened?'

'They get a bit carried away, don't they? They need a bit of telling.'

He went back to the lawn.

I was icing the cake when Charles came in, crying.

'What's wrong?' I asked.

Dan walked in, hot and laughing. 'He banged his face in battle.'

'Never mind, old chap,' Max said. He and Dan exchanged wry smiles. Max handed Dan a beer.

'What did you bang it on?' I asked. I touched the bruise on his cheek.

'His gun,' Charles said loudly, pointing at Dan.

'Never mind,' Max said again, and hustled the boys towards the table.

Charles cheered up and the party carried on. Afterwards Max and I drank some wine. I wanted to talk to him but he went to sleep in his chair when I was in the middle of telling him something. I read a book, watched some TV. I looked at myself in the mirror and wondered whether my face was getting old.

We were sitting on the benches, waiting for the boys to come out of class. Karen said, 'I'm going to set up my own business. Selling designer children's clothes?'

Dan nudged me. 'There's a book I want to lend you.' We were sitting close together. I could feel the muscles in his arm.

Some boys came tearing out. Dan got up and went over. 'Excuse me,' he said to Tom. 'Don't you know you're not allowed to run?'

Tom looked down. The boys shifted uneasily.

'I don't want to see you doing it again,' he said. He took hold of Tom's arm. 'Is that clear?'

He came back. 'They need boundaries. Boys respond to that.'

Karen sighed sententiously. 'It's a fact.'

'For example . . .' Dan went on. He stopped. 'Just a minute.'

The boys were play fighting. Dan walked over to them very fast. He took hold of two and pulled them apart, then he pushed the other boys into a line. He walked up and down, talking.

Charles started to walk away. Dan glanced from him to the other boys. Then he jogged after Charles. Charles looked behind and began to run. Dan ran faster, caught hold of his arm, and Charles fell onto the concrete. Dan held him down, hard, for a moment. Then he half got up, went down again, and did a mock wrestling hold.

He came back, pushing Charles ahead of him.

'Here's your villain,' he said. He was breathing hard, his face red and sweaty. He thrust Charles at me, his knees skinned where he'd fallen on the concrete. 'I think your mother wants to talk to you,' he said. He winked at me and Karen.

'What do you think you're doing?' I said to Dan.

'We'll make him a decent citizen,' Dan said.

'No,' I said. 'We're going.' We started to walk away. I hugged Charles's shoulders.

Dan came up behind us. He put his hand on my shoulder. 'Is there a problem?' he said.

'He's my son. You don't tell him what to do. I do.'

Dan began to shake. He leaned over me. I had a sense of how tall and muscular he was. 'I think we're all entitled to set appropriate standards,' he said.

'He's my son. If he needs telling, I'll tell him.'

Dan clenched his fists. He came up very close. 'I think we all . . .' He choked. I'd never seen him angry before.

'You do not tell him what to do, and you do not touch him. Ever!' I hurried Charles away. We got into the car. I looked into the rear-view mirror, into my own eyes. I thought of Dan shaking, his face screwed up. I looked at Charles. He didn't say anything.

The next day Dan handed me an envelope, his hands trembling. I took it and walked away.

I read it. It was long and articulate. Dan apologised. He realised that an issue had arisen between us. He was confident that, though we might have some different ideas about appropriate discipline and standards of behaviour, we could acknowledge them, work through them, and go on making sure the boys progressed well. He and I understood each other. We had the same aims and goals. It was natural there might be the odd situation where we would diverge, but we knew we were mostly in agreement. It would be a shame if anything affected the great friendship between the boys. Dan realised his expectations were high (and he didn't think unrealistically so), but he was perfectly able to be flexible if others didn't have the same . . .

The letter ran on, repeating itself. It was bullying, full of jargon. It was elaborate and strenuous. Under the surface it threatened, it accused. It aimed to send me scurrying, flustered and apologising, to heal the rift. I had the sense of Dan clutching at something he desperately wanted, a sense almost of hysteria. I thought of the other fathers I knew. They were busy, preoccupied with their adult worlds. They cared about their children. But they didn't take much notice of their children's friends. I sat by the pool, reading the letter again. I couldn't believe I'd been such a fool.

Dan stayed away from us for a week. Then one morning he came across the playground. His face was white and strained. He talked very fast.

'Hope that's all sorted out? Tom's been at me about his website. We haven't had the photo of Charles yet. Could I just have a picture of him? Tom will be really pleased.' He took a digital camera out of his bag.

'No,' I said.

'No?' He blinked.

'And the videos you've taken of Charles — at sports, at swimming. I want you to give them to me.'

He knew what I was saying. He gave me a look of such hatred I backed away. His face burned.

In the days after that, all I could think about was how to keep Dan away from Charles. I couldn't tell anyone, because I had no real evidence. I didn't want to hurt Tom. It made me cold to think that I'd pushed Charles to play with Tom. I kept coming back to the fact that Charles had kept his distance. He had kept away from Dan.

The boys were to go on a swimming trip. Parents were invited, but Max and I were going to a wedding. I said to Max, 'You go to the wedding and I'll go on the school trip.'

Max said, 'Are you out of your mind?'

I sat Max down and told him about Dan. I said I'd realised Dan was fixated on Charles. 'He flattered me. He made me think he liked me, but all the time it was Charles. Just watch him. You watch. He never takes his eyes off Charles.'

Max sighed impatiently. 'He seems like a normal guy to me.' The discussion went on and on. We ended up shouting at each other.

The next day I went to Charles's teacher. She looked at me expectantly and I got nervous. My voice shook. I tried to explain but I muddled it badly. I could tell she thought I was nuts.

'You see, I think Dan wants to *hurt* Charles,' I finished up. I was whispering. I couldn't bring myself to be more frank.

The teacher looked at me in silence. Then she told me an anecdote about a school trip to the zoo. It wasn't connected to anything I'd said. It was as if she thought she was saving me from embarrassment. I left feeling idiotic. I knew what I was trying to tell her was true, but why should she believe me? I had no hard facts. There was so much I couldn't say and so little that I could.

That day after school I went to Dan. I made myself look friendly and relaxed. We said a few neutral things, then I asked him casually, 'Are you going on the swimming trip?'

His expression was pleasant. 'No, I have to work,' he said.

I decided to go with Max to the wedding.

Next morning the parents gathered outside the class. Dan was there, carrying a backpack. 'I got the day off after all,' he said, and he smiled. I was shocked by the smile. It said everything: that there was war between us; there was hatred. I felt it in my stomach, the violence of it. No one would have noticed or understood. They saw Dan Weston smiling at me, in the jolly crowd of parents and boys.

I went to Karen. I said, 'Can you do something for me? Can you take Charles in your group and make sure Dan Weston doesn't go near him?'

She opened her mouth, amazed.

'It's important. Don't let Dan near Charles.'

Max was waiting in the car. He gave a blast on the horn. Karen looked, mystified, over at Dan, smiling and joking with the other parents.

'Please,' I said.

'All right.' She put her hand on my arm. I hurried away.

After the wedding, Max and I were sitting in the car. I said to him, 'This can't go on.' I was thinking about Dan, the school.

Max was drunk. He said, 'No it can't.'

'I'm going to take Charles out of King's.'

Max said, 'What? Over my dead body!' He thumped the steering wheel. He wouldn't hear of it. He had gone to the school. His father and grandfather. Hell would freeze over . . .

'The situation is impossible.'

Max leaned over to me. 'It is impossible. Because *you're* impossible.'

I sat for a moment in silence. 'I know what's going to happen,' I said finally. We looked at each other. We knew each other very well. Without saying anything we agreed.

Max and I separated. He tried to stop me changing Charles's school, but in the end he had to give in. Charles didn't mind. He was pleased — relieved — to go back to his ordinary, homely state primary. He'd been happier there with his old friends. He gave up golf lessons. Max junior started at the primary school too.

I kept the house. Max and I had so much money the split didn't hurt us much. At least, I didn't think so. I knew how lucky I was. Max complained bitterly about finances. I played on his meanness when we were arguing about Charles changing schools. I told him what a saving it would be. After six months Max got himself a new girlfriend. Really he'd had her all along.

When Charles and Max junior have friends after school I say to them, 'Off you go. Do what you like. Go and play under the house!'

It's a silly private joke of mine, but it makes me feel happy.

Karen tells me that Dan took Tom out of school too, soon after Charles left. He did it without warning and they disappeared.

I don't know where they are now. Maybe Dan Weston's turned up at your child's school. Or maybe that blue-eyed security guard is stationed right outside the building where you work. You've got to keep an eye out. The world is full of strange people.

Extraordinary things can be harder to spot than ordinary ones. But it's the extraordinary things that jolt you into taking action. I'm happier now than I've been for years. I've got Dan Weston to thank for that.

Max tells everyone that I'm mad and impossible. He says I'll use any excuse to get my own way. I know people may have trouble believing what I've said, about being followed through the supermarket by a murderer, about Dan wanting Charles not me, and my being too vain and stupid to realise until it was nearly too late. But it's true. I've written it down, because every word of it is true.

the doctor

When I was examining a patient one morning an ant ran up the speculum. I concealed a flash of boyish laughter, panic. I angled the light, trying to find it. It had disappeared up there. One of the patient's round tanned knees brushed my ear. She had her baby in a car seat on the floor. She was staring at the ceiling, one hand behind her head.

I gave up, eased the speculum out. Decided it couldn't do any harm.

'That's fine,' I said. 'You can get dressed now.' I took her arm and helped her up. She let out a long breath and smiled.

I waited until she came out from behind the curtain. She was open-faced, plump, happy. The baby had round cheeks and silvery hair.

She listened to what I was saying. She was in perfect health, I told her. And there were no problems with the beautiful child.

'The birth was so hard,' she said. She smiled at the baby. 'She took until 6 a.m. to arrive, remember?'

'Ah, 6 a.m.' Often I have forgotten. There are so many. But I did remember the birth of her child, because, just before it, I'd delivered a baby whose father was drunk. I was on call for the public patients that night. There was a scene. The drunken father insulted a nurse. Security was called. The baby came while the husband was arguing with the midwife. I congratulated the mother. The nurses did too.

Then, around 5.30 a.m., I went to her, my private patient. Her husband, some lawyer or stockbroker, hovered anxiously near. The birth was straightforward. Every time I did something for this couple, they thanked me.

I walked her out to reception. She looked at me. You don't talk about these things, but I know a few of my obstetric patients fall in love with me, just a bit. I've been there, helped them, at their finest hour. Also, in a funny sort of way, it's a bit like we've had sex back there in my consulting rooms. I don't mean sexual gratification. But the level of intimacy, the amount they reveal to me, it's significant. They think about it. A few fall in love for a while, and then they forget. You get the odd one who won't let go. But they're rare. I have Clarice, my secretary, to protect me. And a big photo of my wife Karen on my desk, just to keep things clear.

Off she went, to the gleaming SUV. She turned and smiled again. Such trust. There you go with an ant up you, I thought. My mouth twitched. But that's the thing. I have bad thoughts, funny thoughts, savage thoughts. I have power over people. But I don't hurt them. They know I will never hurt them.

I straightened my face, because Viola was looking at me. Every time I came out of my room that young woman did nothing but stare.

I got home late. I turned into the drive. The bedroom light was on upstairs. Karen would be getting ready. I drove past the cypress trees, the flowerbeds, looking up at the house. It's two-storey, handsome, the return veranda covered in flowering wisteria. The new deck furniture out there by the pool, spotlights in the garden lighting up the ferns. If you spend long enough in my game you end up with money. Karen is always planning holidays, renovating. You end up wondering what to spend your money on.

Karen is a good person. She has done a lot for worthy causes. Our names — Dr Simon Lampton and Ms Karen Rutherford — are on the Gold List of sponsors for the opera, the theatre, the children's hospital. That night we had tickets for the ballet. I don't really go for ballet. The theatre all dark and suddenly a skinny figure hurtling 'expressively' across the stage. I have private thoughts: pretty ridiculous *you* look. Afterwards we come out and mingle with the other Gold List patrons, dressed up and full of our own virtue. I like the warmth and light, the crowd, the uniform — suits and evening dresses. We're armoured. I always have to wait for Karen. She stays on until the last moments, networking.

In front of me, men in leotards formed a circle and clasped one another. There was thunder and lightning, then the whistle of a train. The dancers mimed sorrow and pain. Karen was leaning forward, looking at the programme. On the other side her friend elbowed her and whispered: Trish, with her designer clothes and gold jewellery, her fluttering lashes, dyed blonde hair.

I can't stand Trish.

After the performance Karen said, 'Trish will drive me home. We've got things to talk about.' A fundraiser. They would linger over coffee, planning. Trish fluttered her fingers at me. She wore layers of shiny ruffled material. Her hair was platinum, afro. Once, at a party at her house, I talked to her husband. He gestured at the guests and said, 'Most of the wealth of this country is represented here.'

'Really,' I said.

Someone switched on an outside light. The women's hands went to their faces. I saw teeth, eyes. Teeth and eyes.

I started driving home. But then I went a different way. I drove down to the end of Queen Street, then up to the top, slowly. I turned onto Karangahape Road. I was putting off going home to the empty house. The streets were quiet; light rain made blurred loops of the streetlights. There were small crowds outside dark doorways, bouncers letting people in. I slowed down outside the Owl Bar. Two men were arguing. The taller man, dressed in a shabby coat, flared jeans and sandals, was leaning over a short, fat man, jabbing his finger into his shoulder. Someone tooted behind me. I pulled in to the kerb. The tall man shoved and shouted. I looked at his sour, disappointed mouth, his thick helmet of black hair. His glasses hung on a plastic chain around his neck. He came near my car. I slid down in my seat. He took a comb out of his pocket and slicked back his hair. His fingers were long, mobile — piano player's hands. He buttoned up his coat, fiddled with his glasses. He held them up and looked towards my car. I didn't breathe. He took a bottle out of his bag and swigged. He peered around, looked up at the rain drifting, falling. His body was swaying. I had never seen a face so bitter, so thwarted and sad. Never back then, never since. I watched until my father had finished drinking, pulled the tattered coat tighter around himself, and walked back into the bar.

I drove home. Karen came home and got into bed beside me. I put my arms around her. I told her: 'I love you with all my heart.'

My mother said, 'He was mathematical, musical. Played the piano. Did the cryptic crossword in three minutes flat. He could have got scholarships, gone on to university. He wasted it all. He said it was because he had to go out to work when he was too young, and then we were married and you children were born. He kept changing jobs because he had no staying power.'

She said, 'It's no use being a genius if you just drink it all away.'

He drank and they fought. He came home and broke things. We listened through the wall. I remember the boozy raving, the pacing, the bitter rage. 'You're tone deaf,' he said. 'Your voice is *dead*. The only thing you love is money.'

'You're no use to anyone,' she told him. She sold his piano. He came home from work to find it gone.

He drank for three days. He followed us to my aunt's. She called the police. He shouted as he was led away. He was going to kill my aunt, kill us, then himself. My mother said, 'Just yourself will do.' She was steely, contained, determined. She looked after us well. When I graduated she told me, 'You're set for life. Your father should be pleased. But he won't be able to bear it. He'll look at you and see what he could have been.'

I thought, I look at him and see what *I* could have been. Instead, I was a doctor. It was a happy day, my graduation. My mother and sisters and Karen and I spent it together. It was as if we'd all made good . . .

After the ballet I woke up in the night. I'd dreamed my father was standing at the end of the bed, raising his glasses to his face. Here I was in my tasteful bedroom, between expensive sheets, my beautiful wife next to me. He was seeing what he could have been.

But the dream had turned bad. Instead of triumph, I felt fear. I dreamed that I looked at him, and saw what I am.

About five years ago I moved into my current consulting rooms. I share a floor with other specialists. Our practice is modern and friendly. I rush between the hospital and my private rooms. I'm often called out late at night. I sweep through the empty streets in my big car, through suburbs washed with rain. I enjoy the silence before the crisis, before my date in the corridors of pain. I'm used to seeing women in agony. They plead and scream, they swear and cry. I touch them somewhere neutral, on the shoulder, or on the foot. I control them. I take away their pain.

At the public clinic the patients are overweight, tattooed and smoky. They present with diabetes, pierced genitalia, venereal diseases. They are not armoured with nice accents and designer clothes. But I find them more restful than the hectic matrons of Remuera and Parnell, who make every consultation a social event. Sometimes, when I get home from my private clinic, I feel as if I've been at a seven-hour cocktail party, without booze.

One day my secretary told me, 'There's a man on the phone. He says he's your father.'

My hands started shaking. I went into my room and took the call. I heard voices and music. The slurred voice said, 'Working hard?'

I tried to treat him like pain. To assess the situation from a long way off.

'It must be good,' he said. 'All those women. All that money.' The voice trailed off. He made a sound, like a sob. 'You're just like your mother . . .'

'I can't talk to you,' I said.

What do I know about him? I remember waiting outside his work to give him a birthday present. I was nine or ten. He took the present, opened it, but he didn't seem to see it. I found myself explaining what it was. He laughed a bit; he looked everywhere but at my face. I was puzzled. When I tried to talk to him he slid away from the subject. He made wild, irrelevant assertions, daring anyone to disagree. He had a high, strange laugh. When others made a joke he looked pompous and high-minded, but he laughed when nothing was funny, or when something was sad or brutal or shocking. He never answered a single question I asked.

He was musical. He was clever. Those were the only things I knew about him. I never saw a genuine expression, or heard a real voice. Can alcohol do that much damage — can it make a personality disappear? Or had he been shadowy, incomplete, wrong all along?

'He's been arrested again,' my mother said. He bounced between dry-out facilities and the courts. He hit rock bottom and stayed there. Then I learned he was working part time driving taxis. A mate was lending him his cab. Can you imagine it — that drunk, driving your wife, your daughter around? We talked about it. Karen was sorry for him. She didn't want him to be poor. She has a kind nature. But she said his drunkenness made it dangerous for people and he ought to be stopped. What could we do about it, though? I practised not thinking about it. I became very good at that.

I was sitting in my room dictating notes. The young assistant Viola came in with some files. She was tall, curvy, with straight sandy hair and an intense way of looking, her head turned sideways, her blue eyes fixed. She looked me in the eye for too long. I turned away. Each time I came out to reception she would stare like this, and when I turned away I saw her looking at me in the window's reflection. It was hard to communicate with her. It was as if she wasn't listening; she was thinking.

'Got that?' I asked.

She looked startled and blushed. Then she gave me a goofy, crazy smile and backed away.

I closed the door. What a weird woman, I thought. She wasn't like this with everyone. She liked me. It was flattering, but it worried me. She didn't seem to care about normal rules. What would Clarice think? I hadn't done anything but I felt furtive, guilty.

After work I was going to drive to the gym. Viola was standing by my car.

'All right?' I said.

'My car's broken down.'

'Have you called someone?'

'Not yet.' She gasped and laughed. There was something about her craziness, her helpless, raw ineptitude. It gave me a funny, dizzy feeling, as if everything I'd built around myself had fallen away. A long look passed between us. I saw myself pulling her into the stairwell, pushing her against the wall, my mouth against hers. She saw my expression; she blinked. Then she gave me an uncanny smile. I ran my hand through my hair. I picked up my sports bag and turned away.

She watched as I drove past, her expression fixed, dreamy, wild. I drove to the gym. I worked it off. I burned the moment away.

Then I went home to Karen and watched her making phonecalls. I thought how much I loved her. Karen is never embarrassed or shy or awkward. She always knows what to say. I never feel a fool when I'm with her, never feel ashamed.

She is tough and competent. She is *of the world*. Not like lawless, staring Viola, asking too much, asking for trouble. Now Karen was going through my accounts, with the hard, humourless look she has when she's thinking about money.

'Want to know how much you made this month?'

I laughed. I think of Karen as *golden*. She leaned back on the couch and I lay on top of her, ran my hands through her yellow hair.

It was late on a Sunday night. Karen and I were in the bedroom upstairs. I was reading; she was watching TV with the sound turned down. The phone rang. I answered it and heard her voice, soft, urgent. 'Dr Lampton?'

I registered her ridiculous formality. Everyone called me Simon. Perhaps she thought it was some kind of disguise.

'Viola,' I said, with a flash of guilt. Then I was really angry. I went to hang up.

'I'm with a man,' she said.

'What?' I grappled with the phone.

She whispered, 'He says he's your father.'

My hands started to shake.

'I was walking home from the pub. He stopped his taxi and asked if I wanted a ride. We started talking. I told him what my job was. He asked were you Dr Lampton . . . and he said he was your father.'

'Where are you?'

'I'm in his flat. He invited me. He's drinking. He's getting . . . angry.'

'Angry?'

'Is he violent?' she asked.

I got up off the bed. Karen sat up and stared.

'Oh, Christ. Just leave.'

There was a pause. 'He won't let me,' she whispered.

Again I went to hang up. But if he injured her . . . She was asking for help. He was my father. She had me. I raged at her silently. There was a bang, cursing, in the background. I started. 'Viola? Are you there?'

'He says he hates you, hates everything.'

'Okay. Just wait. I'll help.'

'All right,' she said, being brave. I saw myself punching her. Then I pictured *him* punching her. I was on the verge of tears. 'Don't worry, darling,' I said.

Karen caught my arm. 'What is going on? Who's "darling"? Simon!' she shouted after me. I dressed, ran downstairs, got in my car.

On the way I rang the police. I must have made it sound serious. When I turned into the street there were patrol cars, and police on the wooden fire escape. They had Viola in the yard, and further up the stairs my father was arguing.

I said to Viola, 'Are you all right?'

My father was taken past. 'I've done nothing,' he said to his escort. 'She knows it.' He wrenched himself close to me, amazed. 'Why are *you* here? Did you call the cops? I could lose my job. I've got debts. You've done this. It's a trick.'

He was pulled away, shouting.

Viola said, 'I didn't want to call the police.'

I rounded on her. 'Well, they're here now. What did you think you were doing?' I watched as my father was shoved into the police car. I was calming down. I was starting to think.

She said, 'I thought it'd be all right to go to his house. He said he was going to have a party with some musicians. It wasn't like going with a stranger, because he said he was your *father*.'

'Everyone's a stranger. Was he drunk?'

She hesitated. 'A bit, maybe.'

I leaned down to her. I said, 'He's a drunk who drives a taxi. He has to be stopped. He's going to kill someone.'

'You want him to lose his job?'

'You think he shouldn't lose it?' I took her arm and pushed her towards the cops.

The sergeant said to me, 'You'll need to make a statement.'

'Gladly,' I said.

But in the car I said to Viola, 'How did you know my number?'

'I remembered it from work.'

'How did you call without him knowing?'

'He was pacing around the kitchen, raving about you, your mother, what bastards people were. I picked up the phone — he didn't even notice. He's crazy. I was *frightened*.' I glanced at her. She saw my expression and looked stunned. I felt fear come off her — fear of me. I stopped driving so fast and said, 'This is a situation. We need to get through it. He stopped you leaving. Anything else?'

'He kissed me.' She shivered.

'That's assault.' I pictured it: him kissing Viola.

'We'll get him,' I said. 'He won't be hurting anyone again.'

At the police station I had a talk with a senior sergeant. I told him everything.

'He's known to us,' the man said. He went from one room to another, came back. He told me what my father was saying. He said, 'It's a long chance, him picking up your young friend.' There was a silence. I wondered what my father had said. The sergeant looked at me steadily. I could tell he was turning over the possibility that Viola and I were connected in this, that we were in league.

'I can hardly believe it myself,' I said. Just get through this, I thought. Just see it through.

He said, 'But we can get something out of it. We can finally ban him from the cabs.'

I went into the room where Viola was sitting.

'Tell them everything,' I said. 'The drinking. The kiss. Everything.' I looked hard at her. 'Don't leave anything out.'

Afterwards I got her back in the car and drove her to our house. The thing would have to be explained to Karen.

Karen had all the lights blazing. Viola blinked. She looked extremely young, foolish and vulnerable.

Karen said, 'So this is the "darling".'

Viola's mouth turned up in a mad grin. She looked rudely around the room, as if storing up detail.

In a caustic voice I explained what had happened, adding that I had feared for Viola's safety, and that the word 'darling' had been meant to reassure. I made it plain that I was at the end of my tether, that I was upset.

Karen looked contrite, then ironic. She said sharply, 'How did she know our home number?'

'I remembered it from work,' Viola said.

Was there a simper in her answer? She looked from me to Karen. She smiled. I jumped out of my chair. Was she enjoying this — torturing us, making trouble between us?

But she couldn't have contrived it. She couldn't have known she was going to meet my father. He'd admitted that he'd been cruising around, that he'd stopped for her on a whim; also that they'd never met before. It was sheer chance — although it *would* be Viola he found, walking in the night alone. I thought about it. She should have refused the lift. But he was a taxi driver. She would have assumed he was after a fare. Then she trusted him because he was connected to me. And she'd been frightened. I'd heard it in her voice. My father was violent, drunk. It couldn't be her fault.

Could it?

I paced to the window and back. Karen looked at her watch, then at me. She raised her eyebrows.

'I'll take her home,' I said.

'Can I go to the toilet?' Viola asked. I was repelled by her silly tone, furious. We waited while she used the lavatory. She came out. She had redone her makeup. I saw Karen coldly noting this. Viola grinned cheerfully and said, 'Right then.'

I saw Karen's angry face at the window as we walked down the drive.

I asked for Viola's address and drove there. I waited for her to get out but she stared at her hands and said, 'When your father was talking about you he said, "I bet my son doesn't like trouble. I bet he likes everything nice and polite, but I'm trouble and *you've walked into it.*" That was when I got frightened.'

I laughed angrily. 'Now who's got trouble,' I said.

'He said, "I bet no one at his work knows about me. What can you and I do about that?" '

I remembered something. When he was being marched past he pushed back his hair with his fingers. A nervous gesture, despairing. I have the same thick black hair. I have the same mannerism. It steadies my hands.

'I feel sorry for him,' she said in a treacly voice.

I was afraid then. She'd invaded my life at its most painful centre. She'd been let loose in it.

I reached across, pushed open the door and told her to go.

I drove home.

Karen and I went to bed and lay close together, talking for a long time.

My secretary helped us move Viola on to another job. The police charged my father with indecent assault. Indecent? A single kiss is enough, the senior sergeant told me. It was a way of getting him out of the taxis. He promised to make sure Viola fronted up at court as a witness. As far as I know, she kept the whole thing secret. She never told a soul.

I only heard from her again once. A few months after my father was banned from the cabs, just before he took too many pills one night and died, Viola rang me at home. We had guests for dinner. I took the phone out of the room. I controlled my trembling hands. She sounded as if she'd nerved herself up. She said, 'You could look back on this, after a long time . . .'

I wanted to shout at her, I have a life. *A whole life.* And you . . .

She was still talking. I cut her off. 'You've got a lifetime of opportunities ahead of you,' I said.

'Opportunity?' she said. 'That's what I meant. You could ask, that night, who wanted what from whom?'

I started to walk back towards the dining room.

'I can't talk to you,' I said.

plane sailing

Plane sailing: The art of determining a ship's position on the theory that she is moving on a plane.

I gave my baby the middle name Max after his father. He already has a son called Max. Max junior. My son is Matthew Max Grace. He never sleeps.

Well, he does sleep, but in restless snatches. He tosses and turns and makes loud snuffling noises, then wakes with a loud wail. He has never slept through a whole night. People warned me about this. They said it would be hard bringing up a child on my own. They urged me to consider it carefully. They must have been mad if they thought I wouldn't do it.

When I first took Matthew home from hospital I had to go to the supermarket, and I went to pieces in the aisles. I wanted to hang on to a shelf, crying. I thought I would fall, that the floor was lurching under my feet. I got through it. I made it home with my shopping, then I stayed in the house for two days, recovering. I've always been independent, reasonably cool under fire. Interesting to find that a trip to the supermarket could be harrowing, terrifying, defeating.

A month later, when I was walking along Upland Road pushing Matthew in his pram, I saw a ship in the sky over Mt Hobson. It was three-masted, gold, with glittering rigging, like a picture in a child's storybook. It hung in the air, sails rippling, banners flying, and the air around it glowed, pearly white. I watched it sail over the edge of the mountain, disappearing into the blue distance, the shimmer of the sky.

I went for a check-up with the obstetrician, Dr Lampton. I didn't tell him about the ship specifically, but I mentioned that I'd had very little sleep. I said something about the edges of reality getting a bit blurred. He gave me a long, cool, assessing look. Then he asked me some careful questions about my mood.

'I'm happy,' I told him. And it was true.

When I think back to how it was before . . . I was in love with Max but he had a wife and two sons, Max junior and Charles, and a big house, and a settled family life, and although I knew this when I began having an affair with him, I still hoped that he would leave it all for me. He wasn't getting on well with his wife. He suspected she was seeing someone — there was a man hanging round, and he was hurt by this, although he said, 'Of course I don't find her sexually attractive any more.' He was tall, handsome, elegant, beautifully dressed; he had a habit that I found irresistible of coming out with shocking statements in his patrician King's School drawl, and I longed to take him to my stolid, timid mother's house in Penrose, just so he could horrify her with some dreadful, languid dismissal: 'What a *bastard* so-and-so is, just a *bastard.*'

He smoked cigarettes, and though I begged him not to (I'm a dentist — 'You don't want to get oral cancer, darling,' I said) I found this habit endearing too, his fierce disregard for niceties and pieties, his refusal to care what other people thought.

I liked being seen out with him; even, I'm ashamed to say, liked the throbbing, ostentatious racket of his Porsche Turbo.

We'd been an ordinary, middle-income family — my father was a clerk, my mother worked in a shop — and I was excited by Max's wealth and glamour. It wasn't that I was materialistic. It was just that he was rather . . . sensational. I loved him. I suppose I always will. I can't say it without tears. I go into Matthew's bedroom and look down at his face. His eyes move while he sleeps. Sometimes he half opens them and looks from side to side, wildly, under his lids, like a crazy little animal. He gnashes furiously on his dummy, plugged in to his dreams.

I was so in love with Max that I spied on his family. It was summer. They lounged out by the pool. I could hear the boys shouting and fighting. I watched Max's wife cooking dinner. I'd go cold at work the next day, imagining the embarrassment if I'd been caught. But still I'd end up driving towards his house. One night he rang my mobile when I was two houses down from his. He wanted to come to my place. I had to race to my car and drive home before he got there. When we were in bed a bit later I kept laughing. He said primly that I sounded hysterical. Then he propped his head on his hand and told me he'd been talking to his wife. He was going to rent a townhouse. They'd agreed to separate.

I hid a rush of tears. I chattered excitedly. What about? I suppose — how pathetic — I started making plans. He left, moody and preoccupied. I was full of hot sympathy. I glowed. Poor Max, how hard it would be for him, starting all over again. I wondered what would be a decent period of time before I could move into the townhouse too. I saw myself being kind, nobly considerate, when his poor wife came to drop off the boys . . .

Soon after he'd moved to his new place, I got tired of waiting for him to call. I went there. He'd been ironing his shirts. He threw himself down on the bed, tired, surly, unwelcoming. He gestured at the ironing, 'Want to do them for me?'

I hesitated. I said I would. He watched me from the bed, his expression cold and mocking; he was forcing me into a parody of what he knew I wanted: domestic bliss. I was upset, chilled. Later I rang him. Then the tears, recriminations. His coldness. Did I — I cringe to think of it now — did I appeal, plead? He turned evasive, hanging up, leaving his phone off the hook. There were a few more unsatisfactory meetings until he finally came clean. He said he had met someone new. He was seeing someone else.

After he told me I walked home to my flat. There's a kind of horror in finding out you're not loved. Imagine discovering that someone you love wants to kill you. It feels like that, doesn't it, the end of an affair? He doesn't care if he never sees you again, doesn't care if you live or die. I remember how the world turned, in an instant, into a dark, pitiless place. I discovered that I minded living by myself. I heard noises in the night and was afraid.

During my check-up, when I told Dr Lampton I was happy, I was remembering the moment when I realised I was pregnant. To be left alone, grieving, and then to find there was something that wasn't lost! Everything broken, in pieces, and then I discovered . . . Oh my child, my treasure. Out of the ruins. I say these ridiculous, half-joking things to myself, out of happiness. My treasure, my precious jewel.

Okay, his father was a bastard, but he was a classy one. I'm sure my son will be devilishly handsome.

When Matthew was seven months old I needed money to pay the mortgage, and I didn't want to lose my place in the city dental practice, which had been filled until then by a locum. My mother was retired, and offered to look after Matthew during the day. He was healthy, thriving, radiant — and nocturnal. The district nurse gave me a book on infant sleep problems. I read: 'Only a tiny percentage of children will not respond to these techniques.' My son (his perverse father's child) belonged to that small, rugged group. He slept slightly longer stretches, that was all. And then the loud wail, the rattling at the bars of the cot, the stunned roll out of bed, the glazed, blundering hours when all options — ignoring, soothing, feeding — were exhausted. Watching the sun come up, sitting on his bedroom floor. Black silhouettes on the ridge of Mt Hobson. A finger of sun moving across the floor.

The nurse told me 'leave him to cry'. My neighbours held out for a fortnight before they began to complain. They went so far as to insinuate that I was ill-treating my boy. How he screamed, left to himself. As though he were being torn away from the world.

At work I took things slowly, stopping often to double-check. What was it I told nice Dr Lampton — that the edges of reality sometimes got a bit blurred? I never lost my grip; it was just that my dreams sometimes *entered* reality and ran alongside, so that I might see some light, bubbly, surreal thing at the edge of a perfectly prosaic scene and blink, and secretly watch it, as it glided slowly away . . .

People have recurring dreams in which their teeth fall out. They're meant to have a particular meaning, although I've forgotten what for the moment. Anyway, I was the dreamer who pulled out people's teeth. I hope I don't sound cavalier. I believe I was perfectly competent. To try to explain that strange time, my dreamtime: I felt I was living on the junction between two different planes, the sleeping and the waking, and at odd moments I could see into both. I kept all this to myself. God. Of course I did.

It was summer again, long hot days, the city emptier than usual. It was a good time to go back to work, there was a relaxed, holiday mood among the secretaries and hygienists, who gathered at the front desk to chatter about their sunburn and their boyfriends; the upstairs consulting rooms were hot in the afternoons as the sun angled in, and I got away as soon as I could after work so I could take Matthew and my mother to the waterfront for a late swim. At the beach I relaxed, and the afternoon turned drowsily, pleasantly incoherent. My mother eating an icecream. My son's hands patting the surface of the water. The dazzle off the sea. Sounds muted in the mellow air, cloud shadows on Rangitoto Island.

One day at midday, storm clouds moved over the city.

There was something bruised and greenish about the sunlight before it dimmed and disappeared. The dark was surprising. It was hot. The secretaries had been whispering about the next patient I was to see: Scott Roysmith, the newsreader. Our practice was near the TV studio, and we saw a lot of their staff, but Roysmith hadn't been in before.

For a moment that morning, I'd been surprised he'd booked himself in with me. Why surprised? Because I gave him such a terrible time every night. I was irritated by his mannerisms. Watching the TV news I'd often startled Matthew by giving Roysmith strident tellings-off. He was obviously clever but there was something naïve about him. He could be perky or melodramatically pompous; most often he was excessively cosy and cute. Yes, cute. He had a combination of blink and smile that said: What an ingratiating chap I am; I am *unassailable* in my charm. His flirting, his over-egging, was unnecessary. Stop hamming it up, I wanted to tell him. Please, play it straight!

Night after night I'd snapped and nagged at Roysmith, and now here he came, bounding up the stairs, full of beans, open-faced, holding out his hand to shake mine.

'Goodness me! The sky's looking peculiar! Great to meet you,' he said, or 'exclaimed'. His hair bristled with the humidity. I felt a little snag of sympathy for him. His hair was over-large; it sat on top of his head like a brown turban. Beneath it, the bridge of his teeth was too narrow for his mouth. He glanced away, smiling. His hand was slightly damp. Probably he hated seeing the dentist.

I invited him to sit. 'What can we do for you today?'

He settled himself, made some adjustment of his face before he answered. He held the edges of the armchair. How strange it must be to have been previewed, to be reviewed, by the people you meet. I saw myself two nights ago, hurling a cushion at his face.

He said in his soft drawl, 'I've had a woonderful chap I've always gone to.'

I looked at the form he'd filled in. 'Yes. Mr Dumbleton.'

'He's over Ponsonby way. Do you know him? Dentist . . . artist, fisherman, raconteur. Just a great bloke. We got on like a hoouuse on fire, for yeeeears.'

I nodded. He shifted on his seat, leaned forward. 'But he's had enough. He wants to retire. He's going to write novels. Marvellous! And I thought, *Bugger*. I'll have to find myself another dentist!'

I thought, because of his job, he thinks I think I know him. So he doesn't try to break the ice; instead he tries to 'be himself', so that I will 'recognise' him.

'Do you have a particular problem?' I asked.

'Well, I've got a bit of a dodgy old tooth back there. I think I might have a hole. Two, actually.'

'How long have you being seeing Dumbleton — Mr Dumbleton?'

'Six years.'

I glanced at Rowan, my assistant. I hoped Bryce Dumbleton's novels were better than his dentistry.

I explained what I would do: examination, X-rays and so on.

'Goodness gracious me, it's humid!' he said. The sky had got darker. There was a rumble of thunder, the air crumpling. Rowan, a tall, slim Indian woman, came forward to prepare him.

'Lovely to meet you,' he said. I caught her flustered little tremor of nervousness — his fame — also his look of faint humiliation as he was pushed back, swathed, cranked to horizontal in the chair. Patients, feeling helpless, stare at Rowan's beautiful hands, at her pretty necklace, as if everything very near has become intensely important. When I lean over them they close their eyes, open them, laugh, look around for Rowan, but she has gone, withdrawing silently behind the screen, where she sits at her computer, ready to appear when I need her.

I adjusted him, and the light. I looked in. There was a lot of plaque — so much so that his gums had receded in places. He had a couple of other issues, things that should have been taken care of earlier. (What a hack that Dumbleton was.) I told him I would take X-rays. I leaned over him, my arm around the head that appeared every night in my sitting room. I said, 'Open, wider, now bite gently down,' and the mouth that was so familiar with its jawing and joking bit down, and opened, and I shone my light in there, picked, probed, scraped, prepared him for another X-ray, and the sky outside seemed to swell in the square of window and become astonishingly black. There was a boom of thunder, abrupt, close, and he started, his head against my arm, and laughed, and tried to say something, 'Goodness...' and I said, dreamily, holding him steady, my eye on that glossy black square of glass, 'Don't.'

'Ug?' he asked. I had his jaw clamped between my fingers.

'Don't say anything.'

He looked at me.

'Just now,' I added, holding him.

He nodded. Co-operative.

'Less is more,' I murmured.

His eyes flicked up. Rolled around. He wrinkled his nose.

Lightning flashed. There was another roll of thunder. We watched the rain, light at first, then big heavy drops, hissing past the window. I thought, how I love the rain, the warm, blind, melancholy.

He tried to speak again. 'No,' I said. I held him gently for three more seconds. We were very close. Then I let him go.

'What do you mean "less is more"?' He cleared his throat and spoke thickly.

'Oh, I don't know. It's true, though, don't you think?'

He lay back, puzzled but obedient.

'And bite gently down.'

His hair was stiff, spiked up at the front with a hint of widow's peak. He looked like a hedgehog. I smiled. He moved. I held him, let him go.

I said I would give him a quick clean, then we would look at his X-rays on the computer. 'Do you have sensitive teeth?' I asked, turning to my tools.

'Not that I know of,' he said gamely.

The storm had a kind of weight; it seemed to be right over the building: thunder followed lightning in quick succession, paper flew up into the air and whirled around and floated down. From the street below came the mournful swishing and tooting of stop-start cars.

'Auckland rain,' I said, and silenced his reply by inserting my instrument, the one with the most powerful head, into his mouth, and working it along a section of his lower front teeth. He strained away from it, more sensitive than he'd let on. Those neglected gums. I stopped. 'Too rough?' I changed the head. 'Try this.' He nodded and settled against my arm.

I looked down at his face. I did my best not to hurt him, but he flinched and his forehead was sweaty. I mopped it with a paper towel. I let him rinse and spit. Bloody water swirled into the plughole. Thunder cracked, the sound echoing in the deep spaces between the buildings. He put up his hand; his many tiny reflections slid across the rounded silver surfaces of the instruments. I hummed as I worked. Quiet humming, the buzz of the machine. I moved his big, boyish head this way and that. He was calming down. But a corresponding hum started, began high-pitched then droned lower and slower; we looked at each other and heard the machinery dying, the instruments letting out a last whine of exhausted momentum. The device went silent in my hand. The lights flickered, the neon tubes buzzed, and blinked off.

Roysmith's face was pale in the half light. He raised his head. 'Goodness gracious . . .' I put my hand over his mouth, gently. With a tissue, I pressed down on his bloody lips.

'It's a power cut,' I said. I left my fingers on his lower lip, just for a second. He gazed up, wondering. The thunder cracked. The rain streamed down. We were silent, looking at each other.

'What do we do now?' he said.

'Shall we wait for a minute?'

'Well, I'm quite comfortable here!'

'I love the rain,' I said. Along the dark corridor people

scampered and laughed and chattered. Rowan looked in.

'It's all down the street,' she said.

'Blackout at noon,' Roysmith said absently. He put his hand behind his head.

I leaned against the top of the chair, watching the clouds moving, swelling, in the square of window.

He closed his eyes. 'So dark. It's like being in bed.'

I had a fancy that the sky, full of its own essence, was pressing against the window, that it would burst through and flow into the air of the room like ink in water, languorous swirls of sky, of rain.

'I watch you on TV,' I said, murmured, in the quietness. Swish and rush of the rain, the laden air.

'Oh yes,' he said, and yawned.

I yawned too.

He laughed. 'I don't get much sleep. Kids. Have you got kids?'

'I have a baby who never sleeps.'

'Aaah. It's a bugger, isn't it?'

We heard a sudden blast of car horns.

When I blinked, particles in my eyes exploded, sprayed out to a point, then began to sink through the darkness, rising, falling with my eyes.

'We'll have to reschedule,' I said. The air seemed to bend when I spoke, sensitive to sound.

His eyes were closed. 'Let's wait a bit longer. Goodness gracious me, I've got . . .'

'Don't say that.'

He opened his eyes, jutted his chin and looked up at me.

'Those exclamations . . .' The air turned over on itself, spun, swirled, flew out in all directions. 'They're too cute. On TV.'

'Exclamations?'

'Less is more.'

'Jesus!'

He was silent for a moment.

I said, 'I used to listen when you were on the radio. I liked those long openers you did. On Afghanistan, on America.

Preachy but good.'

'Glad you approve of something.' But he said it dreamily. 'I liked radio. Now I see my face on billboards, on the back of buses. My big face, riding away. Or I look at the back of the bus and my face isn't there.'

'Must be strange.'

'I shouldn't be looking, should I? To check if I'm on the back of the bus.'

'Why not?'

'Seems egocentric,' he said, vaguely anxious.

'It sounds normal to me.'

Lightning, another crump of thunder.

I told him, 'There was a big storm last year, up north. It was night. The storm was right over the house, but the sky over the sea was clear, and when the lightning flashed, the sky was lit up — blue. Bright blue sky, in the middle of the night.'

'How surreal! Once, on a camping trip, my partner Theodora Davis and I . . .'

But there was a great welling surge in the building, the neon panels buzzed and flickered, the instruments jerked and whined, and we were blinking at each other in the white glare. We looked away: he at the ceiling, I at the floor.

I finished cleaning. Rowan told him he would have to come back for his X-rays; the computers were down. He said he would make an appointment. I saw him to the stairs. We smiled at each other.

'Lovely to meet you,' he said.

'Yes,' I said, and meant it.

Later, as I stood out on the shiny wet street, buses surged past, and I watched Roysmith's face borne away through the curtains of rain; he was real and unreal too — part of the other world that entered my waking days, the secret, the dreamtime one.

That evening Matthew took up a lot of my attention. By the time I'd got him properly settled it was late. I turned on the news. Roysmith appeared. The room was dark; his face hung in the square of bright light. I lay on my sofa. Outside the rain had thinned into drifting showers, falling through the orange streetlights. I dozed.

I dreamed someone was banging on the front door. I sat up. Roysmith looked at me, blinked, gestured. The knock started up again. I went to the door and opened it, not very wide.

A thickset man with tattooed hands and wild hair stood on the doorstep, the rain falling behind him.

I looked at him. He said, 'You need to come out and shift your car. We're moving a house up your street. Your car's in the way.'

I peered out. The street was empty. There was no one around.

He said, impatient, 'You got a note in your box today.'

'I didn't.'

'Yeah, you did. You got to come and move your car.'

I rubbed my eyes. 'I don't know who you are. It's late. I can't just come outside with you.'

He reared back, indignant, not believing I would argue. 'I'm from Farr. Farr's House Movers. You got a note.'

'I didn't.' Hadn't.

'Your car's going to get *crushed*. There's no way you can leave it there.'

'I'm alone in here with my baby. I can't just come out.'

'You got a letter!'

'Where's your ID?'

'I don't need ID. I'm from . . .'

I closed the door.

He swore and walked away up the path. He slammed the gate.

I watched him go off up the road. There were no trucks, no workmen out there. Could they be moving a house up this narrow street? I had seen them moving one along Remuera Road recently. Amazing how they could put a whole wooden bungalow on the back of a truck. I looked at Roysmith. A man has come in the night. If I don't come outside he will squash my car. You smile, you look down at the paper in your hands.

It does sound amusing, I know. But can I ignore him? I need, I value my car! Roysmith shakes his head, looks grave. Indeed, he acknowledges, something must be done.

I dithered. Then I thought of asking the police. I rang the station, was put through to an orchestra, made a cup of tea while it played. Finally a policeman answered. He asked for my name. He told me my address.

'A strange man's come to my door . . .' I said.

'At eleven o'clock at night!'

I paused, surprised. I supposed I was being assessed. Perhaps a drunk or mad person would begin to rant at this point, encouraged by the expression of sympathy. I pressed on, explaining. 'I'd just like to know,' I finished up, 'is it possible they could be moving a house up the street? Will my car be squashed?'

'He was threatening, you say?'

'Aggressive.' I paced on the wooden floor.

'What's that banging? Is he banging on the door?'

'No, he's gone away.'

'Good. One moment.' The orchestra again. He came back on. 'I can't find anything about a house being moved. Don't go outside with this man. I'll send someone to find out what's going on.'

I thanked him and hung up. Outside the street was silent, empty, the rain drifting. I went to bed, left the curtains open, Roysmith watching the street.

I dreamed Roysmith was warning me of something, his head framed by the TV. 'Don't go outside,' I begged him. 'I'm alone. Stay in there. Stay with me.'

Someone was knocking on the door. I pulled on jeans and a shirt. A voice said, 'Police.'

There were two cops, one young and handsome, the other older, sallow, bored.

'You'll have to move your car,' the younger one said.

I swayed, dizzy. There was a film in front of my eyes.

He told me, 'Farr's are moving a house up the street.'

'I'll get my keys,' I said.

I went out into the drenched garden. I backed my car into the neighbour's driveway. I passed the sitting-room windows. Roysmith had gone. When I came back the young policeman was feeling the glass panel in my front door. It moved when he pressed it.

'That's not secure at all,' he said. 'It's not safe.'

I said, 'Want to stay the night then?'

'Sorry, I'm on duty.' He grinned.

The older cop fidgeted sourly. 'We gotta go,' he told me.

They left. I stood on my doorstep. I waited. The dripping garden, the stormy sky. Something scurrying in the bushes. Orange lights flashed in the branches of the trees, the wind roared. Thunder over Mt Hobson. And then it came over the crest of the hill, a wooden bungalow under tow, a large, slow, stout vessel lit by blinking lights, struts creaking, planks groaning; crewed by torch-lit men, it sailed by in the drifting dark, cruised grandly on up the rain-slicked street, slid over the swell of Upland Road and was gone, into the liquid night.

gratitude

I saw my cousin Juliet last week. I hadn't seen her for years. She came into the place where I work and we talked. It reminded me of one holiday when I was eight, and we went to stay at her brother's house in the country. She'd always lived out of Auckland and I didn't know her very well. Her brother was much older, grown up. His name was Stephen. He and his wife Derryn lived near Gisborne, where he was working as a fisherman.

We drove down with Juliet's parents, my aunt and uncle. They were going to leave us there for a week while they went on a trip by themselves. We got to the house in the evening. Stephen was tall, with a beard. He talked in a low, mumbling voice, shifting around on his feet, his smile baffled and harassed — he was as shy as I was. Juliet went ahead into the house. She had been there before.

The house was tiny, weatherboard, with peeling paint. There was a rusty old truck on the grass outside, with weeds growing up into the cab and a cat sitting on the roof. Derryn drifted out, carrying a baby. She was thin and freckly, and her mouth naturally turned down, which gave her a disappointed look. She was wearing a floppy jersey and flared cotton trousers, and her feet were bare. She shifted the baby on her hip.

My aunt and uncle stayed for coffee, then we waved them off. The baby started to grizzle. Derryn hitched him up higher on her hip. She didn't say anything. Stephen gave us his perplexed smile. We followed Derryn inside.

I was too shy to talk to Stephen and Derryn so I whispered to Juliet.

She was fierce with me. She was two years older. She said, 'Why are you whispering?'

'Where should I put my bag?'

Juliet asked where we were going to sleep. Derryn said, 'I'll show you.'

We followed her out the back door and down the garden path. There was a stationwagon parked by some bushes. I thought she was going to drive us somewhere, and I hoped it would be nice.

'In there,' Derryn said. She pointed at the car. 'Did you bring sleeping bags?'

'Oh goody,' Juliet said. She gave me a hard look.

'The seats fold down,' Derryn added. She gazed off across the garden. Her eyes were bloodshot.

Juliet got in and started pushing down the seats. When I turned around Derryn had gone.

I climbed into the car. The vinyl was warm and sticky, and gave off a strong brownish reek; in the days that followed I would spend many hours lying on those musty seats, tracing lines in the vinyl with my fingers, the springs beneath me letting out little excrucited squeaks and cracks, the windscreen above, with its splattered blobs of dirt and leaves, making patterns of jungly light on the ancient dashboard.

Juliet put her stereo on the seat and switched on her favourite tape, the soundtrack of *Jesus Christ Superstar*. We lay and listened for a while.

'What about a pillow?' I said.

Juliet had a round face and curly hair and gaps between her teeth. 'A pillow?' she said in a dangerous voice.

'Oh, don't worry about it,' I said. There was a pungent ashtray in the door, crammed with mashed and crooked butts.

'Your Highness needs a pillow,' Juliet said. I said nothing. She yawned.

I could see a clothesline with sheets blowing in the wind, and beyond that a paddock stretching away to the rainy sky. I wondered what the time was. I was hungry.

'Let's get out,' she said.

We went around the garden. The rain stopped and the sun broke through the clouds. We looked at a couple of pigs in the paddock and stroked the cat sitting on top of the old truck. Behind the truck was an enclosure made of wooden stakes stuck in the ground. Inside it was a bath. Juliet said it was connected by a pipe to inside the house. There were melted candles on a stand, a soap dish, a scattered array of shampoo bottles. A path made of wooden boards led from the enclosure to the back door. I walked on the slats — and stopped short. Derryn was standing in the doorway.

'Dinnertime,' she said. She turned away. We followed. Stephen was sitting at the table. The baby was in a highchair.

Derryn came slowly out of the kitchen. Everything she did was slow. She smelled strongly of some kind of herb. She shared the food around. The meat was tough and the vegetables were raw in the middle.

Stephen looked up, sighing. His forehead wrinkled with effort when he spoke, as if it was hard for him to frame the words. When he got them half out he swallowed them. He filled the spaces between the words with a breathy, humming noise. His expression was kind but helpless. He asked Juliet about the trip, and I noticed that some of the things she said weren't true. It had been pouring when we stopped for lunch. She said it was 'blazing hot and sunny'. The sea had been rough, churned up by a spring storm, and no one had felt like going in. She told him we'd had 'a long, lovely swim'. Stephen looked at me. I ducked my head. She said we'd had three icecreams, then she corrected it to two. Derryn fed the baby and didn't say anything.

When dinner was over I whispered to Juliet.

'Talk properly,' she said. 'It's down the hall.'

I was glad the toilet wasn't out in the garden, like the bath. Then I wasn't so happy — it meant we couldn't use it during the night. The walls of the bathroom weren't lined. On the exposed wooden frames were rows of spare toilet rolls, and the toilet was one of those big old thrones with a wooden seat and a metal chain; the flush roared and the pipes let out a trumpeting moan, finishing off with a metallic shriek. A dog barked in answer in the garden. I hurried out.

Juliet said ominously, 'We've cleared the table, Viola.'

The plates were piled up on the kitchen bench. Derryn and Stephen, having given Juliet a torch and two pillows, had gone away into another room. We went out into the garden. I could hear the dog moving around on its chain. Behind a lighted window Derryn was carrying the baby back and forth. We went down to the car. Juliet brought out bags of sweets and chips and turned her stereo on. The wind blew in the trees. I saw a torch moving far away, across the paddock.

Juliet was restless. 'Let's get out,' she said.

We crept through the garden. The night was cloudy and dark. A light was shining through the wooden stakes of the enclosure. Stephen was sitting in the bath. Steam rose and curled through the flickering light from the row of candles; he held a small cigarette between his finger and thumb and drew deeply on it, and a rich grassy smell blew through the garden. The moon came out, riding between the black clouds. The top of the old truck looked like a skull in the moonlight.

Back in the car I pulled out my pyjamas.

Juliet said, 'What are they for?'

She grabbed them and held them up. They were juvenile, embarrassing yellow. Happy faces, flowers.

'Nice,' she said. She lay back and hitched her thumbs into the belt of her shorts. She was wearing the clothes she always had on: boy's shorts, a sleeveless checked top, and sandals. She had strong brown arms. Her fingernails were bitten down to the quick and her hands were broad and powerful.

I stuffed the pyjamas in my bag. A little squall of rain drummed on the roof. Brief desolation. I thought of my mother carefully packing my bag, fresh clothes for each day. She'd said, 'You'll have a nice time. Juliet's almost your age.'

'Do you ever change your clothes?' I asked, politely.

'Why bother?'

We heard a weird, coughing, retching sound.

'Possums,' she said. I wriggled on the creaking vinyl. I needed the loo. I climbed out and went behind a bush. Light rain fell. Juliet turned the torch on in the car. I looked at the small stationwagon, its back rammed up into the shrubbery, a song from *Jesus Christ Superstar* floating tinnily out over the garden.

Juliet wound down the window. 'Look,' she called. She was shining the torch on a possum, its round dazzled eyes and damp nose.

Juliet wound her window up and I ran back, afraid that she would lock the door.

I slept. At dawn the pigs started making noises; a rooster crowed along the road and I woke up, smelling the ashtray. A cigarette butt had stuck to a strand of my hair. I removed it and sniffed it, sat up and looked over the dashboard, past the washing line, to the paddock. On the far side was a row of tall thin trees that grew along the edge of the river. The sky was white, the air mild and humid. It was strange to have slept in my clothes. I prodded Juliet but she was lying on her back, snoring, and she pushed me away.

I got out. There was a roaring of wind in the trees. Stephen came out of the house. He looked in my direction, wrinkled his forehead in his baffled way, mumbled something to himself and walked past me carrying a big plastic box. He was wearing white gumboots. He loaded the box into his van and drove away, and I had the sudden ghostly sense that I was not physically present in the bright, windy morning, that if I had been closer he might have walked right through me, feeling no more than a ripple of air.

Juliet was awake. She said, 'Look what I've got.' There was money in her hand.

'My mum gave me some money,' I said. I looked for my purse and saw it on Juliet's lap.

I looked down. 'Is that my money?' I whispered. The ghostly feeling again.

'Our money,' she said.

She tossed over my purse. It was pink. It was my best possession; I hadn't thought of it as babyish — now, naturally, it looked grotesque.

'Our money,' she said again. 'There's yours . . . and then there's mine!' She produced a bigger note. 'Look how much we've got altogether.'

I wiped my eyes. 'That's a real lot,' I said. Outside a beam of sunlight shone down through the trees, full of insects and dust. An involuntary sigh rose in my chest. My spirits lifted. I'd never had so much money before.

'There's a shop near here.' Juliet waved the money. 'Now we've got to hide it while we have breakfast.'

She decided to hide it in the engine. She opened the bonnet. With manly grunts, wiping the sweat from her brow with the inside of her forearm, she wedged the money down behind some pipe or tube. She straightened up, nodding humourlessly, her hands black with grease.

We trailed up to the house and put some toast on for ourselves. Derryn had been staring out the window; now she turned and peered, as though attempting to gauge just what we were actually doing there. 'Do you want breakfast?' she asked, with a pale, wondering little laugh.

I swallowed. I was already eating toast. 'Do you mean there's something else?' I said.

'Something else?'

'I've got some toast,' I said desperately.

'You've gone really red, Viola,' Juliet said.

'Oh, yeah . . .' Derryn said. She stirred her fingers through the baby's hair. There was a dreamy silence. A cow mooed outside. I was still hungry. There were a couple of spotty bananas on the bench. When no one was looking I took one and put it down the back of my pants.

Derryn said, 'Come into my room, girls.'

We followed her into a bedroom with Indian material hung around the walls and an unmade bed. Clothes and books were scattered on the floor.

'Sit down,' Derryn said.

We sat. The banana broke apart in my trousers. I could smell it.

'Look at these pictures,' Derryn said. 'We went to India.' There were photos of Stephen, one of Derryn on a bed with her eyes closed, looking dead, the skin of her face stretched and waxy, faintly yellow. I feigned interest, desperately aware of the smashed fruit welling up out of my waistband.

'Do you want this?' Derryn asked. She was holding a piece of bright-coloured cloth. 'You'd look nice in it, Viola. With your blonde hair.'

The baby tottered past the bed with no pants on. Outside the dog barked and jumped on its chain. The baby peed on the floor.

Juliet elbowed me. We got up.

'Thank you,' I said.

Derryn looked at me. 'Oh, yeah,' she said.

Back at the car, I secretly scooped bits of banana out of my underpants and ate them; also secretly, I tried to clean my trousers with a leaf. We got the money out of the engine and set off to the shop.

The sun came out. The flax and the cabbage trees were tossing in the strong wind and the bright light struck off the leaves. Juliet walked on the gravel road in her bare feet. We cut through the paddocks and Juliet walked in the cowpats, her feet turning green.

The shop was cool and dark and musty. In the gloomy back was a shelf with toys. We bought two plastic soldiers with parachutes attached to them, and a bag of sweets. Outside we inspected the plastic men. I liked them very much. We walked back, eating lollies.

On the way back there was a tin barn and, behind it, a paddock. We sat on the fence, and I noticed there was something strange about the grass. Juliet got down to have a look. There were lots of piles of something horrible and bloody and meaty dotted about the paddock.

'It's afterbirth,' Juliet said. 'It comes out of sheep when they've had lambs.' She picked some of it up with a stick. I shrank away.

'That'll come out of you, if you have babies,' she said.

'Where are the sheep?' I asked.

'In another paddock.'

'Where are the lambs?'

'Cooked. That's what we had last night. Dead lamb!' Juliet threw a piece of afterbirth up in the air.

'Give me another lolly,' I begged.

'There's only one left.'

'Can I have it?'

Juliet said cunningly, 'It's greedy to ask for the last one.'

I looked at her.

'I tidied up the car this morning,' she said. 'You were off somewhere being lazy. And I washed your plate for you.'

'Bite the lolly in half,' I said.

'I closed the front door after you. And cleared the table. You must think people are your servants.'

'I don't!'

She held out the sweet, censorious. I took it.

'You probably don't want to be selfish all your life . . .'

I ate the lolly.

Her mouth dropped open. 'Well! I've never met such a self-absorbed little person in my life. Don't you know that people are making an effort on your behalf *all the time*? The *sacrifices* people make? Is that how you repay them?'

'You're copying,' I said, the sweet lodged, bulging, in one cheek.

'I am not!'

'That's grown-ups' words.'

'So what if they are?' she said, furious.

'What shall we do now?' I was cheerful.

Juliet sulked. Then she said, 'We'll go to the river.'

'Let's get some food first.'

She put her hands on her hips. 'Honestly. Do you ever stop thinking about eating? You're going to eat us out of house and home!'

We went to the empty house. Rummaging amid the crammed contents of the fridge, Juliet extracted a plate of meat delicately furred with blue mould, a rubber carrot, a quivering bowl of an unidentifiable jelly-like substance. A tureen of treacly brown snot had a spoon sticking out of it, its cracked handle strapped with a Band-Aid. We settled for apples, though their skins were wrinkled, and two stiff slices of bread.

Behind the dead truck there was a gap in the hedge. We climbed through, and a path wound away through the tall grass. In some places the grass was as high as our chests. It would have been nice to lie down in it and look up at the sky. But I wanted to see the river.

When we got to it I was surprised — I'd imagined something you could jump across in places, but it was a broad, swift stretch of brown water, and the trees on the far side were a long way away.

We sat on a log and ate our supplies.

Juliet said, 'Gotta go.'

'Where?' I said dreamily. I could have fallen asleep in the hot sun.

'Toilet,' Juliet said. She cleared her throat in a tough way and spat.

I sat up. 'Shall we go back?'

'I'll go behind a bush. Leaves are as good as toilet paper in the out-of-doors.' She gazed at the sky, prim.

A long pause. Juliet behind the bush. The river moving over its stones. The birds twittering. A sudden flurry of the foliage, branches snapping, the bush violently thrust to one side as if she'd overbalanced wrestling with her leaves. A snigger began rising in me, a wave of weakness, hot, quivering.

She emerged, red-faced. 'What?' she demanded. Her glare of puzzlement and annoyance — her incomprehension, her grimness — finished me off, and I shook with exquisite mirth, helpless, my eyes full of hot tears. She stalked off, muttering.

I lay in the grass, watching the clouds move across the sky. I heard her shout. Along the bank was a little beach made of mud and stones, and a dinghy pulled up. Juliet was untying it.

'Give me a hand, you gibbering idiot,' she said.

We got the knots undone and turned the boat over. The oars were underneath.

'Let's go for a row,' she said.

I looked at the water. 'I don't know,' I said.

'What are you worried about?'

I didn't want to. But I was sorry I'd laughed so much and I didn't want her to go on being angry. She steadied the boat while I got in, then she pushed off and took hold of the oars.

As soon as we were free of the bank we started to be swept downstream. Juliet put her feet against the seat and pulled hard on the oars. We were close to the bank at first, floating over weeds and stones and submerged logs. The river had seemed to move slowly; now we were on it I understood how powerful it was. Sticks and branches floated quickly by; there were waves, eddies, sudden whorls in the surface. The bank was getting further away. Juliet was fighting the current. I felt the tug of her rowing, then the stronger force of the river pulling the boat where it wanted us to go, towards the middle of itself.

'Where does the river end?' I asked.

'At the sea.'

The river curved around and flowed faster. We were a long way out now, and as it changed direction a strong wind hit us. Waves blew over the sides and slopped on our legs. I gasped when the cold water hit me. The river had widened out. We were being swept into the middle of an estuary.

The current was going in all directions. First we were pulled one way, then another. The boat tossed and spray broke over us. We could see the sea ahead. The wind was so strong now we were drenched every time we hit a wave.

Juliet shouted, 'Viola! The tide's going out. It's pulling us. You'll have to help me!'

I got alongside her on the seat and took one of the oars. I began to snivel. My mouth was full of water. The wind whipped our faces, blew water into our mouths. It tasted salty. At the first strokes my shoulders hurt and I stopped pulling.

Juliet slapped my arm. 'Row!' she shouted. 'You miserable, whining kid — row or I'll kill you.'

I rowed and cried, Juliet yelling in my ear. A wave broke right over us; we shouted with the shock of it. I wondered what would happen when we met the sea. There were surf waves at the beach where the river churned out into it. The sky was hot, dark, grey, with metallic curtains of rain sweeping across it.

Something changed — the wind. It started blowing in our faces. We rowed hard, and for the first time it felt as if our strokes were moving the boat. I sobbed and rowed, closing my eyes tight. The waves were wetting us with every stroke and water was pooling in the bottom of the boat. I wanted to be sick. A wave lifted and slapped us down, and Juliet fell off the seat. Her elbow was scratched and bloody. She kept turning and looking behind, and yelling at me to keep going. If I stopped she shouted in my ear. I felt the water get calmer, then the boat hitting the bottom. Juliet leapt out and pulled me onto the mudflat. I crouched down.

The wind blew stinging sand onto our legs and faces. There was nothing to tie the boat to. I looked at the wide brown sweep of water rushing to meet the sea.

Juliet put a stone on top of the boat rope.

'The tide will wash it away,' I said.

'You want to pull it all the way back?' For the first time she was close to tears.

I shook my head. I didn't know how far we'd come, but it

had to be a long way.

'Whose boat is it?'

'Stephen's,' she snapped. She wiped her face angrily.

We crossed the mudflat and started along the riverbank. We walked and walked. I began to blubber again. Juliet said, 'You'd better not tell. If you tell them we went on the river I'll murder you.' She said I was 'selfish'. If I hadn't panicked we would have been fine. If I told any adults I would be dead.

I cried so much I felt light and washed out. I trudged behind her, my eyes fixed on her wet shirt. I thought we must have missed the path; at one point I insisted I must lie down but Juliet lashed me on with words. When I slowed she dragged me. We got back to the path in the end.

We walked through the long grass to the gap in the hedge. Juliet signalled to me to be quiet. She poked her head through, making sure we wouldn't be seen. We stumbled down to the car.

She turned on the stereo. I got changed, and my clothes seemed small and fussy, all pleats and buttons and zips. Juliet climbed out and draped my wet things on the bonnet.

I wound down the window. She'd hung my underpants on the radio aerial.

'I'm *still* having to do everything for you,' she said.

'It's raining,' I pointed out, dully.

She stood out in the rain and gave me a spiel about gratitude. About how you have to appreciate what people do for you. How people are making an effort for you all the time. I remember thinking that adults must have said those things to her a lot. I looked over at the house. A solitary hen pecked near the front door. There was no one around.

She took out the toys we'd bought. 'Tomorrow we'll go to the shop and buy two more, shall we?'

We lay listening to the radio, the doors closed to keep out the rain. It was hot and fuggy. I dozed. Later we went up to the house.

Derryn opened the front door, the baby on her hip. 'Want some dinner?' she said.

'What are we having?' Juliet asked in an innocent voice.

'Oh . . . lamb? Yeah.' Derryn drifted into the kitchen.

'Remember,' Juliet said, 'if you tell I'll kill you.' She gave me a shove.

I had trouble eating dinner because I was thinking about the sheep losing their lambs when they gave birth, and how their afterbirth got left all over the field. Juliet fixed me with intent, warning stares.

After that, Derryn and Stephen disappeared and we took the torch and went down to the car. Too tired to watch Stephen smoking in the bath, we lay listening to the possums. Tomorrow, Juliet said, we could swim in the surf. And after that, she told me, as I was drifting away into dreams of the powerful, whirling river, she had something *really scary* to show me in the barn.

That was more than ten years ago. I remember the scene just before we left. Stephen didn't use the dinghy much — he did his fishing on a big sea-going boat — but he'd gone down to the river and found it gone. I remember him arguing with Derryn. He was trying to get her to care about it. He said, 'I *can't* buy another one. We haven't got any money.' He stressed the word 'money' sarcastically — probably it was a concept she refused or was unable to understand. I remember when he called us in and asked if we knew anything about it. Juliet said, 'What boat?' and pinched me so hard that I had a purple bruise afterwards. I remember how I repeated, grinning woodenly, 'What boat?' and the way Stephen turned away with a final, disgusted shrug, giving up on us all.

I never went back there. I'm a student now. I've got myself a temporary job setting up computer programs in a big medical practice. And last week Juliet turned up to see the gynaecologist I work for, Dr Lampton. I hadn't seen her in a long time; she lives in a small country town down south. She'd been given a referral to see a city specialist.

I sat down next to her in the waiting room. She was the same tough old Juliet — short hair, no makeup, dressed in shapeless, mannish clothes. She was wary at first, embarrassed perhaps by the fact of her appointment, as if she feared I might have access to her file. 'I hate doctors,' she said dismissively, looking away. But she told me about Stephen and Derryn, who had split up — Derryn had wanted to stay in the country, but he couldn't stand it any more. I wanted to say I'd never told anyone about how we'd lost his boat, but in the end I didn't mention it. She looked sideways at my dress and my painted nails with her old scornful eye.

When her name was called she flinched, then gave me a quick nod, raising her chin with a scoffing look, like a boy dismissing a feeble girl. She always acted tougher than I was, but I'm not so sure. There are different ways of being tough. She doesn't know what I'm like, not really.

Anyway, there was no need to mention the boat, because she knew I'd never told. I'm not a snitch, after all.

I've never got anyone into trouble in my life.

parallel universe

I was standing outside the house looking in. I could see my girlfriend, Lee, walking from the sitting room to the kitchen and back again. She was talking on the phone. I slapped my palm against the glass. She looked at me and walked out of the room. It was a warm, rainy night. I sat down on a deckchair and looked at the garden, spiky palm trees and bushes covered with sticky, heavily scented flowers. A car droned by on the road. I put my head in my hands. I rubbed my hand over the bald spot that was starting on my scalp. I had the idea I might take the dog for a run until things calmed down, but I was wearing jeans and the wrong shoes.

I sat for another ten minutes. The front door opened and Lee came out wearing a jacket and carrying a bag. She had her keys in her hand.

I thought she was going to shut the door. I got up and ran for it. She jumped back, as if I was going to attack her. She was all melodrama. I got hold of the door. She looked at me, her face pale and pinched. Her eyes were red.

'You're a bastard,' she said.

I shrugged. I felt better hanging on to the door.

'I'm going,' Lee said.

I looked at her. Her hair was straggly. Her coat was open and one of her shirt buttons was done up wrong.

'Give me your key,' I said.

Her eyes filled with tears. 'You *are* a bastard.'

I just kept hanging on to the door. I realised how angry it had made me, being locked out of my own house. The house I leased, anyway. It was my name on the rent papers. She stood there pretending to arrange something in her bag. She was tiny and slim, with a runner's frame. She looked about twelve years old. I thought, one minute you've locked me out and you're screaming down the phone about me to God knows who, now you're giving me that face. As if I'm the cruellest man in the world.

She dropped her purse and stamped her foot. Her shoulders shook. This was the moment, she was signalling, that I should take her in my arms and pull her gently inside and tell her I couldn't live without her. And then, my face covered with her tears, we would make love. Etcetera. This was the way it had always worked.

I said, 'Well. What are you waiting for?'

She let out a little wail. She looked like she was going to run back into the house.

'Off you go, then,' I said. It was like a dream. I held out my hand. 'Give me the key.'

Her last look at me was so full of pain that it pulled some strange chord in my head. She wrenched the house key off the ring, threw it at me and ran down the drive to her little Daihatsu. I watched her drive away. I went inside. I put the key on my own keyring. I sat down. The dog, my old black Lab, heaved himself up beside me, groaned, and put his snout on my knee, commiserating.

I was thinking about that last wounded look of Lee's; the way it had struck me, like a sound in my head. I wondered about it. I supposed I'd had a feeling of cruelty. Why would I be cruel to little Lee? We'd had angry scenes before, and it had always ended happily enough. Usually I'd been insensitive or not listened, or not praised her hair or her clothes. But this time I didn't take her in my arms and say sorry. It had to do with what she'd said to me.

I'd been watching TV. She was making a lot of noise in the background. She came over, turned off the set and pointed her finger at me. She said, 'When are you going to get a proper job?'

Perhaps I heard it then first, the strange note. There was Lee, her hands on her hips, her hair fluffy around her face, her lower lip trembling. I decided to be reasonable. But when I started talking she shouted, 'You don't even own your own house!'

She said this, she shouted at me, after all the time I'd spent explaining to her about cashflow, about creditors, about money men and the hoops you had to jump through to deal with them. After I'd confided in her all year, told her my dreams, my vision for the future. We were going to make money, I'd told her — a lot of it. It just takes time. It takes faith. And then, after I'd bared my soul to her, she came out with something as dull-minded as 'When are you going to get a proper job?' I might as well have been talking to the wall.

She worked as a fitness instructor at a gym. She had clients and she talked about their 'physical issues', like she was a doctor. She pretended to know stuff about 'sports physiology'. It was all nonsense. She made enough money to pay her way, but she had no ideas beyond that. She wasn't a creative person. But I'd really believed she respected the entrepreneur in me.

I could have forgiven her. After all, it was her helplessness that made me fall for her, gave me the feeling she needed shielding from the world. But when she turned off the TV. When she stuck her finger in my face. Demanding answers. And then she made an even bigger mistake. I went outside to cool off, and she locked me out of my house.

When she was on the phone she let me hear her say, 'What if we had a baby? How could he provide for that?'

I suppose she had a plan. I know how these things work.

No doubt she wanted to get pregnant, and had decided to throw her weight around, to get us both in shape for it. She was getting on for thirty. But the thought made something close over in me. My daughters were twelve and ten. They meant the world to me. I got on well with my ex-wives, Adele and Lynn. Lee didn't understand it: that part of my life was sacred to me. It was sealed. I saw my girls regularly and paid for them and was a good father. But sad things had happened and things had changed and we'd moved on, Adele and Lynn and the girls and I. I was sorry it hadn't worked out, but that was life. And now I was free to follow my dreams.

I knew Lee would be back. There would be endless dramas. But she'd gone too far. She would try all sorts of tricks, but I was ready. I was ready.

I was forty, and exceptionally fit. I jogged, swam, worked out. In my teens and twenties I'd had a successful sporting career. It was good while it lasted but sport is never going to carry you far beyond thirty, and for the past ten years I'd been doing what I'm good at: finding a business opportunity and taking it to its full potential. I'd had successes. You have to think laterally. My business partner, Russell, and I made money in textiles. We had a time in the hairdressing industry. Russell had a thing for franchises. We bought and sold property. That year I'd got my eye fixed on property development. With Russell's flair and my creative thinking we could go a long way. We were excited. Russell was a visionary — he saw angles others wouldn't notice. He was the kind of guy who's working on a plan every waking minute. I was feeling good; I was energised. There was only one problem, and it was in the financial sphere. We'd got into a bit of difficulty the year before, to do with a retail business and some creative loans.

Our lawyers, Ridge Sligo, were a great bunch of guys. Jon Sligo, a personal friend of mine, had done a piece of financial magic with a shelf company for us, and now, through no fault of his own, was getting bother about it from the Serious Fraud Office. It was a load of nonsense. There was nothing illegal. The way business gets stifled by this sort of thing is a scandal.

We had confidence in the outcome, but we were stalled. It was frustrating. We couldn't move forward, yet we needed to move to make money. We were like sharks, Russell and I. Stop moving and we die.

I'd told Lee we were in a holding pattern, and how in business you have to take risks, and while the rewards can be great, it's often the creative people who get it in the neck when things go wrong. In the meantime, although Lee didn't know it, I'd borrowed money from my first ex-wife, Adele, who'd been unfortunately widowed after marrying her second husband, and who was well off. Adele was easy-going, and she understood about taking the long view. She hadn't aged very well, but I almost felt like re-marrying her when she gave me that money. After all the bad times and petty fights we'd had, she believed in me. She had faith in my vision. Contrast that with Lee.

Adele was a big, frowsy woman. She took no interest in her appearance any more. Her favourite thing these days was to lie in bed, eating and reading. She had a degree in education and she'd been in teaching most of her life. She had a brain, and I respected her for it. She thought I was flashy and she teased me about my taste for 'bimbos and fast cars', but she knew I was as smart as she was. I'd had too many chances early on to bother with university, that was all.

Adele and I traded books a lot. Lee used to complain when I came home with a book Adele had lent me and read it all weekend. I told Lee she should nourish her mind. She said indignantly, 'I've got a book.' She showed it to me. It was called *One Hundred Ways to Improve Your Breathing*. I told Adele about it and we laughed. Lee's book. Dear oh dear.

Adele liked fiction. I preferred books about science and history. I had a craze for cosmology, and even though most of it was hard to understand I got a kick out of trying to explain things like M-theory to Adele and the girls. One day I went around while they were eating lunch. 'Guess what?' I said. 'The universe we live in is not the only one.'

'Really?' said the girls.

'Get this,' I said. 'The universe is a membrane. The Big Bang was caused by the collision of the membrane of our universe and a parallel universe.'

They listened.

'The very beginning of the Big Bang is called the singularity. Before membrane theory, physicists couldn't calculate back to the moment of the singularity. Now that they've realised there are parallel universes, they can.'

'The singularity,' my daughter said. She liked the mysterious sound of it.

'Also, gravity is weak — this is the latest theory — gravity is weak because it's leaking from our universe to a parallel one.'

'Gravity isn't weak,' Adele said.

'Yes it is. Think about it. You can beat it just by picking up a cup.'

Adele and the girls picked up their cups and put them down. They looked at me.

I told them, 'There could be infinite universes, each with their own laws of physics.'

Adele made a face.

'Girls, how many dimensions do you think there are?'

'Three?'

'No. Eleven!'

I enjoyed these talks we had, and when I went home to Lee and her chatter I used to feel bored and flat. But one night, when I'd been reading about quantum gravity, I had a terrible dream: there was a stuffed toy, a reindeer. I looked at it and it multiplied into infinite repetitions of the same toy, stretching as far as I could see. A voice droned, 'There are an infinite number of universes. And therefore you do not exist. You do not exist. You do not exist . . .'

I think it was a reaction to the abstract ideas I'd been amusing myself with. The subconscious part of my mind was appalled. I sat up, sweating. I woke Lee and tried to explain. She started doing breathing exercises, right there in the bed while I was talking to her.

It was for the best that she'd gone. Let her find some young guy she could have kids with. Better that I didn't spoil her chances of that.

Now I was in a rut. I wanted to be out in the world, launching myself into a new venture, but Russell and I went on being stalled. The Serious Fraud Office swooped in and seized some computers from Ridge Sligo. Those bureaucratic bastards had it in for Jon Sligo and his partner Rick Sheet, just because they were innovative and successful. We had nothing to hide, but all we could do was wait. I thought about selling my car, but the idea was depressing. I missed having Lee in bed. One evening I picked up a woman and had quite a good one-night stand. I had a short fling with my second ex-wife, Lynn, but it was a pretty desultory affair. You can't go back. Lee came around and we had some scenes. She found a hairclip of Lynn's by the side of the bed. She moved her stuff out. I felt directionless. One thing about Terry Carstone: I don't like waiting. I was looking round for something, anything, to get my teeth into.

One day I went up to court with Rick Sheet to watch their barrister argue about the Ridge Sligo computers. There was a dispute about what the SFO could get their hands on. I was sitting in the back with Rick and Russell and I had a feeling. This was good. There was order, there was drama, there was a bit of controlled aggression. There was a lot of complicated legal argument that I didn't understand. I borrowed a pen and paper and took notes. I went home afterwards and read them, and then I called Rick and talked to him. I had ideas I wanted him to run by the barrister. Rick talked about 'precedent' and 'relevance', and I knew he was telling me I didn't know anything. But the next week when we went up the barrister came out with one of the points I'd told Rick to tell him to make. That made me feel good. I started to take more interest, to pay attention to every word. I put my books on cosmology aside, and started dipping into a textbook on evidence I'd borrowed from Rick.

I was spending a bit of time at Adele's, and she and the girls seemed happy to have me. I'd drop in when I'd been walking the dog — the girls loved my old black Lab, even though he was on his last legs. Let's face it, Adele wasn't likely to have any men other than me about. She hadn't had a haircut for months, and she'd grown a bit of a moustache. It was summer and she wore shapeless, sleeveless dresses. But I liked her calm cheerful smile, the way she swung around the house with her graceful walk. She didn't spend all her time putting muck on her face and complaining about being 'bloated' or 'having a fat day' or 'cutting out carbohydrates'. Obviously you wouldn't want to go out with her, but she was a good woman, and I used to feel happy in her sitting room with the bookshelves and the pot plants, and the nice garden outside, and Adele in the kitchen making some high-fat dish and chatting away to the girls.

One day I was having a beer and looking through Adele's shelves when I found a book about a criminal case. I took it down, since anything about the law interested me now. A journalist had researched an Australian murder case and decided that the woman who'd been convicted was innocent. I looked through the photos: the crime scene, the victim, the woman accused, and so on. I took it in to Adele.

'You read this?'

She was eating salami. 'Yes. It's quite diverting.'

'Is it true?'

She tossed her hair back. 'It makes a convincing case,' she said vaguely.

I grabbed another beer. 'Can I borrow it, love?'

'Oh, what's mine is yours,' she said.

There was something in her tone.

I looked at her. 'What do you mean by that?'

'Nothing, Terry.'

I judged it was time to leave. I took the beer and the book, kissed the girls and went off to the gym. After that I sat by the pool at my place and started reading.

I liked the writer, a journalist who'd taken up the case of a woman accused of poisoning three people. The guy was tenacious. He didn't accept what people in authority told him.

He dug deep and discovered evidence the police and the defence lawyers had been too sloppy to uncover. He hadn't succeeded completely, since the woman, as far as I could tell, was still mouldering away in an Australian prison. But the book was, as Adele had said, 'diverting'. It demonstrated something: that you can't trust people just because they're in positions of power. Police, lawyers, judges — are human. They make mistakes. Some are corrupt, some incompetent. (Look at our problems with the Serious Fraud Office.) I read the book pretty much in one sitting. I got energised and made a lot of notes. I wished I had someone to talk to.

I went back to Adele's. She was the only one who'd be interested in my ideas. When I opened the door I heard her say, 'My ex-husband.'

I strolled in and here was a bearded fat guy heaving himself out of his seat and coming to shake hands. I looked at him coolly.

'This is Willem,' Adele said.

'Hello, William.'

'Willem,' he corrected.

I turned; it was a reflex. I was about to go to the kitchen for a beer. I hesitated. The table was set with dishes and a fancy salad.

'You never eat salad,' I said.

Adele said, 'Terry.'

'You eat all that fatty shit.'

I couldn't help it. I was upset. I thought about sitting down and telling Adele *and* Willem about the case of the Australian poisoner. But Adele was moving me towards the door. Behind her, fat Willem coughed and shifted his bulk.

I faced Adele at the door. 'How do you have sex? How do you *connect*? Couple of billiard balls.' I said it aloud.

A look flashed across Adele's face. All that good-natured flab sharpened itself into such fury. Goodness me, I'll never forget it. She closed the door on me.

I got in the car. I thought, you never know about people. Sloppy old Adele. She was so slow and easy, so beyond (I'd thought) wanting a man. Something else I'd observed straight away: she'd waxed off her mo.

No doubt Willem was a gold-digger. I checked my mirrors. This was a new habit. Over the past month I'd got it into my head that those fools at the Serious Fraud Office were following me.

Ridge Sligo's case dragged on. The computers were unavailable while the firm tried to get them back and the Serious Fraud people applied to examine them. I went to court each time there was a hearing and soon I had a file of notes on the case. In the end, Ridge Sligo got the computers back. Russell and I were free to move ahead, and we started putting together ideas in the property sphere. I went back to Adele and borrowed a bit more cash. I didn't need to do much persuading. She'd never cared about money. I think she managed to snare her rich old second husband because she didn't give a single thought to his inherited wealth. I borrowed $10,000 from her — spending money while Russell and Jon Sligo and I set up some deals. Possibly she thought it was a good way to get rid of me. When I was busy I didn't get bored and come visiting all the time.

We had a frantic winter and by the time summer came around again things were going well. Russell and I made a lot of money very quickly, on some sidelines. I was playing the field, living the high life. I had no trouble attracting women, although none of them interested me. I wanted a woman I could talk to, but all I met in bars and clubs were empty-headed types. There was one woman I fancied who worked in an upmarket club, The Land of Opportunity. The Land was one of those high-class places where successful players like Russell and myself ended up after we'd had too much champagne. They had gorgeous hostesses and expensive drinks, and rooms where you could have 'conversation' with the girls. It was basically lap-dancing out the back — they took off their clothes and had a chat, and you told them your sorrows. Like I said, it was a classy place. I never went into those back rooms, but Russell did, the old playboy.

The woman I liked, Claudine Zambucka, worked on the reception at The Land, and the first time I saw her I was knocked over by her eyes. They were pure, pale blue and steady. They made me think of words like 'tundra', 'ice floe' and 'glacier', of beautiful, remote, silent places. I was persistent, and in the end I persuaded her to go out with me. Claudine was cool. She was clever. She kept my interest up. She was working in The Land temporarily because her stepmother owned the place. The only problem was Russell. He liked a simpler type of lady. Claudine made him nervous. He really disliked her.

You could tell Claudine anything. She listened, usually without comment, but when you tested her you found she knew exactly what you were saying. Just like Adele. Only Claudine was beautiful. You didn't feel the kind of *need* in her that you felt with ladies like Lee. There was no hidden agenda. It unnerved me every now and then, the way Claudine didn't conform to the normal patterns. But I was crazy about her.

One night Jon Sligo and Russell and myself were at The Land and Jon told me about a lawyer friend of his, Murray Ray, who acted for criminals. Ray had a client, Andrew Newgate, who'd been convicted of murdering his piano teacher. There were questions about the case. Ray wanted to take an appeal to the Privy Council in London but the family had run out of funds. This interested me, because my craze for legal things was still strong. I got Jon to tell me about it.

Newgate, who was about twenty when he was arrested, had had a long association with his piano teacher, a gay guy who lived alone. The teacher had been found strangled in the back garden of his house. After a long investigation the police had fixed on Newgate, and then, as Jon put it, they'd manufactured a case to fit around their theory. They decided that Newgate and the teacher had been having an affair, and that Newgate had flown into a rage when the teacher had a relationship with someone else. The family, who were respectable, middle-class people, insisted that Newgate wasn't gay. He had girlfriends. They said he'd been fond of the teacher and was upset by his death. Now Newgate had been convicted and spent his time in jail playing on an old keyboard — there was no piano inside — composing music, and hoping that the real criminal would be caught.

'Jesus. That's terrible.' I was struck by the thought of him in his cell, alone, making up tunes in his head. Praying for someone to help him.

'Jon,' I said, 'there's something in this.'

All the rest of the weekend I was thinking about the case. I'd been aware of it, had read about it in the papers on and off. I knew it was a case people argued about and spoke of as a possible miscarriage of justice. On Monday I rang up Murray Ray. I told him that our mutual friend, Jon Sligo, had told me about the case. Ray sounded a bit cautious but he agreed to meet me.

I went to his office in town. Murray Ray was a tall, stooped, greying man with sharp, noticing eyes. He was dressed in a fashionable suit and tie. He was hearty in his manner, but there was something elegant and soft and cunning about him too. I told him I was interested in the plight of Andrew Newgate. I said I'd done a bit of my own research on cases of this nature, and on this case in particular, and that unlike most members of the public I knew the justice system got things wrong. I spoke a bit about the power of the state, and how it was up to ordinary people like me to do anything possible to fight when human rights were being eroded. I had my spiel all worked out. The more I talked the more eloquent I felt, and when I finished I thought I'd done a good job.

He studied his fingernails, considering. 'That's all true. We want to take it further. But there's the issue of funds.'

'I'm a businessman.'

He looked at me, sizing me up.

'Let me meet young Andrew,' I said. 'I hear he is a wonderful pianist.'

A fortnight later Murray Ray drove me to the prison. He'd been reluctant at first, but he'd opened up over the days. I can be extremely persistent when I set my mind to something. He'd let me see his files, and we spent a lot of time talking about Newgate's trial and what had gone wrong. Jon Sligo had been right: the Crown case was full of holes. It was a sieve. The police had acted unfairly and covered up significant pieces of evidence, some of which Murray had only discovered after Newgate's conviction and subsequent appeal. No wonder the family wanted to take the further appeal. They'd set up a group to campaign on Andrew's behalf. They were passionate about their cause but short of resources. I studied the file and took a lot of notes. Once Murray realised how quick I was at cutting to the heart of the matter, how I knew a bit about the law, and how serious I was, he took me more and more into his confidence. He had an assistant, a chain-smoking young guy called Sean, and he had Sean take me through the files page by page. I had that excited feeling I get when I'm starting something new.

When we got into the prison a sense of dread came over me at the sight of the razor wire, the claustrophobic buildings, the lines of surveillance cameras. I felt the ugly, dead weight of it. The feeling turned to apprehension when we were about to meet Newgate. I had a memory of my dream about the infinite parallel universes and the droning voice: 'You do not exist, you do not exist.' I was nervous, rehearsing in my head what I was going to say. I felt the way I feel before making some really important pitch. My lips were dry and my throat closed over. And then the door opened and a fresh-faced, freckly young man came hurrying in.

Andrew Newgate's freckles. Dear oh dear. He was sprinkled; he was strewn with them. Not just on his face but all over his arms and hands. And yet he was a very good-looking boy. He was medium height, with clumsy boyish limbs. You'd think of him as gangly, but he wasn't thin, just awkward. He had big, powerful hands. You could see he'd played sport. (He'd been a keen soccer player, it turned out.) His eyes were steady and he had a nice, willing smile. He'd keep up that smile and then you'd see sadness creep into his face, as if he had moments of pure enjoyment, when he forgot his situation, before reality came back to him.

He listened politely while I introduced myself and told him why I'd come. I was a businessman, I said, but I was also a fellow citizen who had a responsibility to act when the state was presiding over an injustice. I said I had a whole raft of ideas about the case, and why it was full of holes. I got carried away and ran on. Andrew sat up suddenly and said, 'That's good, Mr . . . Carstone. Thank you. It's just . . . I don't want to win.'

'Eh?' I stopped.

'I don't want to *win*, like it's a competition that's got nothing to do with the truth. I want to be *proved innocent*.'

He'd set his chin firmly. He gazed at me with his clear eyes. I was moved. 'Of course,' I said. 'My God, you've suffered. And yet you've kept yourself together. You want to be proved innocent. Of course you do, and you shall. How old are you, Andrew?'

'Twenty-two.'

'My God,' I said again. I'd lost my train of thought. There was something so straight and unaffected about him that it made me feel a fool. Here I was grandstanding, holding forth about his fate while he listened, politely and calmly. What interested me was that he didn't chime in, or make protestations of innocence. He didn't try to add to what I was saying. Let's face it, when you've been in business as long as I have you get to be a fairly cynical judge of character, and no one could put anything over on me without the flags going up. But the way he'd cut across me in that boyish way . . . I looked into his face, into his clear, grave eyes. The kid was an open book. In fact, with his honest outburst he'd shut me right up. I sat staring at him with a kind of subdued respect.

He and Murray talked and I was glad to sit, quietly listening. I was struck by Andrew's plainness and simplicity. Not that he was stupid, but he was softly spoken and calm, and got Murray to explain a number of things he didn't understand. He also asked Murray, very courteously, to help him make some requests of the prison authorities relating to his playing of the keyboard. He frowned with a pain that he quickly suppressed when Murray mentioned the problem of funding his appeal. His parents had died in a car accident when he was a child, and he'd lived with his elderly aunt and uncle. They'd spent all their savings on the case.

It was time to go. I shook his hand, hard. 'We're thinking of you Andrew,' I said.

'Thanks, Mr Carstone.'

'Please. Call me Terry.'

'Terry,' he said, and looked at me with his calm eyes.

In the car I was excited. 'That's a murderer? No way. No way, Murray. I've been around. I've been in business, sporting environments. You name it. Terry Carstone knows people.' I lunged around in my seat. I was energised. 'We're going all the way with this.'

I called Russell. I told him I was going to use a chunk of our money. I called Claudine. 'Baby,' I said, 'I'm on to something meaningful here.'

We went to Murray's office. Over a bottle of wine we talked practicalities.

I would fund the appeal. I could easily meet Murray's expenses, which were very modest. To be honest, Russell and I had more money than we'd ever had. It had been a very good year, and I took my hat off to my partner's genius. Russell could make a deal out of thin air, the dear old cowboy.

I would be part of Andrew's defence team and could study his files at my leisure. I was looking forward to going over them looking for clues. I would leave no stone unturned, I told Murray. He sighed and listened. There were purple shadows under his eyes. He was looking at me the way Jon Sligo did when I had ideas about our computer case. Just because I didn't have a law degree, these guys thought I couldn't be any use. But I had other advantages. I was tenacious and sharp. I could pick up any subject extremely quickly. I was intuitive. I'd been a lot of places in my life and, most important of all, I knew people.

'You want to go to the Privy Council, don't you?' I said cheerfully.

Something flicked up in his eyes. I could see he wanted it more than anything.

'It's a once-in-a-lifetime opportunity,' he said. He looked at his nails. 'You know they're going to stop appeals to the Privy Council soon?'

'Well. Let's make it happen. Springtime in London.'

He smiled coldly. 'And you?'

'I'm going to help that poor young man fight the state.'

He made a wry face. He waited.

We were sitting in his office. The room was growing dark. I could see a ferry crossing the harbour, strung with lights.

'I'm a businessman, Murray,' I said. He didn't move. I was looking at the outline of his body against the window, the harbour behind him.

'What do you want?' he said.

'As my mother used to say, "Nothing more than my rights".'

'Rights.' He turned his hands, studying them.

'Well. Speaking hypothetically, what if there were books? Or interviews, magazine articles and so forth?' I paused.

He looked up sharply. 'You want a cut?'

'A cut?' I hesitated. 'You're right. That would seem fair. But I'm acting on Andrew's behalf.' I thought about Russell, but dismissed the idea. 'Andrew and I would have to share equally.'

Murray switched on a lamp. He picked up a pen and pad. He said, expressionless, 'Let's get it down.'

I sat back and put my feet up on his desk.

We roughed out an agreement and the next day Murray and I took it to Andrew for him to sign. This meeting and the ones that followed between Murray, Andrew and myself only confirmed my first impression. This calm, sensible, nice young guy was a murderer? No way.

I became a regular visitor to the prison, and each time I found Andrew the same. He kept his spirits up, and he was always pleased to see me, in his quiet way. A real bond grew between us. I was his connection to the world. If I ever had any doubts going into the prison, when some fact had come up that I couldn't account for, I always came away refreshed in my conviction that this young man was the simplest and gentlest of souls, and that the injustice he had suffered was enormous.

Murray began his preparations for the Privy Council, and while I didn't neglect the business hours I kept with Russell, I kept right on ploughing through the mountain of files. We spent many hours together in Murray's office as night came on and the harbour went dark and the ferries made their way across to the islands. Sometimes I came home at midnight and Claudine would be letting herself into my house after her evening at The Land, and we would sit on my deck talking about the case. I told her about an idea I had. I knew the Newgate case like the back of my hand now. I didn't know how it was going to turn out but I'd already consulted a number of people in the publishing trade. I was going to write a book.

One night I had that dream again. The endless stuffed toys, the droning voice telling me I didn't exist. It's always hard to describe the atmosphere of dreams, but the bad thing about this one was the horror when I realised that what the voice was saying was true. I woke up feeling ill, and bloody old. It was morning; the sun was streaming into the bedroom. Claudine was sitting up. I reached up and stroked her hair. I was still blurry and spooked with sleep. She looked at me and I saw something in her beautiful eyes. What was it? It reminded me, strangely, of Andrew Newgate. Was it youth, inexperience? (Claudine was about Andrew's age.) No, more than that, it was a look that seemed to go beyond me, as if she was searching for something she couldn't find. Had I seen that look on Andrew's face? And then she smiled, and I had the strange impression (I suppose I was still upset by the nightmare) that her smile wasn't connected to me. That between the smile and me there was nothing but a terrible void.

I got up quickly and went to the bathroom. I looked in the

mirror. I shaved and showered. By the time I'd dressed the spooked feeling had gone. I kissed Claudine, took my briefcase and went out to the car.

I looked at my diary. I was meeting Russell for a power breakfast, and a journalist after that. In the afternoon I'd scheduled Murray Ray and a TV researcher. Our campaign was gaining momentum. We were going to get Andrew in the news. I was gaining a media profile myself, something I knew would be useful for Andrew, and for me when I came to write my book. In the afternoon I'd agreed to go to a school play with Adele and the girls. Life was good. Life was full.

I had another idea up my sleeve, one that made me whistle when I thought about it. I was going to marry Claudine. A girl as good-looking as that wasn't going to come along every day. She would be gaining a lot by hooking up with me. After all, what did she have when she moved in? Nothing but a single suitcase and an old alarm clock, the poor girl. Life was a series of chances and it was up to Terry Carstone to grab them when they came along. To take the life I had, and the breaks that came my way, and use them, in any way I could.

opportunity

When I was nineteen, two of my friends went down to Dunedin to study for a year, and I went with them. We found a flat in the city, and the three of us got on well and were happy. I started doing a diploma in tourism and my friends were enrolled at the university. We used to have fun cooking dinner together when we got home, doing our shopping in the weekends, going to the beach in summer. We kept the flat nice and clean and sometimes we went to cheap furniture places and bought things to make it look brighter. I could have lived there forever, except I had in the back of my mind that one day I'd find a boyfriend and move in with him. On Sundays I went to church by myself. Up in Auckland I'd usually gone with my mother. I've always got on well with her. My father died when I was seventeen, but she and my brothers and I are a tight family, and when I was living down in Dunedin I missed going to church with her and helping her in the dairy she owned with my uncle, her brother, who had come out from Manchester after her.

One day I came home and found my flatmates sitting in the

kitchen looking at a map of England. I didn't say anything at first and they went silent and kept looking at each other. Finally I said, 'What's up?' They told me they'd decided to quit their studies for a year and go to Europe. I listened and nodded and said that sounded great. Then I went away into my room upset, because they hadn't talked about it with me, and hadn't asked me if I wanted to come, and because I didn't know what would happen to our flat.

Dee came in and sat on my bed, and I pretended to be asleep. She told me, 'You'll have lots of time to advertise for new flatmates.'

I sat up and said, 'No, I won't do that. I'm leaving.' I didn't say anything more, just packed my things up and left a few days later. I didn't want new flatmates, because everything about the house was spoiled for me. I knew my friends were closer to each other than to me, because they went to university and I was doing tourism. They used to tease me about going to church and sometimes they made jokes about God, but I'd always thought it was in fun. Now I thought perhaps they'd been snobs all along. I was hurt and I left, but I had a problem then, because I'd always told my mother how happy I was in the flat, and I was too proud to tell her it had gone wrong. So that weekend I answered an ad in the paper and ended up moving in with Reid and Sean.

Sean was a law student and Reid was a policeman. Sean had wanted to be a policeman too, but his eyesight was poor. The first time I met him he showed me his collection of guns. He was proud of his .303, which had a telescopic sight on it. He let me hold it. He had a couple of smaller guns, too, but the .303 was his favourite. He even gave it a name: Melissa. Sean was thin and white-faced and a chain smoker. He fancied me at first and kept touching my hands and wanting to put his arm around me, but I made it clear I wasn't interested. Reid was dark-haired and unusually good-looking. He was a body-builder. He looked nice in his police uniform. Sometimes he walked around the flat in shorts and no shirt. He had a little star tattooed on his shoulder. You could tell he was clever because he was always reading novels. He said he was going to be promoted to detective soon. He wanted to do undercover work. I moved my stuff into the empty room and thought everything would be fine.

I wasn't happy for long. For one thing, Reid and Sean kept the place an absolute pigsty. I used to clean it up, until I noticed something strange about Sean — my cleaning up annoyed him. He would go silent and stare around the room as if I'd messed up some special order of things. Once he said, out of the blue, 'Remember, .303s go through walls.' I asked him what he meant. I was angry. He just gave me a funny smile and walked out of the room. Reid was cheerfully messy. He was always eating, and his sandwiches spilled out everywhere and his kebabs exploded and leaked sauce, but he never noticed. He mixed up health tonics and vitamin drinks and left the stuff puddled all over the floor. I stopped trying to clean up after a while. The flat was up on the fifth floor and sometimes the rubbish wasn't taken out, and it rotted and maggots got in. When I thought of my old flat with its cheerful rooms, I felt depressed. I tried not to think about my two friends, but I was lonely too. I told my mother everything was going well. She liked it that I was living with a policeman. She said I would be nice and safe.

I liked Reid but I wasn't so sure about Sean. There was something about him. The only doubt I had about Reid, apart from his mess, was that he and Sean had been friends since they were kids, and this seemed to put a bit of a shadow on his — Reid's — character.

Sean had a laser fitted to Melissa's telescopic sight. He sat up late at night pointing the red dot at the buildings opposite. He had three or four girlfriends and he made sure they never came to the flat at the same time. They were law students and they got a thrill out of holding the gun, you could tell. I used to stay in my room when Sean's friends came around. Sometimes I came out and sat with the group, but I couldn't really join in. They talked about law and legal cases and about politics, and I didn't know much about that stuff. In my family we talked about who was sick and who was well, who'd lost money, who had big bills to pay, who'd bought a new car. My mother could spend a long time talking about a new fridge or a dishwasher. She and my uncle didn't talk about politics except to say that politicians were no good. They talked a lot about the church, because it was a big part of their lives. Anyway, I felt uncomfortable with the law students, and often I'd go back into my room and watch TV.

After I'd been there a few months things started going badly between me and Sean. He paced and slammed doors when I was vacuuming. He called me into his room and said I'd got makeup on his towels. A couple of times I got so fed up with the rubbish that I threw some of it into the lightwell. The caretaker complained and Sean had me on about that.

One night he came back with one of his girlfriends, and I don't know how it started, but she and I had an argument about God. She started off by saying she'd heard I went to church, and at first I thought she was being friendly. I said did she want to come along, and she thought that was a huge joke. She said there was no God and I said that's your opinion. She said it was a load of bullshit and I said it was a matter of faith. She was a smartarse cow, and drunk too. I was angry and tired, and sad and lonely, and disappointed that I couldn't make any friends in the place. She made a stupid joke about Jesus Christ on the cross and I lost my temper and tossed a cushion at her. It landed on the coffee table and all their glasses and ashtrays went flying, and there was wine and ash all over the floor. She shrieked, Sean shouted at me and I fled into my room.

Everything was quiet when I woke up. It was Friday. I went off to my classes and when I came home there was a note pinned on my door. It was written in blue pen and it was headed up with my name, Lisa Green, and the words Eviction Notice. It said that Sean was giving me notice to quit under some act or other, and that the reason for this was my 'act of violence'. I didn't think there was anything particularly violent about tossing a cushion, but I didn't feel like arguing. I screwed the notice up and walked into the kitchen. The tap was dripping onto some plastic bags in the sink. It made a hollow, empty sound. A trail of brown liquid came out of the bottom of the fridge. It had been a hot day and the air was stale with the sickly smell of old food.

I went into Sean's room. There was a life-size picture of a man on one wall, with a target printed on his chest and another on his head. There were full ashtrays on the unmade bed and a pile of cigarette packets on the chest of drawers. The bed smelled bad. The room was so bleak and ugly I should have been pleased I was getting away, but I wasn't, I was crushed.

That weekend Reid and Sean went away somewhere and the place was empty. I sat out on the balcony in the nights, looking up at the yellow squares of light around me, all the empty windows. I was afraid of the silence, of the empty corridors when I went down through the building, of the sounds of the city in the night. I was too proud to ring my mother and tell her what had happened. There was a sensible voice in my head telling me I needed to try again, to move in with some women next time, but I was all screwed up with loneliness, and too uneasy to sleep properly, and by the end of that weekend I felt fragile, as if something in me had been broken.

Still, I didn't give up. I packed up my room, and I started looking at ads in the paper again. I wanted to move fast, because my sense of failure had grown and I couldn't shake it off. When I went to meet my next lot of flatmates I was ashamed, and felt as if I had to hide my bad history. I was surprised when they rang me to say I could move in, and that they'd chosen me from a big group of applicants.

All this time I'd avoided Reid and Sean, which was easy because we were all busy. If Sean was around he made the odd caustic comment and I ignored him, but Reid seemed as careless and happy as ever; I had the feeling he liked me, and that he thought Sean had been unfair. In my loneliness I'd done a bit of daydreaming about Reid. I thought about how he was always reading novels, which was unusual for a policeman, and about how handsome he was. I imagined him doing heroic things in his job.

I moved my belongings into the new flat, and one day I came back to get the last of it. Sean had kept asking for the key, but I was hanging on to it until I was finished. I had some kitchen things to get, some bowls, plates and cups. I went up to the flat and put it all in a box. The kitchen was worse than ever. I could tell the rubbish hadn't gone out for days. Everything stank.

The front door opened and Reid came in in his police uniform. I said hello.

'What are you doing?' he said. He lounged against the door.

I told him I was getting my stuff.

'You're supposed to be out by now.'

I looked at him. 'I'm getting the last of my things.'

'Are those yours?' he said, looking at the boxes of crockery.

'Of course they're mine.'

He started opening the lids of the boxes.

'Hey!' I said. I couldn't believe what he was doing. 'Do you think I'm a thief? Get away.' I was furious. I pushed his hand off. He straightened up.

'You'd better get out now,' he said.

He picked up the boxes and carried them to the door. 'Now give me the key.'

I ran to the window and threw the key out. He came at me and started pushing me to the door. I struggled but he was very strong. He pushed me out onto the landing. I started to cry. There was a pause, then he reached his hand towards my face, and I thought he was sorry, that my tears had brought him to his senses. But he put his whole hand over my face and gave a sharp push. I flew back and fell on the floor. He threw the boxes out after me, and I heard the bowls and cups crash together inside. He shut the door.

I sat next to my smashed things. I thought: there is

something wrong with me, something bad. The realisation came to me suddenly. My tears dried up and I got a strange, cold feeling. I got up off the floor and walked away, leaving the smashed crockery. I took the bus to my new flat.

I did my best to fit in with my new flatmates. I went all out to pretend I was normal. I prayed to God to help me: let them not know that I am wrong and bad, that I am defective. And He did help me. I got on with life. I hid my failures and, after a while, despite my wrongness, I had some successes. I finished my diploma and moved back to Auckland. I got a good job, and one night in a pub in Parnell I met my husband.

James was an engineering student back then. My sense of wrongness was still strong, and I did all I could to cover it up. I set out to please him. He liked strong, independent women, so I acted like that. He liked lots of sex, and I was happy to oblige. I never thought about what I wanted. I wanted my self to disappear, and in a way it did. I turned myself into a good person by acting it, and even though I still felt deep down that I was bad in some way, I started to be happy.

I loved James, but I wasn't comfortable with his family. With them I had to work hard to hide my flaws. They were very educated. His mother, Jean, was an English teacher and his father was a professor at the university. James told me his mother said I was pretty and charming, but I felt a kind of chill at that because I knew she'd picked me as someone who never read books and who wasn't educated enough for her son. His parents met my mother and uncle and they got on well, but you could tell there was always going to be a problem with conversation. Jean wasn't going to talk about fridges and bills and who was sick and who was well; she wanted to talk about the situation in Iraq, and American foreign policy and Maori issues, and books. My mother always rose to the occasion, because she's no slouch really, and in fact she reads more books than I do, but I was always glad when they got onto some topic they could jog along on, like who said what in the Bible. Jean had read the Bible *as an intellectual exercise.*

They could talk about it for hours, even though my mother took it seriously and Jean regarded all religion as mumbo jumbo.

James and I got married. After a couple of years we had our baby, Michael. James had a job, we had a good flat and Michael was a lovely baby. I didn't feel flawed any more. I felt free.

A long time ago, when my father and mother first came out from England, they went exploring in the Far North, and their favourite place was a small bay where they camped on Maori land. They made such good friends with the Reihana family, who owned the bay, that they came back every year, and eventually they got the money together and built a bach. They used to get a manager into the shop and we'd go up every holiday. My parents spent their days with Marama and Don Reihana and my brothers and I played with their nine kids. Marama and my mother kept each other company while Don and my father went fishing. The women gossiped and looked after the kids. They talked non-stop. Marama was as churchy as my mother, although she wasn't as strait-laced. My parents used to send me and my brothers to stay with the Reihanas some holidays, and sometimes they came down to stay with us. Don and Marama were my parents' first real friends in New Zealand, and they stayed close all the years I was growing up.

When my father died, the Reihanas came down to Auckland. They said, 'We've come to take Alfred home.' They took his body up north. We had a tangi at their marae, and they buried him in the Maori graveyard, in the Reihana line.

James liked our bach, and he and I used it every summer. The Reihanas were still there, and James loved the fact that we could go over all the Maori land because of my family ties to the place. He wanted to be friendly with the Reihanas, although he was a bit awkward with them, whereas I'd known them all my life and just thought of them as family. Anyway, we went up there often and one year we took Jean.

Jean loved the place too. She met old Marama Reihana, and

had a long conversation with her about land rights and Treaty settlements, which my mother wouldn't have done; she would just have settled down for a cosy chat about who was doing what in the family, and all the other local gossip.

Jean was very sociable and could get on with anyone, and she was full of observations. She said Marama's grandchildren were good-looking and chic and that they looked as if they had a bit of French in their family, maybe from de Surville's time. She thought it was interesting that some of the Reihana grandchildren were studying at university. One was even doing a Masters degree. She went on like this and it made me a bit uncomfortable, especially when she went on about the university thing. To me they were the scruffy old Reihanas who we used to give our worn-out furniture to, and I wondered if she was having a dig at me, by implying that even the Maoris were more educated than I was.

We took Jean to the Maori graveyard and she enjoyed washing the tapu off her hands afterwards. She squirted some water on Michael's hands, which reminded me of his christening, when she'd kept fidgeting and making rude jokes about the vicar. She'd made James laugh when it was supposed to be solemn and beautiful.

'So you do tapu but not christenings,' I said.

'They're all just rituals, aren't they?' she said cheerfully. Then she gave James a look, as if she was sorry for him.

One day I said I'd ask Don junior Reihana if he'd drive us up to the beach his family had been given in a land settlement. It's a huge, beautiful beach that you can only get to by four-wheel drive.

Jean said, 'Oh, should you ask? They might think it's *offensive*.'

'Why?' I said, surprised.

'If they think we're ordering them about or something.'

I thought, what's offensive? They're friends. We were always asking them for things, and giving them things, too. If they don't want to they'll say no, like always. So I went ahead and asked, and Don junior said that would be fine, but the next day he didn't turn up. Jean started saying he must be annoyed, but I said not to worry, he'd come on a day when he was ready. I was irritated with her telling me I'd offended someone I knew well and she didn't.

Sure enough, on the third day Don drove up, ready to go. Jean made an elaborate explanation about how we didn't want to be a nuisance. He just smiled and waited for us to get ready.

Jean was delighted to be going on a trip. She got Don talking. He told her how a long time ago his father had gone to the Maori Land Court to protest the sale of some land nearby, but the Maoris who owned it had insisted on selling it to the government, and there'd been bad feeling between the families ever since. I was a bit surprised to hear him talking like this. As long as I could remember, the Reihanas had only talked about fishing and boats and the church, and all the other everyday things that had kept them and my parents absorbed.

We turned off onto a narrow, sandy road. Around the first bend we met a truck. Don stopped to talk to the driver, a one-eyed man. There was a fat woman next to him with tattoos up her arms. On the back were two vicious dogs and a row of silent boys. The boys were ragged and thin, with bad teeth. These people were related to the Reihanas, but they were part of what Marama called the 'bad side of the family'. They lived deep in the pine forest. The children hardly ever made it to school. None of Marama's nine children had a single criminal conviction, and they all, pretty much, had jobs. Some of the 'bad side', on the other hand, were rumoured to be lifelong criminals and, in particular, drug dealers.

Don winked at me as we drove off. 'He's a mean bugger, that Riki. Last year him and his missus were having a fight? He went for her, but she stabbed him in the eye with a toothbrush!' He went off into a big giggle.

Jean said, 'Oh dear. A bit of utu.' They laughed for a while.

We drove into the pine forest. It was dark and cool. The thick pine needles muffled sound and you could only hear the wind sighing. The trees grew so thickly together you could barely see the sky. There wasn't a proper road, only a track that meandered through the trees, over stumps, around bluffs, up and down steep banks. The forest stretched away as far as you could see — dark trunks and orange needles with shafts of light angling down. Sometimes the trees opened out, and there'd be a clearing, and a view of a yard full of old car bodies and a ramshackle house, the windows broken and boarded and the paint peeling, and some kids running towards the jeep, dark little figures against the wall of pines. Sometimes you could hear the whine of a chainsaw, or an axe chopping.

When we passed one of these clearings Jean said in a low voice, 'I wouldn't want to be on my own out here.' There was a house with chickens running about and a face at the window. The wall of the house was green and mouldy. It was hard to understand why anyone would choose to live in such a secret, dark, lonely place.

We drove on for an hour. Then Don accelerated and we roared up a dune into bright light. The beach was beautiful and empty, a stretch of sparkling sea with a little island out from it and lines of long, even waves curling in. Jean ran down the dunes holding Michael's hand and exclaiming how lovely it was. She had a way of throwing herself into things with her whole body, like a kid. 'Let's walk to the end of it,' she called, holding Michael. He put his arms around her and kissed her.

Don wanted to load some wood into the back of the truck so we left him and walked all the way to the rocks at the far end. Jean played with Michael, doing different voices for him and making up a long story. We went for a swim and started walking back.

Jean stopped and shaded her eyes. 'The car's gone.'

'Oh my God,' James said.

'We'll have to walk all the way back. Through those terrible woods.'

'We'll be eaten!'

They went on like this, laughing and joking. Then Jean said, 'It really is gone, you know.'

'Oh shit.'

They looked at me, all giggly.

I said, 'You know he won't have gone.'

James sighed. A special kind of look passed between him and Jean, as if each knew what the other was thinking. Jean went on adding to the story about how we'd been abandoned.

When we got back, Don was driving the truck down the paddock towards the stream. Jean told him we thought he'd gone and made lots of jokes while she got out the picnic and made everyone a sandwich. While we were eating, a big, shiny new SUV came over the dune and cruised down to the flat. Two men got out and Don went to talk to them. He came back.

'That's André and Teina,' he said. 'Bad buggers. They live in the pines further down the coast.'

'How bad are they?' James asked.

'How bad? They're like the Sopranos, bro!' Don said, and went off into a big laugh.

'Really? Drugs?' Jean eyed the two men, who were talking behind their big truck. She was dying to know more.

'Drugs, whatever. You name it.' Don said. 'I keep a polite distance. Hear no evil, see no evil, get no evils!' The three of them laughed at that.

After lunch Jean played with Michael again and we drifted about. James swam and Don and I lay in the grass. André and Teina had moved a bit further off and were sitting in the shade of their truck.

'What are they doing?' I asked.

'They're waiting for some fulla. Someone's cousin from Australia or something.'

I could hear Jean's voice, and Michael shrieking with delight. I went down to look for James. When we came back another car had driven down and André and Teina were talking to a man.

Don was starting to load up. I went a bit closer to the men. André was squat and muscular. Teina was thin, with dreadlocks and heavily tattooed hands. The new arrival was tall and dark, with a bushy beard.

Behind me Jean was telling Don, 'Michael's just like James as a little boy. He's so imaginative.' She often said those things. Michael was handsome like James, stroppy like James, intelligent like James.

I was watching the men. Jean said cheerfully to me, 'Ready for the forest? It's so spooky in there. As if anything could happen. Those terrible little houses. The chopping noises. That *face* at the window.'

I turned, with a sensible smile. 'It's just a whole lot of pine trees,' I said.

She gave me a look; there was a sort of incredulity in it, as well as an appeal. Then she looked cynical and resigned.

'Michael! Where are you, you pirate?' she called.

I went towards André and Teina. They stopped talking and watched me. André's eyes were small and calculating. He gave me a malignant smile. Teina looked irritated, as if he wondered how I dared to interrupt. I went close to the man with the beard.

'Reid,' I said.

He made a small movement, jerking his head back, putting out his hands.

'Who?'

'Reid.'

He looked at André and Teina. 'Who's this?' he asked.

'You were in Dunedin, remember? Just before I left the flat. When you were in the police. '

André and Teina looked at Reid. They didn't move.

'Are you still in the police?' I asked.

'I don't know who this chick is,' Reid said. He started to back away.

'Weren't you going to be a detective?'

All three men were very still. Reid looked at me over the top of his sunglasses. His mouth was open, grimacing.

I smiled at André. I said, 'I was sure it was him. He used to have a little star tattooed on his shoulder.'

I shrugged and walked away.

Don started up the truck. Jean was singing Michael a pirate song. He clapped his little hands. James was fussing about the sand in his shoes.

The water glittered in the afternoon light and long shadows were starting to cross the beach. We drove up the dune onto the track, and the pine forest closed around us.

the mountain

From my hotel room I could see the lights of New Plymouth. There was a house facing me with two horizontal slit windows. They stared at me out of the darkness, yellow eyes.

In the morning we had walked around the boardwalk, from one end of town to the centre, where the Len Lye sculpture, the Wind Wand, stretched high up into the sky. It moved with the wind, it dipped and bobbed. I thought it was beautiful. The surf crashed against the rocky breakwater, spray rose, the light was silvery, the white foam so pure white and cold, rainbows in the spray. Alan took my arm. Two teenage girls watched us, him short and plump in his scarf and black jacket, me much taller in my anorak and jeans, my glasses blurred with sea drops. I wished he would let go of my arm but he was talking and happy and I didn't want to pull away.

Alan said he'd expected a flat, dull, inland town. He never looked at maps. He talked about the sea — so strange, he said, coming from Auckland, to see surf crashing in at the edge of a city. We passed a shopping centre and went into a modern building called Puke Ariki. There was a trendy café where you could sit out on the balcony and watch the Wind Wand moving like a giant flower stalk over the sea. Alan drank wine; I had a Coke. He called it rot-gut: 'A glass of rot-gut for my friend.' When he liked a place, he needed to describe it, and he wasn't satisfied until he'd called attention to every feature and oddity, everything ugly and lovely. I sat and listened, and chimed in sometimes. He wanted to know that I'd registered all the impressions he'd had. If I hadn't, he would explain, describe, until he was sure. He shifted nervously on his seat. He waved his hands for emphasis. Then he sat back, smiling.

We finished our drinks and walked back up the main street. He talked about the mountain, how it had been shrouded in cloud when we'd flown in and been driven from the airport, how it was stubbornly refusing to show itself now.

'The guys in the minibus,' he said, laughing. 'What were all the names?'

We'd been met at the airport by a woman with a hard, flat Australian accent. She was the liaison person for the Taranaki Festival, at which Alan was to perform. He was a pianist, a Bach specialist. In the minivan were another sort of musicians — Kiwi rap artists. The woman had taken out a clipboard and asked for names. Humourless and earnest, they came out with '9-Funk', 'Snoop Rag', 'D-Money'. I could feel Alan laughing. I sat up the front with the woman, and Alan delightedly climbed in the back. He said, 'Are you 9, or Funk, or Snoop?' They corrected him. 'I'm D. He's Rag.' They high-fived and whooped and said 'Yo' and 'Dude'. They invited us to their dance party, which was to start at midnight. Alan enjoyed himself. He liked their strong brown arms, their tattoos, their masculine bravado. He thought they were hunky and sexy. He was titillated.

'See that big lump of cloud there?' the driver said to me. 'That's the mountain. It's beautiful when it comes out.'

The sky was blue, apart from the seething mass of grey-black cloud ahead. I had the idea the cloud was moving around the thing it was hiding, the wisps writhing, rising, plunging. I thought of bees circling a hive.

'Why do the clouds cling to it like that?'

'Dunno,' she said. 'You can go up it.'

In the back someone said, 'Yo, surf's up.'

'Yo,' Alan said.

Funk, an Islander, handsome, massive-featured, said, 'I've got some *random* new lyrics, man.'

'Oh yes?' Alan said, gaily, hilariously.

Funk made a series of snorting sounds — drumbeats. The heads of his crew began to bob in time. He started to deliver a string of Americanisms about dreams, destiny, the 'hood. Alan looked innocently polite. The rap went on, a saga of urban deprivation, gun violence. The heads bobbed. We drove through the beautiful landscape, the sunlit fertile fields. Cows watched us go by.

I asked the driver, 'Is it much further?' I liked her. She was good-looking, tough, at ease. The way she tossed comments back to the rappers, you could tell she would fit in anywhere.

'Nearly there,' she said. I wished I could think of something to say. I spent more time wondering how to talk to people than actually talking. I didn't know how to make people like me. Usually they'd moved on before I'd thought of anything.

We pulled up at the hotel. In the carpark Funk put his arm around Alan and said, 'My man! Dude! You're coming to my party.'

'Absolutely,' Alan said.

'Thank you for the ride,' I said to the driver. It sounded formal, sycophantic. Her phone rang. She got in the van. She said something and I started forward with a protesting 'No!'

She drove away.

Alan and Funk were marching into the foyer. I wondered whether Funk was gay. He was muscular, tattooed, powerful, but his face had a symmetrical beauty that might have communicated something to Alan. Now they were playing with Funk's mobile phone. Perhaps numbers were being exchanged. I followed, feeling awkward. I couldn't join in with the bobbing, chanting group crowding around the front desk, Alan in their midst. The receptionist, who was young and sweet, fluttered her slender fingers and pretended to be going to pieces, and charmed everyone. I stood out on the edge, smiling woodenly. It was like this at parties. You smiled, and yet your smile was contrived, rigged up to show willing, and you felt people sensed this and their own smiles faded and they edged away . . .

Alan elbowed his way out of the group, holding up his room key. They called after him. 'Later, Al! See you tonight!'

We took the stairs. Alan panted and puffed, flinging his scarf around his neck. I thought what a genius he had for friendship. He was generous, easy, flamboyant. People followed him. He made them laugh and feel good. I was proud of him; I liked the way he attracted people. I thought of the driver's words: 'I've just dropped off Alan Reece and his partner.' My protesting 'No!' lost in the abrupt roar of her acceleration. I wanted her to know I wasn't gay. Alan had been my music teacher since I was a boy. He was my gay friend. He was my only friend.

All that day, as we walked around exploring, Alan's arm linked through mine, the mountain stayed hidden.

My parents died in a car crash when I was nine. I moved in with my aunt and uncle. Their children had grown up and moved out, and they were happy to have me. My bedroom had a view of Mt Hobson. There were houses built up against the hillside and at night I couldn't see the houses, only their yellow windows against the mountain's black shape. I had a fantasy that the windows were set in the side of the hill; that it contained a whole city, blazing with light. I imagined people coming out of the mountain in the dark. I remember sitting alone in my room, late, looking across the black valley of the suburb, thinking about the hidden city — its heat, its bustle, its fires. I thought of energy building up in there. Some trigger would set it off, and then the mountain people would spill out. I imagined the people in the houses round about, sleeping, unaware, and then the sudden onslaught. Sometimes I imagined terrible scenes. Houses overrun, people screaming.

When I turned ten my aunt decided I was too old to have her tuck me in any more. Sent to bed each night I went upstairs, switched on the light, put my drink of water on the chest of drawers, then sat on the bed, looking at the walls. No one would come to my room until next morning. Before, my childhood had been a blur of unconscious action. But in the bedroom at my aunt's house every move I made felt deliberate and willed. The hanging of my clothes, the angling of the lamp, the opening of the book.

Here in New Plymouth, in the hotel, I had that old sense of dislocation, where everything was unfamiliar, nothing automatic. I remembered the loneliness of childhood. As an adult, you can look for someone to go to bed with. When you're a child, you've got no choice. You go to bed alone.

I always enjoyed my piano lessons with Alan. After my parents died they were one thing that stayed the same. He lived in a big wooden villa with a terraced garden. The interior was quirky and camp, full of old movie posters and strange objects he'd collected. He had a taste for the grotesque and the weird — he had a stuffed bird and other curios, but he had beautiful things, too: vases and lamps and rugs, hundreds of books, and a large collection of music. It was always dim and quiet and peaceful in Alan's house. I sat at the piano and outside the rain fell and birds hopped on the wet lawn and the garden glowed in the afternoon light. Alan sat among his treasures, in his black velvet jacket and his bright scarf, listening. He sat very still while I played, his eyes unseeing.

He said, 'When I was little I had two aunts who used to take me to horror movies. I was too young to see the films and they terrified me. As soon as I'd recovered from one, they would take me to another.' He laughed.

I thought about this. It seemed like a subtle form of feminine violence. Were the aunts sadistic, or just neglectful? Why didn't his mother intervene? I saw little Alan, shivering between two young women in a dark cinema. Coming out into the light, freshly traumatised. He took refuge in music. He knew he was gay from the age of eight. He knew about loneliness and disorientation. But he had courage and a tough character. He was an optimist. He had gay friends, and I used to think gayness was like a club. If you belonged, you had a common language. I didn't like it when Alan's friends came over. It interrupted our talk, and I was shut out.

We were close. I was one of his best friends, maybe because I was so available. No one else would have come down to New Plymouth with him, just for the fun of the trip. I was studying music at university, didn't have to go to work.

I had flatmates, a few mates at university. I was good at getting on with women, but women tended to be disappointed when I only wanted to be friends. The more time I spent with Alan, the less I had to make other connections. People assumed I was gay when I was with him, and sometimes I thought he exploited that, to keep me to himself. He was always saying how good-looking I was. We got on well because we both loved music. Every now and then I had an uneasy feeling. I wanted a girlfriend. I wasn't part of his world, not properly. And I hadn't made a world of my own.

We went out. On the main street we found a café called the Ultralounge.

Alan was drinking and in a good mood. It was Saturday night. He didn't have to perform until Sunday afternoon. We shared a bottle of wine. After the meal we walked down the town. There were posters advertising a band called Sticky Filth. Taranaki's favourite sons, they were called. Alan was amused by the name and wanted to see them for a laugh, but at the Convention Centre we were told they were sold out. I suggested a quiet bar across the road but Alan rolled his eyes, looking restless and bored. He nosed around the corner, eyeing the entrance to a basement pub, guarded by burly bouncers.

He pointed. 'Let's go in there.'

'Oh God,' I said, but there was no stopping him. I followed him down into a dark, deafening, smelly bar, full of drunk hoons and staggering women. People were setting up instruments on the stage. It was rough: you could sense violence, in the women as well as the men. Alan looked around, pleased and interested. A hefty man with long dreadlocks veered into me threateningly; behind him a woman was dancing and falling. I ordered a couple of strong drinks. The band came out on the stage. Alan nudged me sharply.

The band were young and white — three of them, just boys. They had dreadlocks, but the sides of their heads were shaved. The bass player's face was painted completely black. The lead singer had delicate pixie features and black makeup: smeared eyes, black lips. All three wore clothes cut into rags and spraypainted with words: Hate Fuck Death Kill. The bass player took his place, putting on, as a final touch, an oxygen mask, from which dangled a plastic bag. You got the idea: they were horror men, post-Holocaust men; they were creatures who'd crept out of the rubble after the end of the world. They let loose a roar of sound and the singer began to rasp out the words of a song in a voice so deep and flat and violent you could hardly believe it came out of his slight teenage body.

The audience had changed. The women had retreated to the edges of the room. Now, in front of the stage, the crowd was only male, and they were all doing the same thing, leaning forward and shaking their heads in time, and chanting bits of the chorus, roaring it. I looked across the rows of heads. It was a war dance, a dance of rage. It was atavistic, barbaric, primitive. I felt it vibrating through me — the rasping voice, the answer of the crowd, the rhythmically juddering bodies. I was outside it, appalled by the sound, but it was in me too, filling every part of me. And then it finished and the crowd broke ranks, surged forward, roared, raised fists, then there was another explosion of sound and the rhythmic head-shaking began again. 'Zombie, zombie,' they were chanting. I thought of an ancient scene, smeared warriors in flickering light, weapons splattered with blood. The teenage shaman in his warpaint, calling his people to war.

Alan was pulling my arm, shouting and pointing at the door.

Outside he fanned himself and laughed. My ears were ringing. A man with a shaven head and tattoos on his face came close, looked intently at Alan, and said, 'Hello, sweetie.'

'Hello!' Alan said. The man snarled and lurched away.

Before Alan's performance the next day I sat at a café table drinking coffee. I had half an hour to wait in the Sunday afternoon sunshine. The sky was blue but the mountain was still hidden behind a shroud of mist, the clouds boiling around it, rising, falling. A man came along the street. His hair was tied in a ponytail and he was wearing a dark blue coat. He walked closer, stopped and said, 'Andrew Newgate!'

'Andrew!' I said in surprise.

He sat down, lit a roll-your-own cigarette, inhaled and leaned back, looking at me as if it wasn't at all strange to meet me in New Plymouth after all this time. His eyes were flat blue, expressionless. His hands were grimy, his nails black. His face was grey, unhealthy, finely lined. He looked no different from the time when I'd lived in a flat in Auckland and he, a friend of the landlord, had occupied the spare room out the back, a strange, cold, enigmatic character, talkative but self-enclosed — Andrew. Smith? Smythe? He was a shadow, a no man. The same first name was about all we had in common.

'What are you doing here?'

'I live here,' he told me. 'It's my home town.'

I said I was down for the festival with my friend, the pianist Alan Reece. I came up with a few bits of small talk. Andrew looked at me with his unreadable eyes.

I said, 'Remember the landlord, what a miser he was?'

'I still hear from him.' His tone was hostile.

'Tell him from me he was cheap bastard,' I said, laughing.

He got up. 'Fight your own battles,' he said.

I blinked.

'Good luck to your boyfriend.'

I was angry. 'He's not . . .' But he was walking away.

He looked back once, without expression, a phantom

fading back to the other side. He went around a corner, gone.

I thought about the underground bar, the boys screaming 'Zombie, zombie.'

Waiting for Alan I daydreamed: New Plymouth was a place of goblins, of ghouls.

Alan played brilliantly. There was a big audience. Afterwards he was elated. He held my arm as we moved through the noisy crowd. We had drinks at the bar and he overdid it, with relief and cheerfulness. In the toilets he told me, 'I've gone and got drunk.' We came out into the milling foyer and he grabbed me and kissed me on the cheek. 'They're talking about you because you're so handsome,' he whispered. I pulled away but he held my arm tight, held on.

The driver came for us. We drove through the green fields. Alan nodded and snored, his cheeks flushed, his clothes rumpled. I looked at him sleeping.

The driver said, 'Finally.'

Out the window I saw the mountain. The mist had lifted. Draped with the last wisps of cloud, rising against the blue sky, white and pure, cold and sharp, it appeared to me like an idea once obscured now become clear, something ancient, savage, unforgiving.

terrorism

Peter and I had been seeing each other for a year, spending one week at his place and the next at mine, although lately we'd spent more time at my apartment, mine being spacious with a deck we could sit out on and drink wine in the evenings and look over the sea, the harbour still and glassy through the long, hot summer and the evenings full of golden light turning to soft black shadows, and the voices in the street below, the drowsy summer street. I liked to walk along the marina in the evening and look at the water, the rainbows of oil smearing the surface, the light dancing zigzags on the sides of the boats. Peter strolled, listening to me with his customary expression. He had an air of sweet, hastily assumed politeness, as if you'd startled him out of some dreamy reflection and he was gathering his thoughts, waiting to see what came next. He blinked, widened his blue eyes, smiled, and 'Really?' he would say, turning his head on one side while I laughed and explained myself, refining some statement that his manner had made seem clumsy or too forceful. The laugh always there behind his curved mouth, ready to break out. I felt I was the solid one. I was the solid one.

Sometimes I woke in the night and saw him standing out on the deck, looking at the calm sea, the curtains moving around the open door, his cigarette a little point of fire spiralling into the dark as he threw it away. He was a light sleeper. His night prowling disturbed me; it made me think he was looking for something outside and beyond ourselves. I didn't like to think he wanted freedom. I pretended I didn't know how he drifted about in the night, walked through the rooms, played with his mobile phone, how he lay awake, his arms folded behind his head, his eyes open and unseeing.

At the end of summer we started looking at houses. We'd talked about it on and off. I was eager to share a house but didn't want to seem so. I would have liked to stay in my flat and for Peter to move in — I didn't fancy moving into his cramped bachelor lair — but my landlord had given me notice he wanted to sell my place. Soon the sign would go up and I would have to find somewhere new to live. The sentence hanging over the place gave every evening out on the deck a poignant flavour, and already we were talking about the flat with a sense of nostalgia.

Now I was lying on the bed, the real estate section open in front of me, circling possibilities: the small houses for first-home buyers, the inner-city ones.

Neither of us had owned a house before; we agreed, jokingly, that it was about time. Or was I the one who said those things? Perhaps Peter only listened, then slid away from the subject. 'We can afford it!' I said. I was a senior manager; he was a journalist. Neither of us felt very grown up; secretly we couldn't believe how old we were, and the idea of buying a house made us anxious: was it capitulation, would it tie us too stiflingly together? I could imagine Peter asking himself these questions. I thought about them myself, and I hid how much I wanted it, how desperately I wanted it.

I'd worked my way up: now I was a boss. In my team there were four men and three women. Two of the men had children, but among the women there was agreement: we didn't want children. We cared about our careers; we didn't want to lose what we'd fought to achieve. We didn't like kids — the idea of them was boring and claustrophobic. We were always testing one another, probing for signs of weakening. Mike at work brought his baby in once. It lay in a car seat, its eyes closed, its syrupy mouth open, a tiny string of spit trembling on the glazed bottom lip. Bright felt toys dangled above it — suns and stars. He put his hand on its head. The dip of the fontanelle, little strings of soft hair. Our shrugs, our ironic jokes. Clenched fists. Clenched fists.

I showed Peter the houses I'd circled. We went out in the car. He drove, ironically smoking. We looked at the first house, a suburban box, crammed with beige furniture and pastel reproductions and maidenhair ferns in pots.

'Try to picture it unfurnished,' I said hopelessly.

We snorted our way around two more. I wanted to stop scoffing and take it seriously, but Peter kept making funny jokes. I'd only got him this far by pretending it was a laugh, something he could write about: an amusing afternoon, the hidden secrets of the suburbs. I wanted a villa with a return veranda, or an old workman's cottage with wooden floors and uneven windows and a garden, not a townhouse with cardboard walls and brown carpet. I wanted what the agent didn't have. We went for a coffee. There was a week to go until the election. Hoardings stood along the roads.

In the café I looked through the paper again.

I said, 'I know this house!'

I showed Peter: a big place in Remuera, four bedrooms, a view of Mt Hobson. Marie's house. Marie.

I met her when we were both thirteen. There was to be a mufti day at school and she'd got the day wrong, had turned up in plain clothes when everyone else was in uniform. She was blushing, humiliated, hiding her face behind her long curly hair. Attracted by her distress, unsure whether I was sympathetic or wanting to mock, or just, out of boredom, wanting to get close to someone else's pain, I went and sat beside her, and when she said she was going home to change I offered to go with her. I don't know why. We both got in trouble for it, I remember, taking off without telling anyone, getting on the bus and riding all the way back to the house in Remuera, getting the key from under a rock in the garden, going in and finding Marie's mother at the kitchen table in a dressing gown, crying and taking pills, throwing her head back, tipping the tall glass, and telling us to leave her alone, leave her alone.

'They're getting a divorce,' Marie told me. Her bedroom upstairs was striped with sunlight. I looked over at Mt Hobson, the trees against the hard blue sky. Her walls were covered with posters of The Clash.

All the time I knew Marie her parents were getting a divorce. They fought their way into 1981. Her mother had a secret boyfriend, her father stayed at work and Marie spent a lot of time at my house. That was where she got her political education. It was the time of the Springbok rugby tour. There were protests against the South African team coming to play in New Zealand. Marie's parents were all for the rugby tour — they were right-wing. Her father was a rich businessman, a 'fascist', she said. She liked the political talk in our house. She and I started going on anti-apartheid demonstrations. Her parents forbade it and mine encouraged it — went on the marches themselves. Marie and I prided ourselves on being at the front of the march every time. We were obsessed with The Clash. I got myself a short spiky haircut. We were scornful, fierce, daring, political; we got in trouble at school and relished it; we were best friends.

I looked at the picture of the house where I'd spent so many afternoons.

'Let's go and see it,' I said. I explained: 'We used to go on protest marches. She wasn't allowed. We told her mother we were going shopping. My best friend. Outrageous Marie . . .'

Peter gave me an indulgent look. This was something he did approve of — a sentimental journey, a look back at my past. He enjoyed the thought of me as young, teenage, silly, dizzy. 'Yes! Let's see the house where you played with little Marie.'

I rang the agent. He had finished his open home but would wait and let us in. We drove back, past the election hoardings.

'We're going to have a National government,' I said. I felt depressed about it. 'I wish I could do something.'

'Do?'

'Oh, I don't know.'

'Labour's run a lousy little campaign.'

'So what? What about what matters? What about politics?'

Peter sighed and smiled languidly. 'Politics, well . . .'

When we first met he told me, 'I don't really like opinionated people.' He was — what was he? — too cynical? too fey? for political convictions, too light and subtle and comical. I thought of that Dickens character, Harold Skimpole. 'What use is money to me?' he says. 'What would I do with it? I'm just a child . . .'

The house was huge; we could never have afforded it ourselves. Peter stood in the hallway pretending he was interested in the kitchen, the big sitting room, the lush front garden.

The agent told us, 'A writer lives here. Celia Myers? She's finding the house a bit big for her, now she lives alone.' Outside we heard a car engine beginning to be thrashed into high revs.

Celia Myers! We made faces behind the agent's back. It was the kind of odd, quirky chance Peter's luck often brought him: licence to poke around in the house of a writer, to sift through her cupboards and check out her bookshelves. He specialised in interviews and in-depth profiles and here he had an inside look at the literary dame's life — her gardening shoes at the door, her odd, mixed collection of art, the notes pinned on the fridge, the open diary on the bench, her bedroom with the novels and the earplugs on the bedside table, the old bird off out somewhere, unable to prevent him snooping, only the agent hovering doubtfully behind him as he opened closets and studied shelves, making mental notes, his quick imagination, his sense of humour working. He would notice everything; he would be funny and observant about it all.

I adored him. I wanted to keep hold of him. He'd had a lot of girlfriends, but I thought, I really did think, that we were a good match. There were little blow-ups and tiffs: he could be distracted and impatient, or obscurely offended, and I held back in a way I'd never have been able to when I was younger, careful not to crowd him, not to be demanding. I kept secret my relief at winning him back. We'd had such good times, the whole year. His funny emails. Hilarity in bed on a Sunday morning. Our walks by the marina. Moments when he was suddenly sincere or loving or vulnerable, and I was smitten.

And now I was making my way up to the bedroom, Marie's room, where we'd sat and talked, and jumped around to The Clash, where I'd had the kind of teenage certainty you don't get back, full of rebellion and laughs and the thrill of your own daring.

I wondered what had become of her parents. Perhaps they'd got around to divorcing, sold the house, gone their separate ways. I saw Marie sitting on the floor in the afternoon light, an assortment of objects in front of her: masking tape, scissors, glue, string. I smiled at the memory. She was a terrorist, temperamentally. She always wanted to go too far. I didn't know where she was now, what city, what country. Did she have a husband, children?

Peter came up the stairs. I pointed at the floor. 'Marie, she sat here and . . . I remember it so clearly. It was 1981, during the Springbok tour. Marie wanted to do something. There was some company, aligned with the tour. And she made this thing, sitting here on the floor.'

Peter said, 'I got caught in an anti-apartheid march once. I jumped into an alley while it passed. All the shouting and hooting. The earnest faces.'

'You mean you *hid*?' But I was charmed by his expression, enough to smile, to cover what was sharp in my tone.

The agent came up. In the garden next door a group of youths was standing around an old car. The engine roared; birds flew up from the hedge. The agent half closed his eyes.

Then he smacked his hands against his thighs and made as if to bustle us downstairs. Peter, polite, obedient, turned to go. I said, 'You go on down.' The agent ushered Peter ahead.

Marie. She sat on the floor in the sunny room, while her mother whispered into the phone downstairs, while I lay on her bed and worked on my homework, while the dog lay panting and snuffling by the door, Marie, gluing and pasting and sculpting. She wore rubber gloves. Perhaps she had her tongue stuck out the corner of her mouth. Her long hair pinned up on top of her head.

She finished what she'd been making and put it on the bed next to me.

'That'll teach them,' she said.

It was a malevolent-looking thing. She'd summoned up her knowledge of what it should look like from films and TV, I suppose. She'd always been good at art. A frisson went through me, a little shift, where I thought how it would appear to an innocent person, coming upon it unexpectedly. There were wires, and bits covered with tape that could be . . . could be what? Gelignite, plastic explosive? There was an aerial sticking out of it, a nice touch, the spiky point quivered slightly. It gave — radiated — an impression of sensitivity, of terrible potential. She frowned over it, the little sculptress, turning it critically, this way and that in her gloved hands. It was encased in a wooden box, wires running through and around it. I reached out.

'Don't touch!' she commanded, and, narrowing her eyes, whispered, '*Forensics.*'

We looked at the inert thing. Marie's bomb. Fake, of course, designed to scare, to disrupt, to make an anti-apartheid point: she would place it in the building of the company associated with the Springbok tour. Marie sitting on the floor, the dog's asthmatic wheezing, Marie's mother coming up the wooden stairs, her face through the crack in the door, sharp blue eyes, a look of wry amusement, the silent stare, the retreat. I think back now: did I ever hear Marie's mother say anything, apart from that first time when we came upon her with her water glass and her bottle of pills? Perhaps we saved her that day, coming back. Always after that she was silent, secretive. Just the distracted glance and the footsteps on the wooden stairs, the voice whispering into the phone. I heard the stairs creaking now in the lull between revs, the car in the garden below, its engine exposed, steaming. How old was Marie's mother when we came home that day and found her at the kitchen table? She couldn't have been older than I am now.

'All set?' the agent said.

Marie did exactly what she'd intended. She took her bomb into town, left it in the building, walked away, and succeeded in shutting down the whole of the central city. It was the aerial that made it so effective; this I learned from the TV news. The police, unused to dealing with such things, refrained from using their radios in the ensuing panic, for fear of setting the thing off. There was chaos, evacuation, workplaces shut down. Hours later the army arrived, and — does my memory serve me or am I making this up? — a khaki robot, appearing on the TV news like a jerky green reptile, trundled towards Marie's little creation, picked it up in its metal jaws, carried it delicately out into the street and blew it up. Boom! A small explosion after all.

Marie walking away, her curly hair, her baby face. Her oversized handbag, long earrings, short skirt: the unlikeliest terrorist. Her plump shoulders used to shake with mirth, with terrible laughter. Where was she now? Was she still 'political'? I used to love her, even though she could be distant sometimes, cold suddenly, then warm and generous and kind, tougher than I was. I admired her self-sufficiency. I was soft, compared to Marie. She was my age. Does she have kids? I think she does. She would. She would have got them. Got what she wanted.

You bastard, you fucking Peter Pan, why won't you tell me you want to share a house with me, why won't you say you want to have a baby with me, didn't we have our youth so we could grow up, so we could *leave our childhoods behind*?

'I used to spend a lot of time in this house,' I said, and the agent made a sound, a cluck of impatience, and stood uncertain and annoyed while next door the youths revved the engine again, a high note, a scream.

I went around to her place afterwards, came round here; she was out in the garden burning evidence, like a professional criminal. Masking tape, wires, plastic, glue, went into the garden incinerator, Marie poking them down with a stick. I said I'd seen a TV statement from the anti-tour group HART, denouncing her stunt, calling for restraint. Marie laughed. I did too. Her curly hair blew in the wind. We stood out there in the evening light, the smoke drifting up and over the trees, Mt Hobson on the skyline. Lights coming on in the houses on the hillside, melancholy notes from a piano. Marie's mother's face at the window, turning away. The incinerator, still there, down in the garden, by the lemon tree.

The police vowed to catch the perpetrator at the time, to catch Marie. She showed no signs of being scared. They never did. She was clever, Marie, cleverer than I was, but she didn't go to university as far as I know, didn't take up a career, but disappeared into the suburbs, or to another country. I rang her parents a few times, usually when I was a bit drunk and sentimental and lonely at university, asking for news of her. Once they said she was in Australia, another time she'd moved flats and they didn't have a number. I imagined her with children, a boy and a girl, curly hair, unreliable smiles. I looked down at the garden, the hedge, once clipped, now allowed to grow wild: the artistic hand of Celia Myers. What struck me was how *long* ago it was, how long since I had stood out there with Marie.

Peter walked out onto the lawn. I looked at him. What is it to get pregnant without asking, consulting the man? To take what you want, just take it. Is it opportunism? Is it theft, or female terrorism? Is it a crime?

thin earth

I look back on my marriage, searching for patterns and clues. I think about the good times and the bad times, and I try to work out why things turned out the way they did. Sometimes I get an idea and decide to write it down, although I don't have much faith in my scrawled notes. There's no point talking to Max. He doesn't believe in analysing. 'Best to move on' is what he says. 'No need for post-mortems.'

Last night I had a dream about our trip to Wanganui, when we were still married and Charles was still at King's School. I remembered how I'd loved the town, and how it seemed to have a special flavour, particularly because of the bad thing that had happened there. The way I dwelt on it, as if it had been laid on as a special entertainment just for me! I see myself, hair-trigger alert, alone, running through those silent, dusty small-town streets. And then later, on the trip back, something happened that made me feel — not different, but, I don't know — more reflective. Perhaps I understood better what the bad thing had meant to the people whose lives had been crushed by it.

Anyway, the dream set me off thinking about that holiday. It was high summer in Wanganui. There I was, flustered, one eye on Max junior, the other on the local newspaper spread out on my knees. Max lounged beside me, his gaze fixed on Charles, who stood out on the cricket pitch, a slim, elegant figure in the hot light, poised to deliver his killer bowl . . .

Charles was playing in a four-day cricket tournament. It was just before the end of the school holidays, the hottest days of the year. We'd come down from Auckland with him for the fun of it, to see the town and stay in a motel. Charles and the rest of the team were billeted in the dormitories at Wanganui Collegiate. Karen and Trish's sons were playing; they'd come with their husbands, along with a lot of other parents. They were lined up along the edge of the field with their deckchairs and umbrellas and picnic baskets. It was early but already it was hot, cloudless, still. The grass was faded; the ground was hard and dry. Simon Lampton, strenuously jolly, his nose covered with white zinc, was handing around boxes of juice.

The parents, the milling kids. Karen and Trish waving. I, fiddling with my glasses, looking down at the paper, pretending not to see. I didn't want to sit with those two. I was reading about the murder.

There were streets cordoned off near the river when we'd driven in. It had been on the radio. A young woman, a barmaid, had finished work, stayed for a few drinks, left the bar and vanished. She'd been found in the Whanganui River, floating by the bank. She was twenty-one years old.

'Slow down,' I'd said to Max as we passed. There was a caravan set up, some policemen. Those tapes they use to cordon off crime scenes. I see myself as if from outside, the laden car slowing, my face pressed against the glass.

After we'd unpacked that first day I went for a walk. The motel was by a railway line. Heat rose off the stones, the grass was withered. I looked along the train track to where it disappeared around a bend, the trees forming a green tunnel over it. The streets were quiet, full of misty light. There was hardly anyone about. In the suburban streets around Wanganui

Collegiate there was silence, hush, closed windows and gates, streets so thickly covered by trees that the sun shone down in thin beams of light. Empty gardens. Green shade. Walking, I kept looking behind me. Thinking of that girl.

But it wasn't here she'd been killed, in the prosperous suburbs around the Collegiate, but down near the river, where the houses are small, shabby, poor — tiny workman's cottages, ragged bungalows. These were the streets we'd seen as we drove in. I wanted to go down there.

The police had no early leads. They were 'building a picture' of the girl's life. A 'lovely', 'bubbly' person, she was the daughter of regular churchgoers (Baptist). She was 'always willing to help someone in need'. She had ambitions beyond working in a bar. There was no regular boyfriend, but a wide circle of friends. A popular young woman. Her parents too devastated to comment . . .

That first day of the tournament, Max and I watched the game for an hour or so. I finished reading the paper. 'I might go for a run,' I said.

'It's a bit hot, isn't it?'

'Will you look after Maxie?'

'Yeah.'

Little Max settled down against his father. They looked very alike: handsome father, white-blond child.

I said, 'You know the murder? I think I'll go and look for clues.'

Max laughed.

'Go on, Mummy,' Maxie said. Big Max patted my leg and lay back. I went away feeling happy.

I changed into my running clothes at the motel. The room was stifling. I locked it and set off, across the main street and down towards the river. The further you got from the Collegiate, the poorer and more ramshackle were the houses. The streets were just as empty down here. Occasionally a dog looked up from a porch, or a figure moved between washing lines, behind a slatted blind. I recognised the name of one street: the young woman had lived there with her parents.

There was a tiny Baptist church on the corner, where they'd held her angry, desolate funeral, described in the local paper. I reached the river and stopped. The river was wide, stretching away into a blue summer haze. I ran along the path looking down. Somewhere near the bank, in the shade under the trees, the body had been found, floating. I looked at the long grass along the path, thinking I would find something. I stopped a couple of times to look at bits and pieces lying on the ground, knowing it was foolish yet hoping to find something, a real clue.

A man wearing a hood passed me, his head down, his face hidden. His hands were heavily tattooed. He turned once and looked back, as if he'd sensed me staring. There was the black shadow under the hood, an absence of face. He turned away, with a flounce almost, a quick rotation of the hips, something smooth and furtive. I checked my watch. Murderers often return to the scene of the crime.

I didn't find the exact spot. It was too far along the river. I came to a railway bridge. There were rowing boats and spectators along the bank. I was getting to the end of my strength. Max would be wondering where I was. I rested, watching the boats. Then I turned back.

I went a different way. Three young men sat on a veranda, their feet resting on old beer crates, silently watching me. Two little girls played outside a rundown house, the door open, a shape moving behind the flyscreen. Towards the main road a van pulled out of a liquor wholesaler, nearly running into me. I called out, 'Hey!'

The driver's shaven head sat necklessly on his shoulders. He had a beard, a gold earring. The van's back windows were blacked out and it was daubed with symbols: suns, moons, stars, crosses. Painted along the side, in black Gothic lettering, were the words Sinister Urge. The man glared, reversing out. I saw his face behind the windscreen, reflections of leaves sliding across it. He had missing teeth, a tattoo on his cheek. He drove off with a dramatic little squeal of tyres.

That night in a café on the main street I was describing him to Max. The van with its blacked-out windows, the painted words: Sinister Urge. Imagine him parked outside a school! I said, 'But if he was genuinely sinister, if he wanted to abduct people, he wouldn't want to advertise it, would he? He'd drive an anonymous car. So why just threaten people? Why does he want to *do* that?'

'More wine?' Max said. He was trying to get Maxie to eat his dinner. The little boy was slumped, exhausted, in his chair, red circles of sunburn under his eyes. Max held a piece of garlic bread under his nose. Maxie gave it a weary swipe.

'Did you find any clues?' He signalled for the waitress.

'No. I probably saw the murderer, though.'

'The freak in the van.'

'No, a guy in a hood.'

'Oh, right.'

I looked at Maxie. 'He's sunburnt,' I said.

'Well, while you were looking for *clues* I couldn't find his *hat.*'

'Oh. Sorry.'

Maxie slumped moaning into Max's lap.

We walked back up the main street under the hanging baskets of flowers, Maxie on Max's shoulders, asleep. I looked at his little brown leg, Max's big hand holding it.

'It's so nice to get away, out of Auckland.' I put my hand in Max's back pocket. The town had woken up a bit. Boys cruised down the street in low-slung cars, stereos thumping. There were groups of teenagers. A band was setting up on an outdoor stage. A banner behind them read: Subhuman.

'Jesus, look at them,' Max said. There were three boys, twanging their instruments, testing their microphones in that humourless way they do, 'Two two. One two.' Their faces were painted, their clothes ripped. Their heads were shaven at the sides. Dreadlocks sprouted from the tops of their heads.

Max eyed them. 'Imagine if your kid turned out like *that.*'

One of the boys had black lipstick and eye-paint; another had his face blacked out.

'Fucking nightmare,' Max said. He hitched Maxie up higher.

'You never know,' I said. 'They might be Collegiate old boys.'

'Over my dead body,' Max said vaguely.

One of the boys donned an oxygen mask. Max applauded. 'Oh, tremendous, that. Nice touch.'

I laughed. 'He's got quite a nice little face, the one with the makeup.'

'Nice? God!'

We walked on companionably through the warm dark.

In the night the motel room was hot, pitch black, silent. I woke from dreams that were loud, garish, raucous; they came at me and receded and I lay spinning in the dark before I sensed them coming again, points of light rushing across the blackness, a mad caravan: their flaming torches and whirling figures, their fires.

The next day we went out for breakfast, then to the Collegiate fields. Trish arrived, clambering down from her husband's SUV. She was wearing an extraordinary outfit, all stripes and pleats and ruffles. Maxie stared.

'I've got a red waine hangover!' she called. 'Saimon and Karen haven't even got up yet!' She sank down next to us and talked lazily to Max for a while.

Women liked Max: he had a kind of restless, rogue air. I listened and smiled. I wasn't at ease with Trish; she brayed and talked about money and never stopped fundraising and ordering people about. What was it about her and the Lamptons that made me uncomfortable? Their stifling 'respectability', I suppose. Deep down, some small, fierce part of me despised the way they behaved, although I was faintly shocked at myself. But already I was thinking of running away, down to the river, through the hush of the Collegiate neighbourhood, then the treeless glare of the poor streets with their rickety fences and scruffy gardens, and finally the river with its gorgeous misty distances, its blue beauty glittering under the pearly sky — its beauty and what it held within it, things hidden below the surface, terrible things.

Here came Simon Lampton trudging across the field, a pair of fold-up chairs slung over his shoulder. He stood waiting for Karen, who was carrying a tiny shopping bag. She told him where to put everything. Karen and Trish talked about their night out.

'You were a raiot. You nearly got Saimon into a faight!'

'It wasn't quite like that,' Simon said, embarrassed.

Trish let out a screech of laughter. It carried in the still air. Out on the pitch the boys and their coach looked up. Simon glanced at me, wrinkling his forehead. He was a big, awkward man. He held up his hands, as though to quell the cackling women. Max stretched out, sexy and languid on the grass. I caught Trish eyeing him and giving Karen a look. I imagined them over their red wines, the lewd things they'd say.

I said to Simon, 'Have you been reading about the murder? I went down to the river, where she was found, the dead woman. The town's different down there. It was spooky on the riverbank.'

I stopped. Consternation in his eyes. 'The murder?' he said.

'Yes, I went looking for clues,' I said, trying to charm, ingratiate. Oh, funny little me.

He looked pained. 'How horrible.'

'Mmm, awful. A young woman, bludgeoned to death . . .'

I was getting this all very wrong. There was a look of revulsion on his face.

'It *is* terrible,' I said hastily. 'I'm being frivolous. Sorry.'

He gave a weak smile. Silenced, I watched the cricket. I listened to Max murmuring with the women, his louche, cynical chuckle. Why wasn't I horrified by the idea of the dead girl? I just wanted to go back there. I wanted to go down to the river and find the exact spot this time, where they fought, where he picked her up and threw her dead body down the bank, down into the speckled shallows.

I surprise myself. I can run faster and further than I ever could before. I'm running away from the playing fields, genially dismissed by Max, who doesn't mind looking after Maxie, whom he adores, released from squawking Trish and nervous Simon, running away, down to the river. What is it in me that wants to stand in the very spot? Is it just that I want to be right at the point of something, anything, so long as it is at the highest, hardest pitch of feeling? Or is it that I do not understand something that Simon Lampton does? I remember thinking as I ran: I don't know if Max loves me. I don't know. *How can I know?*

I didn't see the man with the hood again, nor the man with the sinister van, although I looked for them, running each day through the silent, heat-shimmering town. I loved the place; the more I ran through it the more it turned away from me: charming, secretive, elusive. I felt as though I were following some important thing that I couldn't quite catch, only saw it at the corner of my eye, fading into the leafy shadows. In the afternoons, drugged with exercise, I watched the clouds moving across the sky, the boys on the field, thin figures in bright light.

On the fourth day, at lunchtime, Charles ended the tournament by whacking the ball away for four. We clapped and cheered. There were little speeches, a prizegiving. Dependable Simon lugged out a chilly-bin full of iceblocks. And then we were getting in our cars and heading out of town, the boys tired and silent, Max cheerful and smelling of the peppermints he'd sucked to mask the smell of the matey cigarette he'd shared with Trish behind the trees.

We drove past the crime scene, deserted now, the evidence tapes hanging limp, the police caravan with its torn posters. We were heading to Rotorua: the boys had requested a trip to the mudpools. We drove for a long time in contented silence, my hand resting on Max's thigh.

At a motel in Rotorua the boys played minigolf. We sat on the balcony in the hazy evening light. Max smoked, his feet up on the railing, his gaze fixed on the boys. He jumped up to get Maxie a sweatshirt, thumped down long-sufferingly to help free a trapped ball. I remember his smoke curling up into the air, the boys' voices, the tiny thwack and scuttle as the golfballs rattled through their courses. There was an orange streetlight outside the window of our room; it blinked and buzzed in the night like an incensed eye, peering between the blinds while Max and I made love.

The next day at Whakarewarewa, told of the price for a family ticket, Max said, 'You're kidding!'

Something formed, shaped itself up, in the face of the woman in the booth. Lips parted, downturned mouth, nostrils widening.

'Is there a problem?' she said.

Max shrugged, and thrust the money through the hole. The woman fell to hard laughter with one of her colleagues. A whiff of brimstone hung in the air.

'God, Max,' I said. 'Don't have a fight before we're even in.'

He laughed, wiping sweat from his face. Here it was even hotter than Wanganui — boiling water under the earth, white fire pouring out of the sky. It felt as though you could get sunburnt through your hat. Below the bridge children were diving for coins, their brown bodies sleek and shining. Charles and Maxie threw in some coins and the boys surged up onto the bank, shouting, spitting, calling for more. We moved on into the village. Neither Max nor I had been before. We were struck by the bucolic shabbiness of the place, its tumbledown fences and tiny dilapidated buildings. There was none of the touristy artificiality we'd expected.

'It's sort of raw,' Max said wonderingly. Between the buildings there were glimpses of battered cars, washing lines, back doors lined with gumboots and stacks of beer crates.

'Well, it's a real village,' I said

We stood at the edge of a briny blue pool, the water steaming. Bags of corn were cooking at the edge. Heat came up in waves, along with the rich, oddly enjoyable sulphur stink. A woman wandered past with a walkie-talkie and a voice crackled out of it, asking whether the corn was cooked. The boys ran about marvelling at the plopping mudpools, the steaming vents. Across an expanse of rock and clay and scrub, over which clouds of steam wafted, a geyser suddenly shot water high into the air.

The boys shouted and pointed. 'We want to go to the geyser. Over there!'

We walked towards it but came to a locked gate. Trying to find our way we headed up behind the village, past a hall in which a concert was being held for a tour group. A fierce child eyed me from a doorway. Behind a flyscreen, a woman jigged a baby in her arms.

A rough track led up a hill and we followed Max, who was determined to find the geyser for the boys. We walked through low scrub past mudpools, the white clay crusts all pitted, the water letting off waves of steam. I enjoyed the heat. We stood on a point looking down on an emerald-blue pool. Then we walked down into a shallow dip of the land, a crater. Amid the scrub there were white clay banks, bubbling pools, still, chemical-green puddles. A sign said: 'Danger. Thin earth. No responsibility taken.'

I caught up with Charles. 'Listen,' I said.

We could hear water trickling under the earth. I called out to Max.

He waited for me. He'd picked Maxie up.

I said, 'We shouldn't go off the path. There are signs saying "Danger. Thin earth." And listen.'

There was the sound of water running under our feet.

'That water's hot,' I said. 'If you fell through . . .'

Max grinned. 'You'd be cooked.'

'Don't go off the path.'

He was already walking away. Charles ran to catch up. I followed. I heard water again, right under where I was standing. I didn't like it. When I caught up with Max he was putting Maxie up on his shoulders.

'We're going to cut across there,' he told me. 'To get to the geyser.' He pointed across an acre of scrub, steam drifting across it.

'There's no path there. What if you fall through?'

Charles was already walking ahead around the edge of a mudpool.

'You can hear the water under the ground. Listen!'

Charles laughed. 'Don't freak out, Mum.'

I ignored him. I hated him siding with his father, laughing at me. 'Max! You can't take them across there.'

'We'll be fine. Come on.'

Little Maxie watched me patiently, not unsympathetically: poor Mummy, making a fuss again.

'I'm not walking on that,' I said. 'It says not to.'

Max shrugged, and followed Charles across the clay. It looked thin, dry, brittle. I felt frantic watching him.

I couldn't make myself walk where they'd gone. I turned away, my eyes stinging. I was furious, ashamed. I went back along the path. Had I abandoned my own children out of fear? But they were not abandoned. They were with their father. I thought about Max's power, his separateness. His love for the boys, their love for him. That he could carry them away and I would be left with nothing but the sound of my angry pleading, the ground trickling away under my feet.

Thin earth.

I waited at the bridge, watching the local boys diving for coins. The sun was an angry white eye. I waited for a long time. After an hour I walked back over the hill but there was no sign of them. I went to a hut near the gate. Two guards, a young man and young woman in floral shirts, were sitting behind a desk. I asked how I could get to the geyser.

They glanced at each other. 'You can't get to it from here. It belongs to the other guys.'

'Other guys?'

'The neighbours!' They exploded into giggling.

'How do I get there?'

'You have to go round the road, go to their gate and pay them.'

You keep that quiet, don't you? I thought. That the main attraction isn't in your bit of the park. I said, 'Can I borrow your phone?'

They were kind, getting out of the way and letting me ring

Max's cellphone, allowing me go on trying when there was no reply. Then he answered, and suddenly I was calm and reasonable, laughing along as he told me they'd crossed the scrubland and been caught in the neighbouring park without the right ticket, that they'd been briskly ushered out, having viewed the geyser, and were walking all the way back around the road.

I met them coming back. The boys were eating iceblocks. I laughed over my stupid attack of nerves, admired Max's acumen in getting what the boys wanted. Max, adopting a faintly cynical and patronising air, allowed me to praise him.

'Silly old Mummy,' the boys said. We straggled back to the village and opened up the car to let out the heat.

I found myself thinking about the girl in Wanganui. The funeral. Her parents. How it must have been. There were boys playing cricket, the sun was shining, rowboats were racing on the sparkling river, and their daughter was dead. I thought of them, burying their only child. I watched as Max carefully buckled little Maxie into his seat. I thought: I must take care of my boys, love them, guard them. I must take care.

The baking concrete, the furnace glare of the afternoon sun. Max straightens; we face each other over the bonnet of the car. There is something in his expression. A moment of hardness, clarity between us. A bird, turning and turning in the air above us, gives a high, sad, warning cry. I think of that expression Max likes to use: 'Over my dead body.'

He believes, with justification, that I am incompetent and hysterical. These are our roles — I dizzy, he rational. These are the parts we play. But a kind of communication passed between us then, as if, for a moment, we had abandoned our lines and were confronting each other, free of script, on an empty stage. He nodded and stared off at the hillside, absorbing the thing I was telling him.

If you leave me, you go alone. *Over my dead body* will you take them away.

home

I was working in Teulada for my friend Freddie. He owned a couple of bars and nightclubs in the town. I used to work for him in London and after he left and set himself up in Spain he phoned me and told me to come on down, so I packed my bags and went there, and soon I was living in a little house by the sea and working behind the bar at Freddie's, and I was happy to be away from London's cold winter and its dead grey light. Those first mornings in the village, when I woke up and walked out onto the terrace and the light was all golden and buttery and the sun was sparkling on the sea, I felt almost happy — healthy, anyway. I felt more alive than I had for a long time.

It was pretty hectic working for Freddie; he was always off his face, although he managed to run a tight ship and make a lot of money, God knows how. He had a lot of rich friends — people he'd gone to public school with, who used to pass through — and he'd play the host and give them what they wanted: all-night parties, hilarious messy times, lots of drugs. There were always girls reeling off the dance floor, dancing on the sand, wading into the sea, shrieking at one another in their posh voices.

A couple of times I took long trips with Freddie. We drove into France and Germany, stopping along the way at places where Freddie had business or someone he needed to call on. Once he took me to a wake in a chateau in France — his friend's father had died. We'd stopped off in a couple of bars and done a few lines of coke along the way, and by the time we got to the place Freddie was feeling pretty regal. We drove up miles of tree-lined driveway, screeched into the courtyard of the most stupendous mansion, were greeted by a bowing lackey and led through a lot of grand rooms. He showed us into a sort of ballroom where there were a lot of people grouped around, everyone very quiet. I hung back but Freddie took command as usual. He strode up to his friend, the bereaved son and heir, shook his hand and shouted, 'Jonty! Let me be the first to congratulate you!'

I had a girlfriend in Teulada, a good-looking girl called Mimi. She worked in the bar too, and she was nice, but it got on my nerves the way she stuck so close to me, always cooking dinner for me and trying to keep me with her on our nights off. In the end I told her it wasn't working and we'd have to call it off. It made her sad — she spent weeks crying about it — but after a while she went to London and married the bass player of her favourite band. I toughened her up. Set her on her way. That's the way I looked at it. I wished her luck.

Just before I left Teulada a fight broke out in the bar. I came out of the back, pilled up to the eyeballs, and a girl crashed onto the sand at my feet. I just stood there staring at her. There was a big punch-up spilling off the dance floor, and soon people were throwing chairs, bottles, glasses, anything they could get their hands on. In the office Freddie was on the phone to the police, telling them there was a riot. Typically they didn't show up, and we just had to wait for the brawl to run out of steam. There was a lot of clearing up to do afterwards, and plenty of ruined stock. Freddie was up in arms and decided to go to the police station to complain. He marched in and gave them a piece of his mind, said it wasn't good enough and what did they think they were doing, just sitting around while the place was torn to pieces. The next night we were all apprehensive, but people seemed to be behaving themselves. The bar was full and the night was going well. But the police had decided to get their own back on Freddie for the telling-off he'd given them, and the next moment they'd turned up mob-handed, forty of them, with torches and dogs. So there was uproar again. Freddie was in the kitchen holding a dinner plate with six lines of coke on it. He threw it over his shoulder. Then he stuffed some pills under the fridge, but the police saw him and had the fridge lifted up. Freddie was led away shouting, 'It's all for me, officers! I'm an addict!'

I lay low and didn't get arrested. The bar was closed down and I walked the short distance home along the waterfront, hearing the screams and crashes and shouts behind me. The sea was calm and still, and the moon was making a shining path across the water. I got home and had a few drinks. When I went into my room I saw my flatmate had put a letter on my bed. It was from my father. He said it was his seventieth birthday soon (so it is, I thought, glazing over a bit) and would I like to come home so we'd all be there for the party. I lay on my back staring at the ceiling. I thought about home. I thought I might do it. He'd offered to pay the fare.

It took a bit of doing, getting home. I was in a bar in London with all my gear and a transvestite stole my bag with my passport in it. I was off my face at the time, and I cursed myself afterwards for not realising that this creature who was doing funny tricks in front of me, dancing and twirling and making faces, wasn't just trying to make me laugh. I ran out of the bar after her, or him, but it was too late. I had enough cash to live on for a short time, but barely enough. I had to apply for a new passport and it was pretty difficult with hardly any funds or ID. I stayed with a friend of mine in Wanstead; she was into something called Vortex Healing. It was a spiritual thing, to do with lifting the bad karma out of places. She took it very seriously.

'We're a worldwide network,' she told me.

'Yeah,' I said, 'course you are.'

She did a procedure on my back, I don't know what it was, but I felt a kind of weight, a strange burning. I told her and she gave a smug little smile and said that my luck would change. Which it did, actually. I got my passport, and I bought myself a ticket to New Zealand — although I have to confess that by the time I got back it was too late for my father's birthday party.

Just before I left London I'd completely run out of money and I ended up staying with a woman I didn't even know. I met her in a bar; she started buying me drinks and the next thing I knew she was taking me to a poetry reading. I was just biding my time, keeping myself relatively sober so I wouldn't miss my plane. Anyway, I sat around laughing at the poets. The next morning she kicked me out of her bed and I struggled off down to the tube and went to Heathrow. When I got on the plane, in that enclosed space, I realised what a mess I was and I pitied the family sitting next to me. I went to the toilets and had a wash with paper towels, wetting them and doing myself over. It seemed to take ages, bouncing around in the tiny cubicle. I couldn't do much about my clothes, but I took off a couple of layers and left them in the toilet. It was going to be summer where I was going. Auckland. I hadn't been back for years.

I had a sense when I got off the plane that the air was soft, not harsh like the mineral air of London. You could smell plants and even cows. The sky was high, light, wide. The light was too bright. All the functionaries at the airport had new wide-brimmed hats, which looked ridiculous. I'd been away long enough for the place to seem familiar but altered, as if I'd walked into a place that was an approximation of what I remembered. My parents were waiting for me and for a second we were all struck a bit dumb. I was thinking what little old people they looked, and I don't know what they were thinking about me. I was bigger, for one thing, not skinny like I used to be. My brother was there with his wife and baby. Poor old William, he was always the sensible one. When I got outside and saw the police cars painted yellow and orange instead of blue and white like they used to be I said to him, 'Jesus, what have they done to their cars? Is that for Christmas?' He laughed. My mother said my name in her dry, ironic little voice. Dad tried to pick up my suitcase and she hissed at me, 'Help him.' I shook myself out of a bit of a daze and picked up the bag.

Dad drove. My mother screwed herself around and stared at me fiercely.

I said politely, 'So, what have you been doing?'

'Oh, just waiting to die,' she said.

Dad said, 'The trip's quite quick now they've put in more motorway.'

'Indeed,' I said.

William was ahead of us in his stationwagon, its back window crammed with baby equipment.

'What have *you* been doing?' my mother asked.

'Just a lot of drugs, basically,' I said.

My father sighed.

My mother gave me an acid look. 'At least William . . .'

'Thank goodness for William,' I said sincerely.

'Lucy's very nice, you know,' my mother said. That was William's wife.

'My girlfriend left me,' I said. I felt a little pang. I sighed. 'Mimi . . .'

'Mimi!' She thought *that* was a scream. She went on repeating the name. 'Sounds like a poodle,' she said. I said was I supposed to have a girlfriend called Desdemona or Cressida, some bullshit name like that? She snorted.

My father stopped at a red light and turned around. His face was so lined, so baffled. He smiled, wanting to be kind. I stared back for a second, my face fixed, then looked away.

'Green,' Mum said.

Dad wrenched himself around and groped dimly at the

gears. The car shot forward. His thin grey hair straggled over his collar. His shoulders were thinner than they used to be. I'd got more solid; he'd shrunk. I wasn't sure I was going to live to his age, however. Not with all the booze and dope and coke and E I'd put away over the years. I sat looking at the backs of my parents' heads. My body was on London time and I was in a bit of a trance, almost drifting off. I could have done with a line of coke. They'd tried, but they'd failed when it came to me and drugs — failed to stop me, I mean. What they should have done when I was fourteen is sat down and smoked a joint with me. But that piece of common sense was beyond them.

When I was sixteen my friends and I grew a little cannabis plantation. Once we'd harvested it we hid it in the back of the warming cupboard at my place. A few days later I came home to disaster — my parents had discovered my stash. They'd brought it out and piled it on the kitchen bench. My mother had a big spoon and she was stuffing the leaves down the Wastemaster. While I was standing there, stunned at this calamity, she barked at my father, 'On!'

He turned the switch. She forced the dope down into the whirring grinder. At her command he turned it off. She took more leaves from the bench and pushed them down. Then 'On!' she snapped. I came alive at that point, rushed forward and shouted at them to leave my stuff alone. My mother held me off with the big spoon. 'On!' she shouted, and my father reached up obediently with his trembling thumb, pressed the switch, and ground the last fruits of my labour to pulp . . .

A rift opened up after that. Betrayed, I took to my room and began to learn the electric guitar. The house throbbed with my angry chords. A battle raged between my parents' classical music and my own eclectic range — I was particularly fond of one song that burst out with the exhilarating lyric, *Slut! Slut! Dirty Bitch!* I remember my mother beating on my door, shouting at me to turn it down. Oh, it's all a long time ago now. A long time . . .

At each red light my father turned and looked at me

carefully, smiling and sad. My mother fidgeted in her seat and ate peppermints, and screwed her head around, her glasses flashing, to fire questions. How long was I staying? Would I think about coming back for good? Did I have any ideas about getting myself together?

There was a sudden heavy shower, the car sluiced through deep puddles, then the sun came out and the road steamed, and I saw a rainbow riding between the wooden houses — appearing, disappearing, a blur of bright colour, the flash of sun through leaves, diamonds of light.

I nodded off in the middle of lunch. Muttering about time zones I crashed into the bedroom they'd given me — not my old room but William's. Perhaps they couldn't bear to have me back in my old lair. Later, after dreaming uneasily on the single bed, I got up and groped my way downstairs. I was in the kitchen with little idea of where I was, until Dad swam into focus next to me. I was looking at the Wastemaster.

'Poor Sam: you're not up to much, I suppose,' he said. He put an experimental hand on my shoulder. I glanced at it, as though at an insect, then at him, as if to say, what's *that* doing there? He registered my expression and we both smiled — I tightly, he ruefully but with affection. I could see him thinking, difficult old Sam, poor old Sam. An idea swam about in my fuddled mind; I was re-registering my parents, comparing them, having been away so long. My mother and I, we have a kind of carry-on: tough, some might even say obnoxious, but my father is different — more gentle and straightforward. I think William takes after him. He'll be henpecked to death by that wife of his, for sure.

'Shall we get a video tonight?' Dad said.

'Certainly,' I croaked. I felt like falling flat on my face.

Will and Lucy came for dinner with their baby, who was quite a cute little boy. I sat him on my knee and tried to teach him a Spanish football song. I got through the meal with the help of a lot of booze and some racy anecdotes about Spain. I was in good form, my head cleared by the wine. Lucy seemed to find me hilarious. She kept going off into shrieks, which made my mother glare. I'd warmed to Lucy, in fact I was already feverishly imagining an affair with her — Will stumping off to work and Lucy sighing and folding nappies and looking out the window, and I in the driveway with my Spanish tan, my bottle of wine, my gypsy guitar . . .

We gathered in the sitting room after dinner, while Dad fed the tape into the slot. I'd been up the road earlier and got myself a bumper flagon of red. One of those double-sized bottles, I'd thought, would be the way to get through Day One. The film was *The Fugitive*, with Harrison Ford. It's a good movie. I offered wine around, made a bit of suggestive small-talk with Lucy, brushing crumbs off her breast and so on, then we all fell silent. Everything went well except that my mother sighed a lot when I kept getting up to offer more drinks. Soon I discovered everyone was saying no when I offered the bottle, so I shut up and got busy with it myself. At one point I nodded off, still on London time, then abruptly remembered myself and got up with the bottle. I tripped over Will's legs. He said 'Fuck' loudly and made a big thing of rubbing his shin. Lucy was sniggering. I looked over at her, delivered some searing witticism, tripped over a cord and the TV went off. Mum rushed off and came back with cloths. Dad knelt by the TV.

'More wine?' I waved the bottle at them. Some drops went on the carpet. My mother made a high-pitched sound. Lucy was snorting behind her hand. Suavely, I asked if she wanted to go out for a cigarette while the technical problem was sorted out.

'She doesn't smoke,' they all said. There was a bit of an atmosphere.

I climbed over everyone and burst out the French doors. It was nice out there on the deck in the soft night. I had a couple of cigarettes, then went inside. The wine was all finished but I had my eye on a bottle of gin in the kitchen.

To my surprise the TV was still off. 'What about the film? Shall we press on?' I clapped my hands, refreshed by the outside air.

My father was holding a wet cloth. He threw it down, his shoulders hunched. Then he turned and made an inept fist — the fist of a man who could never throw a real punch. 'I should have exercised more discipline with you!' he shouted.

I looked at him in surprise. He was overwrought. Just when it was all going so well. I turned on my heel and went silently outside again. I was thinking: families. Always a drama. I sat on a deckchair and smoked. I went back in and Will and Lucy were sitting at the kitchen table. My parents had gone upstairs.

'All right?' I said.

'Jesus, Sam,' Will said.

I winked at Lucy. Her mouth quivered. I stared hard at her, severely — I knew this would bring her out in shrieks. She was making a tiny noise in her nose, like air being let out of a balloon . . .

'Oh, *shut up*, Lu,' my brother said.

I decided to get fit. I borrowed Will's bike and rode to the top of One Tree Hill. It was beautiful up there, the suburbs sprawled under the cloud shadows, the wind blowing in the dry grass. I rode around the waterfront too, and one day I tried to go for a run, with mixed results. Covering ground, biking mostly, I looked at the places I used to live in long ago. The old flat in Grafton, the big house in Mt Eden. My friends from that time were all gone — some to London, some to Sydney, other places. Some had families — kids. I was left behind in an empty city; that was how it felt when I saw those old places. Sometimes I stopped the bike and stood in a spot and stared, and covered my face with my hands. I'd been transported back to my youth but I was changed and everyone was gone. It was almost too much for me. In the mornings I looked in the mirror and saw what time had done to me. In Spain, I had had no past. There was nothing to look back on, nothing to remind me I wasn't young. I could live for the moment, in unchanging happiness. Here, time whispered at me, it told me terrible things. What have you made of yourself? Where are your friends? Why have you been left behind? In the nights I yearned for Spain; during the day I haunted the old places. I visited them again and again — probing the wound.

There was one group of people who were still about, but I was steering clear of them. For one thing, I didn't have much money; for another, I knew what would happen if I hooked up with those people I knew over in Ponsonby. I would end up getting completely trashed.

I was sitting in a café at the top of Upland Road when I heard tooting. A stationwagon shot around the corner, a woman waving at me out the window. I was pretty sure it was Lisa Green. I went home, guessing she would ring. Sure enough, about an hour later Dad called me to the phone.

'You're staying at your parents' place,' Lisa said laboriously.

'So it would seem.'

'Shall we have a drink or something?'

I agreed to meet her that night at the café up the road. I sat at a table outside so I could smoke. She came walking up the road. She was wearing a leather jacket and jeans, and she was thinner than she used to be. We'd been at school together. We had a thing, briefly, a long time ago; now she was married to an engineer and had a baby son and a house and a mortgage — all that. She showed me a picture of her son, Michael, and her husband, James.

'What have you been doing?' she asked.

'Learning how to use email,' I told her, truthfully.

She fell about at that. 'Learning?'

'I've been leading a simple life,' I said with dignity.

'Obviously!'

I told her about my Spanish village, Freddie, the bar. She bought drinks. She laughed a lot and stared at me, obviously fascinated to see how I'd turned out. I got into my stride and told her about Mimi who'd gone off heartbroken and found the bass player of her dreams, and my new girlfriend who used to be my flatmate but who'd ended up sharing my bed, and about having my passport stolen by a transvestite and being stuck in London with no money or ID, and staying with my friend in Wanstead who'd practised Vortex Healing on my back and given me a funny feeling and good luck, and how I'd missed my father's birthday and how my father had shouted at me after we'd watched *The Fugitive*.

'You're a fugitive,' she said, smiling at me.

She was always a bit sentimental. She had a weak spot for me. She liked listening to me. Plus she thought it was interesting, the way I lived. I had no permanent job, no money, hardly any clothes, no house. I was a bit of a fugitive, it was true. But from what? From the things I hadn't done.

She said, 'You're free. You're not trapped in things. But I always wanted to be . . . anchored.'

'So are you anchored? Or trapped?'

'I'm not trapped,' she said quickly. She shook her head.

I said, 'I keep thinking, if my old friends were here, they'd just pick me up on their motorbikes and we'd go off and do lots of good things.'

She stared. 'But they're all gone,' she said. 'They've grown up. Like me. They've got kids, families.'

Families! I told her about various tricky moments with my parents. I talked about them destroying my dope in the Wastemaster, all those years ago.

'That was the beginning of the rift,' I said darkly.

'But *no one's* parents let them keep dope in the airing cupboard,' she said. 'You can't hold that against them now.'

'Oh, can't I?'

'No!'

'They should have sat down and smoked a joint with me.'

'Oh, rubbish!' She was laughing at me. 'Why don't you try being kind to them, instead of waiting for them to be kind to you? Turn it around, now you're old.'

'Old? I'm not old!'

'All this working in bars. You were so clever at school. Much more than me. Remember how you got A-pluses for everything? Literally!'

'Indeed,' I said politely.

'So why don't you go to university? It's not too late.'

'Oh, I could, I suppose,' I said, staring off. But it was too late, of course.

She frowned, looking stupid and conscientious, like a social worker. I gave her one of my most terrible smiles, and she flinched and grinned madly.

I reminisced a bit more, since she seemed to like it. I told her about the mountains of cocaine, the oceans of booze I'd got through, in my years in Spain. I'd had a lot of wine by this time and was yearning for something stronger. I thought about a trip over to Ponsonby. The trouble was, I didn't have any money.

The bar closed. I walked Lisa down the road. I sang her a Spanish football song. I told her how I wanted to do a line of coke. She didn't do drugs, never had — it was one of her limitations. She'd never got over having a Bible-banger for a mother. When we got to her gate I kissed her on both cheeks.

'That's how we do it in Spain,' I said.

She said fondly, drunkenly, 'I suppose I could drive you home.'

'But that would be illegal!' I said.

I could hear her laughing in the dark as I reeled away.

Now I was wide awake. It was a hot night. I was fizzing with *wants*. I wanted an Everest of coke, an orgy, a fistfight. I decided to walk home the long way, to cool off. I slouched along the street. There were a lot of big houses. I wanted to go to Ponsonby and get my hands on some drugs. I thought about crashing back and asking Lisa for money. I knew she would give it to me, because she liked me so much. But I couldn't do that. I stopped. Something rose in my brain like a hot wave, and I realised I was extremely drunk. I could see across to Mt Hobson, the lights in the houses up the hillside. I couldn't go home to the little single bed and the familiar furniture and my parents' faces in the morning.

I passed a café, its doors closed. I sat on a seat for a while, looking down at the water in the Orakei Basin. I walked on through the dark, still, leafy streets. There was an old Mercedes parked in a driveway. I groped my way along the fence. In front of it was a new Porsche. I went back to the older car and tried the door. It opened. I got in and reached under the dashboard, using my lighter to see. I did a bit of wrenching and pulling, tearing my fingernails in the process. After a lot of work and a fair bit of damage I got the right combination of wires and started the engine.

The motor coughed, throbbed, steadied. I waited for a moment. The house was at the far end of the long drive. No lights came on; there was no sign of life. I backed the car out and onto the road, and eased it away, into the rainy night.

At the bottom of the road workmen were moving a whole house on a truck and I had to wait. A policeman walked towards the car, looked in (my face fixed in nervous rictus, my fingers white on the wheel), then waved me on, and I drove through a slalom of flashing lights and traffic cones and away, towards the west, seeking my line, the lifeline of coke that was waiting for me.

Driving on Shore Road I lit a cigarette, and, as I glanced into the mirror, gasped, froze and jammed my feet down on the pedals. The car swerved and bucked, hit the kerb, juddered along the gutter and mounted the pavement. It crashed into a fence, throwing me forward onto the steering wheel.

There was someone sitting in the back seat.

I couldn't move. I let out a whimper. Blood dripped from my nose. He didn't say anything. I could hear him behind me, breathing.

'I'll get out,' I whispered, nodding to myself. I felt for the door handle. There was still no sound but the breathing. I panicked, wrenched the door open and fell out onto the pavement. As I scrambled up I looked in the back and saw the big, still head silhouetted against the window. He looked at me.

It was a dog, a black Labrador. He must have been asleep on the seat and had sat up, bewildered to find himself on the move. Now he was peering at me enquiringly. I wondered why he hadn't made any noise before, but when I got close I saw from the white hairs on his muzzle that he was very old. I patted him. He turned big innocent eyes on me. He pushed his cold nose into my palm. I got in the back seat with him. I leaned on his musty flank and wept. Oh, Jesus, old dog. Oh, life.

I got back in the driver's seat. I heaved a deep, trembling sigh. My nose was bleeding down my shirt. The snout of the car was wounded too, crushed up against the fence. I connected the wires, started it and backed it onto the road. In the mirror I could see my passenger's big, patient, noble head, swaying as he kept himself upright.

I started driving westwards. But I thought about what would happen if I left the old dog parked in a Ponsonby street. There was no guarantee I'd find him again. Once I met my people over there I would be entering the vortex. I would be gone. He would be lost.

I would have to take him home. But I wasn't sure which street I'd taken him from. I didn't fancy cruising around looking while the roads were full of workmen and police. I pulled over. We sat in silence. He let out a doggy little moan and settled himself down on the seat.

I reached back and opened the door.

'Best you get out here, mate,' I said. 'Before we get any further away.'

He raised his snout and gazed at me sadly.

'Go on, get out! Walkies. Find your way home.'

He made that weary little groan again and put his snout on his paws. I slapped his flank. He didn't move.

Frustrated, I got out and reached in the back door, pulling him. He was a dead weight.

'You stupid lump,' I said, furious. I hit him on the head. He just looked at me. I hit him again. He flinched. I backed away. I wiped my bloody nose on my shirt. I got in the car and said, 'I was going somewhere. Now I can't. Because of you, you fucking cunt.'

He didn't move.

I thought about my family. My parents. Will and Lucy, their baby.

'Sorry,' I said. I put my hands over my face.

I reached over and patted and stroked his head. 'We can't go back to my parents' house,' I explained. 'So what do we do now?' His eyes were large and liquid and trusting. He looked out of the window.

I found a cloth in the glovebox and cleaned my face. I started the car. I zipped my jacket over my bloody shirt.

I said, 'We'll go on a bit of a journey. How about up north? A road trip — it'll be nice.'

I drove in the direction of the harbour bridge. He lay down across the seat.

'Don't worry,' I told him. 'I'll take care of you. Everything's going to be fine.'

the prodigal son

My father grew up poor. He and his twin brother lived in Opotiki, in a house with a dirt floor. Their father left them, and their mother brought the children to South Auckland. She took housekeeping jobs, and worked in a bakery. The old state house where they lived is still there, at Mangere Bridge. My father used to play on the mudflats. He went to Mangere Bridge Primary School.

Their mother, my grandmother, was strict and very religious. She worked hard to give her sons a good upbringing, despite the hardships. My father's twin, Barry Weston, became a vicar. My father had a lot of different jobs before he bought the bakery in Mt Albert that he owned for many years.

Every Sunday my parents took me and my brother Tim to the church where my Uncle Barry was the vicar. We sat in our pew listening to his sermon, my mother in a good-natured, open-mouthed trance, my father with his arms folded, stolid, proud, censorious. He always went up to Barry afterwards, shook his hand, leaned close to his ear and said something that no one else could hear, at which they both laughed. Then they stood together, still as strikingly alike as they'd been when they were boys, and spoke to the people who approached them — the old ladies, the nervous young men, the huge-bosomed matrons.

My father was as much in charge as Barry after the sermon was over. He took people aside and spoke to them, gravely and compassionately, about their problems. He was important in his own right, a member of the vestry and an organiser of church functions. It was said that everything would fall to pieces without Ted to organise it. Barry was the 'dreamy' one, the one who 'couldn't organise his way out of a paper bag'. Ted managed the fairs and the church maintenance, and worked to keep the congregation going. Numbers did dwindle over the years, but there was always a solid core of what Barry called 'worshippers', and even, later, a new generation of married couples who came to the service and enrolled their children in the Sunday School, part of a new wave of conservatism that was supposed to be sweeping the country.

When I was a little boy I was proud of my father and my uncle and I liked standing with them after church. I wanted everyone to know I was Ted Weston's son. But when I was a teenager things changed. There were certain words I began to have a bad feeling about. Worshippers. Ministry. Sharing. My father and Barry had a particular hushed, special way of saying them. It started to grate on me. I noticed other things. When a difficult subject came up, instead of talking about it directly, my father would say to us, 'I'll just tell you a little story.' He'd begin his tale in a low, syrupy voice, and it always ended up with a moral, a lesson we were to take from it.

'So you see,' he'd say, 'I'm just trying to show you . . .'

He and Barry 'showed' adults too, when they came up after church. The worshippers nodded and blinked as they listened to the stories designed to teach them this or that, and they turned out bleak, watery smiles as Ted and Barry encouraged and shared, and praised them for their little triumphs.

'Your son's had so many problems. And now he's doing so well. It must be *wonderful* for you.'

'Having your family around you, Mrs Cranston. It's *wonderful* for you, isn't it?'

'Up and about now, Bob? How *wonderful*.'

Often you sensed that things weren't actually wonderful, or at least were more complex than Barry would allow, but there was something smothering and final about his pronouncements; the parishioner's role was to bob his head, to smile bashfully, and to agree. It was all *wonderful*.

For the most part, the congregation were so humble and obedient that it used to give me a slightly disgusted feeling. I began to dislike being 'shown' things, and to wince at Barry's patronising social worker tone, which he used everywhere, even with ordinary, successful people who were more sophisticated than he was.

Barry used to say, 'I am one who listens.' But he was too busy doing God's work to notice whether people received his pearls of wisdom with gratitude, or with the strained look of someone who had been handed a hideous, inappropriate present and was being forced to be polite about it.

I squirmed about these things, and eventually they put me off the church. My younger brother, Tim, went regularly. He stood in line with Ted and Barry after sermons, and even began to imitate their manner towards the congregation. He was said to be a fine, steady young man, a perfect candidate for the ministry. He was charming and good-looking and polite. He had his sensible, caring tone down pat. The old ladies loved him.

My father had sensed me pulling away from the church, but he knew he could rely on Tim to stick with it. There were no difficult, critical aspects to Tim's character. He was similar to my father, in that he enjoyed lording it over simple people, in a way that would have made my mother embarrassed. Tim couldn't get enough of good works, and after he married, he and his wife kept going to Barry's church and sent their kids to Sunday School there.

Tim and Dad were especially close but that's not to say that I didn't get on with them. We were a happy family. My mother had a sunny nature and if there were things about the church that she disliked she glossed over them. The furthest she went was a little exasperated grimace every now and then, when Dad and Barry were being especially pompous.

At a family barbecue one day the conversation turned to education. I stared out the window, glazed with boredom, as members of the family held forth. Barry and Dad sat together, very upright and dignified, and if anyone got excited, one or other would hold up his hand, gravely shake his head to restrain the hothead cousin or nephew, and offer a little story to show the way. There were predictable elements to the stories. One was that no one was to 'think himself', or get ideas, above his station; we were all equal, and no one should be thought superior even if he had achieved more than other folk. Barry and Dad did not tolerate the sin of pride; they were assiduous levellers.

Barry's son, Dan Weston, a clever, quiet boy of thirteen, had described boys in the lower forms of his school as 'thick'. Barry looked sorrowful.

'It worries me when you talk that way, Dan. People might think you're . . . Let me tell you a little story. A man I knew had a son who was dux of his grammar school. Clever, like you. And do you know what happened to him? Well. The poor boy committed suicide.'

Dan stared strangely at his father.

Barry went on. 'What about that chap we went to school with, Ted? Brilliant scholar — what was his name? Sam, Simon, something? Had a bright future. He went right off the rails. By the end he was . . . Well, put it this way, Dan, *he was going through bins.*'

Barry put his head on one side, his voice clogged with regret, his eyes watchful, hard. 'So I'm just trying to *show* you . . .'

Tim chimed in with some inane platitude. I glanced up, and happened to see Barry give Dad a wink that was patronisingly approving of Tim, but somehow toadish and shrewd too. I was struck by the slyness of the wink, and by

Dad's expression as he acknowledged it. It was as if I'd glimpsed, for the first time, a secret current that ran between my father and uncle, a current that seemed to me, at that moment, to have something to do with the will to power. It was an odd thing to notice, in a flash like that. I wondered about it. Did Dad and Barry wink at each other over the heads of their congregation? Was there cynicism in them, hidden beneath their godliness?

Since he'd grown up poor, Dad had strong feelings about money. He talked about bills when they came in, and he was often up in arms because he thought the electricity company was wasteful and we were paying too much. When I look back, I think money (along with 'hard work') was held up in our house almost as a thing to worship, although Dad would never have admitted that the sin of avarice lurked in our house.

I met my girlfriend Emily at university, and I took her to lunch with my parents to introduce them. Emily was having a dispute with the boss at the café where she worked. Dad didn't like the idea of someone being underpaid and he started to advise her, but she looked distracted, and after a moment she tossed her hair and said, 'Oh, it's only money.' I laughed. Dad stared. She ignored him. I could tell by her glances at me that she knew there was something in the air. He kept staring at her all through lunch. He looked as if he wanted to kill her. He didn't say anything direct to me, but Emily made him bristle, and it took a long time for him to warm to her.

Tim's wife, Alison, was studying to be an eye surgeon. Tim had a patchy series of jobs before deciding to become a real estate agent, specialising in commercial property. He talked a lot about his ventures and made himself out to be a terrific entrepreneur, but I got the impression he wasn't consistently successful, and that he relied on Alison to bring in the serious money. There was something striving and fake about him, striding around with his briefcase, shouting into his mobile phone. He'd looked much the same when he was a little boy playing grown-ups. My notion of Tim, if I ever thought about it, was that he was incompetent in most things he tried because he wasn't very bright, but that he had such an aggressive, energetic personality that he managed to convince people he knew what he was doing. He liked telling the family about the tough business calls he'd made. 'Someone has to make the hard decisions,' he'd say. Among our extended family it was understood that Tim was the sensible one in money matters. I was supposed to be bit of a spendthrift, what with my posh, flighty girlfriend and my refusal to participate in long discussions about bills and bargains and the right appliances to buy.

I studied law and started working in a firm after I'd qualified. I had a mostly permanent relationship with Emily. Tim and Alison had a couple of kids, and bought themselves a house.

We had a bach a few hours' drive away from Auckland and we spent all our holidays there. Dad had a boat he took out fishing and Barry and his family used to come and stay. It was a nice place that my parents had bought when it was just a little shack. They'd built onto it, and made it big enough for the family. We spent all our summers there, swimming, fishing, walking out onto the estuary, having picnics. We used it as often as we could. When Tim was married and I was going out with Emily we shared it, sometimes all squeezing into it together.

A long time ago Dad had got advice about death duties (back when they were still a tax). He was told that the way to avoid paying duties on a property like the bach would be to change the ownership into Tim's and my name; that way there would be no tax on inheritance. He'd seized on the idea, as he always did when there was a prospect of saving money. Papers were drawn up and the bach was transferred from our parents' names into mine and Tim's.

I didn't know it, but that was the start of the trouble that would separate me from Tim forever.

We were a happy family for a long time, and then two blows

struck us. My mother collapsed with a heart attack, and seemed to be recovering in hospital, but died a week later. We were wretched, miserable with grief. Dad was completely crushed. We had the funeral in Auckland, then drove her to the graveyard on the hill above the bach. She was buried there, in sight of the sea.

A year later there was a scandal at the church. A woman whom Barry described as 'known to be unstable' got up in church and shouted, 'Barry Weston, tell them what you done to my son!' There were rumours of a misdemeanour, something sexual. It was hushed up, but it had an impact. Barry left the church, and not long after that he died. It was a heart attack, we were told. After that my father seemed to grow older very quickly. He kept his dignity, but you could see that his power was diminished. He became more reliant on Tim. Tim had the big house and the kids, and Alison was always willing to take care of him. They and Dad went regularly to church together, and Dad carried on working on the vestry.

I, on the other hand, didn't offer Dad much. I avoided the church. I still had a fairly tempestuous relationship with Emily. I lived in a series of flats and never got around to buying a house, and was constantly reminded by Dad and Tim that I should get on the 'property ladder' before it was too late. They shook their heads over my erratic love life and my lack of prudence. I thought they talked as if life was one long, dull preparation for a trouble-free transition to heaven — no spending, no risk-taking, no 'living it up'. 'As soon as you're born you start to die,' Dad liked to say. I rebelled against such joylessness. It made me want things, fiercely: love, risk, choice, excitement, life.

Emily and I went to dinner at Tim's. Dad was there too. Emily and Alison clashed.

Alison said, 'Walk down Queen Street. You'd think you were in Hong Kong.'

Tim said, 'Keep them out. Someone's got to make the tough decisions.'

'The Nazis were good at tough decisions.' Emily said, glaring.

Dad said vaguely, 'Asians? They eat so many veges. They live for a hundred years.'

Afterwards Emily said, 'Why is Tim so rough with your father?'

I bridled, offended. 'Tim's not rough.'

'He orders your father around. He talks to him as if he's stupid. He jerked his head at him, telling him to get out of the way. You saw.'

I denied it. We had a row. I said, 'No one's closer than Dad and Tim. You don't know them.'

'He's rude, though, Tim. He wants people to know he's in charge. And what a redneck he is.'

'You're rude!' I said.

But it had been a deadly evening — if ever the conversation had promised to get interesting Tim and Alison had grimly dragged it back to their staple subjects: appliances (the best TV or Playstation or stereo), property (house prices) or immigration (how foreigners threaten all this). And Tim did have a new air about him, as though, having been little brother for so long, he was enjoying an expansion of his powers. He'd been fierce and loud, almost shouting, about the importance of 'family', for example. He'd seemed to direct his tirade at Emily, who was smiling insultingly across the table at him. And it was true, he had seemed to jerk his head at Dad when Dad was hesitating in the hall . . .

I dropped Emily off at her flat, refusing her invitation to come in. She tried a few sly persuasions but I froze her off. I thought about Tim and felt uneasy.

I got over sulking after a few days. I asked Emily to move into my flat, and then a couple of months later we raised a deposit and bought a small house in Ponsonby. We were heavily mortgaged. Neither of us earned much yet. But the good thing was that Dad and Tim stopped nagging me about throwing my money away on rent.

One day Dad rang and said, 'Tim's talking about selling the bach.'

I laughed. 'That's a good one.'

There was an odd silence.

My stomach started to feel rough. 'He's not serious?'

Dad said slowly, 'Tim says it's worth a lot of money. Rising property values . . .'

'It's worth practically nothing. And he doesn't *need* money. He's loaded. You don't want to sell it, do you?'

'Tim's very sensible about these things,' Dad said.

'You don't want to sell it, do you?' I repeated.

'I want to be buried with your mother,' he said in a neutral voice.

I was at the supermarket when I got a message on my cellphone. Tim's voice played back, rugged, brisk: 'We need to meet and talk about selling this . . . house.'

This house. As though it were any old house, instead of our family bach, where our mother was buried. It was the tone Tim used when he said, 'Someone's got to make the hard decisions.'

I was furious. I went to see him. He was pumped up, important. He told me he could get a good price. 'There's money to be made,' he said.

'I don't want money. I want to keep the place.'

'You can be sentimental. But someone's got to make the hard . . .'

I cut him off. 'You and Alison are rich. What do you need the money for?'

He lost his temper. 'I don't have to tell you how I use my money!'

I appealed to Dad. But he wouldn't say anything. He sat on the window seat, leaning his head against the wall. He looked old and furtive and unhappy. He needed Tim.

I threw myself on Tim's mercy. I begged. I reminded him our mother was buried there, and that Emily and I spent our holidays there. I said I couldn't believe Dad really wanted this.

Tim made a little speech. He was sorry he had to be the strong-minded one, the one to make the realistic financial calls. He reminded me that I had never had a serious attitude when it came to money. I listened to him, to the tone of his voice. I'd always been stronger, effortlessly cleverer than he was. Now he was forcing his will upon me. He knew I couldn't stop him. He sounded positively exhilarated. Behind him my father sat silent, leaning his head against the wall.

I said, 'Where will I go for my holidays?'

He smiled. 'Ali and I like Fiji.'

I stood up in a fury. 'You're not selling it.'

He stepped back. 'Ali and I have seen a solicitor,' he said, blinking rapidly. 'Our name is on the title, yours and mine. I've been advised that I can force you to sell.'

I shouted, 'Your name's on the title as a *tax dodge*. You've got a legal right, but you've got no *moral* right. It's Dad's bach. You can't demand your inheritance before Dad's dead. Dad!' I turned to him.

He put out his hands. 'It's between you two,' he said. His fingers shook. He wouldn't say anything against Tim.

'If I ever have kids I want to show them the old places, take them to Mum's grave. You're supposed to care about "the family".'

He snapped nastily: 'You look after your kids and I'll look after mine.'

It was hopeless.

'You won't do it,' I said.

Tim smiled angrily. He shot a triumphant glance at Dad.

'I'm sorry,' he said.

I couldn't afford to buy Tim out. The bach was sold. It wasn't worth much. Tim and Alison took winter holidays in Fiji, and rented houses in summer. In the holidays Emily and I couldn't decide where to go. We booked motels in some spots, but they made me feel empty and rootless and I didn't like them much. My mother's grave was abandoned. Dad didn't get to visit it again. His eyesight was too bad for him to drive himself.

Tim started driving a new sports car. He and Alison bought a big house with a pool. They sent their kids to expensive private schools. The tiny bit of profit they got from the bach sale was swallowed up, meaninglessly, in the vast swirl of money they made themselves. Selling it had been a gratuitous act, without any financial rationale. But perhaps, for Tim, it wasn't just about the money, but more to do with something he'd inherited from Ted and Barry — the quality I thought I'd seen running like a current between them, and that I'd thought of as the will to power.

Dad wouldn't let me go off about it. He said, 'Everyone's got their own opinion.' And 'Tim's very steady about money.'

He still spent a lot of time with Tim, and if he had any thoughts he kept them to himself. It must have hurt him that he couldn't visit his wife's grave. But he was old. He had to look after himself.

I refused to have anything to do with Tim, and avoided our extended family for fear of meeting him. Dad grumbled about it, but he didn't go so far as to try to persuade me to see Tim. He realised that would be useless.

Emily and I decided to get married. We had the wedding in the church, and I invited the whole family except Tim and Alison. After the ceremony we walked outside and I was shocked to see Tim standing near the door, greeting people as if he'd been invited.

I said to Dad, 'What's he doing here?'

'I asked him to come. Say a word to him. Go on.' Dad looked sly, moist-eyed.

'No,' I said. I watched Tim shake hands, smile, 'share' with an admiring group of uncles and aunts.

I was angry, but I tried to put him out of my mind, for Emily's sake. We went to Dad's house, where the reception was to be held. There was catered food and hired waiters and it all looked very nice. Emily was bursting with excitement and good humour. Tim was nowhere to be seen. I cheered up and started enjoying the party.

Then I turned and Tim was walking towards me.

'Dad,' I said, 'tell him to go away.'

'Son, son,' he said, shocked, censorious, laying his hand on my arm.

Tim was followed by a crowd of admirers — aunts, uncles and cousins I hadn't seen for years. He was holding a glass of champagne high as he threaded through the crowd, and the relatives swooped along behind him, chattering excitedly: the common folk following the charming prince. He arrived; the group packed around him. He was buoyed up by the wine and the adoring looks of his aunts and girl cousins. He was wearing a glamorous tailored suit and a bright, stylish tie. His cheeks were flushed, his eyes shone and his forehead was speckled with sweat. He stopped in front of me and tilted his face challengingly. He had never looked so handsome.

He turned and raised his glass. 'To my brother,' he said. He put on his church face: self-righteous, stupid, intransigent.

The group raised their glasses for the toast. Then Tim took the arm of one of the blushing girl cousins and made a little speech.

'Many of you haven't seen my brother for a long time. He's been busy. He's probably been living it up!' He winked. 'Anyway, let's drink to his health.'

Then he added, with a flourish, to a ripple of laughter and applause, 'We welcome home . . . the Prodigal Son!'

I turned on my heel and pushed between the murmuring, bright-eyed women, their faces glowing, it seemed to me, with enjoyment and malice.

In the kitchen, later, my rage was starting to subside. I felt weary, cynical.

Dad came in. He stood, twirling an empty wineglass.

I laughed quietly. 'Oh, that's rich,' I said. 'The Prodigal Son . . . That's good. I didn't think the idiot had it in him, to make a joke like that.'

Dad didn't say anything.

I said, 'He demands his inheritance before you've died. He takes it and squanders it on sports cars and swimming pools. He comes to my wedding and you give him the fatted beef sausages, and tell me to welcome him and to forgive. And he calls *me* the Prodigal Son. Oh, it's very good.'

My father eyed me steadily. His cheek twitched.

I leaned close to him and said savagely, 'I say *he's* the Prodigal Son. But he hasn't repented. He's grasping, stupid, cold . . .'

Dad shook his head.

I struggled against myself. I wanted to get control, to go outside to Emily. I said, '*You* made him worship money! You told him he was more "good" than other people. And he was too stupid . . . he wasn't bright enough to see when he wasn't being good but bad! He takes your property and sells it, shouts at you, orders you around. He talks down to you, even though you've got twice the brains. You were right about one thing: you reap what you sow. You've reaped that . . . that fraud.' I gestured towards the garden.

Dad kept his face fixed in a sententious smile. 'My place is not to judge,' he said.

I said, 'You only forgive him because you have to. It's not Christian charity or virtue; it's pure animal need. You don't *dare* fall out with him. If only you'd admit it, if only you'd stop your platitudes and your stories and talk about things as they really are.'

'Animal need! He's my son. I love him. What do you know?'

I laughed coldly. 'Your Prodigal Son.'

'The Prodigal Son is a parable,' Dad began in a smothered voice. He was holding on to the back of a chair. 'It tells us a story of forgiveness and redemption. The Prodigal Son returns, repentant, and the father rejoices, for we must forgive . . .'

'It's all a myth,' I said. 'All of it. The Bible. The parables. Tim's as repentant as a snake. And your forgiveness is . . . need.'

Dad struggled to keep his composure.

'Did any of your Christianity make Tim good? No!'

We were silent, looking at each other.

'God is a myth,' I said.

I felt light-headed suddenly. I couldn't talk to him any more. Sooner or later he would try to tell me a 'little story', and I'd realised, long ago, that his stories were as much about avoiding truths as confronting them.

I left him standing there, old and silent, staring out into the garden, and I went in search of Emily.

storms

I was sitting in the car; the radio was playing a song. I was looking at where a lane runs off the main road. The lane lay ahead of me, a long narrow stretch, with a high bank overgrown with agapanthus on one side and houses on the other. The song played loud. There was no other sound. An old woman came out of a driveway, carrying a shopping bag. She started to walk away from me down the lane. There was a yellow line painted on the lane. She walked along it. I watched her going steadily away. The lane, the yellow line, the old woman's bent shoulders. A girl came out of the bushes on the bank and jumped down onto the lane, landing in a crouch, righting herself in a quick athletic whirl of limbs; the old woman, startled, still walking, turned her whole body, shoulders hunched, head sideways, to look at the girl, then kept walking away. The music played. The girl went into a house. There was a bend in the lane. The old woman reached the bend and was gone.

Sun on the asphalt. Figures in the distance. The absence of

words. The old woman making her way, the whirling girl. The empty lane, the yellow line, the song.

Rob came out of the house, loaded up with bags. 'What's wrong? What? Why don't you help me? See what I've got here. Everything we need! Everything.'

He opened the boot and packed in the gear, tossing a couple of bags on the back seat.

'You relax! Enjoy the drive. This is going to be good. It won't take long to get there. What a beautiful day. Look at the sky!'

We never had children. I always thought there would be time.

'All set?'

Rob got in. He rubbed my shoulder, shook the hair out of his eyes, glanced in the back seat, briskly checking. He saw the newspaper in my lap. The black headline: *Released to Attack Again.*

His expression changed. He went solemn. He put his arms around me.

'Oh, darling. Don't read it. Don't think about it. Look, there's dear old Osama at the window waving goodbye!'

My dog's name was Robbie, but Rob called him Osama bin Laden because he was such a villain of an animal, and because he said I couldn't possibly have a dog with his name. Robbie was barking at the window. My housekeeper would feed and walk him while we were away. I didn't feel bad about leaving him. He was really Raymond's dog.

Rob took the newspaper off my lap and folded it. 'Don't think about anything. No work, no sorrows, just holiday.'

I smiled. 'Okay.'

Everyone said Rob was a lovely man. I met him after a Francis family meeting in Wellington. He was a barrister, a QC. He was divorced, the father of three boys. It was six months since Raymond had left me.

I had been staying at work until late, coming home to the dog and the empty house, sleeping in the study on the top floor because I felt afraid, waking in the night, listening to the whirr of the pool pump and the dog snoring on the floor, and feeling stunned with loneliness. Grief started to feel like fear. I was jumpy. There was an odd side-effect to my rawness: I felt as if every part of me was reaching out for sex. I was washed out, nervous, tired, but I felt I was radiating *need* and that people — men — were responding. The world was suddenly full of sexual currents, looks, glances.

I was glad to go to the Francis meeting because it meant I could stay in a good hotel and forget myself a bit. The meeting was routine, the usual thrashing-out of issues to do with distribution of the family wealth. I went back to the hotel on the second night and Rob was in the bar. He'd been appearing in the Court of Appeal. He was tall, shabbily dressed, with alert, humorous eyes and messy, wavy hair that fell across his forehead. We started talking. He knew who I was, and that I worked in an arm of the Francis Group of companies. He told me a lot about himself. He was humble and funny. His wife had left him. Had 'despaired' of him, he confessed with a rueful laugh. 'She was terribly respectable. She didn't approve of my cigars or my old car or my messy clothes — or anything, really. She stuck it out for decades. Then she went off with a chap, a hugely wealthy *corpse*. She met him at tennis.'

We laughed. We drank a fair bit and I told him I lived alone. At the end of the evening he took my hand and held it hard, and I said something, some cliché about not wanting to spend the night alone.

Afterwards I lay in the hotel dark looking out at the city lights with the feeling that I was utterly lost and that Rob — this stranger beside me — was the only point of reference I had.

We parted casually, but when we were both back in Auckland he started ringing me, and it wasn't long before we were going out together.

I looked at the dog scrabbling along the window. 'You can't have a dog and a boyfriend with the same name!' Rob had said. Recently I was a wife — newspapers called us a 'high-achieving couple'. Now I had a *boyfriend*. I turned the word over in my mind, neutralising the protest that rose, some convulsion of the old self that I would not regain.

Now we were driving up the harbour bridge in Rob's elegant, battered old car, heading to Whangaparaoa. It was summer. We had both taken a week off work. He had borrowed his brother's yacht. We were to set sail, just the two of us. 'Nothing fancy,' he said, winking. 'We'll be at one with the elements!' He joked about my lifestyle — my family wealth, my job. He wasn't materialistic. He liked things to be natural, honest, down to earth. He loved the outdoors and sailing. I wasn't so sure about boats. But I was willing.

'Look at the sky.' I pointed.

There was an intense turquoise haze on the horizon. The sea was navy blue and broken up by choppy waves. Over Rangitoto Island there was a strange configuration of clouds, like great rags hanging in the pearly-blue glare. Below it the colour of the sea had intensified, as if there was a disturbance spreading across the water.

Sudden changes in the light. The wind buffeting the car on the bridge.

'Good sailing weather,' he said.

I smoothed out the paper. *Released to Attack Again.* I looked at the picture of Chase Ihaka, the man who had ruined my marriage.

Rob shook his head. He put his hand over the page. I took it off, gently.

Chase Ihaka was awaiting sentence. He had been convicted of murder. There was an old picture of him, a school photo perhaps — a round-faced, gap-toothed Maori youth with a shock of messy hair, smiling.

The wind hit the side of the car with a roar.

Ihaka, now aged 20, has a substantial list of criminal convictions, having first been arrested for theft when aged just 10. In January last year, the career burglar broke into the substantial Remuera home of prominent businesswoman Jenny Francis and her husband, the filmmaker Raymond Wright. Surprised on the premises by Mr Wright, Ihaka subjected him to a beating that left Mr Wright permanently scarred. Ihaka received a light custodial sentence and . . .

'All right, darling?' Rob said. 'I'll put some music on.'

Released into the community only five months after his conviction for attacking Mr Wright, Ihaka lived on the streets. He had significant drug and alcohol issues, and acquired numerous further convictions for theft, before the night when he broke into the home of Mr Eric Crombie, owner of the Firebrand chain of clothes shops. Mr Crombie was found beaten to death in his kitchen. Ihaka was arrested driving Mr Crombie's car and wearing items of Mr Crombie's clothing. He had bragged to associates about beating Mr Crombie, and admitted the assault when spoken to by police. During his trial, Ihaka claimed that Mr Crombie had made sexual advances to him, and that he had 'lashed out' in reaction to this 'provocation'. The jury rejected this claim, finding him guilty of murder.

Following his conviction, questions are being asked about why this youth was released to attack again, only months after being convicted of the serious assault on Raymond Wright.

Rob looked sideways, shook his head. He patted my arm.

I said, 'Journalists keep ringing. They say, "The man who attacked your husband went on to commit murder. How do you feel about that?" They can't understand why I don't want to comment. But it's done. There's nothing to say.'

'Keep your answerphone on. Screen your calls.'

I remembered going to the hospital. Raymond's face. He was badly hurt; his nose was broken. But it was his expression that struck me most. The bewilderment, vulnerability.

It made it worse for him — my pity. His spirit was damaged. He'd been so frightened. The youth could easily have killed him. He became depressed. A doctor recommended we have counselling together — a mistake, I know that now. It made Raymond shy away from me. I was a witness to his hurt, his shameful tears. To his fall.

I said, 'We'd done all that charity work for street kids. The Francis Foundation, the fundraisers. Raymond did his free film school in South Auckland. All that "reaching out".' I laughed bitterly. 'What rubbish it was.' I looked for a handkerchief. 'Ridiculous . . . sorry.'

'*I'm* sorry,' Rob said. 'Told you not to read it.'

He reached over for the paper and threw it hard into the back seat. I stared at him. We drove in silence for a while.

Rob looked at me. He said in a softer voice, cautiously, 'Just because your husband was attacked doesn't mean the charity wasn't worth it. The Francis Foundation does good things.'

I wound my handkerchief around my fingers. I looked out, white houses against a blue-black sky. 'It was all bullshit,' I said.

At Whangaparaoa I stood on the marina looking at the boats. The wind blew hard and constant, jinking and clinking the lines and struts; there was the sound of straining ropes, the whine of the wind in the masts. The light was bright and the sea was pale, turquoise, stained with patches of darker blue.

I helped Rob to load up the gear. The yacht was small and compact, well kept, with a neat little cabin and a scrubbed wooden deck.

'Snug, eh?' Rob said. He busied himself with ropes. I had been on yachts but had never had anything to do with the actual sailing. Rob sailed a lot. He knew what he was doing.

He started the motor and we chugged out of the harbour. As soon as we hit the open water we felt the force of the wind. Rob shouted instructions. I did what I was told. We raised the sail. We were tacking up the channel. Boats passed us, racing for the harbour. We were the only ones making for open sea. I looked ahead and saw great clouds hanging ahead of us, and then the nose of the boat dipped and I was looking at the churning water. I felt the jolt in my stomach as we ploughed into the wave then, rearing ahead, I saw the clouds again, like a robed phantom with its cloak stretched out to catch us, and I thought I could see matter whirling in the depths of the cloud mass, a fury of agitated air, and then I was looking down again, down into the green water, and felt the plunge in my stomach, as if I had fallen off a cliff, and the sickening pull as we rose.

I held the rail with both hands. I shot out a burning stream of puke, saw it whisked away on the surface. Spray hit me, stinging drops. I retched again, although there was nothing to bring up but miserable strings of bile. Above me the sky loomed like a cathedral, all points and buttresses, ragged banners, a monstrous edifice into which we battled, up and down, rising and plunging. We were well into the channel, heading past the islands. The waves were getting bigger, and the sky ahead had got much darker. The wind was ferocious. Behind me, Rob was all action, but I was so overwhelmed by my physical crisis that I couldn't speak. I assumed he was trying to turn back, and that we would probably die.

I lay on my side along the rail. A green bush-covered island rose and fell. Ropes of sunlight broke though and shone hurtingly bright on the sea around it, a jumbled, foaming mass of pale green. Water came over the side as we hit each wave, showering spray. Rob had edged over to me. He was shouting above the scream of the wind.

'Bit rougher than I thought!' He said something about the weather forecast.

I moaned.

'Feel better?'

'Can we get back?' I said.

'We'll make for Kawau Island. No problem.'

'Let's go back,' I said, but he had gone. I felt angry at the hyperactivity of males, why they needed to complicate everything, drag one on elaborate adventures. But another wave of nausea carried me away from this thought, and I was leaning over the side again, crying my complaints into the sea.

I don't know how long it took to make it to Kawau Island. The wind screamed so hard that it whipped the words out of our mouths. Rob fell over once. There was a trickle of blood on his temple. 'It's nothing!' he shouted. His eyes were screwed up, his hair was blown wild by the wind. His jacket billowed behind him. I wondered how much strain the small boat could take.

I mouthed, 'Sorry!' I meant sorry to have been so useless.

He shook his head and pointed. 'Nearly there,' he shouted. 'Hang on!'

We were passing the coast of the island, heading for the mouth of the harbour. I looked at waves crashing onto rocks, at the dark slopes covered with bush and pine forest. Rob pointed out the harbour mouth, a swirl of silver water with the light shining on it, and above it a sky that was growing intensely black. It looked as if every cloud was hurrying towards that place, the sky gathering energy into itself. Rain was sheeting down, and soon great squalls of it were blowing over us. We made for the harbour, and it was like riding into the end of the world. I did cry then, with fear. Just before we got inside the sheltering edge the sky unleashed itself, and we were blinded with rain, ripped by wind, jerked and tossed and thrown about, both of us shouting, every rope straining and the mast groaning. At the moment when I thought the boat would be ripped to pieces we came about, the sail filled with a jolt and we skimmed sickeningly over the crest of a huge swell. I looked into the green trough and saw fish streaming through the wave. Water slapped into my face, the boat heaved and Rob yelled. The wind slackened, the water became calmer and the rain, although it kept pouring down, stopped lashing our faces. We had entered the bay. I looked back at the jumble of silver and foam and sunlight and rain, and couldn't believe we'd come through it.

Rob made me a gin and tonic. I lay on the deck in the strange, hot light. The sun was shining, yet directly above us the sky was swollen with purple-black clouds. I was light-headed, smiling with relief, with the joy of no longer feeling sick.

'That was the most inadequate weather forecast in history,' Rob repeated.

We listened to the radio. The rough weather wasn't a storm any more; it was a cyclone. There were severe gale warnings in all parts of the country. Rob insisted that it hadn't been predicted at all. I watched him from my invalid's position on the sunny deck. I had an intense feeling of well-being that made me sanguine, careless. I turned over in my mind, detached, the fact that I didn't believe him. I'd lately been avoiding all news except business and finance, and the paper I'd had that morning was the first I'd looked at for days. I thought a cyclone must have been mentioned at least, in marine forecasts, which he said he'd listened to. Perhaps he'd dismissed it as only a possibility, or thought we could outrun it. We had outrun it, and now we were trapped in the harbour at Kawau, a perfect shelter, deep inside the encircling hills of the island. We were protected from the wind, and the sun, when it broke through the vast black clouds, was extraordinarily hot and intense. In the distance on the hills the trees were being lashed by the wind but down here at the jetty we were floating in calm water, the light dancing on the wall of the cabin, clothes hanging on the railings to dry, Rob propping another cushion under my head . . .

I watched him. Everybody said, 'Rob Farnham. What a nice man!' He bustled cheerfully about on the deck, making things ship-shape. I closed my eyes and felt slightly drunk. I was helpless, weak. It was a sensual feeling. I've lost control, I thought. I remembered that first night in the hotel, where I'd thought everything in my old life was gone, and he was the only point of reference I had.

Had he wanted the trip so much that he'd turned a blind eye to an approaching storm?

We swam and lazed on the beach. In the evening we made ourselves a meal and ate it on the deck. We drank a lot of wine. We could hear the wind tearing the trees on the hills, a roar that died as the sun was going down but began to rise much higher as it got dark. In the brief stillness at sunset the sky was a jumbled black mass, cloud piling on cloud, and the air was heavy, humid, full of whirling drops. We were drunk. It got very dark, and there were only the few lights from other boats shining on the water. The roar of the wind deepened and intensified. Rob took a torch and we walked up a track into the pine forest, shining the light on the branches, hearing the whole forest shifting and creaking above us. We walked a long way, towards the top of the hill. Up there the storm was battering the tops, and when Rob shone the torch up the trees were crashing and lurching together. He walked away from me. There was blackness all around him; he walked in a pool of light. A branch fell near me, then another. I went towards him, through the dark. The crashing of the trees was exciting, agitating. Lightning lit up the forest, followed by a boom and crack of thunder. Rob started to sing. Lightning flashed again. We linked arms and marched down the hill, falling about in the deep pine needles, hauling each other up, ignoring the falling branches, laughing, singing drunkenly at the tops of our voices.

Back at the jetty the rain came, great sheets of it, drumming on the deck, hissing into the water. We went into the cabin and dried off. Rob poured some more wine. We sat at the little table, laughing at each other. One of his shoes had disintegrated in the wet. The toe had burst open. 'I've got another pair somewhere,' he said, tugging off the sodden relic.

I had a sudden vision of Raymond's wardrobe. The sharp suits. The lines and lines of fashionable shoes. Raymond loved shopping for clothes. He liked to look good because he had a strong visual sense. Our house was full of good art because we had the money to buy it, and Raymond had good taste. Not that I didn't, but he was the one with the real eye. He had left his paintings, just as he left his dog. Soon we would divide them up, through our lawyers, in a settlement. After Chase Ihaka beat him, his face was no longer symmetrical. He was still handsome. Is. Was. I don't live with Raymond any more. Raymond is not dead but he is gone. He was gone.

When he told me he was leaving I begged him not to go. I said that we could live through this. I said that a burglar, a nobody, should not be allowed to destroy our marriage. I shouted. 'Fuck Chase Ihaka! He's nothing to us!'

I remember Raymond's expression. He despised me. For begging. For wanting our lives to carry on as before, even though everything — words, promises, memories, shared ideas — all the things that had held us together had been spoiled and broken.

By Chase Ihaka.

Those words. I hear them sometimes when I've been asleep and I'm just at the point of waking. I hear them as if it's my own voice, whispering in my head. The smiling brown boy in the photo, gap-toothed, head on one side, the crooked collar of his school uniform resting on his smooth cheek, long eyelashes, the narrow brown eyes. Little man, his mother's lost boy. Little destroyer.

I was in the narrow bunk, squashed up against Rob. I lay with my eyes closed. These days I struggled with that point between sleeping and waking. I often woke with a feeling of dread. There was something all around me, an unpleasant, alien presence. I realised it was a smell. Something heavy, overpowering.

Rob sat up.

'Oh, Christ. Oh, my God.'

I rolled over. I grabbed his arm. 'What is it?'

The floor of the boat was covered with something dark and pungent. I felt sick. My head reeled.

'The engine's leaking. Bloody hell!'

I pulled on some clothes. He said, 'You'd better get out. Get some air, love.'

The morning air whirled with rain. All the trees were tossing and roaring now, even those near the harbour. The sky was heavy with intense black clouds. There were flashes of purple sheet lightning and cracks of thunder: sharp, one after another, like a series of gunshots. It was hot. I breathed in, deeply, to get rid of the taste of the fumes.

After a long time Rob came up. He sat down heavily. 'It's terrible. I can't get at the leak. What a mess.'

'We'd better get the food out,' I said.

He looked blank.

'We can't get back in this weather. We'll need it.'

'Right.' He leaned his face against the rail. 'I've got a blinding headache,' he said.

'It's the fumes.' I laughed. Horrified.

'What a disaster,' he said. He looked bleakly at the hillside.

We worked to pack the supplies into boxes and bring them out onto the deck. We covered them as best we could from the rain. Everything was drenched. Clothes hung dripping from the railings. Cardboard boxes were sodden. One box broke up and cans crashed onto the deck. Some rolled off into the water.

The cabin was uninhabitable. The floor was soaked with fuel, and Rob couldn't figure out how to drain it, or to stop the leak. Some of the bedding had fallen onto the floor and was wet and stained. Packets of food that we'd opened were spoiled.

We got everything out onto the deck. Rain splattered across our faces. Rob got up, grim-faced. He stood with his back to me, staring at the tossing trees. My wet clothes clung to me. My skin hurt, pinched by the shrinking material. There was rain in my eyes. I'd been inclined to laugh, but the discomfort was increasing. I couldn't think how, or where, we were going to spend the days until the storm had passed. Then there was the question of how we were going to get back. If we couldn't fix the engine we would have to steer back into Whangaparaoa under sail, and I knew that wouldn't be easy.

Rob said, 'I know what we'll do. Load up the dinghy.'

'Where are we going?'

'You'll see.' He didn't confer. He wanted to be in charge. He would *provide*. I thought about this.

He rowed around the point and out across the bay. The wind hit us. I stopped talking and leaned forward, resting my elbows on my knees. It was rough out from the shelter of the trees — not as bad as the open sea, but choppy enough to bring the nausea swirling back. Spray broke over us. There were sticks and branches floating in the water. Rob rowed, grunting with effort, muttering to himself, 'There? There? Where's it gone now?'

We were passing a stretch of pine forest that had been cleared for sections. Small houses showed among the trees.

'Here we are,' he said, steering the boat towards the shore. We landed on a tiny jetty. He fastened the rope and pulled me up onto the wooden boards.

'Right. You wait here.'

'Where are you going?' I was concentrating on not being sick.

'I'm going to reconnoitre.'

I sat down with my arms around my knees. I looked through the wooden planks to the green water sluicing below. Nausea broke my thoughts into odd patterns. I thought: children think adults are a different species. But adults sometimes feel as if they are only ten years old. I sat there, hugging my bare legs. Once I'd stopped feeling sick, I decided, I would go behind a tree and relieve myself. I had been reduced to very simple things. I was soaking. I was sick. I was even hungry. My legs looked skinny, ridiculous, in their baggy shorts. My shoes were full of water. How had I let this happen? I could have been in an expensive hotel anywhere in the world. I had a moment of dismay, almost fear. I was letting everything fall away. I was lost. I didn't know the man I was with. Who was he?

Rob came back, crashing down through the pine needles and scrub, bullish, jolly and commanding, in control once more.

'I've got this client . . .' He looked sideways. I waited.

We were standing on the deck of a small house. There was a covered barbecue, a spa pool draped in canvas sheeting. The blinds and curtains were drawn. As he spoke, Rob was looking under plant pots, shifting a doormat, running his hand along the tops of ledges.

'He says to me, if you ever need it, the house is here. He knows I come sailing round Kawau all the time.'

We had hauled our belongings up from the jetty and piled them on the deck.

I said, 'Are you sure this is the right place?'

'Definitely.'

He went around the back of the house. I sat down. I looked at the orange pine needles, the tossing trees. I heard a tearing, wrenching sound, like old iron being ripped. There was a loud bang.

Rob appeared inside the French doors, unlocked them and stepped beaming out onto the deck.

'Madam! Your palace awaits!'

It was really very cosy. There was a double bed with a striped cover. There was linen in the cupboard. Everything worked, once Rob had figured out how to turn on the pump. The water came from a rainwater tank at the back of the house. We unloaded our food in the kitchen and I set about making breakfast. The cooking utensils were expensive, elaborate. Rob took the cover off the barbecue and fiddled with it. I had a sense of relief at the space. I hadn't liked being cramped into the yacht. I was glad to be off the water, too. To stop feeling sick.

The wind shifted the trees, rain drummed on the iron roof.

'So who's this client?'

'Longstanding one. A good guy. Obviously he's not going to turn up, what with the storm.'

'No.'

'But I'll tell him we've been here,' he said innocently.

I'd looked at the bathroom window where Rob had got in. The metal catch was broken off. The frame had been wrenched out.

I thought, with a kind of hilarity, a QC breaking in? There was a mirror over the kitchen sink. I looked at myself. I'd had a feeling, ever since Raymond had gone, that some outer layer had been peeled away. I was raw, open. I had attracted men — Rob. I had allowed him to take me away. I felt like a kid, limping and snivelling one minute, hilarious the next. And when Rob took over, when he finished his breakfast and grinned at me merrily and pulled me onto the bed, I had the sensual feeling of surrender, of allowing everything to fall away.

Rob went out. He said he was going to check on the dinghy. When the storm had died down, he said, we could go back to the wharf and work out what to do about the yacht.

Before he left he'd said, 'There's a shower.'

I lay on the bed. 'Let's not wash,' I said.

He looked shocked. 'Not wash?'

'Oh, all right.' I laughed.

He left. I had a short chilly shower — the water hadn't yet heated up. I lay on the bed. There was a shelf of old detective novels. I pulled up the duvet and lay luxuriously reading. The rain was loud on the roof. Out the window the forest swayed and heaved with the squalls. Sticks clattered onto the deck.

Later we put on the oilskins that were hanging in the laundry and went down to the jetty.

'There's no one in the houses round about,' he said. He held my hand. Our feet sank deep in the pine needles. The bay was wild, grey-green and running with currents. We walked along a path, past the other houses. Their windows were blank, curtained. We came to a point and looked out at the churning water. The trees were thrashing across on the far shore. It occurred to me that a branch might fall on us.

We went back and spread out our clothes to dry. We lay on the striped duvet, listening to the gale.

I woke in the night. It was pitch black. The darkness was unnerving, so absolute that nothing showed. The wind was howling, lifting the iron on the roof. I moved closer to Rob.

A dream had woken me. It was about Raymond.

We got married when we were both twenty-eight. He was handsome. He was a filmmaker. He had directed successful New Zealand films. After we'd been married a couple of years he was invited to make his first film in America. He would go on making films. That wouldn't change.

In the last months of our marriage I'd thought about trying to get pregnant. I needed to get on with it, if I was ever going to. I stopped taking the Pill. I didn't tell him. I wondered if he knew. What with working so much we barely had time for each other. I didn't get pregnant.

I thought about sex. I forced myself to look back. Was I just thinking this way because of what had happened? What was I getting at? When we'd been in bed together and I was happy, had I sensed, once or twice, a kind of distance, almost malice, in his tone, as if he had performed a task, performed it well, and now could be released?

He was a polished performer. He kept some part of himself separate. It was that distance that made me yearn after him, as well as the moments when his vulnerability showed, and I was all the more smitten with him because he tried to keep his dignity, and to hide it. He was the fourth son of a solo mother. He knew what it was like to be talented and poor. That was why he did free film workshops for street kids. There were parts of himself over which he had grown a shell, in order to get on in the world. Old hurts, things he was ashamed of.

Chase Ihaka took away his dignity, and afterwards he couldn't face me, couldn't stand that I had seen him reduced.

He despised me for begging, for not being able to face the fact that everything had changed.

A voice came out of the blackness. 'What are you thinking about?'

'About Raymond,' I said.

He sat up. I couldn't see anything. He got off the bed.

'Where are you going?' I asked.

He didn't say anything.

'Where are you?'

There was no answer. There was only blackness. I heard a sound. He was standing in the room, near me.

'Where are you?'

Silence.

'Oh, turn on the light! Turn on the light! Turn on the light!'

He jumped and snapped it on. He leaned over me, gripping my wrists. 'What's the matter? What's wrong?'

I pulled away. 'You didn't answer. You didn't speak!'

'I was asleep,' he said, wondering. He held me tight. 'You've been dreaming. Just dreams.' He held me in his arms.

'There's no one I can trust.'

'I'm here. You can trust me. I'll turn off the light, shall I?'

The blackness came down. I was shaking. I couldn't get warm.

We stayed in the bach for three days. On the fourth day the wind dropped. There was stillness, quiet. The sky was low and black, shot through with sudden, surprising beams of sunlight. Rob went to the yacht, and came back with the news that a man who had been sheltering at the wharf in his own boat had helped him with the engine, that they had drained the boat as best they could. The man had given him a bit of fuel. If the engine failed we would have to get into the marina under sail. He thought we would make it. The storm had passed. People were leaving the island.

We packed up and tidied the house. I didn't want to leave it. I had grown fond of it. Rob went into the bathroom and hammered the window frame back into place. I pretended not to hear.

'It's been an adventure,' he said.

'It's been great,' I said.

At the wharf the yachts were sailing out. The beach was strewn with branches; the trees hung with broken sticks, paper, plastic bags. The water was brown and churned up. I looked at the yacht. It was stained with oil, sodden, smelly. I was dreading the sail back. I felt nauseated already.

The engine started, and we headed towards the harbour mouth. Rob waved to other boats, whistled, busied himself with ropes and lines. Looking ahead anxiously I saw that the sea was still rough. When we hit the open water I was immediately doubled up with nausea, and the waves seemed to me terrifyingly high, although the wind was moderate. Soon I was lying along the rail, watching the green shoreline rise and fall. Sunbeams shone down on the sea. Rob shouted to point out dolphins. I watched them leaping through the waves. Foam blew in the air. I rested my cheek on the rail. Beyond Kawau the wind strengthened. The boat rose and plunged, hitting the water hard. I felt the sickness rising and rising. I leaned, heaved, and my breakfast hit the water and was whisked away, a curl of matter on the bubbled surface, like a question mark.

I imagined my own body, falling, hitting the surface, whirled away in the current. I looked across at waves, jumbled cloud, grey water lit up silver in the beams of light, birds riding on currents of air. To lie here like a limp rag, weak, sick, drenched, watching the currents, to yearn only to get from this moment to the next, to be *reduced to simple things*. Was this the way to confront what I shied away from most?

Raymond told me the truth just before he left me. He told me as a final, savage assertion of himself, as if I had forced him into a lie all these years. Afterwards, he despised me for pleading with him. For wanting to carry on as before, despite what he'd told me. It was our secret now. He told me what Chase Ihaka had done, and what he had done to him. The brown young man with the gap-toothed smile. His eager face, his shining eyes. The sort of youth the Francis Foundation wanted to help. He was poor. He may have been talented. It didn't matter now. Living on the streets, a thief and an alcoholic, he had started selling himself for sex. He had not broken into our house. Raymond had invited him in.

Had arranged to meet him secretly, at home, while I was at work. Had heard the knock, opened the door, ushered him inside. Made small talk, poured out wine. Drawn him down onto the couch. At what point the youth went crazy — before or after the sex — I do not know. Raymond wouldn't say. I don't know why he exploded in such violence. I know that he did it again, not long after coming out of jail for attacking Raymond, and that the second time, instead of clamming up, he told the police a version of the truth. He said the victim had made sexual advances to him. That he had recoiled and lashed out. He didn't say he went to men's houses all the time. That it was the way he made money, because he was drunk and drugged out and poor.

Raymond was right. We couldn't really have stayed married. In the end I would have had to face up to things.

It was when Chase Ihaka was arrested for murder that I came home to find Raymond waiting for me, drinking, a strange, heightened expression in his eyes.

He told me. In my distress I tried to make bargains. I thought it was something we could solve.

He looked at me with contempt.

'I thought you would guess,' he said.

I never would have guessed. I had faith in our marriage. I wanted children. I wanted to believe.

'You married me for my money,' I said.

I saw him flinch. He laughed scornfully. I looked at his pale, scarred face and saw that it was true. I felt a wave of pure sorrow for him, as well as for myself.

'What about the Foundation? The sheer hypocrisy of you . . .'

But I didn't go on. I had done my begging. He left the house. I watched him walk unsteadily away up the drive.

Perhaps he didn't think he and Chase Ihaka were all that different, in the end.

Rob shouted. He pointed at the land. We were on a tack, heading for the entrance to the harbour. He was going to lower the sail and hope the engine would restart. If it didn't, I couldn't see how we were going to get back in.

At the harbour mouth he tried the engine. It wouldn't start. He tried again. The boat was tossing badly. I staggered against the rail. He shouted some instructions I didn't understand. The current was pushing us towards the shoreline, where there were rocks. The engine made a moaning sound. It coughed. I could see the edge of the marina, the tops of the clinking masts. The boat turned and was hit side on by a wave. I crouched down by the railing. Rob swore and leaned down again, and the engine spluttered and turned over and started, and then he was steering the boat, heading us in through the channel, and as the sun broke out, casting a livid light through the black clouds, we sailed into the calm lanes of the marina.

I was sitting in the car. I was looking along the lane that runs off the main road. It was strewn with leaves, broken branches, bits of paper. The gutters were running with rain. Leaves swirled in the blocked drain. The footpath was flooded.

The dog, Robbie, was at the window, scrabbling, barking.

Rob got out and started unloading my things. He leaned in. 'Getting out?'

We carried my bags to the door.

'The bach. Did you really know who owned it?'

Rob tossed his keys from one hand to the other. 'Sure. He's a client of mine. Lovely bloke.'

There was a silence.

'Shall I come in?' he asked.

I looked at him. A sudden squall blew through the garden, flipping the leaves, driving rain onto the tiles. I looked up at the white sky.

'Yes.'

I unlocked the door. He picked up my bags, whistling, and followed me inside.

values

He said, 'You're fiery. Your whole family's fiery.'

He walked ahead of me through the hall, up the stairs, into the bedroom. I wondered whether he was looking for something or just getting away from me.

He took off his glasses. 'My eyes are killing me,' he said.

I followed him. I should have left him alone, but I had the bad anxiety of the morning after. Last night's dinner party had turned into a row. One of the guests had taken everyone on.

I said, 'Didn't it make you annoyed, the things he was saying? About Palestinians. Calling them terrorists. Refusing to admit that they might have *one tiny* little grievance. And the way you can't just come out and say, "The security wall is a crime".'

Scott looked at me. 'You did say it.'

'What?'

'You said you can't say it. But you did say it.'

'Oh. Well.' I shrugged.

'Just before you told him to leave and never come back.'

'So, do you think he'll be offended?'

'I'd have thought he'd be pretty annoyed.'

'But he's so unreasonable!' I wrung my hands. Oh, these hungover post-mortems. 'Isn't he? Didn't you feel rage when he said those things?'

'I don't feel the need to be enraged. I might argue with him. Rationally.'

'Are you saying I wasn't being rational? I was completely lucid. So was Rachel. You don't care about these things. You don't say anything.'

He said primly, 'I'm quite happy to say things, I just don't feel the need to run the guy out of my house. Throwing things and shouting "Murderer!"'

'You're exaggerating. Why do you take that censorious tone? Because you don't care, or because you're "diplomatic"? Since you're a public figure. Do you think it's corrupting you, all this celebrity? You can't be seen to have opinions any more.'

He said, 'I'm trying to find my wallet. So I can go to work. So I can earn some money.' When he was angry he got quieter, and he smiled. I looked at his smile.

'You're a slave to your image,' I said.

But I'd behaved badly last night, going on arguing. I was being a shrew. 'So, you think he'll be quite annoyed then?'

'I haven't got time to go on and on!' He slammed the door.

'Oh, shit,' I sighed.

We tended to be vehement in my family. My father never backed away from an argument. You could call my mother 'opinionated'. My sister was fiercely political. They were a lot for Scott to deal with. His family were quieter; his father was a retired manager, a reformed alcoholic whose tastes were simple. Having lived through troubled times, he was grateful for a cosy, uneventful life. He and Scott's mother didn't look beyond their routine; they were happy with a DVD of a rubbish blockbuster and an undemanding chat about trivial things. They were proud of Scott, now he was on television. They enjoyed the attention he got. Scott handled the publicity all right. There were a few changes when he switched from radio. He got his hair done at the studio, in a new style. He took more care with his clothes. He was less spontaneous. He thought before he acted.

I walked the kids to kindergarten and school. I said hello to one of the fathers. He was an American. Recently, the preschool children had made flags. Sophie came out with a New Zealand flag. The American boy had made the Stars and Stripes. He said to Sophie, 'My flag's bigger than yours.' His was on a bigger bit of paper. He meant the size. But his father had said, glancing at me, 'Hey, they're all big.' He meant all flags, all countries, were important.

The Iraq war had just started. I didn't like what I thought of as his patronising, world-conqueror's tone. I said, 'Oh, we had one of yours at home. But we've just recently burned it!'

He looked shocked, then let out a single, cynical bark of laughter — 'Ha!' — and walked away, and I laughed and felt oddly melancholy watching him cross the playground, and wished I were a different woman: silent, mysterious, cool.

My father is an architect. He designed our house. We bought it when he and my mother decided to build themselves a new place. It was beautiful. We were lucky, privileged. I thought of it as my fortress. It was built down a hillside, with a walled courtyard at the top to screen out noise from the road. There were three levels, the lowest a big sitting room and kitchen opening onto a garden. Down there, below the road, it was sunny and quiet, the light broken up by mature olive trees. You could see the harbour from the back deck. I had my workroom upstairs, looking over the suburbs, down to the bay. Below and to the right was the deep, cool green space of the neighbours' tennis court, its wire fence overgrown with vines. Women met and played there in the mornings.

When I got back from the school I went to my studio. I'd studied photography at art school, and I had ambitions. I wanted to publish a book of my work, to exhibit. In the meantime I did regular freelance work for magazines and papers. That morning I was going to pick the best from a series of pictures I'd taken of a writer, to go with an interview in a magazine.

The doorbell rang. I ignored it. It rang twice more. I went to the door.

Gerald Francis was walking away from the door. He made a play of 'stopping in his tracks', his expression arch, faintly self-righteous. Telling me he'd known all the time I was inside.

He was a wiry, grey man, aged about fifty. He had intent eyes behind tinted glasses, thin arms and hands all knotted with veins, and one of those beards that grow only around the chin, not on the cheeks. He lived alone in a big peach-coloured bungalow on the other side of our drive. I said hello to him on the street most days. I had the impression of someone heavily, secretly preoccupied. He was always looking beyond, around, checking for data. He noted number-plates of cars that came down the street. He had told me he kept an eye on things. I could be confident that if any burglars were around, he'd be on to them.

I wasn't pleased to see him. I had things to do.

'Hi, Gerald,' I said. I looked at the photograph I was holding in my hand.

'You can shorten it to Gerry.'

He said this mechanically, like something he'd learnt.

'Gerry.'

He was carrying a book. He thought for a moment, turning it over in his hands. He walked inside suddenly, without asking if he could. Taken by surprise, I stood aside, then followed him in. He put the book on the table.

He pointed at it. 'I thought it was time I showed you.'

It was a thick hard-cover journal, bound in dark green, with gold leaf.

He jigged up and down, wringing his sinewy hands.

'There are two of us in the street now,' he said quietly. He ducked to the window and looked out, then veered back to the table.

'Two of us . . .'

'Artists. You and me.'

'Oh.' I stared. 'I'm a photographer.'

'I've seen your work. Mine is in here.' He pointed to the book again.

'Your work.'

He nodded, squeezing his hands together. The veins stood out on his forearms. He swallowed, blinked, swallowed. He couldn't keep still.

'I've put a collection together,' he said.

'I can't really . . .' I protested. 'I haven't got . . .'

He stopped moving. He looked at me.

'Is it . . . are they photographs?' I tried to think of an excuse.

'You'll see.'

'Leave it with me,' I said. 'Leave it here and I'll have a good look at it.' It seemed necessary to say more. 'I'll study it.'

His eyes, behind the tinted glasses, were fixed on me. 'Study it,' he repeated.

I nodded.

He smiled. There were gaps between his teeth. I looked at his wide, thin mouth, the damp lips above the straggly tufts of grey beard. There was something wrong with his smile.

'Study,' he said. 'Collaborate.' He ducked to the window and looked out.

'Right, Gerald. Gerry.'

He jigged from one foot to the other, staring. He said rapidly, 'Your father is a well-known architect, Peter Davis. Your mother owns the furniture store at 4/38 Teed Street. Julie Davis. Your husband is the newsreader, Roysmith. Your sister is an English professor. Rachel. You have two daughters, aged five and three. You hold strong views, politically. What an interesting family.'

A long, curly lock of his hair had come loose. He took hold of it and smoothed it down over his bald head.

I looked at the floor. I said, with effort, 'Actually, Rachel's not a professor. She's a junior lecturer.'

'Ah. Siblings!'

'What do you mean?'

'Ah.'

'What do you mean about political views?'

He looked sly. 'I heard you. Last night. On the deck.'

'Oh, we had a little argument,' I said weakly.

He stepped closer. I could hear the rasp of his skin as he rubbed his dry hands. He looked pious, crafty. 'My own family isn't nearly so interesting. Just ordinary, hard-working people. We've had a few minor successes. In the legal profession . . .'

'I thought you were a photographer,' I said rudely.

The phone rang.

I went towards it. 'I've been waiting for this call; it's important.'

Holding the cordless phone, I managed to waft him towards the door, frowning and nodding as if there was someone important on the line. I thought he was going to stand on the doorstep listening to me talk. I gave him a thumbs-up sign and, nodding, slowly closed the door.

Rachel said, 'Are you there?'

'Wait a minute.'

I ran up to my room and looked out. He was standing by his car, writing in a notebook.

'Sorry. The man from next door . . .'

I told her. She laughed. 'What about last night? Will he ever speak to us again?'

'Probably not.'

'Oh well. Go and have a look at his book.'

I went down and got it. I turned the pages. I was silent, looking at it.

'What's it like?' she asked.

'It's horrible,' I said.

When I was a child I reacted strongly to visual things. I particularly hated clusters. There was a kind of sea-egg that got washed up on the beach: pods with bunched compartments like wasps' nests. I couldn't bear to look at them. I didn't like multiples. Even recently, when the children watched a movie called *Monsters Inc*, I turned away from it, disgusted by the cartoon monsters' multiple eyes.

When I turned the pages of Gerald Francis's book I felt the same kind of revulsion. It was a very odd book he'd put together. There were about a hundred pages, which he'd had printed and elaborately bound. The first section was got up as a family history. There was a text, written by Gerald — odd, disjointed, full of non-sequiturs but more or less understand-able. It started with the first Francis to come from England to New Zealand, and worked its way to the present day. There were photographs of early Francises, and of members of the families they'd married into. The tone was proud. 'Mr Justice Francis, recognised in the profession as an extraordinary intellect, was destined to marry a great beauty, Agnes, eldest daughter of the esteemed Ronald Rowntree, of brewery fame.'

The Francises had made quite a mark. There were three Justice Francises of different generations, also barristers and businessmen. They seemed to have had, as the text tirelessly reiterated, the knack of marrying into families just as wealthy and accomplished as their own.

On the last page of the first section Gerald had allowed space for himself. His biography and photograph were by way of introduction to the second half, which was a presentation of his 'artistic work'. It was the second section that I reacted badly to. It suggested things to me: unwholesomeness, madness.

I read the biography. Gerald Arthur Francis was fifty-one. He was educated at King's School, then Auckland University, where he studied sciences. There was no mention of his having achieved any degree. There was a series of fudging sentences ('world travel', 'commercial ventures') before he turned up 'a partner in his father's shipping business'. He had, 'like many Francises, shown artistic talent from an early age', and, 'having retired from a successful life in the family firm, was able to answer his artistic calling'. There was a full-page black and white photograph of him, intensely smiling, a gleam of moisture on his lip.

I turned to the photographs, which had been professionally reproduced, some in colour and some in black and white. They were accompanied by a text, stranger and more disorganised than that of the first section, in which Gerald detailed his preoccupations. As a boy he had been fascinated by the natural world. Insects were a great craze of his. There followed some arid portraits of unfortunate creatures. A fly on a leaf. A weta with a broken leg, as if he'd mangled it while trying to pose it. A splayed cicada on a white background. He had been, according to his text, a youth with a love of poetry, 'aware of growing feelings for the ladies.' There was a picture of a girl standing by a tree, looking anxious. I wondered, with an uneasy snigger, whether he'd tied her to it. The picture was called *Untamed*. (I rolled my eyes.)

Further on, he'd got more inventive. There were pictures of women's faces, distorted so that they appeared to have more than two eyes. Some had three eyes; some had six. There were bitter titles: *Deception. Trickery*. A stuffed toy sat on a chair in an empty room. (*Loneliness*.) There was a brief attempt at birds, unfocused, blurry, quickly abandoned, perhaps, because he couldn't catch them before photographing them. (*Freedom. Flight*.) The last untitled section was a long burst of walls, rooftops and gardens, the neighbourhood he would see from his own house. I recognised our roof and part of our bathroom skylight. There were some unfocused, neutral shots of women playing tennis on the courts below our house, and then there was a long series of windows.

It was trite, and the text was mad. I didn't know which I disliked more, the manhandled insects or the distorted women's faces. Francis, I learned, had a 'growing reputation', both in New Zealand and overseas. At the end of the book was a page of endorsements. Boyce Drown, a 'well-known figure in the art world', praised the originality of Francis's work. His former art teacher, Mrs Craig Barrymore, was quoted as saying, 'Of all my pupils, Gerald Francis was the one with the spark.' And performance artist and poet Aslan D. Basmac praised 'Gerald Francis's absolute dedication to his craft'.

It was sad; of his distinguished family, he was obviously the non-achiever, the oddball. With his 'book' he sought to include himself in the Francis pantheon, as a great artist.

It was sad but it presented me with a problem: what was I to say when I gave the book back?

'Just chuck it back, say, "Maarvellous", and dash off quick,' Scott said. 'Simple.' He never had a problem with that kind of thing.

'What a nightmare,' Rachel had said, laughing on the phone.

'I said I'd "study" it,' I said. 'Oh, God.'

I put off having to meet him. I walked the girls down the side of the neighbours' tennis court on the way to school, to avoid his house. He would know I was evading him. I kept away from him for two days. Meanwhile the book lay, resplendent in its green and gold binding, on our coffee table.

I was heading for the shortcut when I saw him standing by the wire fence. He was holding a camera. He saw me. I hesitated, but I couldn't turn away now he'd seen me. I hustled the girls on.

I said, 'Hello! I must give you your book.'

The girls looked up, surprised by my tone.

'You've had a chance to . . .'

'It's very interesting,' I said.

He drew me aside, glancing at the girls. He put his head on one side and said, in a sanctimonious whisper, 'We're pretty straightforward, the Francises. Just an ordinary working family. Nothing fancy. Nowhere near as accomplished as your people.' He looked sideways.

'We're not all that wonderful,' I said, edging away.

'Thank you for taking the time . . .' he came closer, '. . . to study my work.'

'It's a pleasure. I'll pop it in your letterbox.'

He came closer still. 'Now that we understand each other . . .'

I knew what he was going to say.

'If you would just put pen to paper. Your thoughts on my work would be greatly appreciated.'

'You mean to stick in the endorsements bit?' I couldn't hide how I felt.

'We artists . . .'

'I'm just a freelance photographer. I take pictures for the *Listener*. My opinion's not important.'

'People know your work. And perhaps your husband might care to . . .'

'We're running late for school.'

I'd exhausted what little cool I had. I pushed the girls ahead. At the end of the path I turned. He was looking after us, lowering his camera, as if he'd just taken a picture of us hurrying away.

I said to Scott, 'He wants you to put a word in too.'

'Well, that's easy. I'll just tell him I've got no eye. I'm the visual equivalent of tone deaf.'

'He's probably listened to you doing arts programmes on the radio.'

'Don't worry about it. Don't complicate things. Just put the book in his box and if he asks for more go all vague.'

The next day I put the book in an envelope and left it in Gerald's letterbox.

It was Saturday. In the afternoon I was trying to free a kite that Sophie and Sarah had got tangled around the struts of the back deck. I had to hang off the deck to get at it. I ripped my fingernail on the nylon, and fell down onto the grass below. The nail was agony.

'Oh, fuck fuck *fuck*.'

Scott leaned out the top window. 'What are you doing?'

'I've broken my bloody *nail*.'

'Jesus!' Scott slammed the window. He was trying to work.

I lay on the grass. I looked up. Gerald was standing on his balcony. He had his camera hung around his neck. He was standing very still.

'There's no need for that kind of language,' he said.

Gerald was sitting in his red hatchback at the top of the drive. I hurried, hoping to get by, but he got out of the car. He had his camera around his neck.

He said, 'Have you seen the crime stats? There were two burglaries in this street last week.' He tapped the camera. 'Any strange cars that stop, I make a note. Any suspicious behaviour. Someone's got to keep an eye out.'

'We're lucky we've got you to do it.' I looked away.

'No one else is going to, are they?'

I didn't say anything.

He came closer. 'I like to help people. Most people don't help others. They can't be bothered.'

'No.'

'I'm not trying to save the world. Not like you and your sister. Goodness me. You've got some big ideas. Quite impressive. I hope I can play a small part. In a quiet way.' He jigged and stared, squeezing his hands together. 'They talk about community. But who cares any more?'

He looked at Sophie and Sarah. 'Where are the *values*?' he said.

I said goodbye. We walked away. I didn't turn around. I wondered whether he was taking our picture. When we were out of earshot I swung the girls' hands and laughed.

Sarah had turned six. We had a birthday party with ten of her friends. It went well, but afterwards she was overwrought. She couldn't find one of her presents and she stood on the deck, screaming that we'd taken it away from her. Sophie was upset too, and set up a wail, then she fell and banged her head on the rail. We managed to soothe them both and get them into bed.

That evening Scott and I sat on the deck drinking wine. We were tired and we ended up having an argument. It blew up out of nothing. I said something negative about his family. He said something bad about mine. I was angry; he marched upstairs shouting at me to 'Fuck off'. I swore back.

The next morning we made it up and peace reigned until I

discovered that Sarah had headlice, which she'd caught at school twice already. We had to go to the chemist for the special shampoo and wash her hair, which made her wail loudly, and comb her with the nit comb, which made her scream.

I sat on the floor with her, soothing her.

'God. It's a war zone,' Scott said. He smiled wearily, holding Sophie in his arms. He kissed the top of her head.

We went to the beach. In a café the woman behind the counter said to Scott, 'Oh, hello!' Then she realised she only knew him from TV. She laughed and blushed. He was charming with her. He shook her hand, and showed off the girls. She praised their beauty and charm.

'Lovely to meet you. Marvellous,' he told her as we left.

It was a beautiful day, and we stayed on the beach most of the afternoon.

When we got back Gerald was sitting in his car, writing in his notebook. Scott waved, but Gerald only stared.

Gerald was bobbing about at the top of the drive. He came towards us. My car was at the garage. I was going to take Sophie to the doctor in Scott's car, then pick Sarah up from school. I saw him point his camera.

I was struggling to carry Sophie and my bag and some gear of Sarah's. 'Hello,' I said.

He smiled. He hunched his shoulders. He looked as though he was bursting with a delicious secret.

'Have you just taken my picture?' I sounded more aggressive than I'd intended. I was harassed. Sophie was feverish. She started to cry. She'd been throwing up all morning.

He said, mechanically, 'Do you think the police come?'

'What?'

'If there's a burglary . . . They don't come. Someone has to collect the evidence.'

'Why is a picture of me evidence?'

He rocked with a sudden funny little laugh. 'Oh ho. You think people want to photograph you. Because your family's so interesting.'

I felt ridiculous. 'Did you take my picture or not?'

He looked beyond me. His expression changed. He began waving, robotically, like a man on the tarmac directing a plane. A council car stopped at the kerb. Behind it, a tow-truck pulled in and parked.

Scott's car was where he'd left it the night before, parked crooked and partly blocking the drive, although there was room to come in and out. A company driver had picked him up that morning.

Gerald frowned. He assumed an official, severe tone. 'This is the vehicle,' he said to the warden. He pointed at Scott's car. At the warden's signal the towie got out and began to fiddle with the car window.

I hitched Sophie up on my hip and lumbered over. 'That's my car. What are you doing?'

'It's an illegal park,' the warden said.

I rounded on Gerald. 'Did you ring them? Why?'

'Take your medication,' he said, looking slyly up at the sky.

'I'll move the car.'

The warden nodded and gestured at the towie, who got back in his truck and drove away.

'I'll still have to write a ticket.'

'But I'm going to move it!'

'It's out of my hands,' the warden said. 'The offence has been committed.'

I went on arguing. Behind me, Gerald said, 'Take your medication.'

I turned to him.

'Why are you doing this?'

'Take your medication,' he repeated. He rocked on his heels. He wouldn't look at me. He stared, enthralled, at the warden.

The warden handed me the ticket. I dragged Sophie into the car. She was wailing. I drove away fast, screeching the wheels.

I rang Scott. He said, 'The man's unbalanced. We'll have to be diplomatic. Don't take him on.'

'I haven't *taken him on*. I haven't done anything to him.'

'Let's just try to keep the heat out of things,' he said carefully.

'I'm trying to deal with him. I'm not creating the problem.'

'I'm sure we can approach it all in a rational way.'

'Are you suggesting I'm not rational?'

We argued. I thought he was making out it was my fault.

It's a war zone, Scott said. Families: how they reverberate with crashes and screams. I was in a café, drinking coffee and thinking about the last few weeks. Sophie had been sick again. Sarah came home with another infestation of nits. Sophie recovered; Sarah got sick. They both cried in the night and needed to be soothed. Sophie insisted on coming into our bed. She screamed and kicked when I tried to give her her antibiotic. They fought with each other, and broke things. Scott was overworked, yet got up every night to one or other child. The lights were always on in our kitchen as we scurried to and fro, like ghosts . . .

My cellphone rang. A woman said, 'Ms Davis? My name is Mary Michaels. I'm a social worker. I have to inform you there has been a notification about your children.'

According to Gerald's complaint, the children were 'running wild'. They 'weren't provided with guidance or restraint'. He was concerned about the 'values' they were being taught. The household was a bedlam of 'swearing and noise'. The parents could be heard making 'frequent threats of violence'. The children were often 'locked in their rooms, pleading for release'. The mother was an 'abusive control freak'. Although he couldn't confirm it, he believed she was 'on medication'.

We talked through the night while the children were asleep. We went over it again and again.

'You could go and talk to him,' I said.

'That might make it worse.'

'We're just helpless, then.' I was knotted up with rage. 'I'll go and talk to him.'

'No!'

'Well, what then?'

Scott rolled over. 'He's mad. They'll realise it. They'll do what they do, and then it will be over. We have to keep calm.'

I paced around the room. 'I am calm.'

I woke in the night wondering what was wrong. I remembered. I lay awake for a long time, then I slept and my dreams were edged with anxiety, with the fear that no one would listen or believe. Where there's smoke there's fire, people say. Mud sticks. And what about Scott's career?

The social workers were coming to the house. We waited. I had tidied. Then untidied. Too much neatness, I thought, might signify a 'control freak'.

I smoothed the children's hair. Scott squeezed my arm. 'Ready?' he said. 'Remember. Act natural!'

They were knocking on the door. I laughed nervously. My throat closed over.

There were two of them, the woman who had rung me, and a man. The children sat demurely on the floor, playing with Lego. I put Sarah's school report on the table.

'Oh, we've rung the school and kindergarten,' Mary Michaels said.

'You've *told* them?'

'They both said your children were delightful. Intelligent. Happy. Well behaved. In fact, they couldn't believe I was ringing.'

We both started talking at once. 'Well, of course. Gerald is mad. Seriously mad. None of what he says is true . . .'

The man said, 'We hear all kinds of stories. From all sides.'

Scott said, 'We are absolutely furious. We have instructed a lawyer. We intend to sue him. And we want you to prosecute him for making a false complaint.'

The man held up one hand. 'We have a procedure to follow.'

'You can see this is a malicious complaint.'

'We get told all kinds of things.'

There was a silence.

The man leafed through a file. 'We're running police and domestic violence checks. I assume we won't find anything there?'

'Jesus. Of course not!'

I rushed in, 'You should investigate *him*. He had a book of photos. He wanted me to write an endorsement in it. He patrols the neighbourhood looking for burglars. He . . .'

The man held his hand up again. 'Our brief is to check on the welfare of the children. Not the adults' quarrels.'

'But the background's important, surely. The reason for the complaint.'

'We hear all sorts of things.'

'Well, do you listen to them?'

'We certainly do.' He gave me a long, pointed look.

Scott put his hand on my arm.

Mary Michaels said brightly to Scott, 'Sarah's school report is certainly excellent.'

She had told me that once a notification was made, it could never be erased. I thought about this. We were 'on file'. All our middle-class conscientiousness — the ban on smacking, the minute control of diet and environment, the finger painting and nature walks and birthday parties, all our slavish, adoring love of our little girls had ended up here, in interrogation, humiliating inspection, a social worker saying 'violence' and 'police' and making notes on a file that would be kept forever.

'The children are our whole life,' I said stupidly.

Mary Michaels nodded, smiled.

The man said heavily, 'When the grown-ups make complaints about each other, it's the children in need who suffer.'

There was another silence.

'He's the one who's made the complaint,' Scott pointed out.

The man looked aggrieved. 'When I have to sort out between warring mums and dads, and find out who's telling the truth, it takes me away from my real job. Caring for the kids.'

Scott sat forward impatiently. '*We'd* rather not be here. *He's* got us here, by making a false complaint. Once you're satisfied about the children, I want you to prosecute him.'

'We'll look into that,' the man said. 'Among other things.'

Mary Michaels said, soothing, 'We'll speak to our manager. We can issue a warning to people who make false complaints.'

The man said, 'You'll appreciate, we can't assume someone's a certain kind of person just because they've got a certain kind of job.' He looked meaningly at Mary Michaels. He was accusing her of sucking up to Scott. He wasn't going to be told what to do. The woman was freer, more flexible. But she was junior to him.

I said to her, 'You talked to Gerald. I bet you could tell there's something wrong with him.'

'You should stay away from him,' she said. 'Don't be tempted to get into an argument. It may be what he wants.'

'We have a job to do,' the man broke in.

He picked up Sarah's school report. He put on a pair of glasses. Sophie stood up, bored. She leaned on me and grumbled and I quietened her.

The man said, 'It's a good report.'

'And the social bits,' I said. 'Happy, friendly, co-operative.'

The man looked over his glasses at the kids. His tone softened. 'We have a full schedule. A lot of people to see . . .'

'Is that it?' I'd expected more. Some interrogation of the children.

'I think we're finished,' the man said.

We stood up. We shook hands all round.

'Thank you for your time. We'll be in touch,' they said, as if we'd just tried to sell them something.

I rang Rachel. I told her everything. 'Can you believe it?' I said.

'What a creep,' she said. She sounded subdued. I could sense her shying away. She'd always been hypersensitive. She didn't like ugliness, unpleasantness. It made me go on and on, trying to win her over. In the end she said she had to go, she had work to do. I was depressed afterwards. I thought about the taint Gerald had put on us.

'Are you going to tell your parents?' I asked Scott.

He hesitated.

'Surely you're going to tell them?' I'd told mine. They were sympathetic, horrified.

'Why aren't you going to?' I pressed him.

'It doesn't matter, does it?'

'You think they won't believe us?' I knew I should leave it but I couldn't. I was angry. His parents suddenly seemed stupid to me. Hostile simpletons. The sort of people who would go on about 'values' while letting themselves off all kinds of crimes.

'I don't want to hear any crap about my family,' Scott said. He walked away.

We went to a lawyer, who drew up defamation papers. As soon as our documents were served on him, Gerald rang the law firm to find out if they were genuine. He must have thought we were playing a trick on him, the kind of trick he'd played on us.

Two weeks later a letter came from the social workers. The case had been investigated. No problems were found and no action would be taken. The department wished us well. The enquiry would be closed.

But the file remained. It could never be erased.

Scott came home. I showed him the letter.

He said, 'They won't prosecute Gerald. They say people have to feel free to notify.'

'They think we're throwing our weight around. They're not going to be dictated to.'

He said, 'We have to keep calm about it, remember.'

'That mad bastard,' I said.

'Don't talk like that. We have to be rational.'

'I am bloody rational.'

'And don't swear. That's what got us into trouble in the first place.'

'*What*? You swear all the time. *He* got us into trouble. Because he's mad.'

'We don't want anyone knowing about this. What'll he do next — go to the media? Do you realise what he could do to us? Don't provoke him.'

'Why would I provoke him?'

'Because you're fiery.'

'What's that supposed to mean? I have never provoked him.'

'Shut up!'

He walked away, pressing his hands to his eyes.

I was in my room, working. Scott rang, excited.

'Gerald went to a lawyer. He's signed an apology, in exchange for us not suing him. Saying he shouldn't have made a notification.'

I leaned my forehead against the doorframe. 'Oh, that's wonderful. Brilliant.'

'We can get it put on the file,' he said.

The file that lasts *forever*. I looked over at Gerald's house. 'One day he's going to pay.'

'We'll just keep away from him,' Scott said. 'We will *not* get carried away.'

'Let's go out to dinner.'

'Good idea. Oh no, I can't. I've got the banquet.'

'Oh yes. Well. It's good news. I'll see you. In the morning, I suppose.'

I picked up the girls and took them to swimming. We bought pizza on the way home. I was so pleased about Gerald's apology that I let them have all kinds of treats. We had a festive little dinner.

'Where's Daddy?' they clamoured.

'At a do. A fancy banquet for work.'

I read to them and put them to bed. I opened the window and looked out at the rainy dark. I went around the house locking up. Through the trees I saw Gerald pass his kitchen window. I went to bed. The rain was getting heavier; it drummed on the roof, overflowing the guttering and spouting into the garden.

I got up. It was 3 a.m. I walked through the rooms. The house was dark and cool. I watched the silvery water coursing down the glass in the sitting room, the liquid shadows streaming down the walls. I looked out at the street. A taxi was driving away.

Scott was standing in the rain, wearing his black and white dinner suit. He tilted his face to the heavy downpour, swaying a bit on his feet. He wiped the drops from his face, loosened his black bow tie. He turned.

He took hold of Gerald's wooden letterbox, wrenching and ripping it back and forth until its pole came out of the ground. He put his whole body into it. He held it high and smashed it on the road. He kept smashing it until it broke into pieces. He threw the pieces over the hedge. He spat on the road.

He leaned one hand against the lamppost. Rain streamed down through the light. He stood there, as if lost in thought.

I went back to bed. He came in quietly and sat down on the side of the bed.

I rolled over. 'How was it?'

'Just the usual. Long speeches. Not too bad.'

'Anything interesting?'

'No.'

I ran my hand over his back. 'How did you get so wet?'

'I walked some of the way. I was thinking.'

'About Gerald?'

'No. Not about him.'

He took his clothes off and got into bed. He put his arms around me. We lay in the dark, listening to the rain.

free will

We were on to the second course when the light changed in the room. Two long shafts of gold fell across the floor and the room was lit up; the bleached faces along the table looked exhausted already. Sandy's cheeks were dry, perspiration beading her upper lip; Dave was red-eyed, his face creased in a foolish smile. George had surrendered to a blank moment and was gazing out at the milky skin of the sea, the container ships out there with their toy colours, the gulls lined along the rusty railing. There had been a sudden shower; now the sun appeared like a white disc, slicing through the cloud. George sighed and gathered himself, and turned to Miranda. I saw him brace himself against her bright scrutiny, the amused malice of her gaze. She was intelligent; cleverness expressed itself in her tiny eyes, in her sensual, brutal mouth. Such fools she made of us.

Before lunch George had given the usual reminders. Miranda is an important client. She must be shown a good time. Miranda can give us work — more work than you could ever imagine. She is courted by many firms. The competition is fierce. She must be wined and dined, until dawn if necessary. Calls had been made to spouses. Belts loosened. The afternoon, the evening, had been written off. Lunch with Miranda: you never knew when you'd get home.

No one could match her stamina. She and her deputy, Mark Venn, dined out on law firms, and always they drank the lawyers under the table. They watched, with spiteful amusement, as lawyers crashed and burned, trying to show them a good time. Midnight would find Miranda Hill sipping a cocktail, upright and smiling, amid the human wreckage of the group who had treated her to lunch. Lunch would have turned into dinner, dinner into cocktails, and finally the last ones standing would escort Ms Hill to some exclusive bar, where she and Venn would gossip languidly — usually on the subject of bungling lawyers — before stepping over the bodies of their hosts and strolling off to a cab. The next day, on receiving the shame-faced, hungover phone call — its gruesome jokes, its wincing joviality: 'So, feel like throwing a bit of something our way?' — Ms Hill might release one small snippet of work. Or not. It depended on whether you'd shown her a good time. If not, the following evening, she might let slip the odd detail of last night's 'debacle', her new companions writhing with sycophantic mirth over their rivals' embarrassing collapse.

That's business.

She was looking at me. George had seated me opposite her: she was said to like young men. There was a crease between her plump arm and her fleshy hand, as if a string had been tied tight around her wrist. Her eyes were deep-set. Beneath the mask of round cheeks, long lashes and the frame of glossy brown curls, her real nature — hard, alert and vigilant — was watching. I smiled vaguely and looked beyond her to the sea, so calm that it gave off an oily glow. A seagull turned against the bright sky, the reflection of the water rippled on the wall. There was the creak of ropes, of boats shifting against the wharf. Miranda broke the leg of her crayfish with a tiny crack and sucked out the flesh. The music CD had stuck, a tune had begun to repeat itself, now there was an unnatural hush as the waiters rushed to change it. Sandy laughed out loud and covered her mouth. Mark and Miranda exchanged a look over her head. I had not drunk much wine but already it was too much; I felt dazed in the heat and the bright light, at one remove from the company. This would not do: I had to last the distance. I looked around for the carafe of water, and resolved to drink no more. Miranda reached across and filled my wine glass.

'Cheers,' she said.

'Cheers,' I replied, and obediently drank, and looked at the golden bars of light lying across the table near us. Miranda and Mark had arrived an hour late. The afternoon shadows were lengthening on the wharf. Already the lunch crowd was emptying out.

George clapped his hands and began an anecdote. He wasn't naturally jolly. I heard the strain in his voice. He was a tall, thin, mournful man, diligent, polite, often ridiculed for his awkwardness. Miranda watched him perform, unsmiling, cracking the legs of her crayfish. The waiters put on a fresh CD, and George was obliged to talk over music that was hectic, too loud.

He finished his story. He gave a pained flourish with his big hands. Miranda and Mark looked not at him, but at each other. The waiter was sent for more wine.

I excused myself. In the gents I splashed water on my face. My phone rang in my pocket. Its screen registered three missed calls. I answered.

My secretary Cheryl said, 'Hi, Sean. How's it going?'

'Yeah, good,' I said, leaning there, against the wall.

'I've got a woman here wanting to see you. I told her you're busy. She says she'll wait.'

'Who is she?'

'She's not a client. She's . . .' There was a pause.

'She's . . . ?'

'She says she's a *friend*.'

'Name?'

'Frances Leigh?'

'Don't know her.'

'Well, she's plonked herself in reception. She's . . .'

'She's *what*?'

There was something Cheryl wanted to say. 'She's . . .'

'Tell her to ring me tomorrow.'

'She won't go away. She's . . .'

'Put her on,' I said, irritated.

A voice came on the line, husky, calm. 'Hello? It's Frances. I used to work at Penn's.'

'Oh. Hi.' (You? Why?)

'I need to see you now.'

I wondered whether it was a prank dreamed up by Miranda Hill and Mark Venn, a trick they played on junior solicitors, that they would hoot over at future dinners.

Confusion. I stammered. 'Now? Why?'

I pictured her. Frances. Dark hair, nice figure. Efficient behind the bar, easy with the punters, wide smile, good teeth. The barmaid at Penn's.

'We have something to discuss,' she said.

'Look, I'm at lunch with clients.'

'You remember that night?'

I closed my eyes. That night at Penn's. Six months, a year ago? We'd been talking over the bar while she worked. Midnight, I the only customer left and she invited me out the back. There was a tiny flat upstairs, a studio. It was raining hard. We sat on a balcony, the rain ran off the veranda roof in streams, she said she didn't live here but stayed the night sometimes, we drank vodka and there was a dartboard on the back of the door. Late in the night I spilled a glass of vodka, felt it running down my chest as cold as rain. We played darts; we slept together on a futon on the floor. And I woke the next morning at dawn and ran away home . . .

I hadn't seen her since. She didn't work at Penn's any more. She rang once but I put her off. I had to keep it a secret from my girlfriend at the time, Jane.

'Frances,' I said. 'I can't see you now, I'm working.'

'Where are you?'

'I'm at the Waterfront Café. Busy. I'll ring you tomorrow.'

'I'm coming down,' she said.

'No, no, I'm working!'

'Be outside in ten minutes or I'll come in.'

I went back to the table, sweating. I picked up a glass and drank down some wine, felt my stomach cringe, the soft blow to my brain. George was looking at me. He'd hoped I would be good with Miranda. *Why did I tell Frances where I was?* Stupidity. Would she make a scene? Was she the kind of woman to make a scene? I would have to go outside in ten minutes, to head her off. I would pretend I wanted to smoke.

Miranda put her head back and laughed. Even her teeth looked plump, glistening there in the soft, cushiony mouth. Her cheeks were flushed. Only her eyes were hard: tiny black chips of rock.

I drained my glass. Miranda said, 'Do you like working with George?' Mark Venn focused his attention on me.

'George? George is great.'

George looked down at the table, faintly smiling.

Miranda and Mark glanced at each other.

I said, 'George has worked all over the world. London, New York. He's the man.' I looked out at the street.

Mark sat back, neutral. Miranda picked her teeth. The idea was to get me drunk, to see whether I would come out with some dreadful indiscretion that they could store away for future reference.

I checked my watch; ten minutes had passed. I considered sitting it out: surely Frances wouldn't dare walk in on a business lunch. I would be safe here, biding my time, trying not to drink too much. I wanted to help George, to protect him.

Miranda was saying something about wine. I looked beyond her and saw Frances's face in the reflection of the window: she was pushing open the glass door. She came in, shaking rain off herself, said something to a waiter and stood behind the bar, searching, her expression fixed. Miranda saw me looking. She turned. The waiter surged forward reflexively and took her empty plate.

I said, 'Can you excuse me for a minute, Miranda.'

'Again?' She smiled, not nicely.

'I won't be a second.'

As I disengaged myself from the seat, accidentally tugging the tablecloth, a knife clattered to the floor and I caught George's look of dismay, the faintest hint of reproach. I turned away.

Frances was holding an umbrella. Her hair was wet. She was wearing tight black clothes with a denim jacket over the top. Her expression was determined. I realised what my secretary had not been able to bring herself to say.

I looked back at the table. Sandy was standing, red-faced, acting out some story. There was a wave of loud guffawing.

I took Frances by the arm and hustled her to the stairs.

'We'll go up here,' I said.

She walked ahead of me. Numbly I watched her negotiate the stairs; she took each step with an effortful swivel of the hips, using the umbrella as a walking stick, stabbing it loudly on the wooden steps. I pushed her ahead into the empty upstairs bar. A kind of blurred panic had taken over; I wanted, urgently, to get to the point of what it was she wanted so I could hurry back downstairs, get away.

We sat down facing each other. I ordered a glass of wine. She asked for an iced water.

'We've got clients downstairs. I'll have to be quick.'

She seemed, once seated, to sink into a torpor. She gazed, blinking, at the harbour. Seagulls squawked along the balcony rail.

'So, when's it due?' I blurted.

She smiled, patted the swollen bulge of her stomach. 'Tonight,' she said.

'*Tonight?*'

She laughed.

I was angry. 'Look, Frances. I can't stay. I'm working. What do you want?'

'I need your help,' she said. I stared. The waiter put a glass in front of me and I picked it up and drank deeply, steeling myself against her, gathering my nerves.

'I'm having the baby tonight.'

'But how can you know that — don't you have to wait for it to . . . come on?' I couldn't hide my irritation.

She laid a hand on my arm. She spoke slowly, like a nurse soothing some frail hysteric. 'It's going to be induced. It's overdue. The doctor is going to bring it on. I go into the hospital tonight and he'll give me drugs to start the labour. I've hired myself an obstetrician. I borrowed the money . . .'

I took a breath. Asking: it was like jumping off the high diving board, the moment when you wished you hadn't made the leap, the plunge, the awful shock of impact . . . 'What's it got to do with me?'

'It's your baby,' she said.

I set down my glass with a crack. 'Oh no. No.'

She sat back, her hands resting on the tight bulge.

'From that *one night*?'

'Yes.'

'Oh, Christ. It's not possible. No.'

'I need your help,' she said again. 'A friend was going to come to the labour with me. She can't come. She's stuck in Wellington. And that leaves you.'

I closed my eyes. It was a dream. In a moment it would unravel and splinter and I would wake and blink and the dreadful weight would lift.

'It should be you at the birth,' she said. 'I mean, he is your baby.' She smoothed her shirt with a competent, blunt little hand.

'How do you know that? Why should I believe you?'

'Well, you can have a test done.'

I leaned my elbows on the table, hands on my temples. 'But to spring it on me now. To not tell me, not warn me. Not consult me. This is outrageous.' I rose.

'I'm sorry. I know I've gone about it all wrong. Please sit down.' She was flushed, pleading, plucking my sleeve. There were patches of sweat on her forehead. Her breathing was harsh. 'I was going to do it all on my own. I did ring you after that night but you weren't interested. I got the impression you had someone else. And I didn't have the heart to get rid of it.'

I sat, laughed. 'Oh, this is unbelievable. We've got clients sitting downstairs and here I am . . . this is too much.' I drained my glass, wiped my hands nervously on my jacket. 'You can't do this,' I said. 'You can't do this to a person. It's *not right.*'

She looked down. The parting in her hair was crooked. Her neck and shoulders were thinner, more delicate than I remembered, as if the outrageously jutting bulge in her midriff had consumed all her energy.

'I'm sorry,' she said. 'I wanted to have someone with me. I've got to be there at seven tonight. National Women's Hospital. It is a weird thought, isn't it, you turn up and they . . .'

I stood up. 'No, *I'm* sorry. I can't . . . do this. Do you want me to get you a cab?'

She looked down. She sighed and shivered, pushing the glass of iced water away. 'Yes.' She gathered up her umbrella and her bag and stood looking desolately out at the sea.

I told the barman to order a taxi. I walked her downstairs. At the door I took hold of her upper arm, pretending to steady her; I was afraid she would run into the restaurant and screamingly denounce me. She was silent. The rain had come on again, falling thick through the laden afternoon air. She stood under her umbrella smiling at the ground. I felt the delicate chill of the rain on my scalp and remembered how I'd spilled that glass of vodka, how it had streamed cold down my chest inside my shirt, and she'd laughed and said, 'Smooth,' and I'd said, 'Clumsy hands.' And she'd told me about a philosophy paper she'd done where they'd discussed a kind of madness called 'alien hand', where people think they can't control their own hand. 'Their hand attacks them!' she said. 'It lies in wait and then boom, it's around their neck!' We played darts. Drunk, clowning around, I pretended to be attacked by my own hand. Outside, the cyclone beat against the windows.

Rain streaming down the glass, rain on the harbour, on the winter sea . . .

'Wish me luck,' she said.

I slammed the taxi door.

She was a student. Arts, a BA. She was paying for her studies working in bars. She lived in a flat somewhere; also she'd said she came from Wellington . . .

I sat down facing Miranda. I was light-headed. My glass was empty again. Sandy hiccupped, giggled. She was making up for my failure with Miranda; she was being the life and soul.

'No. No. You told it wrong,' she was insisting. She got up — why did she find it necessary to stand, as if we were in a classroom? — and began some idiotic joke. She twined her fingers, acting something out. George was waving the menu and calling, with grotesque jollity, for dessert wine. Formality was breaking down; the rot was setting in. Miranda swapped seats. Now Mark Venn was studying me with his calculating eyes. Frances: had she called the baby a 'he'? Sudden misery. I shifted in my seat; the image of Frances was like a fly that I shook off, only to find it settling again, the exquisite pressure of it tickling my flaring nerves. I was hot. I fidgeted, couldn't keep still.

'How's it going?' The quiet Venn was tall, hard-faced, athletic, his dark hair slicked back off his forehead. There was something sly and knowing, almost intimate in the way he was looking at me. He sipped his coffee with a little finger coyly crooked. He was said to have an interest in — what was it, interior decorating? Furniture? George had said to me, 'Talk about his interests.'

'Still into antiques?' I said.

He launched immediately: bargains, the way to spot a fake, traps for the unwary. I bided my time; I was drinking now to cure the thrills of adrenalin that were running through me; I was trying to separate myself from my nerves. I was still afraid that Frances would come back. Every few seconds I glanced beyond Mark to the street door, expecting to see her drenched, outraged, avenging figure. Was it guilt I felt? But how could I be guilty, when I had done nothing, *nothing* wrong? I experienced a moment when something definitely loosened in me; I let go and drifted outwards — in other words, I was drunk. Mark and I sighed and grimaced at each other, and he said with sudden candour, flicking his eyes over at Miranda, 'She's only just got started, mate. She's on for a big night.'

On one side George, 'roaring with laughter', on the other Sandy covering her mouth with a look of fright, like a child about to be sick. Miranda lolled sleekly between them, cocktail in hand. Dave's hair was sticking up, his tie was loose. Miranda was taking an interest in him now. She picked a crumb off her jacket and eyed him, her head on one side. Out in the harbour a single ray of light lit up a patch of water. I could see birds wheeling above it, and a small boat making its way towards the wharf, trailing its foamy wake.

How could life begin so haphazardly; how could it depend on something so fleeting as spilled vodka, random talk, darts, the rain? 'It's too late to go now,' she'd said. 'If you go home now you'll drown,' and I pulled her against my sodden chest, and the wind crashed the open door against the veranda wall and a sign was blowing down the empty street, tumbling over and over. We slept with the door open. At dawn the rain was still coming down, and when I walked home in the early morning the street was strewn with wet leaves, sticks, paper, broken umbrellas. Strange night: I slept much of the next day, woke in the late afternoon and lay thinking about her. Strange, intense girl, sitting on the edge of the futon, a dart in her hand, drunk but lucid, telling me about 'alien hands' . . . 'Okay. Concentrate! More vodka? It goes like this: If you have alien hand syndrome, the part of the brain that gives the sensation of control over the hand is damaged. You think the hand is controlling itself. You never know when it'll go for you. Now. It's known that the electrical charges that precede all limb movements occur *before* you consciously decide to move your limb. So your "decision" to move your hand, your "free will", is actually an illusion. Your choice has already been made before, by your brain. People with this syndrome have lost the illusion of free will. So they're closer to the reality of how much we're responsible for our actions than the rest of us!'

George was standing over me. 'We're off,' he said, resolute, and named the pricey tapas bar Miranda had chosen. He helped her with her coat. Sandy swayed against Mark's arm, Dave sighed and stifled a burp.

Miranda stood under the roof talking on her phone. Serenely she turned her barrel-shaped calf this way and that, inspecting her witchy shoe. George danced out into the rain, opened the cab door for her and waited while she got in. She was still on the phone, not looking at him. He closed the door with an anxious nod.

In the cab she snapped her phone shut and said, 'That was Simon Grey from Billington Watts. He's in the bar at Mollie's.'

George winced. 'It's far more fun where we're going. Eh, Dave? Sandy?'

'Simon Grey's so boring,' Sandy said in a high voice.

'Oh, I don't know,' Miranda said languidly. 'Remember that night with Simon, Mark?'

'How could I forget?' Mark said.

'You know he had that . . . thing with the Law Society. What a mess.' George glanced at me. Two humiliated red spots had appeared on his cheeks. Normally he would never stoop to this: slander, currying favour.

'Yes, but he gives wonderful parties,' Miranda said sweetly.

There was a silence. George screwed up a receipt and threw it on the floor of the cab.

I turned on her. I'd had enough. 'Are you coming with us or do you want another cab?'

George jerked his head up. 'Well, it's up to Miranda, of course . . .'

Miranda gave me a long, amused look.

'Let's forget Simon Grey,' she said finally.

Mark laughed. His hard thigh pressed against mine.

We rode in silence through the rainy night. George threw some money at the driver, leapt out and rushed around to help Miranda out. She allowed herself to be led down into the hot, crowded subterranean bar. She sat sipping an elaborate drink, bending her head to George, who was talking non-stop in her ear. Mark popped tapas into his mouth and listened to Sandy, who seemed to want to climb into his lap. George paused and gave me a bleak, relieved smile. Dave was talking about cars; I pretended to listen. Someone handed me a glass of wine. I drank it, caring not. I drank another. There was a disturbance up at the bar, some pushing and shoving. A bouncer arrived. On a TV above the bar, Scott Roysmith was soundlessly reading the news. I had been drinking since one o'clock.

I was on my feet. I put my hand on George's shoulder.

'I'll be back, mate,' I slurred.

'Where are you off to?' Miranda's shiny little black eyes fastened on me. I leaned down.

'It's a secret,' I said in her ear.

She laughed. George smiled uncertainly, made apologetic shrugs. I kept my eyes on Miranda as I backed away. She didn't drop her gaze until I turned and pushed my way out into the street.

I got to a cab. 'National Women's,' I said.

'Where?'

I said it again. He got the idea. Grumbling, he started off. I got him to stop on the way. I came out with cans of beer in a plastic shopping bag and a meat pie, which I ate, to his disgust, in the back of the cab.

He let me off outside the main building. I strode into the foyer. At the information booth I couldn't think of the right word. 'Where women have babies,' I finally said. Directed to Maternity I waited for the lift with an aged couple who shot doubtful glances at me and moved closer together. I rode up to Maternity and stood, getting my bearings, in the hall. A woman in a pink tracksuit walked out of a room. She asked me who I wanted.

'Frances,' I said. There was a long pause. Her eyes travelled down to my plastic shopping bag.

'Frances . . . Leigh.' I came out with it, triumphant.

Casting backward glances, she led me along a corridor. 'Wait here,' she said. There was a brief conversation. She came out. 'You can go in,' she said. She gave me a severe look and retreated not very far along the hall.

Frances was sitting on the bed wearing a hospital gown. She stood up awkwardly. The gown made the bulge in her front look even bigger.

I stood there, holding the shopping bag. I gestured at her stomach. 'You'll be glad to get it out,' I said.

She grinned. 'It's huge, isn't it?' Then she put her hand over her mouth. 'You came.'

'Course.' I set the bag down with a crash. 'It was touch and go, actually. What with the client lunch and all.' I had no idea what I was going to say next.

She went on grinning. She smoothed the front of her gown.

'Want to sit down?' she said.

'Yeah, actually. Thanks.' I fell onto the bed. She poured me a paper cup of water out of a plastic jug.

The woman in the pink tracksuit marched in. 'Doctor's here,' she said.

The doctor was tall, with thick black hair and a mild, shy expression. He was dressed in jeans and a jersey that had three woolly sheep embroidered on the chest.

I stood up, reeled, righted myself. I leaned against the high bed. He held out his hand.

'Simon Lampton,' he said.

His handshake, like his outfit, was gentle, non-threatening. Big softie, I thought. Woolly sheep. All rigged up not to scare the ladies.

He spoke soothingly. 'How are you, Frances? Good. Now, we're just going to insert the pessary, and that should get us under way. Labour probably won't get started until later. Tomorrow morning, even. So you can both try to get a good night's sleep.' He glanced at me, as if to say, and *you* need it.

'Bottom half off,' rapped the midwife.

Embarrassed, Frances wriggled about under the gown. She screwed her underpants into a ball. The midwife took them and handed them to me.

'Thanks!' I said.

Doctor and midwife exchanged a look. 'Here we go,' he said. He put on surgical gloves, took a small, bullet-shaped object from a packet and reached between Frances's legs. She shrank back. He murmured something, pursed his lips, looked up at the ceiling. Then he nodded, snapped off the glove and straightened up. 'All done.'

We looked at him blankly.

'I'll be back when you get started. In the meantime, get some sleep.'

He left. The midwife stood over us. 'Right. You can both go to bed. There's a mattress for you in the cupboard,' she said to me.

I got it out, dropped it on the floor and fell on top of it. Frances laughed. The midwife made a tsking sound. She said to Frances, 'Any trouble, ring the buzzer.' She went out, giving me a glare.

We lay down. The room was full of striped shadows. There were conversations, footsteps in the corridor outside. I heard her turning over, sighing. I drifted off, then woke. I wondered how much time had gone by. Minutes? Hours? As quietly as I could, I reached for my bag and eased out a can. The ring-pull gave the tiniest scrape. There was a long hiss.

She sat up. 'Are you opening a beer?'

I kept quiet. She coughed.

'Feel anything yet?' I said.

She poked her head over the side of the bed. 'I can't feel anything. It's not meant to start until morning. I can't sleep.'

'Me neither.'

'Shall we go out?'

'Out? Where?'

'Down the shop. Get some magazines.'

'Okay.' I was willing. I got up, sipping the beer. She was pulling on a top and a pair of jeans.

'Come on.' She went to the door and looked out. I hid the can under my jacket and we went to the lifts. 'Might bring it on, going for a walk,' she said, frowning, sensible.

I half expected to be challenged in the foyer, but no one seemed to notice me strolling out with one of the inmates. There were other pregnant women about, a group of them smoking outside, each in similar pose: one hand massaging the small of the back, the other holding the fag.

'Smoking when they're pregnant! I don't know. What's the world . . .'

Frances smiled and said, 'Shh.'

I hitched my shopping bag over my shoulder. There was a fine, drifting mist of rain. We walked slowly, close together. The night seemed to have gone on forever; it was an age since I'd talked antiques with Mark Venn. And yet the weariness and confusion I'd felt in the taxi had left me; I was braced by the last beer — by braced I suppose I mean freshly drunk. I held on to my bag of beers — I clutched it very tight. I dreaded the morning so, that I felt a swooning sort of love for the night: the rainy air, the spotlit gardens, the black shadows across the pavements. Walking on the quiet street, in the velvety dark, the wind sighing in the trees, it was possible to forget so many things . . .

We got to the main road. There wasn't much traffic but there was a roar that got louder and, as we waited at the intersection, a procession came slowly into view: jeeps emblazoned with warning signs, then an enormous truck lit up with revolving orange lights and, improbably, mounted on the back of the truck, a whole wooden bungalow. We watched it sail past, towards the south. Then we crossed to the petrol station.

Frances browsed along the shelves. She chose a couple of magazines. I bought two pies and a packet of crisps. The man behind the counter said, 'When's the baby due?'

'Tonight,' she said. She slapped a packet of mints on the counter.

He nodded, neutral.

On the way out we confronted the full-length reflection of ourselves — I in my wrinkled suit, loosened tie and crooked collar; she with her strangely distorted form, her back unnaturally swayed, walking her awkward waddle.

I carried the supplies. I offered her a pie. She shook her head. She'd gone silent. Back in the dark street that led to the main gate she wanted to rest on a wall. I opened a beer.

'Feel anything yet?'

'I'm not sure.'

There was something in her tone. I gathered up the bags. 'We'd better go back.'

I finished the beer in the foyer. As soon as we got out of the lift the woman in pink sprang out. 'Where have you been?' She sniffed. 'The *pub*?'

Frances said, 'Something's happening.'

'Already?' The woman bent over her, with a scandalised look at me.

'Feel how hard it is.' Frances put her hands on her stomach. Her face crumpled.

'Right. Let's get you back in the room. *You*,' she pointed at me, 'get in there and behave. And no drinking!'

I sat on the end of the bed. The midwife came in wheeling a contraption — a gas canister on wheels. There was a tube, and a mask connected to it.

'You're having strong contractions. Breathe into this,' she told Frances. Frances breathed in and out. Her eyes glazed over. She shook her head and pulled the mask off. 'No, it's terrible, it makes everything go blurred.' She ducked her head, clenched her teeth and made a grinding, growling sound. She opened her eyes. 'Oh, hell,' she said.

'Time to get the doctor,' the midwife said. She went out.

Frances was swearing softly. I sat near her. I had a strange sensation, as if alarm, fear even, were near me, wanting to get into my head.

'I get you anything?' I whispered. 'Pie? Beer?'

She laughed, wild-eyed, then she said in a high voice, 'Oh, it's coming again.' She clutched my hand, ducked her head, gritted her teeth and made the growling sound, digging her fingernails into my palm. She banged her forehead against my arm, swearing. After a time she looked up at me and said, 'This is unbelievable. You're not going to leave, are you?'

'No,' I said. I sat there while she cried and swore and mangled my hand. I don't know how long we sat there. Hours, maybe. My hand was raw.

The doctor arrived. 'Come on a bit sooner than we thought, eh?' There was a crease down the side of his face and his hair was rumpled. His eyes were swollen. He snapped on some gloves, then he and the midwife waited, casting looks at each other, while Frances went into another contraction, moaning and clenching her fists. When she came out of it he had a brisk look between her legs.

'Mmm, hmm.' He and the midwife conferred.

I sat looking out at the city, Mt Eden on the skyline. I felt so dazed, so incredulous, suddenly so *put upon*. I considered getting up and walking out of the room, out of the building. I resolved to do it. In half an hour I would be at home, hiding my face in the pillow. There was no point in explaining. I would just go.

Frances cried out. The doctor stepped back, a small instrument in his hand, like a crochet hook.

I started up. 'What are you doing?'

'I've broken the waters. Didn't you hear me saying?' He and the midwife looked at me doubtfully. They exchanged a glance. 'We're just helping Frances along.'

Frances was making small whimpering sounds and rocking back and forth.

'Are you all right?' I asked her.

The midwife snapped, 'Honestly. She's having a baby, for heaven's sake. Can't you make yourself useful?'

'Go to hell,' I muttered.

'I *beg* your pardon?'

'Now, let's concentrate on Frances,' the doctor said.

'Oh, God,' Frances moaned.

'Right,' the doctor said. 'I'll be back.'

'You're not leaving. Look at her!'

'It's perfectly normal; she's doing well. I have another patient to look in on.' There was a pause. 'Excuse me,' he said. I stepped out of his way. He looked at the midwife. She rolled her eyes.

Frances was making strange noises. Her eyes were bulging; tendons stood out on her neck. 'Good, good,' the midwife said. 'You're doing fine.'

I said, 'It's not good. She looks terrible. Can't you do something? She's in agony.'

The midwife whispered savagely, '*Will* you please settle down. You're supposed to encourage her.'

'I can't stand it,' I said.

'Then perhaps you'd better go outside.' Icy, she pointed at the door.

'Fine!'

I picked up my shopping bag and lurched out, crashing my shoulder against the door. Behind me Frances wailed something, imploring.

'Don't worry . . . do him good,' I heard the midwife say.

I walked down the stairs and out through the foyer. The rain was whirling around the streetlights. I opened a can and drank. The sky was just perceptibly lighter, the black turning to dark grey, and I could make out flying tatters of clouds. The wind had got up, roaring in the trees on the edge of One Tree Hill. I stood out there in the warm, dark, howling dawn, dipping my head to my drink, and I couldn't make out, in the deeps of my mind, what to do. I began to walk away. I reached the main road. I stood under the streetlight. Two possibilities: to cross to the petrol station and call a taxi, or turn and go back along the dark road. I couldn't remember now, drunk as I was, what she'd told me about free will. Was it that everything had been decided already, by my brain? That free will was an illusion? If that was the case, I could only wait to see what I would do.

The answer came to me, and relief with it: I would get in a taxi, I would go home and in the morning the dream would splinter and fade . . . The rain surprised me, sweeping up the road like a silver curtain; I stopped on the kerb, the spiky, sudden drops drumming on my head. Paper blew along the street, tumbling over and over; cold rain streamed down my neck. A dartboard, spilled vodka, rain falling on a winter sea; the wind blew the door against the veranda wall; *if you go home now you'll drown* . . .

In the foyer I chucked away the empty can, took a breath and swung up the stairs two at a time. I opened the door; the doctor and midwife looked up. Frances turned her white, sweat-streaked face to me, her mouth open in a soundless howl. The doctor stood up; I thought he was going to bar me from coming close. I was ready to push him, to stand my ground: I can hold my own in a fight! Instead he put his hand on my arm.

'The head,' he said, pulling me towards the bed.

I advanced, quivering. I looked between Frances's legs. I saw a rubbery circle; within it, a round, grey ball. And then the midwife said something sharp and the doctor pushed me out of the way and angled in with both hands. Frances let out a stream of sobbing swear words, straining with all her might. For a long stalled moment the doctor seemed to wrestle, almost to wrench, then suddenly he stepped back and he was holding the blue-grey, blood-streaked rubbery doll, its arms lolling free. I wanted to cry out, 'Why is it blue? Oh, it's dead, isn't it?' and Frances held up her head to look and let it drop, as if she, too, saw that the worst had happened. I closed my eyes. And then I heard the small cries, and the midwife announcing, 'There you are, madam. A healthy boy,' as she placed the hot, slippery, flailing soul on his mother's chest.

'Congratulations,' the doctor said. 'Time of birth, 5 a.m.'

The baby panted up at me, his eyes swollen and his face streaked with blood. His skin was changing from that terrible blue-grey, turning pale. His eyes were slate, the colour of a kingfisher's wing. He had small strings of hair, wrinkled hands that were too large for him, a watchful look. He regarded me. What did he see? What first impression was I printing on his brain? The midwife picked him up. She inspected him, weighed him, wiped him and wrapped him in a cloth. The parcelled child was returned to Frances, who had propped herself up on pillows. She sat there, holding the oblong bundle. We all three looked at one another: Frances, I, and the strangely calm child.

'Shouldn't he be crying?'

The doctor murmured, writing on a form, 'They're often nice and quiet after an easy birth.'

Easy? *Easy*? A bloodbath!

The midwife snapped, 'If *you* want to hold him you'd better sit down.'

I looked at her. I sat down. She put him in my arms. 'You've got quite a responsibility now,' she said. 'Haven't you.'

I looked down at the child's face.

'Less of the drinking . . .'

'Oh, shut up, you dragon.'

'*What* did you say?'

'Get out of my face,' I said. 'Bugger off.' But I spoke quietly, looking at the baby.

'Right. That's it. I'm calling security!' She took the baby, gave him to Frances and marched out. The doctor kept on filling in his form. He looked at his watch. There was a silence.

Frances said dreamily from the bed, 'Is she really calling security?' She had her head close to the baby's; now she looked up, a glazed, blissful expression on her face.

'I'd say so,' the doctor said. He came close and touched the baby's head.

'Isn't he lovely?' Frances said.

'He is. He's very nice,' he said.

'Thank you,' I said.

'You're welcome.' He smiled.

'Will you get me some things from home?' Frances asked me. 'Some stuff I forgot to bring?'

There was the crackle of a radio. A uniformed security guard stood at the door. He made me come out into the corridor. He listed my crimes. Drunkenness. Abusiveness. Foul language. Strict alcohol ban . . .

I steadied myself against the wall. 'I had to get through it,' I said.

I heard Frances say, 'They can't throw him out now.'

'Any more trouble and you're out of here,' the guard finished. He confiscated my last cans of beer.

'Yes, yes,' I said.

I walked back into the room. Out the window the sky was a jumble of black cloud, thin beams of early morning light shining on the slopes of the hill. The baby was making sounds. Frances leaned down, whispering to him.

'What do you want me to get for you?' I said.

She told me, while the midwife and doctor looked on.

I went close to her. 'See you soon.' I touched the baby's head. I went out. Halfway along the corridor I stopped. I ran back.

'But what's your address?' I said.

She laughed. 'Oh, I forgot . . .' She told me. She said, 'The key's under the orange pot on the deck.'

The midwife stood by, hands on hips, shaking her head. I thanked Dr Lampton and left.

It was all misty outside, sun breaking through the wisps and ribbons of cloud, the wet trees and grass glittering with silver drops. When I looked up at the dawn sky I had the strangest feeling, a great welling pressure in my chest — for a moment I thought I would fall over . . .

Then I walked across the carpark, looking for a taxi. What address to give the driver, Frances's or mine? She would know that I simply waited for my brain to decide, and so, have no regrets.

going back to the end

When I was twenty-two and working for a newspaper, my boss, a married man of thirty-four, was the hero of the piece of fiction I worked on obsessively, day and night. This fiction never made it onto paper: it was my life.

I fell in love with him when I saw him spying on me with binoculars from the building in which we worked. I lived on the top floor of the flat across the street. In the early mornings I would go out onto the roof terrace to drink a cup of coffee. One day the sun penetrated the mirror glass of his office and there he was, staring out, holding the binoculars to his face. I had no doubt he was looking at me. My 'novel', at least the novel about him, began that day. I was already a fantasist — my life was one long, continuous fiction. That day a new project began, page one opened, and my hapless boss was trapped within it. From then on, nothing he did would be free of significance. Every move he made was scrutinised, analysed and noted by the obsessive junior down the hall. Was he aware that he had become the hero of that common phenomenon, the autobiographical first work? He might have noticed that the atmosphere had changed, changed utterly. He might have begun to suspect that his previously ordinary junior had gone completely mad.

Why did he become the 'hero' so suddenly that day? I hadn't paid much attention to him before. It was the binoculars. They were an irresistible fictional hook. There he was, taking a secret interest. At the very least wondering why I was lounging on that dingy roof terrace, instead of hurrying in to work. With a single expression of curiosity he had made the leap and entered the fiction. And this was no detached, third-person narrative I was cooking up. The *other* central character, the heroine, of course, was me.

I worked in a small internal office. I laboured over my assignments. I never wrote a word of fiction. Rather, I lived it. Every element of my life, every conversation and event, played its part in my fantasy. I couldn't go into my boss's office without being keyed up to the highest pitch of anticipation. What would happen today? What turn would the story take? I believed there would be a happy ending. But there were setbacks and difficulties along the way. The fact that he wanted to get work done was a constant problem. What baffled, impatient looks he gave me! And the fact that he *would* get in his car every evening and drive home to his wife. I got discouraged sometimes, when my plotlines didn't produce the expected effect, when dialogue faltered and scenes fell flat. I sat in the office or the lunchroom, stewing over my secret drama, editing and re-editing the day's projected scenes, while around me people worked and chatted and lived their ordinary lives. I made complex calculations: if I make this happen, then his reaction will be this. If I contrive x, then y will be the result. Friday night drinks were always interesting, because when tipsy I am prone to be inventive . . .

As I got deeper into the work I became more intense and solitary, more engaged in the fictional world. How did it end? Well, I can say this now quite coolly: I failed in art and love. The project spun away from me. I couldn't control my hero.

I failed to win my man.

Was I mad?

There are descriptions for my behaviour: unrequited love, erotomania. But my madness was quite particular, and one thing was required for me to lose it. I needed to begin to write novels. When I started to write fiction, I stopped living it, and I became entirely sane. All my fantasies poured onto the page; all my scheming went into getting my characters from one place to another. I met my husband and had a baby, and from that point on my feelings became secondary to the child's. I ceased to take notice of myself. I lost myself. *I did not want myself back.*

I became a writer. I had some successes. I lived as much of a literary life as you could in this small city. I worked hard.

I'm a widow now. I'm an old woman. When I look at my daughters I recall my young self. I was glad to leave her behind. But how intense her life was. Bright colours, black miseries. Rage and joy. She was crazy, all right. She was insane.

I'm old, but it's only in the last few years that I've begun to feel it. A year ago I had a health scare. I began to have trouble breathing. Doctors told me it was heart failure. I had an operation, during which my faulty heart valve was replaced with a pig's valve. I was weak for a long time afterwards. The very thought of my heart frightened me. It made me worry about what would happen next. But I worked hard on getting fit and made good progress. I got pretty much back to normal, and tried my best to forget the whole episode.

I've always had a routine. In the summer it's dependent on the tides. At high tide I go down for a swim at the waterfront. If the tide's out in the morning, I go for a walk instead — I've always needed to get exercise before settling down to work. There's a marker in the harbour that I used to swim to before I had my heart trouble. It's a long way out, and I always used to feel triumphant when I got back after reaching it. I've missed the feeling of accomplishment that swimming out there gave me. But it's such a long way . . .

This summer my neighbours have been annoying me, playing loud music, fixing cars in their driveway. I stopped in at the local real estate office and told the agent, Mr Lye, that I was thinking of selling my house. Yesterday he rang and told me he had some clients who would like to look around. I agreed to be out the following morning.

At nine o'clock I walked up and dropped off a set of keys for Mr Lye. Since I couldn't work I decided to do some errands. I caught the bus down to the shopping centre and went into a big department store, intending to buy a new kettle. A couple of other things caught my eye. I browsed for a while.

On the way out I went to find the ladies'. In the cubicle there was no hook, so I put my handbag on the floor. I heard someone come in. A toilet flushed. A tap ran, and the hand-dryer roared. And then footsteps, and a hand snaked under the partition. Like a live thing in itself, an animal, lightning quick, it felt around, grabbed my bag and pulled it into the next cubicle. I snatched at the bag, nearly caught it — there was a tug as it was wrenched under — and it was gone. Footsteps running away. I cried out and stood up, pulling at my clothes. I flung open the door. There was no one, just the empty white room, and my own astonished face in the mirror.

I clutched my hands to my heart. I listened to the beats thudding in my chest. Before my operation I would have burst out of the lavatory and given chase. But now . . . my heart throbbed so. My own expression in the mirror frightened me.

I straightened my clothes. I walked out into the mall, and into a shop.

'I've been robbed,' I said.

A teenage girl regarded me, stopped in the act of folding a pair of jeans.

I felt a tremor go through me. This wouldn't do. I was embarrassed.

'Are you okay?' she asked. Her tone grated; it was insulting.

'Is there a . . . security person?' Oh, this was intolerable. I sat down heavily on a bench on which there were piled many pairs of trousers. The girl came out from behind her counter. She was wearing tight shorts and high heels. There was a diamond stud in her nose.

'Are you okay?' she said again. In her voice an equal measure of syrup and derision, as if she couldn't decide whether I was a deserving case or a drunk. She made significant eyes at another girl, who came down from a ladder carrying a pile of clothes.

'I need to make a complaint. For insurance purposes,' I said in an absurd, haughty voice. My eyes burned. If only the girl would stop staring at me, I could pull myself together. I looked away. I said, more normally, 'I was in the ladies' and someone snatched my bag. I need to complain to someone. I'm just not sure to whom.' There. I was myself again.

The girl who'd come down the ladder did a little shriek. 'Not again! Taylor, ring the police.' To me, 'It happened last week outside the supermarket.' She put her hand on my shoulder, gesturing at the other girl. 'Taylor, get security too.'

The girl called Taylor clomped away. The other bent over me, keeping up a stream of talk. 'It's unbelievable. I was just saying to Taylor the other day . . .'

I began to think about what I'd lost. My wallet, all my cards. Keys. Fifty dollars cash. Two letters I'd been meaning to post. In the zip compartment, floppy disks with my latest stories. I'd printed some of them out. Most were stored on my computer, but were they all? There were other things on the disks too. Letters . . . I pressed my fingers against my temples.

'It's not the end of the world,' I said.

A security guard came. Then a policeman. He said, 'Can you describe the person?'

'It was a hand.'

'A hand?' He glanced at the two girls.

'It was brown. A woman's, of course. It couldn't be a man's, could it?'

There was a silence. They were all looking at me.

'I was in the lavatory. The hand came under the partition. By the time I'd got out there was no one there.'

'Ah . . .' The policeman wrote in his notebook. The security guard said he was going off to look at 'footage.'

'Footage?'

'They'll be on the camera. Name, date of birth?'

I supplied details.

The policeman said, 'I'll give you a lift home.'

'No.' I rose. 'I'm perfectly all right. I'll get the bus.'

'How're you going to pay for it?' Taylor said, smartly.

I blushed. 'Oh. No handbag, no money.' I felt ridiculous. I needed to get away. 'I'll go to the bank and sort it out first.'

I managed to extricate myself. Their concern was humiliating. I couldn't bear little Taylor's mocking smiles.

I went to the ASB in the mall and explained the situation. They cancelled my old cards. They asked a series of questions, security passwords and so on. They promised me that new cards would be on their way.

The policeman was waiting for me. He led me to his car. Odd to travel without one's handbag. I kept reaching for it. I had him drop me on the main road, so I could pick up my keys.

I walked along the street. It had been a week of those hard, bright days at the end of summer, when the light has altered and autumn is in the air, the gardens shining in the clear light and everything very beautiful. But now the weather had changed again. There were black clouds, sudden showers, gusts of wind roaring in the trees. Leaves were falling onto the pavement.

I got the keys from the estate agent and hurried home. Mr Lye's card was on the dining room table. The house was bright and warm, the light falling in stripes along the hall. I didn't really want to sell it.

I rang the insurance company. I made myself a snack and turned on my computer, intending to get some work done.

At two o'clock the phone rang.

'Mrs Myers?' A male voice: soft, breathy, full of warm concern. 'This is Trent from Armadale Security? Just ringing about your bag that wuz stolen?'

'Yes?'

'Just to inform you, ma'am, that we have found your bag in the carpark area.'

'Oh, good!'

'There's good news and bad news, Mrs Myers. The wallet and cards are there but I'm very sorry the cash is gone.'

'Oh, never mind the cash. What about the disks?'

'I'm not sure, ma'am. But would you like to collect it? Just come to Information at the mall, the booth on the ground floor near the main entrance.'

'Yes, I'll come.'

'Are you able to come today? Only the booth shuts at four.'

I told him I'd come in an hour.

I took the car, using the key on the set I'd lent Mr Lye. I had my mind on the floppy disks in the bag. I wasn't efficient with storing work and I was sure there was material on them that I should keep. I wondered whether I'd become less organised since my heart operation. The thought made me anxious.

I parked and found the information booth.

I smiled at the woman. 'I'm Celia Myers. I've come to collect my bag.'

She looked blank. She fluttered her eyes. 'A bag?'

'My handbag was stolen here this morning. It's been found. A Trent from security told me to pick it up.'

She looked under the counter. 'We don't have bag here.'

I leaned on the desk while she picked up the phone and made a tentative explanation. 'She say her bag was stolen here? She got call, come here? No? No call?'

She put down the phone, shaking her head.

'I've come all the way down here. Can you ask someone who knows what's going on.'

'Sorry.'

'Sorry. Sorry. The bag has disks in it. Important work stuff. Understand? Where is Trent?'

'I don't know . . . Trent?'

'Get me a security guard.'

I waited, agitated. He came out, slouching, eating a sandwich, a different man from the one that morning. I explained.

'I know there was an incident,' he said. 'I'll have to check.'

'This is so inefficient!' I could feel my heart banging in my chest. I saw myself reflected in a shop window. An elderly woman, angry, fists pressed against her collarbone. I straightened up.

'Probably just some wires crossed, Mrs . . . ?'

'Myers. Mrs *Myers.*'

He spoke into his radio. Then to me. 'There's nothing about a bag.'

'You've got my number. Ring me when you've got your . . . act together!'

I hurried away. I stood by my car. I had the strangest feeling. My eyes filled with tears.

Why do I feel so raw? Is it the way people speak to me, their patronising tone? Is it because I feel my heart, because I'm suddenly aware that it beats?

I sat in the car. Honestly. Get a grip. It was life. Things like this happened all the time. People committed crimes. People were inefficient. One got mucked about.

But these moments of feeling so unnerved. It was like dropping an outer shield I'd worn all my adult life – like returning to my raw younger self. I had an odd, fearful sense that something — what? — was wearing thin. If I should become weak in some way, lose my focus . . .. would fiction and life blur again, would I lose the control I had over my work? It was another way of saying I was afraid of death . . .

Oh, what nonsense. I drove out of the carpark, fast.

I would buy a new bag. I'd cancelled my cards already; no point in getting them back. I would just not worry about the disks. Everything was stored on my computer. Forget it. Let them keep the bag.

I pulled in to the garage. I walked down the path. The front door was open. My heart sank. Was I forgetting simple things now? The door one week; next, forgetting to put on my trousers. Oh, really. All this brooding, it was maudlin. I needed to ring an old friend, go out, have a drink.

There was an alien smell in the hall. I recognised it: sweat.

'Oh dear,' a dim little voice rattled in my head. 'Oh dear.'

And then I understood what had happened.

They had really been very efficient. My stereo, my precious CDs. Paintings: a Pat Hanly. A small McCahon. A Louise Henderson. Gone, all gone. Kitchen things: appliances, some expensive bowls. The TV and DVD player. Ornaments. My favourite, most valuable vase. I walked upstairs very calmly, pressing my hands against my chest, thinking perhaps they'd got tired; perhaps they had no room in their vehicle . . .

But of course the computer was gone.

I sat on the bed. When I was sure I could speak clearly I rang my daughter, Dee.

'I've been very stupid and gullible,' I told her. And then a terrible fear took hold of me. I ran downstairs as fast as I could and closed the front door. But it was no use locking it: 'they' had my keys! 'Trent' had simply got my address from the letters in the stolen bag, had rung and tricked me into going to the mall, then, once I was out of the way, had let himself into the house.

I went out onto the deck. It started to rain. I lifted my face to the white sky. So many feelings at once . . . I had to get them under control. When I was young I was abnormally sensitive. I would have been overwhelmed by that sensitivity if I hadn't been able to write. If I began to flounder, if I couldn't write any more . . .

Dee had said practical things. Ring the police. Get a locksmith straight away. Change the locks. Insurance would cover everything. She was coming over to help me sort things out.

I felt unable to go back in the house and wait for her. It wasn't just the thought of the burglary, or the misery of the lost computer. I felt a deeper sense of anguish, unreality. And

I thought, suddenly, I must go for a swim.

I took my gear from the laundry and got in the car. I drove away.

There were black clouds over the harbour. The wind was blowing the sea into choppy waves. Out in the gulf, Rangitoto Island wore a shroud of mist. It was past high tide and there was only one other swimmer, a young man in a wetsuit who swam out powerfully, past the buoys and away towards the next beach. I got changed, and the wind blew cold against my damp swimsuit. I hid my keys, checking that no one saw.

There was rain falling out at sea. The islands were indistinct, distant. The water wasn't too cold, after the first shock. I struck out, swimming my usual mixture of overarm, breaststroke and backstroke. The rain began pattering around me. I was calmed by my slow breathing, by the rhythm of the exercise. I swam to the first buoy and paused to look back. The beach was deserted. The cars drove slowly on the waterfront road, headlights on because of the heavy shower. The sea was rougher now. I looked at the distant marker I used to swim to, before my heart problem. It was a long way out. I thought for a moment. I swam towards it.

I ploughed through the chop, swimming on my back for a while, turning to make sure of my direction. The outgoing tide threatened to carry me off course, beyond the marker. I had to readjust by swimming across the current. I stopped once, treading water, and looked back at the wet beach and the drooping trees and the cars with their lights on. The sky was heavy, whirling with water; the afternoon was collapsing into early, rainy dusk. Waves splashed into my face. I thought of Dee, walking around in the dark, plundered house, calling my name. I was out in the channel now, pushing against the tide. The marker was still a distance away, and for a while I made so little headway that I thought I wouldn't be able to reach it. And then it was closer, and still closer, and finally I was there, gasping, hanging on to the green, barnacled wood.

The sea rose and washed against me, splashing stinging water up my nose. Another shower swept across, the drops hissing on the surface. I was alone, far away. I could feel the shush shush of my heart. The sea heaved and broke against the marker, the rain blurred my eyes. Far away at the port a container ship showed its lights. It was frightening to be out here so late. I looked at the bush slopes of Rangitoto, rising up to the crater. I thought of striking out towards it. Swimming toward the black volcanic rocks, the silence of its cold stone shores. Above me gulls were flying. They skimmed down to the waves, swooped up into the rainy air, turning, pearly white against the grey sky. I was filled with fierce happiness. My eyes stung with tears. I said something out loud, something stupid and dramatic. And then salt water splashed into my face, bringing me to my senses, and I set off overarm, counting the strokes in my head.

It took a long time to get back. Halfway back I grew tired, and could only do a slow breaststroke. There was a hot heaviness in my chest. When my feet finally touched the sand I looked back at the lonely marker out in the channel, surrounded by rough water. That I had been all the way out there, in this weather. I laughed. I wanted to punch my fist in the air. But when I raised my arm it felt so strangely heavy and sore . . .

I dressed and drove home. I was light-headed, shivering. My heart was going full tilt. I turned on the radio and sang at the top of my voice to a ridiculous pop song. I did something wrong at the lights. There was a squeal of brakes. Someone tooted long and hard. I parked outside the house and hurried down the path.

Dee had been waiting at the window. She came out.

'Where have you been? It's terrible. Your paintings. The computer — all gone.'

I flew to her. 'Dee. It was marvellous. I went out there, all the way. The sea . . .'

I put my arms around her, folded her in my happiness. 'It was wonderful.'

Oh, Dee made all sorts of responsible noises. Said I was 'hysterical.' Made hot sweet tea. She even stood, frowning, like a pretend nurse, and listened to my pulse. It 'sounded funny', she announced. She went upstairs and made a phonecall, said she wanted to take me to the doctor. I sat on my sofa with a blanket over my knees, looking at the patch on the wall where my Pat Hanly used to hang.

She came back in.

'I'm so sorry about the burglary,' she said.

I smiled at her dreamily. I took her hand. My head was light. I was dizzy, seeing stars. I could hear a strange, new banging in my heart, a little drum of happiness.

'You're a funny colour,' she said, alarmed. She fiddled with the rug on my knees.

I said, 'It was magical out there. Frightening — the dark coming down, the rain, the beach so far away . . .'

'But your computer,' she said. 'Was there work on it? Your stories . . .'

'Stories?' The idea of writing seemed distant, unfamiliar. There was something bright and swelling and immediate in the way. I heard her voice, although, funny, I couldn't see her very well.

'Your *Opportunity* stories. Remember you told me: they "contain all your crimes".'

I had a rush of feeling, irritation almost. Didn't she understand? I hadn't felt like this since I was young.

'I'm alive,' I said. 'I'm *alive*. What do I care about those?'